WHAT PEOPLE

OREADS

A lyrical coming-of-age novel, *Oreads* is a bittersweet journey depicted so vividly that readers see the fog on the mountains, smell the ripening corn, and feel the conflicted passions of characters who can't escape, yet can't go home again. A work to savor.

Susan Hubbard, author of seven fiction books including *The Season of Risks, Blue Money* (Janet Heidinger Kafka Prize) and *Walking on Ice* (AWP Short Fiction Prize). Her stories have appeared in TriQuarterly, The Mississippi Review, Ploughshares, and several other journals. She is Professor of English at the University of Central Florida.

John Lavelle is one savvy, insightful, and fearless writer. The world of *Oreads* is far more vivid, chilling, and compelling than the one you're living in. Trust me. Lavelle's Vietnam-era northern Appalachia is a forbidding landscape of shattered lives and broken dreams where a desperate woman gets one last chance to save herself and her children. This is nightmare material of the first order, at once exhilarating and profoundly disturbing. It'll leave you breathless.

John Dufresne, author of two short story collections, *The Way That Water Enters Stone* and *Johnny Too Bad,* and the novels *Louisiana Power & Light, Love Warps the Mind a Little,* both New York Times Notable Books of the Year, Deep in the Shade of Paradise, and Requiem, Mass. His books on writing, *The Lie That Tells a Truth* and *Is Life Like This?* are used in many university writing programs. He's the editor of the anthology *Blue Christmas.* His short stories have twice been named Best American Mystery Stories, in 2007 and 2010. His play *Trailerville* was produced at the Blue Heron Theater in New York in 2005.

He's a professor at Florida International University in Miami. He is a 2013 Guggenheim Fellow in Fiction. His new novel is *No Regrets, Coyote*.

Oreads

Oreads

John F. Lavelle

Winchester, UK
Washington, USA

First published by Roundfire Books, 2016
Roundfire Books is an imprint of John Hunt Publishing Ltd., Laurel House, Station Approach,
Alresford, Hants, SO24 9JH, UK
office1@jhpbooks.net
www.johnhuntpublishing.com
www.roundfire-books.com

For distributor details and how to order please visit the 'Ordering' section on our website.

Text copyright: John F. Lavelle 2015

ISBN: 978 1 78535 183 9
Library of Congress Control Number: 2015941042

A CIP catalogue record for this book is available from the British Library.

Design: Stuart Davies

Printed in the USA by Edwards Brothers Malloy

We operate a distinctive and ethical publishing philosophy in all
areas of our business, from our global network of authors to
production and worldwide distribution.

Oreads

Whirl up, sea—
whirl your pointed pines,
splash your great pines
on our rocks,
hurl your green over us,
cover us with your pools of fir.
H.D

Chapter 1

The late summer beyond the kitchen window lay heavy on the Allegheny Mountains. Cassie slid the last of the heavy earthen dinner plates into the brown-gray water, wanting to get at the fry pan and be done with the supper dishes. Life seemed to overflow outside, the birthing and seeding, fruit ripening, the corn crowned with small golden rainbows, pregnant with large bulbous ears, their silken hair browning in the sun. The sticky sweet odor of it, the sour-sweet taste of the drying hay, and the scent of the cows freed from their maternal burden of milk, plodding to their night pasture, drifted through the window on the warm evening breeze.

Cassie's fingers had turned pink and wrinkled from the washing. The small calluses dotting her palms, earned from hoeing and weeding the garden, were now white. The tepid water smelled of detergent and pepper. She twisted the dishcloth to get the food scraps out of it and plunged it into the water to the top of the sunken plate.

Cassie's mother swayed next to her with the rhythm of the work, taking dishes from Cassie, drying them, and putting them away in the cupboards. She said, as if speaking to no one in particular, "I think the corn might just be about ready," her voice absentmindedly soft. Her mother always spoke quietly when she'd caught the tempo of work, but still, her voice carried a raspy texture like rough cloth, the sound of a life lived outdoors. Her words rolled with the cadence of a song.

The heat from the day and the cooking lingered in the kitchen of the small, unpainted, and weathered-gray house that sat on a thin strip of bottom-land that twisted between two steep mountain ranges. Cassie had long ago settled into the summer, putting away the duties of school with her school clothes, now living as her mother did, tending the garden and the house, also picking up the rhythm of the days, the weeks, the months out of school while her father and Ben tended the farm and picked up work as carpenters during the good weather, and during their free time splitting and stacking wood in the shed that leaned against the rear wall of the house where they also kept a porcelain-white wringer washer and an old chest freezer.

"Yes'm," Cassie replied repeating the absentminded lilt, not so much caught up in the dance of her work but in the possibilities of the evening to come. Past the kitchen window, the bread-crust-brown curtains, the two little blue and brown glass bottles sitting on the sill, a newly potted philodendron reaching its way across the ledge, past the lilac bushes, the tractor-tire flower garden overflowing with impatiens, her brother Ben leaned against the open door of Jimmy Marshall's old station wagon parked on a dusty patch of driveway in a square of sparse lawn surrounded by a green wall of corn. The sun rested low in the sky casting long shadows of the boys waiting in the bronze tint of the August summer's evening as they listened to the radio. Cassie could make out the tune to "Carrie Anne" but not the words.

Jimmy said something. Purdy, sitting on the passenger's side smoking a cigarette, flicked the ashes between his feet. He glanced down at his watch. Ben turned toward the window, cupping his hands around his mouth. "Cassie, you about ready? We got to get going here pretty soon."

Cassie leaned across the sink toward the window pressing against her mother. "I'm coming, Ben. It'll be just a minute."

Her mother nudged Cassie away from the window. "Just hold your horses. You got plenty of time before you got to be going. If you were so worried about getting there early you'd of ate faster."

"Ma." Cassie handed her mother the washed dish. She rubbed her nose against her upper arm still smelling of the lilac soap from her bath. Ben and the boys would be angry and never take her along again.

"Now, I'm just teasing," her mother said. She held the plate tilted like a church tambourine, running the towel over the rim, then the front, then the back, the same each time. "You're so fired up about going to that dance, you ain't coming close to getting these dishes washed right. I had to dry most of them clean."

Cassie plunged the large black skillet she'd used to fry the pork chops into the brown water. "What if Darlene gets there early and I ain't there? Ceilia's boyfriend's going to drop her off."

Her mother still watched her son. "That girl ain't been early to nothing in all her life. Neither was her sister, excepting maybe her first birthday."

Cassie scrubbed at the crusted-on remnants of the pork chops with a pad of steel wool, feeling for the baked-on food in the brown water. "I'll be making everyone late."

"Ain't no dance going to be starting without no band." Her mother held the plate up toward the window, squinting across the surface. "Why you want to ride all the way across the county just to listen to your brother sing? Don't you hear enough of him here? Lord knows I get tired of that caterwauling. Now country music, that's music—Patsy Cline, Hank Williams." Her mother lowered the plate to look across the summer-ripe fields.

A muscle knotted in Cassie's upper arm as she scrubbed. "Kids don't pay to hear country music. Besides, most places Ben plays, I can't go." Cassie stretched her arm above her head, working out the cramp, letting streamlets of water run down her arm, dropping her arm before they reached her elbow.

The heavy ceramic dish clanged against the others as her mother slid it onto a stack sitting in the open cupboard. "Well, most of the places they play ain't fitting for a good woman."

Cassie turned the skillet and scrubbed the bottom, then handed it to her mother. Her mother pursed her lips and passed the skillet back to Cassie.

Cassie dunked the pan back into the water and began to re-scrub the spots still dirty, splashing water onto the counter and her clothes. "I know, but Ben won't ever take me anywhere if I make him late."

Her mother nudged her away from the sink. "Go. Lord knows you're getting more useless by the minute."

Cassie ran up the stairs into her bedroom squeezing between her bed and dresser. The house had been divvied up into six cramped rooms: three minuscule bedrooms, Cassie's and Ben's upstairs with a bathroom just big enough for a toilet, bath, and sink. The kitchen where they ate, a small living room with a potbelly stove to heat the house, and their parents' bedroom filled the downstairs.

She slipped her blouse over her head then wiggled out of her denim cut-offs, carefully pulling on her stockings, attaching them to her garters. Stockings were expensive. She'd only been allowed to wear them since her fourteenth birthday that past January. She slid the dress she'd sewn three weeks before over her head. She'd made it from a bolt of burnt-orange cotton cloth she'd bought with extra money from picking berries. She'd fashioned a small collar and covered the buttons, four of them up the front, and stitched two breast pockets. The hem was the shortest she'd ever worn, a full three inches above the knees. Cassie leaned over her dresser to brush on mascara and pencil on eyeliner. She'd had to talk her mother into letting her wear this much makeup. Her father was still not happy about it. She pulled the clips out of her hair and let it fall down halfway to the small of her back, brushing it quickly, grabbing her small purse and shoes, then running down the stairs and out onto the kitchen stoop to slip on her shoes, rushing to the boys and climbing into the station wagon.

The band was playing at a large state-run campground in the mountains surrounding a man-made lake. At seven o'clock they opened with "Light My Fire." Cassie sat on a stool she'd found in a corner of the dance hall while she waited for Darlene and watched people dance. She'd placed the stool next to Guy, their drummer, so people would know she was with the band. The dancers were mostly campers from the cities dressed in bright new store-bought clothes and smelling of expensive perfume and cologne. They generally danced with others from the cities. Maybe it was her clothes, or her hair, or makeup that gave her away, though boys asked her once in a while, especially when she danced with Darlene. But she really had nothing in common with boys from the city, nothing she could say to them, nothing they'd understand.

Almost an hour after the band had started, Darlene appeared standing next to the doorman, still a bit little-girl gawky, though she swore her long thin legs were her most attractive feature. She wore her favorite corduroy skirt, too short for Cassie's taste, and a white sleeveless shell. Darlene twisted a thin gold chain attached to a crucifix around her finger. She always wore it around her long neck, which Darlene thought to be her second-best feature, the reason she kept her bleached-blonde hair short. She argued with the doorman.

As far as Ben was concerned, Darlene wore too much makeup and not enough skirt, flirted too much, and there were rumors she'd gone all the way. Everyone knew her big sister had. He'd told Cassie he wouldn't be surprised if Ceilia ended up shacking-up with that man she'd been going with.

Cassie grabbed Darlene's hand, pulling her into the building walking her over to a small picnic table sitting under the low eaves. "Late again." Cassie sat on the table so she could see over the heads of the dancers, using the bench as a footstool, pulling the skirt of her dress down below her knees.

"Aren't we testy." Darlene reached for Cassie's hand. "Come on, let's dance." She pulled Cassie out onto the floor finding a spot in the middle. Darlene took stock of the room as they danced, scrutinizing the small groups of boys holding close to territory they'd staked out in the slowly filling building.

The band played "Mustang Sally" and "Strange Brew" to finish the first set. They set down their instruments and switched the amps to standby, then walked away to the concession booth at the other end of the pavilion as people worked their way toward the exit as if on cue.

"Aw," Darlene said. "I just got here. Make them play more. I ain't even stinky yet."

"Darlene." Cassie turned to walk toward the picnic table.

Darlene followed, catching Cassie in two strides. "I'm going to get a drink. You want one?"

Cassie had a dollar in her purse that she'd saved from berry picking, selling the blueberries to a roadside stand. Usually her father took the berries to the stand and she never asked for the money unless she wanted to buy cloth for a dress or blouse, but she'd been with him when he'd stopped and he'd been talking to the owner and had let her conduct the transaction. The owner's wife had given her a dollar extra that Cassie had hidden. She'd felt guilty about hiding the money and almost told her father, but he didn't understand how hard it was to be a girl nowadays. "No." If she saved it she could buy some new makeup, or a new pair of stockings.

Cassie walked over to the open window behind the drums to let the late-evening breeze cool her while Darlene went off to the concession stand. The reddened sun had begun to slide behind the western mountains, the sky bleeding blue through red to purple, the eastern sky fading into black.

A motorcycle barked as it slowed, the driver dressed in jeans and a denim jacket leaned the bike into the parking lot, the crack of its exhaust echoing off the surrounding hills. Once he'd parked, several of the local boys meandered over to him and the bike. Ben called them lot flies. They sat in their cars, or on them, listening to the music rather than pay the dollar admission. Their type had always been there, he'd said. Now a new type of person sat in the parking lot with them or on the lawns, a type who also didn't pay the price of admission. They wore beads and tiny sunglasses and let their hair grow long. Ben called them hippies.

Cassie really didn't believe that. Real hippies didn't live in West Virginia.

As the boys scrutinized the bike, a small pain pulsed beneath Cassie's breastbone, the same feeling she got when she thought she'd forgotten her homework or lost her purse, but it was for something different, something far off and distant.

"What're you looking at?" Darlene asked coming up behind her.

Cassie jumped away from the window, partially because Darlene had scared her, partially because she didn't want Darlene to know who she'd been staring at or what she'd been thinking and feeling. "Oh, nothing, really."

Darlene inspected the parking lot. "Nothing, my ass. Them's a bunch of local boys. Mighty fine bunch I might add too, except for maybe Chad and Hank."

Cassie peeked through the screen again. The driver was buckling his helmet to the front forks. "Which one's Chad? Which one's Hank?"

Darlene stepped back. "Then there's Hank's little brother, Terry. He's the worst of them all because he's so good looking. He's the big tall one with all the muscles. But he's a love 'em and leave 'em sort of guy." Darlene smiled and shrugged. "So they tell me."

"Which one's he?" Cassie asked. A boy passed around a pack of cigarettes. Several boys gently picked one from the pack as if they were sticks of brittle sugar candy. Another boy held up a silver lighter. The ones with the cigarettes took turns dipping the tip of the cigarette into the flame, smoke blowing out the sides of their mouths like an old tractor trying to start.

Darlene swatted Cassie's arm. "God, Cassie, I swear your folks found you under a cabbage patch."

Cassie rubbed at the pink spot on her arm from Darlene's slap. "Darlene McAlester, what are you implying?"

Darlene stuck her face near Cassie's and wrinkled her nose.

"I'm implying you're too sweet a thing to be messing around with the likes of those boys."

Cassie nodded toward the parking lot. "Who's that boy there, the one's got the motorcycle?"

Darlene leaned her head near the screen and studied the boy. "I don't rightly know. I seen him once or twice around, I think. Bike seems pretty new. It means he's a working-saving sort of guy. His clothes don't look like his pa's rich."

Cassie edged closer to the screen. It smelled ashy of long-sitting dust. He wore a navy-colored button-down shirt. "You can't tell all that just from looking at him?"

The motorcycle rider and two other boys started up the path to the pavilion. Cassie backed away from the window. "Oh, God, they're coming this way."

Darlene grabbed Cassie's sleeve, pulling her back to the window. "Not yet, honey. They're too far away to see us. Let's get a good look."

Cassie clung to the windowsill as they walked by, a warm watery wave flowing from her head down her body as the boy with the motorcycle came into better focus.

The boy Cassie thought to be Hank spoke to the owner of the motorcycle. "You getting something to drink, Jake?" Jake nodded as he stepped around the corner of the building.

His name was Jake and he smiled openly and had clear eyes. The other two boys appeared to be Darlene's kind of men—dangerous. Terry worried Cassie. She'd seen boys like that in school, but she wondered what it would be like to be his girlfriend, to know your man could take care of himself, to not have to be afraid for him. Then again, a man like that wanted a certain kind of woman.

Jake paid his money and walked into the building. He looked at least Ben's age as he scrutinized the room as if searching for something, his gaze lighting on Cassie and Darlene for a second.

"He noticed you," Darlene sang.

Cassie brushed nonexistent crumbs from her dress. "I'm sitting down. Darlene, you sitting or not?" Cassie sat on the bench of the table opposite the dance floor now not feeling so pretty. Darlene followed, glancing boldly back at Jake, who watched her and Cassie. Cassie sat her purse on her lap staring at her hands. They seemed so small. "There ain't no reason he'd be interested in me."

"Why not?" Darlene sat down on the table, hiding Cassie from the rest of the people in the pavilion. "You ain't exactly a wilting flower." Darlene took a slow drink of her soda and seemed to think about it for a minute. "So? What kind of girl you think he wants?"

"Look at all those girls from the city," Cassie said. "They got store-bought clothes and real makeup, just like China dolls. They're like walking picture ads from a magazine." Her fingers played with the hem of her dress. "I ain't hardly been on a date yet." She measured where it ended above her knees and compared it to hems of other girls standing on the dance floor. "I've only been kissed a couple of times and some of those don't count because they were just boys being silly."

Darlene leaned back, bracing herself with a long arm. "I ain't never seen you acting like this. You've danced with a bunch of boys. You've been held in their arms."

"Not really." Cassie peeked around Darlene as Jake walked over to stand with Hank and Terry at the concession booth next to Ben.

Darlene stared sideways at Jake and the others, then back to Cassie. "Now, it ain't what you got that matters. It's how you use what you got."

Cassie's face reddened. "I could never do that." She set her purse on the table and played with the snap. The chrome had worn off and the brass showed through.

Darlene laughed. "Don't kid yourself, honey, you ain't got that." She slid down onto the bench, then swung her legs under the table to face Cassie. "But you got a lot. Like, you're real pretty, in a church-going sort of way."

Jake said something to the girl at the counter. The girl smiled back at him. Cassie pulled at a strand of her hair. She'd lose him before she ever had a chance to get to know him. The girl brought back a soda and opened the can. Jake counted out some change. The girl smiled again.

"What a floozy," Cassie said.

"Who? Oh, her. You're right about that." Darlene sipped her drink then handed it to Cassie.

Cassie bent the straw toward her to take a polite sip. "She don't have to be so brazen." She rubbed the cold can against her wrist then handed it back.

Soon Ben and the others returned, picking up their instruments, checking the mikes, Jimmy strumming a few chords on the guitar. The people standing outside started to file back in reminding Cassie of the cows coming home at milking time. Cassie pulled the skirt of her dress down over her knees and laid her chin on the table again.

Her brother flicked a switch on an amplifier, and then walked over to his mike, tapping it. A loud knocking sound thumped from the speakers. To Cassie, Ben was grown. He had a job when he wasn't in school. He didn't earn much money, but that was because he worked only when their father worked, and their father worked sporadically, taking ill several times a month.

People staked out unmarked spots, a strange intricate pecking order depending on who they were attracted to and who they attracted: the dance before a dance.

"I wouldn't know what to do if he did come over and ask me to dance," Cassie said.

Darlene stretched her legs in anticipation of the music. "You dance with him, you fool."

"That ain't what I mean, Miss Dee."

The chatter on the dance floor increased with each person who reentered the building. The band started to play "The Letter." Darlene pulled Cassie down the dance floor away from the band where Hank and Terry danced with a couple of girls. Nearby, Jake spoke to another boy, one slightly more rotund and pinked-faced than Darlene would settle for.

People crowded the floor blocking Cassie's line of sight to Jake. She had hopes Darlene would attract either Terry or his brother and then she could meet Jake and talk to him. At least he would know her name. She could introduce him to the band. Maybe Jake and Ben could become friends and then maybe he could fall in love with her when she grew a little more. She could beg, plead with Darlene. She could talk her into it. Darlene had her ways. She had no talent for being Darlene, but those people better off than her or Darlene's folks saw little difference in her family and Darlene's. They called Cassie and her family dirt farmers, working a farm that made no money, scratching out a living they'd say, but it was more than scratching out, it was living in a way she loved. Darlene came from a long line of women having the ability to mix men and booze and produce children. Men were attracted to the Tillman women, her mother's maiden name. Men left just as quickly as they came.

Whenever Cassie got a chance, she glanced at Jake. If he looked in her direction, she quickly turned away. The chubby, blonde boy speaking to Jake noticed her looking and smiled. Cassie turned away, heat rising to her face. Darlene would have smiled at Jake, given him a little wink, not bothering with him again until he came over begging her to dance.

When the song ended Darlene nodded toward the chubby boy. "You got yourself a big fish there, anyway."

Cassie grimaced, glancing at the boy who still stared at her, moving away as if already sure he was going to come over and talk to her and then Jake would end up with Darlene and that would ruin everything. "It's what I get for wanting something too much that I shouldn't be wanting." Cassie turned her back to the boy, brushing her hair behind her shoulders.

Darlene pulled at her necklace as if trying to saw her neck in half. "If you can't get one you mise well get the tuther."

People were starting to pair off, some girls finding excuses to move away from the boys they'd found not to their liking. Some boys stood awkwardly away from the girls they'd been coerced into dancing with. Others stood close to the new person of their dreams.

"Please don't say that." Cassie peeked quickly over her shoulder at the boy, hoping he wouldn't notice, hoping he had quit looking at her, but he still stared. "You're a bad person, Miss Dee. Lord knows why I permit your presence."

"Well, darlin'." Darlene overemphasized the dropped ending in a mock southern drawl, something they played at in school, satirizing some of the more well-to-do girls who put on airs. Darlene flicked her wrist daintily. "It's because, secretly, you're envious of little ole' me."

Cassie mimicked her. "Why, surely, I am not."

"You are too, honey child," Darlene said, rolling her eyes as the band began the first chords to "Massachusetts."

"We've got to get off the floor." Cassie grabbed Darlene's hand, dragging her back toward the sanctuary of the table where a couple now sat. Finding a small corner to wedge herself and Darlene into, Cassie turned her back to the dance floor. Fast dances were flirtations. A slow dance was romance, and romance should be taken seriously, the way it was in movies and songs.

Young men bit their lower lips as they nervously scanned the room for their future mates. Young women sought their future in the eyes of the approaching men, or kept their eyes to the floor, or hid inside a cloister of their same sex as some boys did. Some, of fainter hearts, hid in the bathroom or walked outside.

Darlene peered over Cassie's head. "Here he comes."

Cassie stood still understanding the implication. "Who?"

Darlene smiled at the approaching boy. "Lover boy. He's

homing in."

Couples on the floor fitted arms around each other, synchronizing their bodies.

"He could want you," Cassie said.

New partners' clumsy feet took first unsure shuffling steps.

Darlene said. "I ain't the one who's been smiling at him all night." Darlene backed away from Cassie as if to signal she made no claims on her.

Cassie reached out for Darlene's hand. "What am I going to do, Dee?" She measured the boy's advance by the change of expression on Darlene's face.

Darlene shrugged her shoulders. "Dance with him. Get engaged, get married, have kids, you know, all that shit."

"What are you talking about? Oh, God, I've got to leave," she said.

"Too late." Darlene smiled at the boy coming up behind Cassie. Cassie stared into her eyes, trying to catch the reflection of her doom.

"Excuse me,"

A finger tapped Cassie gently on her shoulder, the muscles in her back instinctively tightening. She turned slowly around, staring down at scrubbed and polished shoes, faded-but-clean blue jeans. He wore a denim coat and a button-down, navy-colored shirt. Flecks of gold swam in his brown eyes, the same gold as in his hair. His cheekbones were high and his jaw strong. A noise buzzed in her head louder than the amplified music. Cassie wasn't sure if she could move from the spot she stood, let alone dance.

"May I have this dance?" he said, his voice no longer sounding like a boy's, but not yet as deep as her father's.

Cassie nodded and then led him out onto the dance floor to turn and half expect him not to be there. Jake reached for her hand. Suddenly she wanted to step backwards, to go back home, to sit on their old sofa with her mother as she always did and watch television while her father slept in his chair, but she took his hand. He pressed the other lightly against her waist. The warmth of it seeped through her dress, touching her skin, cradling her as if he were picking her up off the floor and moving her along. She didn't remember any other boy's hand being this large or strong. As they danced Jake looked down at her, stepping closer, slipping his hand around her back and gently pulling her toward him. He smelled of the same aftershave her father wore. Cassie wanted to be even closer to him, to lay her head against his chest, to hear his heart beat, but she didn't know how to go about this, or why she needed to do it.

When the music stopped he said, "My name's Jake, Jake McCullom." He let his hand slip from her side, shoving it into his coat pocket.

Not knowing what else to do, she held out her hand. "I'm Cassie Wolphe."

He shook her hand and laughed. "Nice to meet you Cassie Wolphe. Come here often?"

"Only when Ben's playing." She nodded toward her brother.

"Ben? Oh, the singer." Jake slid a half-step back. "Do you like him?"

"He's my brother." The half-step meant he thought she might be taken.

Jake stepped closer seeming a bit more confident. "Probably go to a lot of dances. Meet a lot of people."

Cassie pulled her dress away from the small of her back still feeling the touch of his calloused hands. "I go to some. I meet some interesting people sometimes. You come up here often?"

Jake shifted from his left to his right leg. "No, not too much. A couple of times a year." A drop of sweat dribbled down his right temple.

"Then you must meet a lot of people, too." How many times, how many girls? The band started to play a fast song.

Jake leaned close to her ear. Cassie stiffened, fearing he was about to kiss her. He shouted over the music, "I'm sorry, I don't know how to dance fast."

She shouted back, "That's okay. Why don't we just sit down?" He led her away to a table in a different part of the room. They sat quietly while the band played, speaking mostly between songs, Jake telling her he lived on the other side of the county from her, that his father owned a small farm like her father's. He had an older sister, Evie, and a little brother named Chet. He earned the money for his motorcycle by working for the other farmers in the area, haying and plowing, sometimes doing all the chores if the farmer needed a day off. He was seventeen and going to be a senior in school, Cassie worrying she might be a little young for him.

Jake shouted over the deafening pitch of the music. "Do you want to go for a walk?" He made a motion with his two fingers as if walking on air.

The mountain air had cooled, now heavy with campfire smoke. Droplets of dew already coalesced on the surfaces of benches and rocks and clung to the grass. People stood near the building, smoking cigarettes, talking—boys seriously, girls politely. Further away, beyond the yellow glare of the light above the door and the crowd, a couple kissed under a tall yellow pine, Cassie figuring them for city. Nobody from the country would be stupid enough to lean against a pine tree with its lower branches cut off.

Cassie and Jake walked silently side by side down to the sand beach, their shoes shuffling through the wetting grass, the night swallowing up the sound of the band, a weak breeze blowing off the lake, smelling of fish and seaweed. Hidden crickets chirped and far off a single bullfrog croaked sporadically at the dark edge of the water.

They sat on a bench that smelled slightly of coconut oil as the full moon lingered over the mountain, its reflection rippling across the placid surface of the lake. Down near the water a girl giggled.

Jake asked, "How old are you?"

Cassie had no time to prepare, to set herself for what would come. After she'd found out he was so much older than her, three years, she'd been trying to find a way to tell him her age or to avoid it altogether. She stuttered, trying to answer. "I'm fourteen—going on fifteen this January."

Jake said nothing, seemingly to search the black surface of the water and the silhouettes of the new lovers. He didn't appear troubled by her age, but neither had he said it didn't matter.

Cassie stared out at the water. The moon rippled across the quiet black surface. She glanced sideways at Jake for a second, trying to guess what he might be thinking, wanting to plead with him to give her a chance, but if he kissed her, he would know she was just a girl. She didn't even know how to kiss like a woman. Were you supposed to kiss firmly or softly? Were you supposed to kiss with your mouth open or closed? He was handsome. He'd probably kissed a lot of women.

Jake slid his hand under hers, their fingers sliding together. Cassie relaxed. He didn't think she was too little, but now she wasn't sure why he'd be interested in her and then her cousin Rancy came to mind and maybe she'd been caught again. If she refused, Jake could get angry. Who would save her? Ben was a large enough boy to seem like he could take care of himself, but he'd never been in a fight. He really didn't have much courage. Jimmy, on the other hand, had no fear. Cassie didn't know if he would protect her. He certainly protected Ben when they played at the bars. If you messed with Ben you messed with Jimmy, and if you messed with Jimmy you messed with his bigger brothers and his pa, who thought nothing of spending a weekend in jail for busting a nose or two. Darlene would let Jake kiss her. She would have to let him kiss her, and then get back inside as quickly as possible.

"Are you cold? You're shivering." Jake removed his jacket.

"Here, take my coat."

"Yes, maybe we should go back." She could take his coat and stay outside, give him another opportunity to kiss her. It was wrong and foolish, but, strangely, she desperately wanted Jake to kiss her. "I don't want to get into trouble, you know. Ben will come searching for me if I don't get back soon."

"I hope I didn't do anything wrong," Jake said. He held his jacket out by the shoulders, waiting to help her put it on.

"I'll be all right." Wearing a boy's jacket meant they were a couple, they'd made out. If the world thought she'd been necking with a boy she'd just met, that'd be just wrong. Dee would have worn the coat like a badge of honor.

Outside the pavilion little knots of couples and gatherings of people stared intently toward a group of men in the shadows. The band had stopped playing, too early to be a break. Cassie searched the crowd for Ben spotting him standing at the edge of the shadows with Purdy whose thin face glowed red and angry in the light of his cigarette. Guy stood next to the building talking to Darlene.

Cassie searched for the familiar shapes of the men that would be there, hoping desperately they weren't, making out the dark silhouette of Jimmy, his older brother, father, and the two Park Police officers who were always at the dance keeping things in order. Another man, larger than any of them, shouldered in to the group. Rancy was back from the service. Cassie almost bolted toward the lake and the dark, twitched a bit, took a half step. If she hadn't been holding Jake's had she probably couldn't have stopped herself. Cassie could almost smell the tension radiating from the men like the air before a lightning strike. Jimmy bounced in and out of the small group, attempting to keep his father and brother from taking the band's money. They'd done it before when they'd been short on drinking cash and when the band played bars, Jimmy let the bartenders know not to let his kin run up a tab.

"Let's go in." Jake gently pulled at her hand.

"No," she said. "I'm a little bit warm. Let's stay outside for a minute." She tried to seem calm, her heart racing. She'd put Jake into real danger by being with her. She'd heard that Rancy's decision to join the service had something to do with a girl of less-than-good reputation trying to refuse his advances. If the girl had been good, he would have never gotten the choice of jail time or the armed services. Maybe people believed the girl had it coming? Cassie shuddered to think about what he'd done to the girl. When Cassie let herself think those thoughts, she half expected, even hoped, someone would have killed him by now, then she prayed for forgiveness for thinking that way.

Ben and the others boys would never tell Rancy she'd come along, but there was nothing they could do to protect her if she was spotted.

Dee watched her intently from her place across the gravel yard. Darlene didn't know about Rancy. Only Ben had any idea and he really didn't know it all, at least Cassie hoped not.

Three girls walked across the lawn near Rancy. He turned to watch them.

"Let's go in." Cassie pulled Jake across the yard as quickly as she could without being obvious. Rancy said something to the girls. They abruptly changed direction, stumbling over each other like frightened hens. Cassie swore she heard the crack of his hard laugh.

She dragged Jake to a far corner of the room, keeping him between herself and the windows facing the men. One of the police pointed toward the parking lot. All five men turned and disappeared into the dark.

Her brother and the boys returned, Ben searching the room for her. When he found her he mouthed, "He's gone."

After the break the band played mostly slow songs. Ben had seen her holding hands and had smiled at her from behind the microphone while she danced with Jake. He winked at her. She winked back, happy that her brother approved. As the night went on, Cassie and Jake danced closer, their steps smoother until she knew his next step for certain. The warmth of his body seemed so natural. Her hands pressed against the muscles of his back—good, strong, heavy muscles from farming.

The last notes of "A Whiter Shade of Pale" had been played. People started filing out of the building, knowing the dance was over. The pain in her chest was there again only ten times worse. Jake fumbled with the keys to his motorcycle. "I suppose I should be going," he said. "Come and see my bike."

Cassie took his hand knowing truthfully what he was asking. People milled around in small groups of couples and odd singles on the hardscrabble of the yard outside the building. The singles flowed like a sluggish river toward the parking lot or to the main path skirting the shore of the lake to the campground. They laughed, giggled, talked, and yelled, the tips of their cigarettes dancing sprites floating in the dark.

As Cassie and Jake turned the corner of the building, he said, "I was wondering, you know, if I could stop over to your house sometime. I mean if it's okay with you and your parents?"

Cassie had been watching the path, wondering if she'd ever see him again. "Yes," she said. "Yes, that'd be okay. When?" she said, now worried she'd spoken too quickly.

Groups of couples disintegrated two by two and wandered off to their private darkness, quieter, more subdued than the singles.

Jake walked slower. "How about tomorrow? You go to church?"

"Yeah." She wanted to look into his eyes, but he kept moving, searching. Her heart pounded in her chest. Her hand perspired in his. "We get home around one." She spoke as if asking questions. "Dinner's over about three, so's if you come about four it'd be all right, I think?"

He bit down on his lower lip. "Should I call first?"

"No, just come over." Now he'd certainly think her too forward, but they didn't have a phone. "It'd be best if you met my mother and father."

They stopped in the darkest spot along the path between two lights. It was time for him to kiss her. Cassie swallowed hard. Her legs shook. Jake's arms slid around her waist. She gazed up at him, not quite knowing what to expect, afraid of his kiss, afraid he'd change his mind. He kissed her. Her hands slid up his arms, over his shoulders, around his neck. Ever so slightly he pulled his head back. Their lips parted and ever so slightly she tugged on his neck and kissed him again before she knew she'd done it. Her breath was gone. All she wanted to do was to kiss him, to melt into him. She had felt these feelings before, only alone, only wisps of them at sunset as the sun turned orange and the sky dusky, stained with color, or deep into a clear night when the sky became an endless field of stars, and now they coursed through her like a spring flood. She pulled away.

He pulled her against his chest. It moved in and out in long breaths. She closed her eyes and listened for his heart. It was beating quickly. Cassie hoped, like hers pounding in her chest for him, his beat for her. She wanted to kiss him again and again, to hold him, to feel how they fit perfectly together. She turned away. If she looked at him she would kiss him again. "Who's that on your bike?"

"What? Oh, damn. Oh, I'm sorry. I've got to go. I'm sorry, it's someone I know." Jake stepped toward the lot as car doors opened and shut, engines started, goodbyes were shouted over car roofs and from open windows. Tires of cars squealed as people drove away.

"I'll see you tomorrow." She let his hand slide from hers.

Jake started to walk down the path. "I'll be there about four," he called.

"Okay," she said. She laughed.

Jake laughed, also. He walked back up the path and kissed her again. "I don't want you to forget me."

"In a day?"

"Yes," he said. "I don't want you to forget me in a day, for an hour, for a minute, or even a second."

She shook her head. "No, I won't."

"Are you sure?" he asked taking two steps toward the lot.

"Yes." She wanted him to know for certain. "Jake?"

"Yes?" he said again, walking back to her. She kissed him, her hand on the side of his face. People walked by. She didn't care. She was in love for the first time and forever.

"Cassie," Jake said.

"Yes?" He bent down and kissed her.

Oh, God, she thought.

"Good-bye," he said. Jake walked away.

She smiled weakly and waved as he walked toward the skinny kid with the scraggly blonde hair sitting on his motorcycle. The boy said something to Jake as he approached. Jake grabbed him by the collar of his shirt and lifted him partially off his motorcycle. The boy put his hands against Jake's chest but didn't push, Jake letting him go, waving his hands as he spoke to the boy. The boy was his little brother. Cassie knew. She knew Jake. She knew him well, as well as she knew her father's farm, the hills that surrounded her, the time when the berries came ripe and the time to cut willow branches to make the rough baskets she used to carry vegetables in from the garden. The mountains were as much a part of Jake as they were her.

Chapter 2

Cassie lingered between waking and sleeping, the pictures of her dreams blending with the soft sounds of the beginning of the country day, the morning pre-dawn chill floating over a damp forest floor. She thought she heard the wind blowing up out of the valleys, rushing along the stone faces of the mountain to rustle the gray-green leaves of the birch trees standing like frozen streaks of lightning on the ridge above her father's farm. She had dreamt of the lazy morning feeding of the fish in the holes and eddies of the streams, turtles crawling from their burrows to a place in the sun, the buzz of an early-rising bee, the birth of a calf in a high meadow dotted with rock more ancient than man.

Had she imagined Jake? Not all had been a dream. Some of the last night might have been not so much a dream as a hope, a wish, but what she wanted him to be did not have much bearing on who he was. His name, Jake McCullom, and he was seventeen. She tried not to think of him, to put too much stock into one night, but how could she not? She could still feel him in the tips of her fingers, the muscles of his arms and shoulders where she had held him as they danced, the taste of his lips. She had a sense of the size and shape of his body against hers. She'd floated alone in her dream, but Jake had been all around her, warm and soft, the same feeling she'd had last night when she'd kissed him.

Cassie took her tea out to the front porch. The clover and dandelions of the lawn sparkled with thousands of diamonds of dew and the air smelling sweetly wet. The green needles of wild onions bordered the country road. In the morning the breeze was tinted with the smell of them. The far-side field lay fallow, sloping away from the road with blue dots of thistle flowers mingling with all the shades of the green of mountain plants, spattered with the reds and yellows of paintbrushes, and the white of wild mustard, and Queen Anne's lace. The meadow ran up the side of the hill to the woods. The bank of a small stream, a yellowish-tan line, split the ripening field.

Her mother gently shoved open the screen door with her foot. "Good morning, Cassie." She stepped out onto the porch, blinking at the brilliant light.

"Nice morning, ain't it?" Cassie slid to the side of the bench, making room for her mother to sit, knowing she would, and hoping to speak to her but too afraid to start.

"It's lovely, like every morning." They stared out at the mountains, daughter and mother listening to the birds, watching the erratic flights of butterflies. Trees climbed stubbornly upwards until the mountains became too steep, leaving only gray outcrops of rock to the tree-covered summit and the blue morning sky.

Cassie's mother held an old porcelain cup in her right hand, its matching saucer tucked under her chin as she sipped at her hot tea. She hadn't dabbed on the flowery-smelling perfume she wore on Sunday that Cassie now associated with the day and church as much as with her mother. Her mother's gray-streaked hair, pulled against her head, was as long as Cassie's and now Cassie equaled her mother's short five foot height.

Cassie said, "Ma, how'd you know it was Pa? How'd you know it was him that was going to be your husband?"

Her mother gazed out at the lawn as if searching for the answer. "Oh, I don't know. I just knew, that's all. It ain't like I'd known that many boys."

"You think you got to know a lot of boys before you know when the right one's come along?" Cassie asked.

"No," her mother said. She glanced down at the skirt of her dress, picked an errant thread off near the hem and dropped it off to the side. "As a matter of fact, it probably don't help at all, but today ain't yesterday." She sat quietly for a moment. "This is about the boy you met last night."

A car drove slowly up the road, a neighbor. Both women

waved.

"How'd you know?" Cassie asked. "Oh, Ben, he can't never keep a secret."

"Not when it comes to his baby sister," her mother said. "What's this boy like?" Once again the saucer went under her chin, the cup to her lips.

Cassie took a quick sip of her tea. "He's got a motorcycle."

Deep lines from years of working in the sun cut down each side of her mother's mouth. Wrinkles sprayed from the corners of her eyes and shadowed her cheeks. She sipped at her tea and swallowed before answering. "A motorcycle? I don't know if I like the sound of that."

"No, no, it's not like that. He's like us." As her mother had done, Cassie searched for the answers she needed out on the lawn and in the sky.

Her mother smiled. "You mean he's in the sun all day, like he works the land?"

"Well, yeah, but he dresses like us. His clothes ain't nothing fancy, but they're clean and he's real polite."

Her mother examined the mountains, the smile gone from her face. "You really like this boy?"

"I think I do." Cassie smiled, too flushed with the memory of Jake to keep it secret. "We hit it off real well."

Her mother sat her cup in her lap. "Cassie, honey, you ever been in love before?"

"No, I don't think so." Cassie searched her mother's face trying to understand what her mother wanted to know and to know if she would need to defend her love. "I mean I don't know if I love him. There's been boys I liked in school, but not like this. It just seems that when we danced—oh, I don't know."

Her mother gently brushed away the wind-blown strands of hair from Cassie's face. "You got a lot of time."

Cassie sat still while her mother fixed her hair. "I'm over fourteen. That ain't so young."

Her mother sat back to search her daughter's face. "Maybe it's not, but there's some people who's pretty young at fourteen."

Cassie tucked her hair behind her ears. "Some people's pretty young at thirty."

"Lord knows that's true." Her mother lifted the cup and saucer from her lap. "It's life that makes you old. What I mean is mature." She stared down into the cup.

Cassie turned the word over in her mind, trying to understand exactly what her mother meant. "I don't know, he seems pretty responsible. Seems like he takes life pretty serious."

"And what if you're wrong?" her mother asked.

"I'll know," Cassie said, but how would she know for sure, or would her heart lie to her head, or her head lie for her heart?

"It takes time, Cassie. You have to have patience." Her mother set her cup on the bench. She took Cassie's cup from her and reached for her hand. "Cassie, I know you know what goes on in men's minds. I ain't saying it's bad. It's just nature, but you've got to see the rest of it, too. Women rear the children, keep the nests. It's the men who provide the labor."

Cassie's mother's hands were so familiar to her, and she'd heard her mother's speech before, but it still brought a sense of comfort, knowing who she was and how she fit.

Her mother said, "I guess what I'm trying to say is that men's lot is different from ours. In its own way it's as hard. The world has a way of beating even the strongest men down. We can see the fruits of our labor grow into young men and women while they watch as their life slowly slips away." Cassie's mother spoke in long one-breath sentences, inhaling slowly between each. "What I'm trying to say is, a good man is hard enough to find and he'll take care of you and yours as long as he's able. But it ain't only that. You've got to know that it's the man and not what he can do. I knowed some women who thought they could up and throw a man away when they were done with 'em, but God's got a way of evening things out."

The last part was new. Cassie wasn't sure why her mother had spoken that way. She'd stay with her man through fire and storm—once she knew who he was. "I ain't nothing like that," Cassie said. "If it of been that way, I know a couple of town boys who'd been better prospects."

Her mother set her jaw. "Now don't you go hanging around any of those boys. You know what they're up to." She gazed up to the summit again, searching. "It can be wonderful, but it can be so full of heartache, good heartache and bad. You got to take the good with the bad." Her mother passed Cassie her tea.

Cassie smiled, the feel of Jake, how she felt in his arms coming back to her. "Jake's a good man. I can tell by the way he talks. He's real polite and he don't flirt or brag."

Her mother gazed sternly at her daughter her lines on her forehead deepening. "Maybe he's a good man and maybe he'll bring to you a lot of caring and loving. What can you give to him?"

Cassie turned away from her mother, not wanting her to be able to read her heart. "I know what you mean, Ma." She didn't want to be reminded of it, not now, not today, of the old fear, of the older responsibility.

"In case you don't, all I got to say is sometimes the urge gets mighty strong, especially when you think he's the one. I know you're a good girl, but you got to remember that you ain't got much, but you got yourself." Her mother cleared her throat. "That's what you bring to your wedding night. He brings the future. You bring the past."

Cassie picked up her cup. The tea was getting cold. She drank it to avoid looking directly at her mother afraid her mother might see the doubt in her eyes, that her daughter wasn't sure what kind of girl she was or would become.

Her mother touched Cassie's face with the knuckle of her index finger. Cassie pressed her cheek against it, feeling the roughness of the skin, loving her for it.

"It's been this way forever and there's no sense thinking you can mess with it." Cassie's mother stood, balancing her cup and saucer with her left hand, smoothing her dress out with the other. "It's time to get ready for church."

"Ma?" Cassie touched her mother's arm. "He's supposed to come over today."

"That's good. That's real good, Cassie." Her mother went back into the house.

Cassie drank the last of her tea. Was her mother right? Above her the sunlight struck the tops of the mountains, inching its way down into the valley. Some things never changed, like the mountains, but some things did, like the creeks. They changed all the time and sometimes they were dry and sometimes they flooded. Did the same rules always apply?

The church was a half-hour away. Cassie rode in the back seat behind her father. Dust floated through the rusted holes into the passenger compartment of the old two-tone, green and black 1957 Plymouth station wagon. She hated how the dust got into her hair and on her skin. It smelled ashy, like a long-dead fire. The car had no radio, but even if it had, no one could have heard it over the sound of the engine, the loud humming of the old snow tires, and the banging of all the old worn parts of the car.

"Ben," Cassie's father shouted. "How was the dance last night?"

"Okay. Cassie met a boy." Ben laughed.

"Ben?" Cassie glanced into the mirror, but her father stared out at the road.

Her mother gazed out at the fields. "Looks like it's about time for a second cutting."

"And he's got a motorcycle," Ben said.

"Ben, stop it," Cassie said. Still her father said nothing. She brushed at her cotton dress. Sometimes she hated how Ben teased her. Her mother said it was his way of showing he loved her, but sometimes it was downright cruel, and Ben had ruined

27

everything. Now her father would think she'd been keeping secrets and maybe send Jake home. She wanted to cry, but you didn't cry over trivial things. You cried for sorrow and not for pain. You endured pain.

"Cassie asked him to come over," her mother said. Now her mother was teasing her.

"Oh, I see," her father said. He turned slowly onto a county highway, and then peered up into the mirror. "When were you planning to let me know?"

Cassie met his stare. "I was going to tell you soon if people'd leave me alone."

He glanced at the road and then back to her. "I suppose you're expecting me to let you go riding all over the county with him. You got chores to do."

Cassie said, "He's a good boy. You'll see. Honestly, he's real polite. He lives across the county outside of Chauserville."

Her father said nothing. His decision wouldn't come now, or even when Jake arrived. Sometimes her father thought too much. It was part of the illness, or the illness was from too much thinking. A strange, dark cloud descended on him once or twice a month and kept him from working. He could barely climb out of bed. Cassie served him dinner in a darkened room, her father's red and swollen eyes staring weakly back at her. The sadness scared her. But because of the illness Jake would come over. If her father had been in better health to afford a phone, he could make her call Jake, or worse, he could call Jake's parents. Her father could still go to Mrs. Fowley's house and use her phone, or make her, but borrowing a phone meant not only were you too poor to afford one, but it was akin to admitting it.

They attended the First Evangelical Church of Christ. Cassie's father's sister, Aunt Teresa, went to the same church, sitting in the upper-left section of the church, in the pews with the other well-to-do people of the parish. The Beglows and Cantrells sat there too, along with other flatland dairy farmers. Cassie knew the

Cantrells' boy Judd from school, but he never went to church anymore. He was what Darlene called a looker, but even she cut a wide path around him. Darlene liked to say too much inbreeding caused his craziness, that their class of people needed to quit marrying each other so much and get some new blood into their veins. Judd had always been in trouble in school, picking fights all the time.

Other people were ignored when attempting to sit in the left -front section, talked over as if they weren't there. Only a little time needed to pass before people got the idea you sat there by invitation only.

As they neared the church, Cassie's mother said, "Oh God, there's Teresa. Who's she got with her?" Her mother pulled herself forward to get a better view of the couple. "It looks like a soldier? Why, it must be Rancy." Her gaze followed the pair as her husband slowed down and pulled into the parking lot. "He's cleaned up kind of nice."

"Only on the outside," Ben said.

Cassie's father steered their car into a parking spot. "Well, he's going to church. He ain't done that in a while."

Teresa and Rancy waited for them next to Teresa's new pink 1967 Impala. Cassie slouched down in the back seat. Her aunt had always reminded Cassie of a soft dumpling, a just-risen loaf of unbaked bread. Teresa never went outside that Cassie could remember. Her uncle Carl took care of the lawns, gardens, and farm. Teresa busied herself in their big farmhouse, growing large to fit it.

Everyone knew Carl and his boy never got along. They could never have made the ride over without getting into a fight. Maybe Rancy had changed? Cassie doubted it. Zebras don't change their stripes. They could dress him up all they wanted. They could give him a fancy uniform, but underneath he was who he was.

Teresa waited until they had all gotten out of the car.

"Calvin." She raised her voice not so much as to be impolite, but to get Cassie's father's attention. "Calvin, how are you, Cal? You remember Rancy, don't you?"

Her father walked over to his older sister. "Why, of course, Teresa." Cassie had hoped he might have waved or shouted hello and gone in the direction of the church doors.

Teresa blushed slightly. "Well, I know you wouldn't forget. It's just he's gone and changed so much since he volunteered for the service. I thought you just might not recognize him." Teresa and her son maneuvered to stand between Cassie, her family, and the church.

Rancy reached over and shook his uncle's hand. "The Marines have made a man out of me. That's something you ought to be thinking about, Ben." Rancy grabbed Ben's hand. The index finger of Ben's other hand touched the scar on his chin, the one Rancy had given him when they were children.

"Here's my little Cassie," Rancy said. "You're all growed up and prettier than ever. I got a lot of friends in the service I'd a have to kill to keep them away from you."

"Hello, Rancy," she said. "You ain't been gone that long." Cassie stood away from him, fearing what might come next, although she was somewhat safe as long as they were out in public. If she'd allowed herself to hate anyone it would be him, her own cousin, flesh and blood, and her very own torment.

He squared up in front of her. "No, I guess I ain't, but it's been a while since I seen any of you. You'd think you'd of missed me a little bit. Give your cousin a kiss hello."

"No thanks." Cassie backed away, making a conscious effort to keep her hands at her side.

"Come on now, Cassie, don't you be shy," Teresa said. "Ain't he a man? You should hope you get yourself one like this someday." She patted her son on the arm. "Now just give your long-lost cousin a kiss."

Rancy grabbed Cassie by her upper arms and leaned over to

kiss her. She turned so he kissed her cheek. His face flushed red when he backed away.

"Why, you're blushing, Cassie." Teresa giggled.

Her father stared at the big man. Ben and Cassie's mother blushed. Teresa doted on her son and the families had always been close even through the arguments Rancy caused. Cassie's father believed in the sanctity of kin. Family was all you really had and cousins were the next things to brothers and sisters.

The kiss shamed Cassie, but nothing would be accomplished by protesting.

Teresa turned to Cassie's mother. "Hello, Gertrude. That's a nice dress you got there. How would you all like to come to dinner?"

Cassie thought of swearing under her breath. She even half-thought of the words. She was sure Ben was cussing a blue streak.

"That's mighty nice of you to invite us," Cassie's father said. Cassie's father loved his sister. He also hated being around her, but no more than Cassie hated being around Rancy. "I know Gertie would just love to get out of cooking, but you see, Cassie's already invited someone over after dinner."

A straight thin smile crossed Rancy's face. "If it's one of her little girlfriends, she can come too."

"Well, you see it's not. It's a beau."

"Pa," Cassie cried. He lifted his hand for her to be quiet.

Teresa turned to her brother. "Cal, she's a little young to be having a serious beau."

Rancy's gaze turned from Cassie. "Ma, I'm not going to stand around all day. I'm going in." He walked up the steps of the church and into the interior.

Ben let out a long breath, running his hand through his hair. Cassie's mother fussed with her purse.

"Now, Teresa, I remember you courting a few when you was her age," Cassie's father said.

"Why, I never." She laughed. From what Cassie had heard, Teresa had had only one boyfriend and that was Uncle Carl. Teresa had been on her way to becoming an old maid when Carl came along.

Teresa seemed beside herself, fidgeting with her purse, touching a few dark hairs on her chin. "Cassie, oh, dear, Cassie, I should of had you over more. I could of taught you the proper way to entertain a beau."

"I bet you could of," her mother said. "Now, Teresa, let me help you up the steps." She touched Cassie's aunt's elbow and pointed her to the church as if Teresa weighed nothing at all.

"Why, thank you, Gertie. You know I didn't mean nothing by it. I never had a little girl of my own. I like to think of her as one of the family."

Cassie's mother walked beside her sister-in-law. "She is, Teresa."

"Well, I mean I always wanted her to be like my little girl. You know I just loved to dress her up and comb her hair." Cassie swore she saw a tear falling from Teresa's left eye. Her father and Ben were smiling, but inside they were laughing. She would have laughed too if the joke hadn't been mostly on her.

After the church service was finished, Cassie filed out of church behind her mother, father, and Ben who was still groggy from the nap he had taken. Below the steps, lined up on the left side of the walk like a wedding line, stood Teresa and Rancy. She could make out the green color of his uniform through the spaces between people. Cassie moved to the side of her father, away from Rancy.

Her aunt grasped her father's hand as they passed. "Calvin, you must come over for coffee at the least. Carl's been making his fry cakes just for Ben and his little Cassie. You've got to come over. He'll be so disappointed if he doesn't see them."

Her father patted the top of her white doughy hand. "Teresa, we got things to do."

Teresa spoke quietly. "My boy leaves for Vietnam, next month. I don't know when I'll be seeing him again. I just want someone to see my boy in maybe his finest hour going to fight for his country. My friends—my so-called friends—they just can't abide my boy's strong personality, and you know Carl and Rancy ain't got along in a while. You're family, my only family."

Her mother stepped in front of Cassie's father. "Teresa, sure we'll come over for coffee and fry cakes, but you got to promise that we only stay for an hour or so. Cassie and I truly need to clean the house up for her new beau."

"Well, of course, Gertie," Teresa said. "I know how one must get things in order for proper entertaining. There must be a heap of work to getting your place in order and all." Cassie's mother grinned at her sister-in-law's remarks, but turned and walked to the car.

Teresa's farm sat in a wide valley with enough flat land to grow corn, wheat, and oats for the needs of the ninety head of dairy cattle, leaving some to sell as a cash crop. The gently sloping hills around the farm allowed for the growing of twenty acres of burley tobacco and enough pasture for grazing. Teresa had seen to it that everyone in two counties knew the farm paid for itself. Every four years or so she had the barn and outbuildings painted red with white trim without the need for tobacco advertising. She had the house painted white.

Teresa kept most of her antiques on display, the furniture, rugs, lamps, desks, piano, and fixtures, purchased by all the Wolphes occupying the house before her. To Cassie they were her ancestors, or at least the remains of them. Each and every piece whispered to her of long-ago life, of which she was the culmination.

Uncle Carl greeted them at the door, shaking Ben's hand and hugging Cassie. The house smelled of hot grease, flour, sugar, and the aroma of percolated coffee. Carl was a big man gone almost completely bald. A starched, white shirt bagged across his shoulders but tightened around his middle. A pair of dark slacks and a brown belt with a brass horseshoe buckle hung below his stomach.

"Sit down, sit down," he said, motioning toward the table. "The coffee's on and the cakes are real fresh. First batch just come out of the deep fry." Carl was a farm boy who entertained his friends and family at the kitchen table, using the dining room for formal dinners, but always back to the kitchen afterwards for coffee and dessert.

"How you been?" Cassie's father asked. They didn't shake hands—smiles were enough.

The porcelain teacup, Cassie's since she could remember, sat on its saucer on the table. Rancy sat down next to Cassie's cup. Carl handed Cassie the plate of doughnuts. "Here, honey, why don't you pass these while I pour the coffee?"

Cassie served Rancy at arm's length. When everyone had taken a cake, Ben took two, Cassie set the plate down on the table. She walked slowly back to her chair next to Rancy. Uncle Carl's old yellowing mug sat in her place and her cup sat two chairs away.

Carl talked about the farm to Ben and her father, and asked about Jake when he heard. That was Uncle Carl's way. He generally loved people and seemed interested in what they did and had to say. The farm made him happy. It would have made Cassie happy too if her father had taken it back after he war.

"Excuse me," Cassie said after her second cup of coffee, pushing herself away from the table, walking through a living room heavy with the odor of furniture polish and potpourri, to the stairwell, up to the landing, turning left, then down the hall to the bathroom smelling of thickly scented soaps Teresa bought in a fancy store in the city. Cassie locked the door.

She flushed the toilet, put the seat down, washed her hands and scrutinized herself in the mirror. Her hair could use a good brushing. Cassie unlocked the door and twisted the knob. The door flew open. She jumped away from it.

"Well now, Cassie girl," Rancy said. "Very long time no see." He still had crooked teeth. They were white now, changed from the sickly yellow they'd been before the Marines cleaned them. "That weren't much of a kiss you gave me for my welcome home. And after all we mean to each other, too. Hardly no tongue at all."

Cassie backed further into the bathroom. She'd been so careful. Why had she let her guard down now? Cassie held her arms over her breasts. "Just leave me alone, Rancy," she whispered.

He stepped closer to her. "Now, you know you don't want me to do that. Remember all the good times we had as kids. You was just a skinny little thing then. Not worth fucking with. Now you got some meat on your bones. Don't tell me you've forgotten?" He slid his finger across her bare upper arm.

Cassie cringed and moved away from him. "I remember all the time."

Rancy grinned and stepped in front of her, reaching for her shoulders.

Cassie sat down on the toilet seat, trying to curl into a ball. "Why do you do this?"

"Because I know how much you sweet little things like it," he said. "You act all innocent, but I know better, don't I?" He brushed her hair away from her neck. She slapped him. Rancy held his open hand near Cassie's throat. "You stupid little bitch. Don't you know they taught me how to kill people with just my hands."

Cassie pressed her chin against her chest trying to protect the opening of her dress. "Just leave me alone. I didn't do nothing for you to act this way."

"Oh, and I thought you loved me," he said. "Here I told my best buddies that when I got home you and I was going to fuck all night." Rancy slid his fingers through her hair.

"Ain't you done enough already?"

"Not hardly enough, honey." Rancy leaned over to kiss her neck. Cassie ducked out of his way, toward the open door. He grabbed at her hair. She yanked hard, her hair slipping through his hands. She ran into the hall.

Uncle Carl turned the corner of the landing as Rancy came out of the bathroom. "Cassie," he said loudly. "I think your folks are getting ready to go." Her uncle walked past her as she scurried by. His eyes turned dark and narrowed, focusing on his son. "What you doing?"

Cassie turned and walked down the stairs. She heard Rancy say, "Get out of my way, old man. I ain't afraid of you no more."

The ride home felt dustier and longer than it had ever been. She needed to think about Jake, to get her mind off her cousin. Rancy would be gone for a year. How could he be so different? Ben, her father, and Jake seemed gentle, almost too much so. Sometimes she worried that Ben and her father didn't have what it took to be really strong. Whatever her brother and father were made of, Rancy had none of it. Maybe because of that, they never suspected him.

Jake would be the first boy she'd ever had over to the house. Her folks getting to know him seemed important. The feeling was strange, though, to have a man attracted to her, really attracted, as if he saw a different person, a grown person who stood in the same place she did, that looked like her, sounded like her, but was different.

At home Cassie changed into blue jeans and a blouse. She would have rather stayed in her dress, but if her father consented to let her go for a ride she'd better be ready. There was no sense in giving him time to change his mind.

After supper she sat on the front porch, waiting. The wind blew at the tops of the trees, rushing down the side of the west mountain, absorbing the scent of the pines and the musty smell of the day-warmed forest. It charged across the valley floor, over the pools of the drying creek, through the fields of ripening seed pods of the wildflowers, crashing headlong into the ridge of the eastern range, climbing to the summit and disappearing over the top.

A little after four the deep chatter of a motorcycle exhaust cut up through the mountains. She stood up, then sat back down. The sound grew louder like rolling thunder, slowly, inevitably making its way up the valley to her. If she stayed on the porch she could greet him like an old friend, but they weren't old friends. If she went inside now, pretended she had to fix her hair, then he could arrive, knock on the door and ask for her.

Cassie walked stiffly through the living room, through the kitchen and up to her bedroom. Jake shifted the motorcycle down, the motorcycle growling like a haltered beast. The bike idled in front of the house. Was their name on the mailbox still legible? Should she rush out or not? Finally the bike came up the driveway.

"You can come down now, he's here," her mother said.

"I was just getting ready." Cassie pushed her hair behind her shoulders and waited for him to knock. It came from the back door, a good sign. "Hi," she said through the screen.

"Hello, Cassie." Jake stood a few steps away from the door, fidgeting with the straps of an old white helmet. He wore his faded denim jacket, a red, cotton pullover, and blue jeans, everything clean and pressed. He smelled of the same cologne he'd worn last night.

Cassie stood for a second behind the screen, not knowing what else to do. She'd been the little girl who had run and jumped around the yard while her mother hung the wash, who rode on her father's lap while he turned the garden with the old tractor, Ben's little sister who held his hand when crossing the road. She had a feeling she would open the door and something would end.

"I'm fine," she said. "Would you like to come in?" Cassie

swung open the screen door. He followed her into the living room. She introduced him to her mother and father.

Ben came down from his bedroom. When he saw Jake, he said, "Hey, how's the motorcycle? I bet that thing goes really fast."

"I don't really know," Jake said. He bounced the helmet lightly against his knee as he spoke. "I just bought it for transportation."

Ben sat down on the arm of the chair, next to his mother. "Really?" he said. "How'd you get all the money for the bike? Must of cost a pretty penny."

"I work for some farmers. Been saving for almost two years." Jake smiled at Cassie's brother, but to her, it was looking more like a trial with Ben cross examining Jake while her parents sat in judgment. Jake said, "My pa knew of a cousin who died in Vietnam and talked his father into selling it cheap."

Ben stood up, turning to walk out of the living room. "Well, some of us get lucky. Got to write down some words to some songs. Nice seeing you again, Jake."

Cassie wanted it over. It wasn't just Jake on trial. Her ability to choose a good man was being weighed. "Jake and I are going out on the porch, if nobody minds."

"Well, be my guests," her father said, reaching for the paper he'd gotten from Carl.

When Cassie and Jake were sitting on the front porch alone, peering out at the mountains, Jake said, "You look very nice today, Cassie."

"Thank you. I can't believe that Ben." Cassie wished she had the courage to study Jake's face, to peer into his eyes. If she did, she could see what was in his heart.

"He pretty much got everything out of the way real quick."

"But he was just being mean. Sometimes he gets like that." There were feelings she had never felt before, and she realized they had to do with her, only with her. Jake might not feel anything towards her other than the hope of satisfying some physical desire. She had seen the young bulls in the fields, the birds and squirrels in the springtime. She understood what bees meant to flowers. She had dismissed boys like that with little acknowledgment.

She studied Jake's face for a full two seconds. His eyes were set deeply, the line of his forehead bent slightly and curved sharply into the break of the nose.

He turned toward her. She stared up at the rounded peaks, invisible under a canopy of hardwood in full bloom. She tried her best to hold still, to offer herself to his eyes, but it scared her, this man examining her.

A couple of small butterflies fluttered like tiny fairies from flower to flower in the field across the road, the mountains towering above. Jake reached for her hand. Cassie intertwined her fingers in his. He blushed. She relaxed. She wanted so much for him to kiss her and yet she feared he would try. Her mother or father might be keeping an eye on her if only to see what might happen. They would think him too bold.

Jake said, "Do you think your father would mind if I took you for a ride on my bike?"

"I'll ask." There were times, if she asked just right, her father couldn't refuse her. She'd learned that sometimes women did have power over men's hearts. The trick was to never ask for too much, or for the impossible.

Jake slid to the edge of the bench as if to get up. "I should most likely be the one to ask," he said.

Cassie laid her hand on top of his feeling the strength in it. "Let me ask, just this once. When they get to know you better you can do the asking."

Cassie left him on the front porch in the care of the high hills where the trees swayed in a gentle dance. Her father sat at the table in front of an empty cup. Her mother stood at the sink, her back to him. She glanced over her shoulder as her daughter walked in. Cassie sat down opposite her father. He seemed to be waiting for something. "Pa? Jake would like to take me for a little ride on his bike. I told him I'd ask. He wanted to."

Her father glanced over to her mother as if not sure what to say. "I don't much like those things," her father said. "If I let you go and you get hurt, I'd never forgive myself."

Her mother didn't turn around, but stared out of the kitchen window at Jake's bike.

Cassie folded her hands and placed them on her lap. She tried her best to appear like the little girl her father couldn't refuse. "Jake's a good boy. I know he'd never do anything that'd get me hurt."

Her father sighed. "Sometimes things happen that we can't control." He glanced again at his wife's back. His shoulders slumped just slightly. "Only for a couple of hours. You've got a lot of work tomorrow."

"Oh, thank you, Pa. We'll be good, I swear." Cassie kissed him on his cheek.

Cassie had dug out Ben's old denim jacket one he'd outgrown. She'd laid it on her bed in case she did go for as ride. She'd remembered it last night on the way home, Darlene and her separated by an amplifier. Darlene jabbered constantly at Ben and the boys while Cassie sat quietly remembering Jake, wondering if it had all been a dream—not the dancing, or the holding, or even the kissing, but the believing.

Jake smiled when he saw the jacket. He gave her a helmet and helped her strap it on when she couldn't get the hang of the double rings on the strap.

They rode around on country roads. The wind and the noise from the engine were louder than the music of the night before. The air rushed by warmed from the sun, cooled by the shadow of the mountains and the water from unseen streams. The sun played a game of hide and seek, ducking behind mountaintops, or peeking at them through green leaves. And the earth moved, tilting up slowly, smoothly heaving all its rocks and trees, deer and squirrel, its creeks and sky to the whim of the motorcycle.

And she was close to Jake, touching him, rushing through the country with its sweet sticky smell of ripening corn, the pungent odor of manure spread on hayed fields.

At a crossroads a small Volkswagen bus made its way toward them from the opposite direction, wallowing over the small dips and rises of the road. Yellow, orange, and green peace signs and flowers had been scrawled across it. It stopped at the corner. Over the idling exhaust of the motorcycle the sound of singing could be heard coming from the van.

As the van passed, the passengers shouted, "Peace, love— man." Hands with two fingers forming a vee, stuck out of the windows,.

Jake glanced at Cassie. She shrugged, pointing to her right. "I think this way goes to the Mill Pond Road?" He turned the way she pointed. They came to another crossroads. She pointed left. Cassie wasn't sure where they were, but she liked the game. She pointed to another road wondering how long he would take directions.

When they had ridden for an hour in the hills, the bike slowed as if the air had thickened. Cassie pressed into Jake's back, worried something had gone wrong. Jake stopped, turned around and headed back east. He slowed again and pulled off the road onto an overgrown rutted lane that clung to a creek piercing a narrow opening between two steep hills.

In the hollow, on a small rise, sat the remains of an old house whose burned timbers were crumbled into what was left of a cellar. A brick chimney jutted above ground level. Weeds and vines clung to the remains, devouring it decade by decade. A small tree peeked its head out from the cellar.

Jake stopped the bike and shut the engine off. Cassie jumped from the bike to stand several feet away, struggling to take off her helmet.

"Hey," he said. "This is kind of nice."

"Yes." Cassie dug at the strap. Jake walked toward her. She

smiled, but moved slowly back, keeping several steps away from him.

"I thought we'd stop and talk," he said.

"About what?" She didn't really know Jake.

"Oh, I don't know, about school and stuff." Jake walked away from the motorcycle and sat on the grass. Cassie followed, sitting several feet away, looking around. There was really no way out.

When the wind blew from the direction of the old foundation, it smelled of burnt timbers, flowers, and grass. There was no sign of a barn, or equipment shed. Both hills, opposite each other, were too steep to plow. They cascaded down to the creek. The land had been cleared for cattle not so long ago the scrub bushes had had much chance to reclaim the pastures. Tufts of long, thick-bladed grass, exploding in growth, spotted the sweeping green carpet of the side hill. A few small scrubs, gray-barked and twisted, shielded with thorns, grew stunted in the steep meadows.

"I wonder whose place this was?" Jake twisted around to gaze up toward the foundation.

Cassie shrugged, but remembered how clever Rancy could be.

Higher, crowning the hills, tall maple and oak stood crowded together, limbs rubbing limbs, walling the hollow. Their small hardwood saplings dotted the edges of the fields. Here and there a scraggly, thin, white line of a birch tree lurched its way towards the sky.

"It's so sad here," she said. "Whatever happened here must of hurt a lot of people."

"Yeah, they were probably real good people too."

A gentle wind rustled the leaves of the tall trees. The stream flowed out of the woods at the upper closed end of the valley where the open hollow melted back together, water splashing onto small round-worn rocks, churning over itself, tumbling through the brilliance of the grass-covered hills and disappearing into the hole in the woods at the opposite end.

Jake pulled at a blade of grass. "Your mother and father are nice."

"They are," Cassie said. "I can't believe they let me go riding."

He broke the stem off and started to shred it from the bottom. "I'm not getting you in trouble, am I? Maybe we should be getting going?"

Cassie stood and walked toward the creek. "No, it's all right. Just as long as I'm home before sundown."

"Then I say we've got about fifteen minutes before we got to go. That is, if you haven't gotten me too lost."

Cassie glanced back at Jake. "You're lost?"

"No, not really." He walked toward her. "See that big hill over there."

"Which one?" Jake kept moving closer to her. Her instinct was to move away, but she wanted to trust him. "Over there. The one that juts up." He pointed to a tall ridge higher than the others.

She sighted down his arm. "Oh, yeah, that's the hill outside our house."

"Yep, I figure if I keep working toward it, I'll get you home." He wandered down to the small creek and sat down.

Cassie followed, sitting a foot away, her arms wrapped around her legs.

"Cassie, I'm really glad I met you." Jake moved closer, their hips almost touching, his right arm braced against the hill behind her. His left arm moved around her and he gently pulled her closer.

Cassie let go of her knees to keep herself from falling into him. Jake leaned over and kissed her.

She wasn't scared anymore, and when he kissed her again, her eyes were closed and she lost her sense of the horizon. Cassie kissed him with her mouth open, with her mouth closed. She kissed his neck. He kissed hers. They weren't sitting on the steep bank as much as lying on it. Between kisses and after a long breath, Cassie said, "I think we should go."

"Are you sure?" he asked, slightly breathless. His lips were still only inches from hers, his breath warm in her nostrils.

She pushed him gently away. "I don't want to get into trouble on the first day."

They rode back west toward her house. Cassie wanted to lay her head on his shoulder, to close her eyes and just feel him next to her. But it was too soon, even though she was sure she loved him. There was a proper time and place for everything. Her mother had told her that and her mother knew more than she did.

Jake said his good-byes to her parents and Ben. When Cassie and Jake stood with the screen between them, Cassie needed to kiss him so much it ached inside her, and when he left, a part of her, a newly discovered part, left with him.

Chapter 3

People stood in the cold smoking cigarettes next to their cars as wind-blown snow stung their faces just to see how the other world, the one on TV, had reached its hand down into the valleys and hollows of rural West Virginia, along the ridges and bottom land, and had bled the life out of one of their own. Those who'd parked too far away to see the procession stood in the road waiting to see an honest-to-God casualty of war. No one spoke.

Above Cassie, her mother, Darlene and a line of black-clothed mourners, six men, including Ben and her father, all John Wayne Arnow's cousins or uncles, clutched the handles of the walnut coffin. They bulled it up the steep, snow-covered path to the grave site. Gravestones poked through the snow like gray and black buoys in a white sea. The men stepped their way up the slope, each man marching in the other's tracks. More gawkers in fogged-windowed cars entered through the cemetery gates, some getting out to take pictures.

Two soldiers walked behind them, an army soldier and Rancy. Cassie's father had told her the Marines had given Rancy leave from the war to bury his cousin and comrade. In actuality John Wayne wasn't related at all, but since J.W. was Teresa's brother's nephew, she had gone down to the post office where the selective service office was housed and made such a fuss Rancy had been sent home to attend the funeral.

John Wayne Arnow had only been a shadow out of Cassie's childhood. He had always been in the Army, always in uniform. Men left all the time from the hills to serve their country, but they came back and settled down to kit and kin, but not J.W. Cassie had heard relatives call him a career soldier, a lifer. Uncle Bill had always been proud of his son, but he had spoken of the time when J.W. would retire out of the service and come back to run the farm and maybe settle down, with a local girl. Anna had worried there'd be none his age left.

An area of about thirty feet in diameter had been shoveled clear. Gold-painted chairs for Anna, Bill, and a few of the older neighbors were arranged in arcs around a green-rug-trimmed, eight-by-five-foot hole.

A few dry snowflakes rested on the pallbearers and the under-taker's dark-clothed shoulders. Rancy stood erect next the other soldier, taller and fuller-chested than the man in green, as though he'd been born to be a soldier.

Reverend Francis spoke with his head bowed. Darlene, who didn't really know John Wayne, cried openly in heaving sobs, not caring who saw. She had come to comfort Cassie and to stay the night—to be a part of it all. Ben cried. Now tears welled up in Cassie's eyes despite her effort to stop them. She would have cried openly if it hadn't been for Rancy. A funeral didn't matter. She had to be on guard. Rancy was quick enough to get to her, some way.

The reverend finished his prayer. Rancy and the soldier folded the flag with a precision Cassie would not have thought possible for Rancy. The soldier handed Anna the flag. She grasped the thick triangle of white-starred, blue cloth while her eyes searched the soldier's face seeking an answer. Rancy stood next to him. His eyes peered down on Anna, unblinking. Anna burst into long, air-gasping sobs.

Three rows of gravestones away a high-school boy in a suit, tie, and black galoshes played taps. When the boy finished, someone from above, from the skeletal woods, or behind a grave-stone, echoed him back. The men from the VFW shot off their rifles.

Ben and Cassie's father came and stood by her, Darlene, and her mother as people began to drift slowly back down to their cars. Cassie's father took his wife's arm and Ben walked between Darlene and Cassie. They were both crying, sniffing tears in the cold air. Darlene laid her head on Ben's shoulder. He put his arm around her and held Cassie's hand. It'd been a long time since Ben had held her hand.

At Anna's, salads and pies littered the tables and counters. A freshly cured ham, smelling of cloves and caramelized sugar, baked and sliced, sat in the center of her large dining room table. Cassie, Darlene, Ben, her mother, and father were crowded into the living room along with several more distant relatives. They spoke quietly catching up on family news, the fried odor of an antiquated furnace tinting the air. The closed house sat stifling hot—human body hot, moist and heavy maybe what death felt like, the earth closing in on you.

Rancy and a group of older men crowded around the kitchen table a dozen feet from the living room. A bottle of whiskey sat in the middle of the table, Rancy's white hat shoved against it. Cassie listened as they told war stories. The stories were about killing. The other men's stories were mostly about cousins or brothers in World War II or Korea.

Rancy said, "Well, I been there about two weeks and I hadn't even fired my weapon yet." He quickly glanced over to Cassie. She turned away. "Hell, I hadn't even been in the bush but a couple of times." He spoke loudly as if he wanted her to hear. "I thought I was going to spend the war filling sandbags." He stopped his story for a second to rest his arm on the back of his chair. The top two buttons of his coat were undone. Slowly he brought his whiskey up to his mouth, sipped it, and then smacked his lips.

"One day we were woke up early," Rancy said. "They crammed us all into a Huey—that's a helicopter—and dropped us off in the middle of the jungle." He paused. Several men leaned forward. A man pulled his chair back and crossed an ankle over a knee. "We must have tramped through swamp and muck for ten miles. I was sure no one had any idea where we were going. Then they tell us to shut up and get down. We were right outside of a village." Rancy took another slow sip of whiskey. "They get us double-timing it into this little shit-hole and I see another platoon is coming in from the other side."

A heavyset man to his left offered him a cigarette. He waved it off. "Now, we're rousting out the natives. You have never seen any smaller people in your life. I thought, them people ain't even worth killing, let alone dying over. Well, we're shoving a bunch of them little yellow bastards around with the business ends of our M-16s when another grunt screams, 'She's got a weapon.'" Rancy played with his drink, turning it around on the table, glaring at the men and smiling. "I turn and there's this little slanty-eyed girl with this big old rifle. She lets off one round and jumps behind a hut. Can you believe it?" he said, smiling broadly. Rancy laughed. He pounded his fist on the table. "She jumped behind a straw hut. Well, I empty my clip through the corner of that hut where I figure she just might be. When we get around the hut, there she was lying dead."

"I'll be damned," one of the drinkers said. Another man coughed twice.

Rancy glanced around the table again. "Yep, I know what ya'll thinking. You're thinking Rancy's done killed a woman. Well, I said that too. I said, shit, my first kill and it's a little girl. My sergeant comes up to the body and kicks it over. He says, 'Soldier, that ain't no girl. That's the enemy.'" Rancy tilted his head back and drained his drink. He sat his glass on the table. A man filled it for him again.

Cassie had never seen Rancy around anyone except Teresa and Carl or her family. He seemed at home among men. More than at home, he seemed to draw men to him. There was admiration in their looks or if not, at least respect. She could almost see him leading men into battle, fearless and inhumanly cruel. Was that what men respected?

Rancy grabbed the bottle and poured more whiskey into his glass. "The moral of the story is, sometimes women aren't women, they're the enemy."

Cassie turned away.

Her father reclined in an old rocker watching the snow fall, a glass of whiskey in his hand. He hadn't touched his drink, but was peering beyond the yard, down its slope to the automobiles parked along the road.

Cassie left Darlene quietly talking to Ben and sat down next to her father. "Pa?" He had the look again of his sickness

Cassie's father stared down at his drink. He set it on the windowsill. "It's time we got going." He touched her knee. "Cassie, would you get the coats?"

Cassie walked upstairs to the bedroom where Uncle Bill had stacked all the coats of the quests on a bed. She rustled through the pile reeking of barn, wood smoke, of body odor, and old people's perfume. Cassie picked out Darlene's and her family's coats and turned to leave. Rancy stepped into the room and closed the door. Cassie clutched the coats in front of her.

"Been a while," he said. He moved from the door to Cassie with two quick steps.

"Not long enough." She turned her head, avoiding his stare.

"Aren't you at least glad your cousin ain't dead?" Rancy touched her cheek with one finger.

Cassie jerked away.

"Now, that ain't how a man like me ought to be treated." His face beamed red with the effects of the whiskey.

Cassie moved to her left, the coats in front of her. "You don't deserve no better."

Rancy stretched his arm out to his side, the amount of space she'd moved. "Everyone treats me with respect now. You know why?"

Cassie stepped back in front of him, away from his hand. "No," she said.

"Because they fear me. They know I like to do my job and they know I'm good at it."

"What job?" Cassie asked.

Rancy sat back on his heels. "Killing. And they pay me for it."

Cassie backed up a step, knowing the bed sat behind her, but she needed room. "That ain't nothing to be proud of."

Rancy grinned, his teeth still white. "Those old fools around that table think so. Hell," he said, backing up a half step, "I was born for this. People give me what I want or I take it from them." He stepped forward quickly. The backs of Cassie's calves touched the muslin of the bedspread.

She stood unable to move, to think of a defense. She didn't even have a straw hut in front of her.

Rancy ran his finger under her chin, down into the small vee of her neckline, pushing the coats out of the way. His voice was soft. "You know, I could stay here, not go back that's what they tell me, but then I'd lose out on almost a half a year of killing." Rancy undid her top button. His finger traced a line down her chest. "Damn, though," he said, as he touched the next button. "You could just change my mind." He undid the button spreading the opening with his hand.

Cassie's legs shook. There was a cruelty in his eyes she'd never seen before, not even when he'd been younger.

Suddenly Rancy grabbed two coats from her and stepped away. He swung around as the door opened.

Teresa stood in the opening. "There you are, Rancy. What are you two up to?"

"Why, Ma," he said. "I'm just helping little Cassie with the coats." Rancy walked past his mother, through the open door.

Cassie clutched her coat against her chest trying to secretly button up her dress. She followed Teresa, trembling, unable to speak as she handed out the coats with Rancy, who smiled, standing next to her shaking hands as if they were a couple. He kissed Darlene good-bye. She giggled over it.

The family rode in silence halfway home before her mother spoke, the words soft in the winter silence and the hum of snow tires over hard-packed snow. "Well, it was a nice funeral."

Cassie's father glanced back at Cassie. Darlene used Ben's shoulder as a pillow. "You watch, Teresa's going to get her boy killed off, too," he said. "Thinks the service will make a man of him."

Ben glanced at Cassie. "I heard J.W. was shot up bad," Ben said. "Did you see him, Pa?"

"Ben." Cassie's mother turned to stare over the seat at her son. "Don't you go asking your pa things you got no reason to." She turned to her husband, and brushed the shoulder of his coat. "Don't pay no attention to him, Cal. You been through enough already."

Cassie expected to see her father's eyes wide with anger reflecting from the rearview mirror. When he glanced back at her, his eyes were glazed over, as if he were getting ready to cry.

He said, "J.W. didn't suffer much, or I don't think he knew he suffered. He got hit plenty of times by something big. I figure it was one of those fifty-caliber machine-guns, not one of those oversize squirrel guns they use now." Her father wiped at the fogging windshield. "Probably after the second or third slug hit him he was like a chicken whose neck is wrung."

"Pa, that's a terrible thing to say," Cassie's mother said. She gazed out at the road for a minute, then back to her husband.

"There's some decisions to be made soon," he said. "You know Teresa didn't think I was much of a man. I could of got a draft exemption to keep the farm running since there was only me and her and Ma, who was sickly. The farm was damn near as big as it is now. Just like Rancy, she hustled me off to the service. Told me I was shaming them all by trying to get a deferment." Her father shoved his hand between the defroster vents and the windshield. He fussed with the heater buttons, jiggling the direction slide.

Cassie's mother said, "And all she was doing was trying to steal the farm. If the truth's to be told, let's not hedge it. Didn't tell Carl he ought to be going to the war."

They rode quietly in the early evening as the sunlight weakened. Cassie's father glanced back at his son. "I thought I fooled her. Got myself a job as a mechanic because I worked on the farm machinery so much. I got sent over to Africa to fix Patton's tanks. There weren't much fixing to them. They either ran or they'd been blown up. They put me in one right up on the front lines." Cassie's father wiped the windshield with the back of his hand again. "There'd be German tanks shooting at you and fools walking beside them shooting at you. You'd be shooting back trying to kill every last one because you was so scared that they'd get you. It was the only way you knew how to save your neck."

Cassie gazed into the mirror, needing to see his eyes to know if they were the same eyes she saw peering out of the darkness at her in the days of his sickness. Her father glanced into the rearview mirror. His eyes seemed to be pleading with hers, making the peculiar contact of a stranger, not father to daughter. Horror showed in them, the fear of a boy.

"It ain't nothing like you see in the movies. Man's got the same thing in him a hog's got and pretty much looks butchered when they get shot up." Cassie's father felt for the stream of hot air once again. This time he only glanced at the heater buttons. "You don't congratulate each other. You just try and get something else before it gets you. Ain't nothing louder than shrapnel hitting the outside of a tank, excepting maybe getting blowed up. Once in a while a bullet would get in and bang around inside. It weren't nothing but desert, good for nothing. Oh, God, did it soak up a man's blood."

Her mother leaned against her door and quietly cried.

"I got hit," her father said.

"You got shot?" Cassie gasped. Ben leaned forward, pushing Darlene's head from his shoulder.

Her father glanced up at her. "Not really shot. One of those bullets got inside and bounced off a couple of walls and hit me in the helmet. Knocked me for a loop. The artillery was blowing us to bits. The Germans was blowing us to bits. We was blowing them to bits." Cassie's father cleared his throat a few times. "Yeah—I was hurt plenty bad. We couldn't go no further. It was a standoff. Just shooting at anything we seen. I was still trying to load the gun even though I couldn't see straight." Cassie's father became quiet. He drove for a mile before he spoke again. He glanced at her in the mirror. "I was on my knees. I couldn't get my balance, or maybe I'd a got out of there. They said it was my concussion that made me piss my pants, but I'd pissed them long before that."

Darlene said, "That must of been horrible."

"Lenny, our driver, just leaned over and quit driving," her father said. "To this day I don't know how they got him, but he was dead. Sometimes I think he died of fright. Butch stuck his head out and started shooting all the Germans. When he stopped firing all I could see was his legs twitching. I threw up. He'd been like my big brother since I'd gotten to Africa."

Ben appeared astonished. Cassie didn't know if it was because he never knew his father had actually fought in the war or that war was like that.

"I knew he was dead. I knew we was all dead. I had my pistol out but I couldn't focus to aim it. I was just hoping it wouldn't hurt too much." Her father laughed. "One of the other guys was swinging the turret all around and someone was firing except they weren't waiting for me to load."

Cassie watched his eyes in the mirror even though she would rather have not, but he expected her to be there. She had always been there.

Cassie's mother said. "It's time to stop. You're getting yourself all upset."

Cassie's father reached over and patted his wife's hand. "I'm feeling fine. Ben's my boy. He's going to need to know because he's going to be needing to be making some decisions."

Cassie's father always drove on his side of the road even though there were no cars coming and the road was high-crowned and the snow tried to tug them toward the ditch. "I guess we won the battle because all the sounds of killing were dying down. Someone pulled Butch's body out. You should of seen the look on the soldier's face when he saw me pointing my forty-five at him. Took Mike or Frank five minutes to convince me they was Americans. They got me out of the tank and started patching me up. The bullet was still in my helmet. They put three green guys in and sent it off. It never came back. They gave me a medal for bravery. Can you beat that?"

They passed people who didn't have tractors, working with shovels at the plowed drifts that held in their cars. Heavy white clouds of breath poured from their open mouths as they struggled with their shovels against the hard-packed snow.

"Wow," Darlene said. "You must of been really proud."

"I could never get myself to get back into another tank. My legs would give out and I'd piss my pants and start crying like a baby, so gave me a medical discharge." He stared out at the road.

Cassie's mother reached over and held his hand. "Nobody ever needed to know."

Cassie's father glanced back at his son. "Ben, soon you're going to have to sign up for the draft."

Ben grabbed the back of the front seat and pulled himself forward. "I don't have to."

"No, you best. They got ways of finding you." Cassie's father pulled his hand away from his wife's, grabbing onto the steering wheel. "People are saying they're taking every able-bodied man around here when he turns nineteen." Her father tapped the brakes to feel which way the car might slide as they approached a corner. "Sign up. We'll try and get you a deferment. I don't give a shit what anybody says."

Cassie's mother brushed at her coat. She watched the

countryside go by. Cassie figured she was trying hard not to be a part of the conversation.

Cassie's father cleared his throat. "If you get four-F there'll be no problem, but I don't think you will. Look it here, I ain't one of those longhaired hippies on television and I believe in defending this country, but if this country wants to go on fighting all the time let it. Them boys like Rancy can go and have themselves a good time, but we ain't got no reason to be fighting a war just for those big government people in Washington."

Cassie stared into the mirror but her father wasn't looking there now. She wasn't partial to either side of the argument whether people ought to be fighting, but it just didn't seem like they needed to take a side that'd cause trouble.

"Hell, ain't no Vietnam people attacking us," her father continued. "Ben, I want you to go to Canada. If you get one-A, go. I love you and I'd rather you're safe in another country than six feet under. Better thought a live coward than a dead hero."

Cassie said, "We'd never see him again."

Her father glanced into the mirror, his eyes clearer. "We'd come and visit."

"When?" Cassie's mother cried. She pulled her small frame up in the seat and leaned nearer her husband. "We never have the money to go cross the county, let alone to another country. We'd lose him forever."

"Damn it," Cassie's father said. "I'd rather that than visit his grave every day. John Wayne was black and all bloated up like a dead cow. It about killed old Bill."

They drove on in silence. The tires hummed rhythmically over the snow-packed road. The heated air smelled of dust and a pinhole leak of antifreeze and the heated rubber odor of her mother's white boots.

Ben had slid back in the seat and Darlene was using his shoulder for a pillow again. "I heard Rancy tell he's got a woman over there," Ben said.

Cassie said, "It must be real bad over there for a woman to put up with the likes of Rancy." She shivered, imagining Rancy's hand on some poor Asian woman. Her father wiped at the window again. He finally opened the wing window. The cold air swept in feeling of snow.

Chapter 4

The snow had stopped by the time they pulled into the driveway, her father banging the car over the plowed drift blocking the entrance. Behind the clouds the sun was setting turning the sky a cold gray-blue and the Earth a cold metallic white. Her father or Ben would start the tractor and clear the driveway. The house sat cooling from the stoked fire of the morning, the air smelling of dried wood and plaster, the house feeling as if it needed to be warmed by a big fire, the air needing the smells of cooking, people talking and laughing, and the faint odor of their bodies.

After hanging their coats and arranging their boots in a straight line with the others, Darlene and Cassie crowded into her bedroom, Darlene stripping down to her underwear, a black bra and matching bikini panties.

Cassie turned away embarrassed by her friend's easy acceptance of her own nakedness and the fact Darlene looked good in those kind of underwear, like the models in a fashion magazine. "I'll go change in the bathroom," Cassie said.

"Why, Cassie, you seen more than this in gym class." Darlene danced in place. "Don't I look pretty?"

Cassie stared at the floor. "Yes, you look very pretty." She grabbed a pullover and a pair of jeans from her dresser drawer, glancing up only once. "I'm going to change in the bathroom." Cassie wore the same type of cotton underwear she'd worn since the day she'd gotten out of diapers. The underclothes that had hung on mannequins in the women's clothing stores weren't for her. Those kind were meant to be seen.

Darlene snapped the waistband of her panties against her flat stomach. "Well, aren't we the shy one all of a sudden?"

Cassie pushed by her. "You're crazy. You know that?" But Darlene wasn't and that bothered Cassie, Darlene's easy acceptance of the outside world.

After supper Cassie washed the dishes while Darlene dried. Afterwards they sat at the table talking, thinking about making a pot of tea, when Ben and her father came in from the chores, stomping the snow off their boots in the breezeway, letting the cold air squeeze under the door and sweep along the floor. Ben laid a gallon jug of raw milk on the table and sat next to Darlene. "Mrs. Fowley didn't come get her milk tonight."

Cassie's father poured himself a cup of coffee. "Maybe someone ought to go over there and see if she's okay."

"Sure, Pa, me and Miss Dee will be glad to do it." Cassie moved away from the table.

"Thanks." Her father took her seat.

The sky had started to clear. The moon was still down, but the snow seemed to give off its own blue light and the air was turning colder, smelling of ice. Cassie and Darlene had dressed in extra sweaters, and pants, boots, coats, hats, and mittens. Darlene adjusted her hat around her ears, and then fluffed her bangs. "It's really sad about your cousin John Wayne." She followed Cassie to the road. "I feel sorry for Rancy, too."

Cassie had decided a while ago not to think about today. Anyhow, Rancy would be going back overseas and maybe he'd end up like J.W. Then she shook her head, sorry she'd thought such a terrible thing.

Darlene pulled at the belt loops of her inner pants, then her outer ones. "Boy, you don't like him much do you?"

"I did, once," Cassie said. "You know how sometimes you think someone is special. You know, when you're a little girl."

"You mean like a crush."

Under a thick layer of powder the tire-packed snow made a soft crunching sound as they walked in the quiet night. "Yeah, I used to think Rancy was special," Cassie said. "I used to talk my way into staying over when I was little and I'd sneak into bed with him."

"Cassie, you didn't?" Darlene said.

The snow on the road was still not plowed. Six inches of snow on a weekend night wasn't enough to call out the plows for overtime. "No, no, we didn't know nothing like that at all. I used to sleep with Ben sometimes when I was scared, so it didn't mean all that much." Cassie hesitated for a minute thinking about it all, what it had meant, what Rancy thought it might have meant. "But Rancy learned what it was supposed to mean. By then he was getting pretty mean and I was staying clear. Sort of like a bull calf. They're real nice when they're little." A small ache started in her lower right arm. She hugged the bottle to her, sliding her arm up and resting the jug on her left arm while she thought of how Rancy had repaid her for her caring. "He's a terrible man."

Darlene reached down between her legs and pushed the crotch of her pants up. "Cassie Marie," Darlene said. "I can't believe you're being so cruel. That's just not like you. Rancy's serving our country."

"Cruel? He's cruel." Cassie took a breath. "We use to go to Teresa's house almost every Sunday for dinner. Rancy used to hit Ben and me all the time and then tell everybody we were lying."

Darlene stepped ahead of Cassie, turning around and walking backwards. "So, you tell on him?"

"Teresa believed him all the time. It just caused her and Pa to start fighting." Maybe the story was too complicated to make any sense. Darlene wouldn't understand, but she didn't want Darlene to think she was a cruel person. "I accidentally knocked a plant off Teresa's porch. Rancy took the blame. Uncle Carl wailed on him something fierce. I've never seen anyone get a beating that bad. I thought he killed him. Now I wished he did."

The maternal warmth of the milk seeped into Cassie's clothing against her stomach, hinting of the meaning of herself and her body, the one she was only now coming to understand. "For a long time I thought he was really something. I made him pies and everything. I even let him be mean to me." Cassie stared off into the hills. She might end the story there, but it wasn't the end of the story, just the beginning and the end was somewhere in the gray future. Maybe it would end in the same way John Wayne's ended. Cassie didn't want to wish for anyone's death, but if she wished Rancy wouldn't die in Vietnam, then she wished his torment on herself and that could only end tragically.

"When I was about ten," Cassie said, shrugging her shoulders trying to put her choice of wishing someone dead, or her life as a living hell, out of her mind. "It must of been around Easter because I had brand-new store-bought clothes right down to underwear and socks. Teresa always bought them for me. Rancy was fifteen, dirty and pimply faced. Ben and me always made ourselves scarce around the farm so's he wouldn't find us, but about then Rancy was making himself pretty scarce too. It got so he was never around. I guess that's why I was in the barn when Rancy found me."

Darlene bit at the sleeve of her sweater underneath her coat, pulling it down. "That sounds bad."

Cassie shook her head. "You don't know, Dee. I must of forgotten all about him. He chased me up into the loft so's he could peek up my dress. He was teasing me about my new underwear. When he got up to the loft he knocked me down and took them off of me. I was so mad I got up and slapped him right across the face."

Darlene leaned into Cassie as if wanting to see her eyes in the dark. "What'd he do?"

"He laughed. Then he grabbed the hem of my dress real quick and pulled it off right over my head. I was naked except for my socks and shoes." She blinked twice and squinted to where the stars became long needles of light. "He started laughing at me and saying all I had was baby things. I ran and hid behind some bales in the back of the loft. I begged him to give me my clothes back. He said he was going to steal them and hide them and I'd have to go home naked."

The tin cap of the jug had been rubbed shiny by all the years of twisting. She could stop right there and not tell Darlene anymore, but that wasn't the point of the story. "I begged him, really begged. How could I have ever faced my ma and pa? Dee?" Cassie stopped in the road, in a dark place between the lights of the houses.

Darlene stood away from Cassie, her neck appearing even thinner sticking abruptly out of the layers of heavy clothing.

"Dee, I didn't know nothing about nothing then, you know, but I think I would of done anything he wanted to get my clothes back—anything he wanted. A bad secret's better than the public shame."

Darlene moved closer. "Sometimes not." Darlene breathed hard through her nose, her jaw clamped shut, staring up into the sky as if searching.

"Uncle Carl came in to the barn. He heard us. He told Rancy to get down from there and that he shouldn't have me up there where I could get hurt."

Darlene reached out for the jug as if it were a baby. "Give me the milk. It's my turn to carry it." They walked on silently for a while. Darlene cleared her throat several times before she finally spoke. "Did he, did he you know?" She shrugged her shoulders and smiled a half-smile. "If it hurts too much to say it, just nod."

"No, I never let him get another chance like that. It was bad enough when I started to develop." Cassie stared at the stars filling the dark sky, twinkling like Christmas lights. "He was always grabbing me."

"Why didn't you tell your mom?" Darlene asked.

"You know why," Cassie said. "If I did, he'd say I was lying, or worse. He'd tell them I was one of those girls. You know." Cassie shrugged her shoulders. "Teresa would of taken his side. She'd have loved to put shame on our family."

Darlene shifted the jug, trying to become accustomed to the weight. "Your mom and pa would of taken your side."

"Pa always said kin was special even if they aren't always right. It's all you got. Teresa and Carl is all he's got." The air had started to turn colder and drier. Cassie pulled at the inner seams of her pant legs, trying to pull them down. "There'd been a big row. Who knows what Rancy'd say and Teresa would of spread all sorts of nasty stuff about me and mine. All them people are just waiting for someone like us to screw up so they can belittle us."

"I know what you mean." Darlene tried shoving a mittened finger through the handle of the jug. She gave up and cradled the bottle, blowing a cloud of vapor into the air in a long sigh.

"Oh, Dee, I didn't mean it like that," Cassie said.

"It's all right," Darlene said to the top of the milk jug. "I'm going to show them some day. Just you wait."

They walked up the road toward a small house whose yellow light spread out along the drifted snow. A large dog somewhere far away howled at the cold night sounding lonely. Darlene swung the milk jug back and forth with the rhythm of her walk. She'd been humming quietly to herself. "So, you still a virgin?"

"Darlene, how could you ask that?" Cassie said. The stars sketched the bristly top of the ridges cutting a ragged outline against the starlit sky.

"Well—then—did you ever let Jake, you know—fondle you?"

"Darlene, you're terrible. No."

They walked on toward the light, pant legs rubbing together, swishing rhythmically. Their breath puffed in the frigid air. The light of a car a half-mile behind them reflected off the white landscape. The tires, wrapped in chains, made a Christmassy sound as they churned up the road. The girls moved over to the side next to the bank.

"No? Not even once?" Darlene asked. "You're a cruel girl yourself, Cassie Marie. Poor little Jake comes around all the time holding your hand, a kissing you up and he don't get one little feel." Darlene fell in behind Cassie. The crunching sound of the snow under the front tires mixed with the muffled exhaust noise as the car drew nearer.

"Dee, that's not what good girls do."

Darlene said nothing for a minute. "Well, that's why there's women like my mother and sister, to give them poor men some satisfaction, to ease their pain."

Cassie jumped two steps ahead of Darlene and turned walking backwards as the sedan slid over to the left giving them room as it passed. Cassie tugged her wool hat down over her ears. "Your mom and sister ain't bad girls."

"No, they ain't, but people say they are. My momma said she'd rather wake up alone than go to bed alone. So's I guess it's just your preference."

"What's that supposed to mean?" Cassie played with her breath, watching it roll out of her mouth in white clouds. The night was clean; the stars were clean, owing to no one but themselves. She always felt secure in nights like this, being outside, maybe knowing hardly anyone else bothered with it.

Darlene seemed to ponder the question before she spoke. "I ain't sure, but just maybe there's two kinds of women in the world and men need them both."

Cassie held her mittens to her mouth, breathing into them, letting her breath warm her face. She giggled. "Well, okay, it happened." She knew it'd been wrong, but it just happened.

Darlene stopped. "Okay? Why, Miss Cassie, what kind of a woman are you?"

Cassie put her hands on her hips and stuck her chin out at Darlene. "Well, Miss Dee, it was an accident. We were just kissing and I had on my blue blouse that I don't tuck in, you know." Cassie turned away from Darlene and started walking toward the light. The small red taillights of the automobile, shining through a cloud of wind-blown snow, vanished over a rise.

Darlene caught up to her with a couple of long strides. "So, big deal."

Cassie smiled. Jake's hand had been warm and he'd cradled her in it and had been gentle when she'd closed her eyes. There had been a wonderful sinful pleasure. "His hand got up under it, accidentally."

"That's it?" Darlene said. "Geesh, that ain't petting."

"I know that." Cassie kicked at a small clod of plowed snow that had fallen back into the road. "I didn't make him take his hand out. I guess he just got carried away." She'd been the one who'd gotten a bit carried away but she'd pretended she'd put up with it for Jake. Cassie kicked the irregular snowball harder. It burst apart, small pieces scattering in different directions. "I ain't saying no more. Miss Dee, you're so nosy. I'm not saying anything more."

Darlene stopped walking. "I'm not going another step more with this milk until you tell me truthfully how it felt to have Jake's hands on your titties."

Cassie stood opposite her in the road. "Come on, Darlene, I said more than I should of already."

"Did it feel good? Did you like it?"

"I can't say I didn't like it. It just felt—different." Cassie turned away from Darlene and walked on.

"Different?" Darlene said, catching up again.

"Different," Cassie said.

"Different from what?"

"Different from when Rancy tried to do it."

"Oh," Darlene said.

A patch of yellow light from the single lit window lay over the soft and rounded snow drifts, piercing the blue landscape and lighting the shovel-width path leading to the back door of Mrs. Fowley's house. Despite Cassie's arrival being announced by Mrs. Fowley's dog, she knocked. "Mrs. Fowley," she said. "It's Cassie Wolphe. I got your milk here." She pressed her face close to the glass window of the door. Her breath fogged then crystallized on the surface. "Pa said I ought to bring it to you." The girls waited, listening to the constant yapping of the dog. The strain of the day began to ebb from Cassie now that she was back to doing her normal things.

Darlene said, "Don't that thing ever shut up?"

A light flicked on in the kitchen. Soon the door to the back shed scraped against the jamb as it opened. A shadow of a small woman in a shawl shuffled to the outside door. "Hello, Cassie." Mrs. Fowley's voice, weak and scratchy with a slight vibrato, and the shaking in her hands, suggested a life lived longer than her body could manage.

Cassie raised a mittened hand. "Hi, Mrs. Fowley. This here's my friend Darlene McAlester." Darlene nodded.

The old woman smiled as if awakening from some long sleep. "Come in." She turned and shuffled back toward the kitchen door. "Get yourselves out of the cold. My bones get so tired of this cold." Cats scattered from under their feet. Without looking back to Cassie the old woman shuffled to the far end of the kitchen to an old stove sequestered in the corner. She opened the fire door and slipped a chunk of wood onto the dying embers. A newer four-burner propane kitchen range sat next to it. "Robby thinks I should go down to Richmond with him, but what would I do there?" She nodded toward the table. "You girls sit down and I'll make some cocoa."

Cassie leaned against an old chair, bracing herself against a moving floor of cats searching for hiding places. "Oh, thanks, Mrs. Fowley, but we best get going. It's starting to clear up and it's getting colder out there."

Darlene opened the refrigerator door to place the jug of milk inside next to several tins of cat food covered with aluminum foil. She wrinkled up her nose at the open cans making sure Cassie saw her and Mrs. Fowley didn't. Then she smiled and adjusted her cap.

Cassie smelled wood smoke. The flue was starting to clog.

She'd mention it to her father. He'd come over, or send Ben to clean it. Her brother never minded helping Mrs. Fowley. It gave him an excuse to stay for the cocoa and maybe some homemade cookies.

The house was old, bigger than Cassie's, full of old furniture, dark wooden things with sweeping backs and velvet cloth. The barn had been knocked down by the weight of a heavy snow pack sometime before Cassie had been born, Mrs. Fowley having sold off the livestock and machinery years before after her husband died and Robby had moved to Richmond. She lived off her husband's army pension, renting the land and selling off timber once in a while.

Her lamps, with red cloth shades and ornate tassels, cast rosy shadows on washout wallpaper, the flowers having faded to white silhouettes in the parlor, covered with the faint gray of smoke or the yellow of cooking in the kitchen. As long as Cassie had been alive, Mrs. Fowley had owned the same furniture, but a new color TV sat in the front room.

Cassie's family's black and white TV had quit working a year ago last July. Even with Ben's help putting in extra money, her father didn't have the money for a new one until that Christmas, the color one. Cassie had almost lost interest in television altogether, reading the romance novels and fashion magazines Darlene gave her, reading Jake's letters over and over. Now her family seemed to have become addicted to television. Lately, though, she'd been watching it more to know the kind of clothes and hairstyles other kids wore and to see some of the neat things people had, but she worried that maybe they had too much. Some of the town kids in school thought too much of what they had and the clothes they wore and less how they treated people like her and Darlene. She still preferred to listen to the radio.

Cassie peeked into Mrs. Fowley's extra room, her sewing room, a woman's room with a cutting table with drawers for patterns and buttons, pins, and scissors. Cassie hoped to have one after she was married. Someday, her father had said, he would turn the woodshed into a room like that. But in a couple years Ben and she would be gone and then what would be the use? She didn't know. It was a ways away, two years and even though Jake loved her, he'd never mentioned anything about ever getting married. But he would—someday. She could feel it in her heart and the way he talked. He had plans now and they included having kids, which took a wife, meaning she'd be gone before her father ever got to the room.

Mrs. Fowley shuffled toward the backdoor, Cassie and Darlene stepping around the cats, the bolder or more desperate ones now rubbing up against their boots. The small yapping dog had disappeared. The girls squeezed between the open door and Mrs. Fowley. "McAlester?" Mrs. Fowley asked. "That name does sound familiar."

"Bye, Mrs. Fowley," Cassie said and shut the door, afraid of what Mrs. Fowley might remember and not wanting Darlene to have to explain her family.

A large silver moon rose over the high dark horizon dwarfing the mountains, hovering over the crystallized valley, the craters sharp enough to see with the naked eye. Cassie turned toward the meadow behind the house.

"Where're we going?" Darlene asked, following behind her.

"We're cutting across the field," Cassie said. "The snow's beautiful in a full moon." She stepped off the path into snow up to her knees, gazing at the mountains and the moon. The land lay soft and silver, the hills bristling with the black trunks of trees, the stars sparkling on the high horizon and the world asleep. Jake and she had kissed in the snow and let the moon shine on their faces. It all seemed to be another world for Jake and her and now Darlene. Cassie suddenly missed Jake more then she had all day and she'd missed him a lot all day.

Across the field of rolling drifts shone the muted light of her parents' kitchen. Cassie and Darlene stomped toward the faraway light, treading through the snow into drifts past their waist, getting stuck and depending on each other for help, laughing at almost nothing but of being out in the night and the snow.

Darlene scanned the field for little valleys between the drifts. "What're you going to do if Jake gets drafted?" Darlene pushed through a drift leaning hard forward.

Cassie had been tracking behind her. She stopped planted up to her thighs in snow, understanding the words, not understanding why she hadn't thought of it before, and why Jake had never mentioned it. He wasn't eighteen yet, but sometime he'd have to go.

Darlene's face shone ghostly silver-white, beautiful in the fullness of it, her eyes dark shadows with the spark of a moon's reflection. "I didn't mean nothing." Darlene offered Cassie her hand. "Don't worry, it's a long way off. Maybe he'll go to Canada? You going to go with him, if he does?"

Cassie seized Darlene's hand, steadying herself as she stepped through the drift, shaking her head slowly. "No, no there's nothing I can do." There'd always been a war, maybe always would be. It wasn't supposedly part of her world, but J.W. was dead. Rancy could be soon, and maybe Jake, someday. "Jake would never go to Canada. He'd even go to Vietnam if he had to." But she needed to believe it couldn't happen.

Darlene nudged Cassie. "Well, Miss I'm-Still-a-Virgin, if you had a couple of kids, they won't take him. Of course, I think you've got to be married or something. I heard they don't take men who are married with two kids."

Cassie stopped for a minute to run the figures through her head. She stepped toward the kitchen light, stepped back, shoving the snow before her in little eddies as she cut a deep erratic path in the drifts. "Oh, but there's not enough time. Even if we get married when I turn sixteen, they'd draft him when he turned nineteen. If I got pregnant on my wedding night, I'd be

only eight months along with the second when they took him."
She turned back to Darlene, searching her face for an answer, but
it was still only ghostly beautiful. "You think they wouldn't take
him if he had one and another one on the way, or you think he's
got to have two in his arms?"

Darlene took several steps toward Cassie's house. "I don't
know. It wouldn't be good for you if he got himself killed and
you had two babies to take care of." She turned to Cassie, pulled
at her mittens, brushed snow from her coat, then smiled, her face
brightening as if increasing the light from the moon. "Hey, if you
don't get married would you do it with him before he left?"

Cassie walked on toward the kitchen light not thinking about
Darlene's question, but about Jake and the war and the changes.

"Serious, Cassie." Darlene stood fast in a drift. "I'm being
serious here." Her face darkened as she turned away from the
moonlight. "You'd send Jake off to war knowing he might never
come back without knowing what it was like to make love to
him?"

Cassie walked back toward her friend, one of the few she'd
ever had in her life, plowing up the snow with her legs. "I don't
know, Dee. Is sleeping with a man that important?"

"Well, how would I know?" Darlene turned and walked away
from Cassie into the field. "I just think it'd be sad—that's all."
Darlene threw her arms in the air. "If I had a man like Jake, I sure
wouldn't let him go halfway around the world to find some
loving with someone else. If a woman'd take Rancy, they'd surely
take Jake. I'd make sure he understood well what he had waiting
over here."

Darlene had a point. The war had been over by the time her
mother had met her father. This war had been going on forever,
and Jake would get drafted unless he went away to college or
Canada, or she had two of his kids. "Ma says I should be saving
myself for my wedding night. She says there're other girls for
that."

A long way off in the field, two deer stepped lightly over the snow. "Yeah, there are," Darlene said brightly, "but if you ever, you know, don't want him no more, send him my way."

Cassie picked up a handful of snow and started to pack it into a ball. "There's no way I'm going to let you at my Jake, you hussy. I seen that sexy underwear you're wearing underneath your clothes." She threw the snowball at Darlene and ran toward her house trying to leap over the snow, leaning into the heaver drifts.

Darlene shouted after her, "Okay, Miss High-and-Mighty, you're going to get yours." Darlene ran her down, shouldering her into a drift. She grabbed Cassie's hair and pushed her face into the snow. "How's this, little missy? I got you now. What you going to do?" She pulled Cassie's head out of the snow.

Cassie glanced over her shoulder at Darlene. "I give up," she said.

"Give up? You don't get to give up that easily. You got yours coming." Darlene shoved her face deeper into the packed snow. "Here's for thinking you're so good because you go to church every Sunday."

Cassie lifted her head and screamed, her face wet.

Darlene pushed Cassie's face down harder into the snow. "And here's for being a lily-white virgin." Darlene's voice turned shrill. She pulled Cassie's head up by her hair.

Cassie spit snow, struggling to wrestle her way out from under Darlene, but the girl was just too tall and strong.

"And here's for those damn big innocent cow eyes of yours." Again Darlene forced Cassie's face down into the snow pack. "And here's for getting all the good men and leaving me all alone."

Cassie screamed as her face was buried deeper, choking on the frozen snow, starting to fear something was wrong.

Darlene held Cassie down as if drowning her. Cassie flailed against the snow, not understanding why her friend played so roughly, and hurt that Darlene would say those things even for fun.

"And calling me a hussy." Darlene stopped. She pulled Cassie's head up, her mouth open and her eyes wide.

Cassie coughed out snow.

"Oh my God," Darlene cried. "Oh my God, Cassie, I didn't mean it."

Cassie blew snow from her nostrils. She rolled over on her back. The snow, like a million needles, pricked Cassie's cheeks as she gasped for breath. The apology made things better and she thought she might understand why someone like Darlene might get mad, being without a father, and how people talked. Sometimes it wasn't fair what some town kids called Darlene behind her back. Dee didn't have life easy and some people could lose their temper when life was so hard. "God, Dee, you're trying to kill me."

Darlene's face was flushed. She leaned over Cassie stretching her wool cap back on over her hair. She pulled Cassie to a sitting position and hugged her. "Oh, thank God you're all right." She wiped the snow from Cassie's cheeks and eyes. "I do love you, you silly girl."

"Don't seem like it from where I'm sitting." Cassie shoved snow into Darlene's face. Darlene spit it out, stood up, and pulled Cassie to her feet. They walked arm in arm the rest of the way back to the house.

They hung their coats in the breezeway, leaving their boots to dry. Music came from Ben's room. He'd borrowed Purdy's new Beatles album. Ben was trying to learn the words to "Lucy in the Sky with Diamonds." It would be a poor song to dance to. Cassie liked simple rock and roll. The band played a lot of the Doors songs because of Purdy's electric organ. They were hard enough to dance to, but the songs the band was learning now had strange rhythms, almost undanceable. The songs were getting just too complicated for her.

Cassie and Darlene shuffled into Cassie's bedroom, their pant

71

legs dripping water. Cassie peeled off her extra sweater and pants. She pulled her nightgown from her drawer and turned to go into the bathroom.

Darlene stepped between Cassie and the doorway. "My God, you're shy."

"No, it's not that. There's just no room in here." Cassie turned away. Darlene could tell it was all a lie.

"More room for the two of us in here than for one in there. What's the matter?"

"Nothing," Cassie said, trying to get around Darlene. "I just got old underclothes on and you got pretty things."

"Yeah, well, I got old underclothes too and it ain't like I don't ever wear them either. You don't want me to look, I won't." Darlene turned her back to Cassie and pulled her sweater over her head.

Cassie, not knowing what else to do, turned her back to Darlene taking off her sweater and pants.

"So, you think I look pretty?" Darlene asked. She held her arms away from her and slowly turned around in her bra and underpants.

Cassie covered herself with her sweater. "Yes, you look very pretty."

"Here," Darlene whispered. She reached behind her and undid the strap to her bra, pulling it off her shoulders and handing it to Cassie. "You try it on." Cassie had never seen another girl this naked before, not even in gym class where she changed as quickly as possible, not talking or looking at the other girls. "Here, don't be chicken." Darlene turned Cassie around to face her mirror. She unsnapped Cassie's bra, pulling it down her arms.

Cassie quickly crossed her arms over her breasts. "Darlene," Cassie whispered.

"Quick, try it on."

Cassie slipped her bra off her arms, laying it on her dresser, quickly sliding her arms into the straps of Darlene's. Darlene grabbed the back and hooked it for her. Cassie adjusted the front. It pushed up against her breasts. "These are hard."

"Yeah, I think they got some metal things in them."

Cassie glanced into the mirror trying to get the bra adjusted. "I think it's a little small."

Darlene stepped backwards her hands to her hips. "Why, Cassie Marie, what are you insinuating?"

"Nothing. It just feels a bit uncomfortable, that's all."

"Yeah, it's damn uncomfortable, but see how they look."

For the first time Cassie connected the image of the bra and the breasts to the image of her face, the same face which had always looked back from the mirror, but her body had changed. "Oh my God. They're huge!" She laughed out loud, covering her mouth with her hand.

"They ain't that big," Darlene said.

"I know, but geesh." She had a woman's cleavage and she appeared, well—sexy. She played with her hair, trying to make herself resemble one of those women she'd seen on the cover of the men's magazines in the drugstore, trying to get it to lay just on the rising curves of her breasts. She hardly recognized the woman in the mirror. Her dark eyes and her winter-white skin softly reflected the light of the lamp, her cheeks still red from the cold.

Darlene whispered, "You're beautiful."

Cassie shook her head despite thinking the same thing. "No, it's just the bra. I bet it could make anyone look good."

Darlene undid the hooks. Cassie took it off. Darlene turned Cassie back toward the mirror. "Look," she whispered. She pulled Cassie's hair behind her shoulders. "You're beautiful. Look at yourself. You're really beautiful. You're everything anybody could want."

Their images stared back at them, one tall and thin, one shorter, but the images had changed from what they had been.

Their bodies curved with waists and hips. Her mother and father, aunts and uncles, all of them had said she was almost full grown, but she had thought they'd meant taller or more responsible. She had never thought of it in this way, and she didn't know why. She had come into womanhood and somehow had not been aware. She understood now Jake's wanting to be alone with her, the kisses, his touching. It wasn't bad, just nature and the girls in the mirror were women or on their way to being women, but what kind of women would they be? She held her breath from the excitement of it all, their future, and something about the shadowy images staring back at her in the faint light scared her as if in these new bodies there was some kind of secret. For some time she'd known someday she'd bear children and being pretty could help her find a husband, but this was different. This was what men stared at, bought magazines for, spent money on. She saw two women in the mirror that men might desire in that way.

Darlene reached around Cassie and hugged her. Darlene's body was warm against her back. Darlene's hard breast pressed against her shoulder blades. Darlene's fingers were smooth and long where they pressed her lower abdomen. Cassie's stomach tightened and Darlene pressed harder. "We best get dressed," Cassie spun out of Darlene's arms and reached for her nightgown. "I'll make us some hot cocoa."

The late movie, *Dracula*, droned on with its black and white film and overly loud and melodramatic music. Their cups and a large bowl that once held popcorn lay empty on the floor beside them. Cassie and Darlene snuggled under a quilt on the floor, using the couch as a backrest. Ben sat on the couch next to Darlene, sharing a corner of their quilt. Winter chill brushed against their cheeks as the house grew colder. The fire had been stoked for the night and their parents had disappeared into their bedroom.

Cassie held the quilt tucked under her chin, the other end wrapped around her feet against the wisps of draft that rushed along the floor. "I don't know why we watch these movies. They scare us half to death."

Darlene pinched Cassie's arm. "Speak for yourself, Miss Scaredy-Pants."

Ben hushed them, motioning toward their parents' bedroom. "You girls just like to see Dracula bite all those women's necks."

"Now what's that supposed to mean?" Darlene asked. She pinched Ben's leg.

He winced in mock pain. "Maybe you want someone to bite your neck," he said just above a whisper as if unsure whether his parents were asleep in the other room.

Cassie glared at Ben. "You know better than that, Ben," she whispered.

Ben leaned forward. "You don't want Jake to bite your neck?"

"She's never going to let Jake touch her neck until they're married," Darlene whispered.

Ben fell back against the couch, bracing his elbow against the arm, leaning his head against his hand. "That's a long ways off. I don't care what anybody says."

They'd played with the argument before, mostly when someone commented on how grown up she'd become. Her mother, aunts and uncles, and even her father believed the time was approaching. What else was there for her? Cassie couldn't understand why Ben refused to see her side. "It ain't that long. Maybe a little more than a year." But now she wasn't sure.

"Come on, Cassie, sixteen? That's way too young," Ben said.

"If I was living a hundred years ago, I'd be half-way through my life by then."

Ben rubbed at the creases on his forehead and stared at the screen. "That's just some stupid statistic."

"Well, I could be," Cassie said.

"I'd let Dracula bite my neck." Darlene smiled at the TV.

"No, you wouldn't." Ben threw a kernel of popcorn at her, bouncing it off her head.

Darlene picked the kernel up and threw it back. "Yes, I would. You get to do anything you want if you're a vampire."

Ben grabbed the back of her neck, gently squeezing it. "Except walk around in the daylight."

Darlene scrunched up her shoulders in defense. "So's you'd sleep in late."

Ben rubbed the spot he'd squeezed. Darlene bent her head forward closing her eyes rolling her head to the rhythm of Ben's fingers. He brushed his hand across her hair, then sat back. "He's got all his women vampires all tied up."

Darlene rolled her head, touching where Ben had rubbed. "Ain't that just like men. They just can't leave nobody have a good time. You get a little uppity and they slap a name like vampire on you and poke a wood stick through your heart. They're always going for the heart too. Then they drop you in a box and throw you in the ground."

The movie was moving to its inevitable end. The only vampire left was Dracula and the town's people were closing in. The fact Dracula lived out in the country and the people from town were after him bothered Cassie a bit because, although Dracula was surely the bad man, she couldn't help but know how he felt, being country and alone and fearing town folk.

Ben said, "Truth is most men's afraid of women. It's a fact."

"How can that be? They can beat us up, no problem," Cassie said.

"Don't no man want anybody to know he beat up a woman."

Darlene turned around and laid her arm against the couch, gazing up at Cassie's brother. "Why're they afraid?"

Ben stared down at her, seeming to think for a moment. "A woman can break your heart and there's nothing you can do about it." He brushed the tips of his fingers against his jeans, wiping off traces of butter. "A woman can make a man feel worthless or she can make him feel like he's the best man in the world."

Darlene used Ben's jeans to wipe her fingers, also. "You afraid of women?"

"Not that way." Ben watched Darlene's fingers run over the heavy cloth above his knee. "Because I'm not what most women are looking for."

"Ben, you're a good man," Cassie said, but she seemed to be interrupting a private conversation.

He cleared his throat and sat up. "Yep, and that ain't what they're looking for. They're looking for some hunk with little brains and no heart. That's why I ain't afraid of them. The woman who finally falls in love with me is going to be a mighty good woman, or mighty desperate."

Darlene stopped wiping her fingers and picked at the greasy kernels crowded at the bottom of the bowl. "So how do you tell?"

"Playing at the bars, the desperate ones are the ones that come cuddling up to you at about two-thirty in the morning. They all want to know your name when closing time comes." He brushed his hand through his hair. "It's the ones that come up to you early that are the good ones."

"I'd still like to be a vampire," Darlene repeated. She nibbled on broken pieces of butter-soaked popcorn.

Cassie had been playing with the ends of the quilt. The stitching had started to unravel. She, or her mother, would need to fix it. "I think vampires are supposed to be bad women."

"Maybe that means that once you go real bad it don't matter," Darlene said.

Ben leaned forward, close to Darlene. "That's what I been saying. Once you learn how to use it, you women got us."

Cassie glared at him. "That's terrible. Good women don't do that." But it was what she had been thinking in her bedroom with Darlene. There was power in the reflection.

Darlene smiled up at Ben. "Look who's talking, Miss I-Don't-Let-No-Man-Touch-Me-Until-He-Marries-Me."

"Darlene," Cassie said. Ben was laughing at her. "It ain't like that at all. I don't have to beat him off of me. And I ain't playing that game." And she wasn't or she hadn't, maybe? She wasn't sure now. Jake had wanted to go farther when they kissed and she let him a little bit, but only because she loved him so much, she thought, but it didn't sound exactly right anymore when she rolled it over in her mind.

"I'm sorry, Cassie," Darlene said. She went back to wiping her fingers on Ben's jeans.

From their parents' bedroom, their mother said, "Don't you young'uns ever plan on going to bed? Ben, I know tomorrow is Sunday, but you still got chores to do."

"Yes-um." Ben bent down and hugged both girls. "You two be good little girls and head beddie-bye."

Darlene gazed up at him. "Who you calling a little girl? Aw, stay up with us and protect your women, you big strong man." Darlene wrapped her arms around his leg, pretending to hold him there.

Ben stood. He stretched his arms over his head, touching the low ceiling.

"Good night, Ben." Cassie pulled the quilt off Darlene and folded it, then placed it on the end of the couch as Ben walked up the stairs to his bedroom.

"Night," Darlene said.

Cassie shut off the TV and the light. She whispered, "Come on, Miss Dee, let's head up."

"Oh, fine, sleepy head." Darlene picked up the bowl and cups. "This movie wasn't all that scary anyway."

"Then why were you screaming like it was?" Cassie ran water into the bowl and then rinsed the cups out. She stacked them to be washed in the morning.

Darlene stood behind her, waiting. "Just for fun. So why were you?"

Cassie stepped carefully into the breezeway trying to avoid any cold drops of water left from the boots. She checked the lock.

"Because you were, that's why. You were scaring me to death. Now go up to bed and I'll shut the light off." Cassie waited at the bottom of the stairs until Darlene disappeared into the bedroom and she heard the bedsprings whine. She shut off the last light and tiptoed up to her room.

The snow on the clear night filled the small rooms with the blue light of the reflected moon. A winter's silence fell over the house. Darlene waited for her in bed, the covers pulled up to her chin.

"Move over," Cassie pulled the blankets back. Darlene slid closer to the wall as Cassie laid down next to her.

"I don't like it here. Let's trade places." Darlene lifted herself up and slid one leg and arm across Cassie.

Cassie slid under her. "Be quiet. Everyone will hear you."

Darlene stretched out above her. "Well, Cassie girl, look where I got you now. If I were a man you'd be in big trouble."

Cassie peered up into Darlene's eyes. "Oh, stop that." She scooted out from under her and turned her face toward the wall.

Darlene laid her head on the one pillow they shared curling her long body around Cassie's, blowing Cassie's hair away from her face. "How can you sleep with all that hair flying around?"

Cassie spoke quietly to the wall. "It don't bother me. Ma puts hers up, but I hate sleeping with a clip or barrette in my hair. It hurts my head."

"It's sure a bother to me." Darlene pulled Cassie's hair behind her ear. "When you're married you might have to do it for Jake."

"Jake likes my hair."

Darlene laid her hand on Cassie's hip. "According to you, he ain't had to sleep with it. I'm the only one gets that privilege. Besides how do you know it'll be Jake you marry?"

"It'll be Jake." Cassie pulled Darlene's hand around her and held it. "I know it. Now go to sleep."

They lay quiet for a minute. The tiredness the long day had brought seeping in to Cassie, Darlene breathing in long soft breaths, her weight and the warmth of her settling on the mattress, Cassie working toward sleep. Would it be like this with a man or did you hold each other in your arms all night?

Darlene spoke softly. "Cassie, you ever, you know, hear of two girls loving?"

Cassie wasn't sure what she meant. "Lots of girls love each other."

"No," Darlene whispered close to Cassie's ear. "I mean, you know—doing it."

"Girls?" Cassie stared at the wall. "I heard mention of it." She was tired but relieved. She wasn't sure, but there had been an ending and a beginning—somewhere, somehow. "Don't quite seem possible or at least worth it. What's the purpose?"

Darlene leaned on her elbow, bending over Cassie. "Well, I guess it ain't really possible, but it's sort of possible." She gently stroked Cassie's hair. "Yeah, but you know—it wouldn't really count, I think?"

Cassie said, "I don't much see the sense of it."

"No, me neither." Darlene laid her head back on the pillow. "Well, good night."

"Good night, Miss Dee."

The moon traveled slowly in the mountain sky, as the stars etched their circular path from horizon to horizon while Cassie slept. She dreamed a strange dream where she stood naked and beautiful in front of her mirror, and Jake, naked behind her, put his arms around her waist. She felt a flush of warmth run through her. His body pressed against her. She wanted to turn, to know what it would feel like to have him inside her. She turned slowly to face Darlene, her gray eyes peering into hers, her kiss warm and moist.

Cassie woke sweating. Someone walked quietly around the kitchen downstairs. It was Ben. She could tell by his steps. Her mother's were light; the floor almost made no noise at all. Her father shuffled more.

Darlene slid out from under the blankets, tiptoeing out of the room and down the stairs. Cassie hoped they wouldn't scare each other in the dark. She fell back to sleep, waking a few minutes later at the sound of the kitchen door opening and closing.

Cassie rolled quietly out of bed and walked downstairs to the breezeway. Darlene's boots were gone. So were Ben's. She peeked outside. There was no one in the yard, only hers and Darlene's old tracks from the evening and several heading toward the barn. Cassie rushed back to her bedroom and knelt at her window. She peered between the shade and glass.

Below in the late moonlight Ben and Darlene were kissing. Her flannel nightgown hung down below her coat, brushing against the snow. They walked toward the barn hand in hand. Cassie crawled back into bed, excited about her brother and best friend being in love.

She woke as Darlene crawled back into bed.

"Is that you, Ben?" Cassie's father said.

"Yeah, Pa."

"You're up mighty early. You got another half-hour to sleep yet."

"I know. I thought I'd make coffee."

"Suit yourself."

A half-hour would make it five-thirty in the morning. What had they done all that time? What could they have done, what they shouldn't have done? Cassie decided Darlene wasn't really that type, but especially not Ben. He was a good man. They were like her and Jake. Cassie curled her body around Darlene's and put her arm around her. Darlene took it and kissed her hand. Cassie snuggled up to Darlene's hair that smelled of chaff.

Chapter 5

Spring had been quietly approaching for some time, first the faint smell of last year's leaves and the carcasses of the dead grasses rotting under the melting snow, the faint pungent odor, the final farewell of a past world, then the sound of the clear water running through the small ditches. The run-off creeks babbling with snowmelt, trickling over rocks, hundreds of unrelated streamlets combined to rush headlong down the hills coalescing into one swollen, rushing creek, its low roar heard day and night.

Soon the song birds returned, and late in the evening the deer came down from their hiding places to feed their winter-thin bodies on the new shoots and show off their newly born young. Finally, spring flowers bloomed, and on the newly warming days the bees, in an ecstatic flurry, rushed in a grand madness from flower to flower.

Cassie had waited for this day, the first warm Saturday in April when Jake's bike was put on the road again and they could escape the vigilance of her parents. A multitude of letters, several well-timed phone calls, and twice-a-month visits had gotten the two of them through a long winter. Jake had taken her to the movies, once during the January thaw, and had brought her home several times for Sunday dinner stopping on a back road for several minutes to and from to talk and neck, but most times they stayed at her home, well chaperoned, their kisses and hugs stolen.

She stood on the front porch near a wood post listening to the deep-throated staccato of the motorcycle echoing off the bluffs, growing steadily louder as Jake worked through the passes, up and over the hills. The bike burst into the valley suddenly like a deer breaking from the woods, leaping along the edge of a field. The engine barked as it decelerated off the mountain. The rhythm of the engine pulsed through the air as Jake neared Mrs. Fowley's house, driving faster then she allowed him to with her, but still, his bravado, his courage thrilled her as he raced around the turns.

Cassie walked through the house to the back door, past her mother busy attaching a sleeve to a shirt for Ben, the soft thudding of the sewing machine adding to the quiet of a house whose family was nearly grown. The dissipating smells of an early lunch hung faintly in the air of the kitchen, and the cool spring breeze swirling in through newly opened windows, brushing aside the curtains, kicked up long-imprisoned dust.

When Jake reached the door she glanced over her shoulder, stepped outside, and kissed him quickly, reaching her arms around his neck so not only their lips kissed, but their bodies, Jake smelling of soap and cologne. She took his hand and led him inside. "Ma, Jake's here."

Cassie and Jake sat on the porch watching spring slowly cover the mountains, the anticipation of finally being able to be alone driving her to need to hold him, kiss him, and to have him kiss her, to touch her, to move her closer to that unknown place of liquid warmth she feared as much as desired. The wispy, yellow-green, spring-young fingers of the willows raked at the brown back of the swollen creek, and the apple trees had begun to thrust out their white and pink flowers with yellow centers. In a couple of weeks the petals would fill the air like snow and the naked seed pods would slowly swell into fruit.

Cassie touched Jake's cheek. Downy stubble tickled her hand above his soft skin.

Jake closed his eyes and pushed her hand against his face. "I love you too much."

"I missed you, Jake." Cassie combed the errant strands of hair falling across his forehead with her fingers, the warmth and texture of his skin registering in quick electric pulses through her finger tips to her brain and down her body. She moved toward him, glancing back to the curtained window. "Later," she whispered. "Later we'll go for a ride." Jake laid his hand on her thigh. The heat and weight of it sent a flood of warmth up her leg. She swallowed hard. She wanted him to kiss her, not quickly like they did when they were home, but the long breathless kisses they kissed in the hollow. "I know, but all things in their own time." She touched her finger to his lips. Jake reached up and held her hand. He kissed it. He'd never done that before. Cassie softly kissed his hand. She didn't know quite why. She rubbed it against her cheek. She sucked in a breath as her body started to float in the way it did when they were alone and he kissed her or touched her. Cassie stood. "Come on." Jake followed her into the house. "Ma, we're going for a ride, if that's all right?"

Her mother glanced out from behind the shirt she held by its shoulders. "You going to be home for supper?"

Jake said, "I thought we'd ride down into Wytheville. I'll buy her supper there."

"No," Cassie said. "We don't need to waste money like that." Wytheville was not where she wanted to go. She didn't want a long ride, just a short ride and a long kiss.

Jake took a half-hour finding large enough stepping-stones so they could cross the flooded creek. Even then, Cassie was afraid to cross without him holding her hand. They spread a green woolen blanket out high on the hill in the new-green grass where the sun had dried the ground to listen to Jake's small portable radio that battled with the sound of the snowmelt-gorged stream, the ground still smelling damp.

They kissed for a while, Cassie removing Jake's hands from the parts of her that sometimes, late at night when she was alone in bed, she admitted she wanted him to touch even though it was wrong. They lie quietly watching clouds pass overhead.

Jake had been staring at the line of trees bordering the far edge of the meadow. "I think there's a crow's nest over there in the woods." He pointed up to where the creek opened onto the fields and slid down between the hills.

Two large black birds floated from a high perch, gliding silently to the ground, picking up a piece of twig or a blade of grass in their mouths, then, after giving Cassie and Jake a suspicious look, pumped their large strong wings, lifting themselves up to the top of a tall tree.

"Yeah, they've got young'uns coming." Her gaze followed the birds into the woods.

Cassie hadn't realized she'd sighed until Jake asked, "What's the matter?"

"I was just wondering." She smiled at him and kissed him then leaned her head against his. "I was just wondering what'd it be like for us."

"You mean making love?" Jake asked.

Cassie pulled her head back to look at him. "No, I mean having a nest." Cassie's heart pounded. She tore at a blade of grass. She hadn't meant for it to be happening here and now and if he avoided answering her, the disappointment would be her own fault, but she wanted so badly, just to be with Jake, now and forever.

"Cassie, you know I plan to marry you. That is, if you'll have me." He said it easily as if it meant nothing at all.

"Are you asking me to marry you?" Cassie had thought about being married to Jake, but never about the actual proposal. She had not thought about wanting the words, but now she wanted them more than anything.

"I guess I am." His gaze followed a crow to the tree. "I don't know when. It'll have to be in a while. I got to graduate from high school and then get a job and then save enough money to get a place for us. It's going to take time."

A great uncertainty about herself and her life lifted. Now there would only be the waiting, the uncertainty of life replaced by the uncertainty of time. "You remember Uncle Bill and Aunt Anna?" Cassie stammered, reaching for his hand, spreading his fingers, running her smaller fingers between his. "He's Ma's brother. Remember J.W. died?" Her heart raced. "They came over Christmas?"

"Yeah, I remember them. He died in the war," Jake said. He leaned back on his elbow, his face flushed.

Cassie cleared her throat, straightened her blouse and pulled down the legs of her jeans trying to give herself time to organize her thoughts, to tell Jake a secret she'd been holding onto since last winter, and to do it in a way he wouldn't think was a bribe or coercion. "Anyway, they were out in the kitchen sipping whiskey and he started asking about you. You know, were you a good boy, did Pa trust you, were you treating his prettiest right. That's what he calls me." She couldn't tell whether Jake was happy or scared. Did men get scared? Once they'd made a decision they pretty much stuck to it. "Ben comes out and asks them what's all the fuss for. And they say because I'm getting all grown up and could be getting time to get married off, seeing how Ma and Anna weren't much older than me when they got married. Then Ben goes and tells them we were a long way from going to the altar, seeing we were both in school still and you didn't have anything but your motorcycle. Pa said, been a lot of people started with less and he couldn't see me finding a boy who'd treat me any better than you."

Cassie laid down on the blanket. She wiggled her shoulders, smoothing down the soft ground underneath. Jake stared down at her. Being with him seemed so natural. "He told Uncle Bill you were a good man and you'd work real hard to make a good life for your wife and kids. We might start with nothing, but we'd do okay. Ma agreed and said there wasn't anything better a woman could do than marry a good man like you. Said she'd be real happy if I married you."

Cassie ran her hand up Jake's arm, rubbing the soft darkening hair, pulling her hand away when she realized what she was feeling, wanting the feeling but knowing what could come of it. "Uncle Bill said you sounded like a mighty fine boy and if we were to get married he'd give us that hunting cabin those city men built on his land up in Hungry Hollow. They never paid him the money they promised so he took it back. Pa said, and Ma agreed, that if you got a good job this winter, when I turn sixteen we could get married."

Jake sat up. "Why didn't you tell me that? How come you kept it a secret?"

Cassie sat up. Jake seemed to have gotten nervous all of a sudden. Maybe the decision was harder for him than her. It had to be. "Because silly." Cassie folded his hand between hers. "I couldn't very well bribe you into marrying me with a house. How'd I ever know you loved me or just took me for the land?"

"I'd never done that. Cassie, you know I truly love you."

In his eyes was shown something beyond a boyfriend, or what a husband might be, something Cassie didn't quite under-stand. "I do now. Oh, God, finally I can tell someone. I've kept this secret from everybody. Well, I mean the two people who mean the most to me in the world, you and Miss Dee." She glanced away to break the connection that had started something bubbling inside her. "You know how quickly she would have blabbed it. She can't keep secrets."

Jake's gaze wandered to one of the crows floating on the wind. "Did you ever see the place?"

Cassie tucked her legs under her. The ground below the blanket gave way a bit. The question seemed odd as if he were deliberating whether it was worth the commitment to her, as if this was some transaction. "No." Was being a husband different than just being a man, like being a wife was different from being just a woman?

"It may not be anything to look at. It might need a lot of work," Jake said.

"Oh, you think so?" Cassie sat back on the blanket. She hoped not, but then how good could it really be if Uncle Bill was giving it away? More than likely just a shack, but if it kept out the rain and held in some heat, Jake could probably fix it up. They just needed a place for a garden, or maybe they'd just make her folk's garden bigger.

Jake laughed and hugged her. "I'm still going to marry you, don't worry. Do you want to go?"

She smiled and said, "You better, now that you got my heart set on it. To the cabin?" The cabin would be theirs, but to claim it now was almost like making love before they were married.

Jake touched her cheek. "If we won't get in trouble with your aunt and uncle, it'd be good to look at it. We could see how much money we need to fix it up."

His fingers had been hot against her cheek as if he were on fire inside. "I don't rightfully know. I don't think they'd mind. Besides, I don't think they'd even know we're there. We could just go and walk around it, see what needs to be done."

Cassie had learned to ride, to anticipate Jake's moves, the same way they danced. A part of her mind turned inward when they rode, noticing her feelings, dreaming, while another part of her danced along with Jake, complementing, agreeing, and acting in unison. She leaned when he leaned. She thrust her upper body forward when he accelerated, back when he braked, not once disturbing her thoughts, but now as the wind rushed past, the sun raced through the trees before them, the flowers and grasses smelling sweet in the youth of spring, perfuming the air, a strange thought came to her, for all intents and purposes, Jake and she were going home.

Less than a mile past her uncle's farm, a dirt road designated as Hungry Hollow Road by a small, green, county sign, ran off up into a narrow rugged valley. Jake turned the bike toward what looked like a box canyon. They passed one small farm in a state of disrepair. Its lean acreage seemed to have been hewn from the woods. The porch of the house had been lost years past, the back end of the barn, collapsed, and deep ruts ran down the steep driveway from the spring run-off. Dingy gray laundry hung from a line strung between two trees, suspended over an unmowed lawn, green stalks sprouting between the brown carcasses of last year's weeds.

A mile further on, the road narrowed to a single lane. Jake braked in front of a rusted pipe-gate that marked the end of the road. He carefully threaded the bike around the post and up a faint tractor-width trail through deep woods.

Where the woods cleared, the sun shone down on a small hillside meadow reflecting off a bright yellow, gingerbread-trimmed, two-story cottage, almost new, and well crafted, with a screened-in front porch. It stood a good story above the sloping hill on a large and solid fieldstone foundation, a steep, tree-covered bluff rising behind it. Long, wide steps with turned newels and spindles reached down the hill like open arms.

Jake shut off the bike. "This is got to be the wrong place," he said as he took off his helmet.

Cassie dismounted, stumbling a bit on the uneven ground, her gaze also transfixed on the cottage. "We're behind his farm. It's just over that hill." She pointed to the south ridge.

Jake pushed the bike into the woods out of sight. "No sense inviting trouble."

"What do you mean?" she asked. They were doing nothing wrong. He'd said so himself.

"If someone happens to come along we should be able to hear them. It'd be a lot easier just to sneak away into the woods than trying to explain ourselves."

"We're just going to look at it." Cassie unbuckled her helmet not taking her eyes off the cottage. It couldn't be right, but it had to be. They hadn't passed another place since that old farm. The cottage was more beautiful than she could have dreamed, but more importantly it meant, despite Ben, shortly after her sixteenth birthday next January she'd be married. Jake would be out of school and have a job by then. She could quit school and be done with it and them.

Jake reached for her helmet. "There's no posted signs, but there's no sense getting anyone upset over nothing." He rebuckled the strap and slid it over the handlebar.

"You sure it's all right?" She whispered the words even though she was sure no one else was around, but sometimes words had a way of echoing around the hills. "I mean, do you think we might get caught? People get in trouble doing things like this."

"Not if you run fast enough."

"Oh, don't you worry. I'm so scared now I'll be running like a rabbit with a fox after him."

Jake held the screen door open for her. Cassie hesitated for a few seconds, worried it was a mistake. She stepped in turning around, peering out at the valley below. The house appeared to float over the trees, sitting where the two ridges melted together and flung themselves out like grasping arms.

"It's so beautiful," she whispered. "Why would anyone ever give this up? A person could live their whole life up here and never come down." The breeze ran up out of the valley, smelling of spring plowing and new growth.

Jake glanced around the porch. "The furniture ain't much good and the floor needs scraping and painting." He scrubbed the toe of his boot against the planks.

Cassie sat down on a faded and dusty wicker couch wiggling her behind to test its sturdiness. A rain-spotted table and two wooden kitchen chairs hid in a corner. A metal glider balanced off the other side of the porch. Cassie laughed. "It ain't so bad."

Jake flicked the heavy padlock several times that run through a large hasp bolted to the front door, letting it bang against the hasp. "I guess your uncle didn't want nobody getting in without him knowing it. Let's look around outside."

Jake led Cassie off the porch. As he rounded the corner he stopped.

"What's the matter?" Cassie asked, but she saw the problem.

An outhouse stood on a level spot on the hill. "I knew it was too good to be true. They probably don't have running water either."

Jake walked slowly up the hill. "Yeah, but that may not be the problem. There might not be a spot for a toilet and tub in the house." He continued walking around the corner of cottage searching for something. "We may have to build on."

"It's got to have a place. We got one and our house isn't as big as this." As she followed Jake to the top of the knoll, Cassie smelled the creek that cut along the bluff beyond the house before hearing it or seeing it.

Jake studied the back lawn looking for signs of springtime flooding.

Cassie saw none. She walked over to the back stoop and stood to look out as if she were standing in the kitchen. "Jake, it's beautiful."

Jake studied the door. "You want to see what's inside?"

"No, we couldn't. How could we? I mean if we were, you know, so inclined." Cassie stepped off the stoop and stared up at the side of the house. "If we didn't think we'd get caught, how could we get in?"

"It ain't getting in that's the problem," Jake said. "It's getting out fast if someone comes. If he's only got a bolt on the backdoor then we can unbolt it." Jake grabbed the doorknob and tried to turn it. The knob held tight. "If someone comes, all we got to do is scamper out and relock the knob lock. Most likely he, or whoever, won't even look to see if the bolt's been moved."

"Jake," Cassie whispered. "You know how to do this stuff? What kind of a man am I going to marry?"

"It ain't like I do this for a living or anything. I seen Pa do it once when we got locked out of our house by mistake."

Jake picked the window behind the glider and with his pocketknife chipped away the glazing prying out the center pane of the upper window.

"You're not going to leave it like that are you?" Cassie asked.

Jake stopped working for a second. "No," he said. "I'll put the glass back in with the wedges and get some glazing at the store and replace it this week. Don't worry."

Inside they stood in the silence, a foreign place she'd never been before and shouldn't be, though half her attention was outside, listening for the noise of a car or a truck, for the warning cry of a crow or jay.

The downstairs consisted of two long rooms divided by an enclosed staircase. In front of them sat a large oak table with four chairs, at the back, the kitchen. The afternoon light streamed in through the windows. The dust they'd disturbed danced like tiny fairies in its beam. The air smelled dry of a house too long closed. Cassie wandered away to the other room as Jake went to check the bolt, her heart pounding. There were stands with vases, and framed pictures of hunters and fishermen hung on the lacquered knotty pine planks that paneled the walls. A gray, stone fireplace, bigger than anything Cassie had ever seen, spread over half a wall. From its place mounted high on the chimney, a large buck's head stared down at her, its multi-pointed antlers reaching into the air almost touching the ceiling. An oriental rug covered oak hardwood boards polished smoother than a dance floor. A large low table, two smaller couches and one large one, all a dark green, made up a square before the fireplace. Ornate brass kerosene lamps, like tall candleholders, sat quietly on dusty tables.

The room exuded richness, comfort, and quiet. Cassie's fingers ran along the dusty fabric of the couches, the smooth hard surfaces of the tables. She leaned against the mammoth fireplace and rubbed her cheek against the cold stone, caressing it, smelling the odor of ashes too long unstoked. What kind of men lived like this? And over it all lorded the large buck. There was power here she'd known nothing about, male power, a potent power controlled and forged—Rancy's sheer madness directed. Where her father had broken under this hammer, these men seemed to have found the strength enough to succeed and to build this chapel and then to leave it all, and to call this precious home a whim.

"Hey, Cassie, come here," Jake shouted. "Come here. See this. You sure he's giving us this lock, stock and barrel?"

"What?" She whispered her reply as if she were in a church. Cassie walked back to the kitchen. "That's what he said." The cupboards lay open, full of pots, pans, and dishes, the drawers full of knives, forks, and spoons. Another kerosene lamp sat on the table, no light on the ceiling none on the walls. "Jake, there's no electricity."

"Yeah, I know. It wouldn't be nothing to wire up the place. More to get the power company to run some poles, though. You know." Jake moved quickly toward the living room. "Wow," he said. "Will you look at this? This looks just like one of those hunting lodges you see in *Field and Stream*."

She hadn't noticed there weren't any electric poles on the ride up. "I know," Cassie replied. "It's beyond anything I've ever seen."

Two doors faced each other at the top of the stairs. Cassie went left, Jake right. The room was plain, large with unadorned, beige walls. Four beds sat in a row like in a hospital ward, the mattresses naked. Cassie entered slowly. An unadorned window looked over the side lawn, across the roof of the outhouse. Cassie placed her palms against the panes and imagined herself standing outside on the sloped side-lawn staring up at herself gazing from a window of a home that was supposed to be devoid of human life. In a way she was a ghost, something out of its place in time. She wished, by closing her eyes and opening them again, it would be a year from now and she would be the woman of this place with all her freedom and responsibility. But now she was just a thief, entering her future self's sanctuary, the place where, in the dark of the night, she would make love to Jake and her children would be conceived, but the image in the glass looking back was the image in the mirror that night with Darlene, not a wife or a mother. She sat on the bed. What would next year be like to lie naked in Jake's arms as the rising sun flooded daylight into their house?

Jake walked into the room. "Hey, there's two sets of bunk beds in there."

"Two sets?" Cassie asked, running her finger along the rough mattress. The number of beds didn't seem important. "What have we done?" she asked.

Jake sat down next to her. "Nothing, really. We broke into our own house."

Cassie tried to smile. "And no one is the wiser. We're beholden to no one." She took his hand and stared up at him, hoping he might read in her eyes the questions she had and would lead her where they might want to go.

In the stillness of the house Jake kissed her. She kissed him back, feeling the solitude of the rooms, knowing no one would see. She wanted to kiss him hard. She wanted to be the woman and not the ghost. They kissed again and again, open mouthed, closed mouth. She let Jake run his hands over her. She was sweating even though Jake had unbuttoned her blouse and slid her bra off her shoulders. He reached down to unbutton her pants. She laid back on the bed. She wanted him to touch her. They were there in the house clandestinely. It thrilled her and scared her and told her who she was, the woman she was to be.

Cassie lay on the bed naked, the rough bare mattress scratching her back. She wanted to laugh loudly, to giggle, but her breath only came in loud rasping gasps. She spoke between the gasps and Jake's kisses. "I love you." She ran her hand down Jake's side. His shirt was off. She hugged him, feeling the softness of his skin, the hardness of his muscle. Cassie moved her hands downward. He was naked and they lay on their wedding bed. His legs moved between hers, gently nudging hers open. She wanted him. "No!" she screamed.

Jake jumped off her. "I'm sorry. I'm sorry. I didn't mean anything."

"No, oh, no." Cassie covered her eyes, rolling over on her stomach, crying.

Jake gathered his clothes running down the stairs.

Cassie cried for a while. She wasn't sure how long. She cried because nothing had happened and because it almost did. She cried for Jake. Darlene was right, she was cruel, unmeaningly so, but she was cruel. But the woman on the bed hadn't been her. It'd been the ghost, the ghost she'd become. The body was hers, but it hadn't been her. She'd been possessed, hardly remembering becoming naked. She certainly didn't remember Jake taking off his clothes. But she'd known all of it, and she'd let it happen because she'd wanted it to happen. He had never seen her naked before. She hadn't cared. And if she had made love, only she and Jake would have known, but then what value would she have? Who would she be?

She turned over on her back and stared up at the cobwebs hanging almost invisibly in the corners, understanding now what boys whispered about and preachers warned about. Whatever she'd felt, had consumed her and even now she wanted to feel it again, and people like Aunt Teresa had been right all along. Maybe even Rancy had known finally she'd burn like fire. She stared at the ceiling and wondered if she had let him see her underpants on purpose. Did she have to go up the ladder? Maybe she had egged him on like she had done with Jake? Had she let Rancy take her clothes off just like she had let Jake? Did she really try to fight him or had it all been play? And those nights curled up against him? She'd have to fight the feelings all her life, just like Uncle Bill and whiskey. If she let herself go, there was no telling what she might do?

Jake sat on the couch, staring into the empty fireplace. Cassie sat down next to him. "Jake? I'm sorry, I didn't mean to do it."

He didn't turn to look at her. "It's not your fault. I should of never gone that far, but you know how men get. Sometimes we just can't stop."

Cassie knew what he meant. She knew all too well. She had those men feelings herself. Cassie reached for his hand. Now she knew, the same flesh of his hand was the same flesh of his body, good, clear skin over good, strong muscles. He was more beautiful naked than dressed, and even now she wished she had seen more. "We've got to think, Jake. We've got to think about what we're doing. We could make a big mistake here."

Jake said, "I know, I know what you mean."

"I want to leave, Jake. Can we leave? I don't ever want to come back here again until we're married. The next time we come here I want it for real."

Chapter 6

The fete had been scheduled for noon, Cassie's father believing it a waste of a good Saturday, but Rancy was family and a war hero. For what, Cassie didn't know. It meant they had to show up. The mill where Jake worked now with his father had scheduled overtime and Jake had to work, Cassie thinking it a good idea anyhow, considering she was sure Rancy hadn't changed a bit over the last year and there was no need for him to be able to put a face to the name Jake McCullom.

Cars and trucks jammed the church parking lot. Men in starched white shirts and baggy pants directed traffic to a side field where automobiles and pickup trucks sat helter-skelter over the hay stubble, men crowding into little groups, their polished shoes hoisted onto rusted bumpers, their hands, lazily draped over raised knees, clutched cigarettes while women ran in a mad rush to and from cars and out and back from the long tent that sheltered three rows of tables draped in white paper table cloths, a short row positioned ninety degrees to the others. Men tended the smoker and the barbecue pits with white hankies neatly folded and stuck into breast or slacks pockets, used to dab politely at their sweating foreheads.

Cassie's mother's gaze swept across the mayhem. "Good Lord. This is all for Rancy?"

Cassie's father steered the car across the field to a spot away from most of the others and further away from the tent than Cassie wanted to walk in the good shoes and the dress that her mother had insisted she wear. Smoke rolled thickly from the chimney of the smoker smelling heavily of seasoned hickory weaving into a blanket of odors with the aroma of fat rendered into liquid dripping down onto the coals, igniting into a flash of light and flame, and barbecue sauce from the chickens, the fire flaring up as the halves were basted and turned. Mrs. VanVleet, the reverend's wife, ushered Cassie and her family to the table of honor to sit next to Carl and Teresa. Even though she was half the age of most of the parishioners, everyone called her Mrs. She'd come from Boston with her husband, a small woman no bigger than Cassie.

Somewhere behind them, in one of the groups of men, was Rancy. Cassie didn't dare turn around, fearing that if he noticed her looking it might spur him into action.

As if by some secret sign, older women, including her mother, scurried out to the tables of food, hurriedly uncovering salads, deviled eggs, beans, relish plates, condiments, rolls, cakes, and cookies. The younger mothers dispersed to round up children. Men slowly coalesced from behind cars, from under trees and from the field where a makeshift game of softball had been trying to form. Other women herded parishioners, including Cassie and her family, and strangers into two lines on each side of the tables. Men and women with full plates started flowing back under the tent to chairs. More pious neighbors elbowed those who tried to start eating before grace.

Rancy slid down beside Cassie, his bulk shaking the tables. He wore a green uniform, the top buttons undone, his face red from drinking. He held two plates in one hand and a large glass of lemonade in the other. "Yep," he said to Cassie. "Nothing like being home. Good food and plump women." He glanced down at her plate. "Now how you going to keep those nice rounded thighs you eating like that?" Rancy pinched her under her ribs. Cassie jumped.

"What's the matter?" her father asked.

"Nothing, Pa, just a bug bite."

Rancy tore off a leg of a chicken sticking it end-ways into his mouth, peeling the meat off the bone with his teeth. "You calling me a bug. I got you a bug. Got a twat worm for you."

"You're worse than an insect," she said. "You don't even know enough not to eat at your own lawn fete until grace is said."

Rancy swallowed his chicken and wiped his mouth on his sleeve. "Why the hell didn't you tell me?" His face colored deeper than the whiskey blush.

"It ain't my job to take care of you," she whispered. People sat talking quietly at their tables, many staring at Rancy and her, sipping politely at their drinks.

"Your kin come home a war hero. You'd think I'd get some respect." He studied the napkin on Cassie's lap. Rancy picked up his napkin and placed it on his lap, nudging Cassie while doing it.

Cassie scowled at him. "I was praying you'd come home in a box." And she'd meant it. Because, she thought, because he'd driven her to it.

"You got any box in mind?" Rancy laughed.

Reverend VanVleet said grace and for a while Rancy was busy eating and Cassie could relax. Soon, though, his attention returned to parts of her body out of sight and all she could do was try to keep her legs closed, fearing, that if her father discovered his nephew was pinching and rubbing his daughter's leg, there'd be hell to pay. Several times she ignored the pokes, knowing Rancy could only do so much in public and some of it was surely penance for the way she'd thought. Soon the pinching stopped, but as he ate and drank with his right hand, his left hand idly rubbed her thigh. Cassie elbowed his arm away when she thought no one was looking. Rancy smiled back at her like a little boy.

After most of the guests were done with their meal, someone shouted "speech" and others followed until Rancy, in embarrassment, stood. "Ah," he said. "Ah, well, I don't go into much for talking. Action's more of my thing." He shuffled from foot to foot. "You know," he said, coughing several times. "I went over there to do my duty and I know you people think I'm some kind of a hero or something. And you all are making all this fuss. But I didn't do nothing a whole bunch of other guys didn't do."

There was clapping and shouting. "I thank you all for coming and making this big fuss. I thank Bob's Used Cars for giving me that fine Mustang."

A man, who Cassie figured to be Bob himself said, "You deserved it. You're an all-American boy, there, Rancy."

Rancy twisted the buttons on his coat. He said, "Well, I appreciate it. And I appreciate Mr. Liskow's giving me that fine job of temporary Assistant Game Warden for the county. "Hell—heck," he said, glancing at the reverend and his wife. "I would of done it for free just to be able to wander out in the woods all day."

Someone else shouted, "Nothing's too good for boys'll fight for this here country instead of turning Commie."

"Well, I ain't never going to turn Commie, that's for sure," Rancy said. There was applause and shouts. Rancy sat down. He let out a long breath and wiped his face. "Well, what'd you think of that?" Rancy asked.

He genuinely looked distressed to Cassie. She felt sorry for him, then angry with herself for thinking anything at all. "You ain't no war hero."

"As much as your old man."

"He don't say he is."

Rancy picked up his tumbler of lemonade drinking it down and then stared at the empty glass. He turned to Cassie, a long straight leering grin across his face. "Yep, they think I done a good job for this country over there. I'd a paid to do it." He moved closer to her. "You know, Cassie, girl, you just don't know how much pleasure choking the life out of a man can bring you." Rancy leaned closer to her, breathing in her ear and on the back of her neck. His hand came around her chair, pressing her toward him. He spoke slowly. "The only thing I enjoy more than choking the life out of a man, is choking the life out of a woman."

Cassie tried to bolt from her chair but Rancy held her as if she were nothing at all, so easily no one could tell he wasn't just hugging her and she wasn't letting him. "Please let me go," she whispered.

Several men approached her and Rancy. The way they were walking and the redness of their faces told Cassie they were well on their way to a drunk. "Rancy," a tall thin man shouted. "Why you hanging around here. Who's this?" he said, pointing to Cassie.

"This here's my cousin." he said. "Ain't she the prettiest thing?"

Another man looked at Cassie and said, "When you're through entertaining the children, how about we go and celebrate your new job?"

Rancy's arm loosened for a second, enough time for Cassie to jump from her chair. She walked as fast as she dare toward the car, past her brother and the reverend's wife discussing a point of theology, as Ben liked to say. It had always sounded like an argument to Cassie.

"Cassie," Rancy shouted.

Cassie glanced back to see him, arm outstretched between two of his buddies, calling to her. She ran to the car. She couldn't breathe, almost feeling Rancy's large hands on her throat, crushing her neck. She wanted to scream, to burst into tears. She leaned against her father's car gasping for air.

The reverend's wife reached her first and held Cassie by her upper arm. She said to Ben, "I think your sister's had a bit too much sun. It might be time to take her home."

Ben said, "I'll go get our folks." He walked off.

On a warm August day Cassie and Jake lay on the woolen blanket in their hollow while the sun baked the land. The odor of parched soil and the smell of the bitter summer grass slowly dying clung to the earth with the constant low buzzing of hidden insects as if the heat and odor had sound. Heavy, white clouds spotted the sky. A storm was on its way. The air had grown thick with moisture and a listless feeling permeated the hollow. Sound seemed deadened. The radio faltered in the heat fading in and out, the white noise giving sound to the heaviness of the air. Rancy was returning to a bad memory again, like the times when their lights had been shut off or they were short on food for a week, but still she found herself and Jake sitting quietly for hours, neither speaking. For two weeks after Rancy's lawn fete even Jake's touch had made her ill, made her feel dirty and cheap. She knew what troubled her, but Jake's troubles were new. Something had changed in him. Maybe she'd started it with her troubles, with talking about Rancy being home from the war, but never about what he'd done. She could never speak of that.

"Look at that cloud, Jake." Cassie pointed towards the sky. "It looks like a face, a clown's face." Rancy was even ruining this part of her life. They needed to believe in themselves and their future to protect themselves from the world of Rancys and his kind.

Jake shaded his eyes with his hand, giving the sky a half-hearted glance. "It don't look like much to me. If it's a face it sure ain't a clown's," he said. "It looks all twisted up. It don't even look much like a face. Don't look much like nothing." Jake leaned over to re-tune the radio, trying to get the station to come in clearer. "Damn it," he said. "I got to get a better radio." He peered up at the hills. "Something with a hundred foot antenna. That's the only way it's going to get any stations stuck in these god-forsaken hills." He fell back onto the blanket sighing heavily.

"Well, it does too. See what you can see in the clouds, Jake." Cassie thought they needed to smile more. Jake seemed to have forgotten how to smile. He did, but only short half smiles as if awakened from some deep thought, and lately Cassie hadn't felt much like smiling either. She loved him more, deeper and differently than when they'd met a year ago, more settled, more mature, more sure they would spend their life together.

Jake searched the sky for a few minutes, studying one cloud and then another. "I don't see anything in them," he finally said. "They're clouds."

"You got to use your imagination. You got to believe." The way her brother and Jake acted now frustrated her. They were quiet, sometimes angry for the littlest things. Cassie wanted to grab hold of them and shake as hard as she could, tell them to knock it off and get back to being her boyfriend and brother.

"The Dock of the Bay" whispered through the static of the radio. "Believe in what?" Jake laid the small radio on a flat spot he'd dug from the hill in the spring. He turned it one way, then the other.

"Jake, is there something wrong?" Grown men talked less than boys, but her father and mother still had their conversations. There was so much to say; so much that needed to be said. The future had been so clear only a few months ago. They had been so sure of themselves, of what they knew, of what they didn't know, but the future was fading to a gray unknown. Cassie had learned a long time ago, though, that dreams and reality were different. Jake seemed to be learning it now.

"It's nothing, just work I guess."

When they went someplace, to the movies, or to the hollow, they walked less hand and hand. Cassie loved him too much, but the world changed despite her, and what was here yesterday could be gone tomorrow. Did he love her deeply, or still? Had his love grown? Lately, at night in bed, she felt alone, needing something—what, she didn't know—listening to the sounds of the backwoods night that had sung to her since birth, the sounds of crickets, of frogs, of wailing cats, the lonely sound of barking dogs, the contented mooing of cattle and the murmur of the night breezes. With great hope comes greater disappointment. She'd lay awake contemplating the thought that the night would end and the dream would be lost in the wakening. "Jake?" The whistling of the birds and the gurgling of the creek seemed to punctuate the silence.

"Yeah?"

"Jake, you still love me?" Cassie sucked in air between her

103

teeth. She'd said it, said what she feared. "It's all right if you don't. I know things happen. I'll understand." She wouldn't. She would never understand if he said he didn't love her.

Jake slid his arms under her, lifting her slightly as if she were a small child. He'd grown stronger from the heavy work of the mill. "Cassie, I'll always love you." He kissed her.

She pulled herself to him. "Then what's the matter?" she asked.

Jake laid her down and settled back on the blanket to peer at the sky. He sighed. "A person needs a God-awful lot of money these days. It ain't the same as it use to be, like when we were young, when our folks were young."

Money trouble. She could deal with money trouble. "Well, it ain't so bad. We get along. Ma and Pa don't have much money but they're happy."

"We should be able to do things, to go places," Jake said. "Just to have a decent car. You can't tell me you don't want those things."

"What's important is us, me and you." Cassie grabbed his hand and brought it close to her face. Small scars sketched white and pink across his hand. Two were still red where he'd been nicked by wood slivers

"Yeah," he said. "That's what's important, me and you." Jake fell silent again for several minutes. "Cassie, you know what I always wanted to do? I always wanted to take a trip." They did take trips: once to Charleston, mostly to Wytheville, maybe someday to Wheeling. "Go all over. See America. You know, Nashville, New York, San Francisco, and Los Angeles. Then maybe Europe and other places." Jake smiled. "You and me, we could go all over. We don't own nothing, or owe anybody nothing. We could even have the bike sent to England if we wanted to. Then after we got tired of there we could go to France. Wouldn't it be great to ride around in Paris? We could stop off at some café and drink wine and maybe have some food we can't even pronounce."

The shadow of a large cloud ran slowly down the hollow, creeping across the trees and grass, people and crows, taking away the sun.

Cassie sat up. "Jake, you don't drink and you don't even speak French. How are you going to order food?"

He turned away from her to stare off into the woods. When he turned back his eyes were wet. "I got my draft card yesterday. They'll be sending me my notice soon."

Now Cassie had to turn away to stare into the dark woods and blink away the moisture. The man she loved could be gone in less than a year. No matter how much she prayed to God, one way or another, her life was going to change. She took several breaths, glanced at the browning grass, the heavy green foliage of the trees, the dried creek, finally asking, "You thinking about going to Canada?"

Jake stood, brushed his hands over the back of his pants, searching the hollow as if looking for a way to escape or place to hide. "No, I'll go. I can't do that to everybody. I mean my folks and everyone couldn't raise their heads if I took off." Jake walked a few steps along the side of the hill then looked up at the heavy clouds above them. He finally said, almost too low for Cassie to hear, "I ain't afraid of dying. I ain't brave, but I ain't a coward either, and I know we all die sometime."

Cassie reached her hand out to him. "Jake, come here. Let's not think of it, now." There was nothing they could do about it. Maybe it was God's will. All they could do was hope.

"I haven't seen nothing yet, Cassie. I ain't lived at all."

She wanted to say it was every man's duty to protect his family, but that would be like sending him away, what Teresa did to her father. And how was he protecting her over there?

"Don't you see it? I mean them protesters got something." As if he'd seen her thoughts in her eyes, Jake said, "I won't be protecting nobody from nothing. Those people just want to be left alone. So do I." He walked a little farther down the hill until he stood below her. "I mean, what is going on? We keep fighting and fighting. It's like this country's forgotten how not to fight. Because of that, I got to die? I mean you don't see any rich kids fighting in Vietnam. They're the ones that got it all and they run and hide in college and when they get out they'll just get richer and we'll be dead. Why is it always the poor that's got to fight for the rich?"

"You don't know that," Cassie said. She reached out with both hands. "Come on back, Jake. Sit down for a minute." Another deep shadow of a dark cloud darkened the hollow. Until her eyes adjusted, it seemed as if night had pressed in.

"I can't kill nobody either. It's crazy. How am I going to live with that?" he said, throwing his arms up and walking toward the dried creek bed. He turned to her again. "I know some wars got to be fought, but those that don't, shouldn't."

Cassie tucked her legs under her, staring down at Jake. Her heart ached for him but what could she do? This was beyond her doing. She would pray every night it didn't happen, but other than that it was beyond any of them. "It's God's will, Jake."

"God's got nothing to do with it." He stared at the ground shaking his head. "If he does then I don't want no part of him." Jake finally smiled up at her. "Those hippies got the right idea."

Now that was crazy. "They don't have any money," Cassie said.

"Not that," he said, walking up the hill toward her. "All they want is to be happy and to live a little. My life could be over in a couple of years and that'd be..." He stopped, as if contemplating the end of his life. "That'd be just a shame."

The clouds above were gathering, boiling toward the heavens. She and Jake seemed to be on their own paths—close, but separate. This was not the time of her mother and father when there were few paths to follow. A decision had to be made. The wrong man wanted her. The right one needed to. The government owned him, like her father, J. W. and Rancy and what had they been promised in exchange? Her? Yes, a woman, a wife, a family, peace and love.

"Jake," Cassie said. "I changed my mind. I want to go back to the cabin." She neatly folded the blanket, picked up the radio and walked down toward the dried creek bed. Even the storm that was brewing wouldn't replenish it. The arid land, its overwhelming need, would soak up almost all the rain.

Jake followed her. "You sure?"

Cassie nodded. She tried not to think about her actions too deeply. But maybe she'd been thinking about it for some time now, since the last time they'd been to the cabin, since Rancy touching her. This was the right way if it must happen at all before her wedding night, and with the right man.

The radio felt hot in her hand. It had been playing for too long, for too many days. She stuffed it into the blanket and strung the blanket to the back of the bike with several bungee cords.

He held the screen door to the porch open for her. "Do you want to go in?" he asked.

Cassie nodded. Jake undid the repaired pane of glass and opened the window. They crawled through it. She walked toward the stairs. By the time Cassie reached the landing, Jake seemed to have guessed her intentions. He took his time, slowly, carefully as if he was giving her time to change her mind. She never did, even as he undressed her, as he undressed himself, as he lay on top of her, as he entered her, slowly and carefully, holding her. She never told him to stop, even when the fire and ecstasy crowded out the feelings of sacrifice, of submission, when thoughts of him and Rancy swirled through her mind, and she found she wanted Jake greedily.

Cassie slept a dreamless sleep, the feel of Jake's bare skin next to her, the smell of him surrounding her. She woke to the dim light of a clouded early evening and the sound of distant thunder rolling down the valley. She murmured and kissed Jake's chest. "What time is it?" Cassie curled up closer, wincing from the pain. She hurt and felt wet.

"It's about six. You slept about an hour and a half. Are you all right?" Jake asked. "Do you want to go home?"

Cassie nodded. "We are home."

"Yes, we are. I love you, Cassie."

"I love you, Jake." She felt safe in his arms, safer then she'd felt for weeks, knowing she'd made love to the right man. She had saved their love and maybe herself. She would miss supper. Her mother would have to make it all by herself. Everyone would be angry with her, not so much they'd say anything, but there would be the looks—the old disapproving looks from her mother and father for not doing her chores, that new stare from her brother, a nasty glaring look of jealousy. She understood it now: the freedom she was gaining was the same freedom he was losing. All her life she had been chained to the rules of what was proper for a girl living under her father's roof. Soon she would gain the freedom of her own house while Jake and Ben found the freedom of being boys lost to the responsibility of being men. Didn't they know she exchanged chains only voluntarily? A plow horse knew there wasn't much difference between a saddle and a plow, but an unbroken colt took a while before it became accustomed to its new life. "We best be getting back," she said.

"Are you sure? We can stay a while longer, you know, if you want?"

Cassie winced again, mostly for show. "No, I don't think so." Even now it could be too late. Even now she could be pregnant.

"Do you need help?" he asked.

"No," she said, but he helped her balance while she put on her jeans. When they were dressed they held each other for a while. Jake drove slower, avoiding as many bumps and holes as he could. She laid her head against his back and tried not to think.

They arrived just at suppertime. Jake took his place at the

table next to Cassie. Cassie's father just stared. Ben had to be called twice from his bedroom.

Cassie had tried to help, but her mother refused. "I done it all. I might as well finish it," she said.

The kitchen was oppressive with the humidity and heat of the day and from the cooking. No one spoke until Ben asked, "So what've you two been doing all day?"

"Oh, nothing," Jake said quickly.

Cassie squeezed his hand. "Oh, just rode around."

"Since early afternoon?" her father asked. He propped his elbows on the table, a knife in his right hand, a fork in his left. "That's a pretty vague answer for a girl who left her chores for her mother to do." He cut a piece of meat, stabbing it with his fork. "What's happening here? You kids seem to be thinking you've got no responsibilities."

Ben dropped his knife on the table. "Man, I'm getting sick of this same old song. All you think we're here for is to slave for you two. We got our own life too, you know."

"It's my fault," Jake blurted out. "I got lost."

"Shit," Ben said.

"Don't use that language at the table, Ben," Cassie's mother said. She put her knife and fork beside her plate. She wiped her lips with a dishtowel and stared at her children.

Ben picked his knife back up and pointed the blade toward Jake, sighting down the blade with his right eye, his left eye closed as if taking aim. "That's a lie, Jake knows every road in this county."

Cassie looked down at her plate. Was the difference so obvious?

Jake smiled across the table at Cassie's brother. "Well, I wasn't in this county. I went up to Allegheny County."

Ben dropped his knife-hand to the table and sat back in his chair, taking a long breath. "What were you doing all the way up there?"

Jake wiped his mouth on a paper napkin. "It was dumb, I know, but I heard there were hippies living up there. I thought it'd be fun to see what they looked like."

Ben laughed. He stabbed at a potato. "Yeah, I heard that, but they're not there."

"I guess not. I didn't find them."

Cassie's mother and father laughed at Jake's joke. "I'll be," Cassie's mother said. "Real live hippies living right here in our neck of the woods. What'll happen next?"

"Well, I got to be running," Ben said. "Playing tonight." He ran up the stairs into his room.

Cassie's mother said, "I hope it ain't in one of those honky-tonks."

"Ma, it ain't that bad," Ben said as he walked back down the stairs pulling on a tie-dyed tee shirt of a multitude of colors and patterns—like the war protesters wore on television. His performing shirts, he called them. Her mother and father didn't like him wearing those shirts. They didn't like the fact he was growing his hair longer either. Ben said it was all for show. It didn't mean anything. He turned to Cassie and Jake. "Next time, go up to the Flat River basin up by Cider Creek. You got to go way up in the hills." As he walked out of the house, Ben said, "It's what you've been looking for, the hippie colony."

Cassie and Jake did the dishes. When they were done, they sat on the front porch under a starless sky below thickening clouds and in the sticky heat of a muggy summer's night. Heat lightning flashed.

"Maybe you ought to get home before it starts to rain," Cassie said.

Jake pulled her closer. "I don't care," he said. "I'd rather stay with you."

Cassie touched his face. "I know, I know, but it's going to be a bad one, this storm coming. I can feel it. I'd rather not have you with me than think I put you in danger. I'd never do anything to hurt you. Besides, I need a father for my unborn child."

"We'll call him Little Jake." He kissed her on the head.

Cassie punched him lightly on the arm. "Go now so I'll know you'll be coming back."

"I'll be coming back," he said. "I'll always be coming back." Jake left, the growl of his motorcycle sounding strangely alone as the light seemed to search its way through the night along the valley and over the hills as if it were going away forever.

Fork lightning jumped from cloud to cloud. Soon it would be raining. Cassie walked inside. Her mother was getting ready for bed. Her father was already sleeping, his snores coming softly from the dark doorway. "Is everyone out of the bathroom?" Cassie asked, knowing no one was left to be in there, but saying it as a friendly warning not to be disturbed. "I want to take a bath. I feel all dirty from the ride today and this heat."

"Be my guest," her mother said. "Just be quiet. Your pa and me are tired."

Cassie soaked in the tub letting the water cool. She put on a light cotton nightgown and then tiptoed through the living room. She sat on the porch as the lightning forked over the hills, hitting the ground somewhere. The air smelled of rain. The sky was thick black. Only when the lightning flashed could she see the clouds boiling above her. She hoped Jake got home okay.

Chapter 7

Making love had hurt a little bit, but she'd expected it. Jake had been Jake, gentle, caring and she had been herself, giving, but there had been something even before her deflowering and after, before the pain and after the pain—Darlene's good—that feeling again, that invisible whirlwind around her as Jake's lips found those spots on her body. She had made every effort not to feel, to give herself to him unselfishly, but before the pain, and after, and even during, there was a want to be bathed in the fire, a greedy, almost insidious feeling—of what? Of pleasure washing over her and she'd devoured it. She whispered to herself, "Admit it, just admit it, you enjoyed it. There is a bit of a devil inside you. At least it was with my husband. At least husband-to-be."

The rain started. First one fat drop fell hard on the porch roof, then another. Soon a hard rain fell. Yellow beams from a car's lights streaked through the deluge, illuminating the heavy drops falling thickly onto the ground. The passenger's side door opened. The interior light went on. Cassie stood up. She walked to the end of the porch just inside the curtain of rain, the lights blinding her. Someone was trying to get out even though the car was still moving.

The automobile stopped in front of her house. Cassie moved back to go inside and wake her father. The door opened again. Darlene flew from the car and across the road.

Ceilia cried from the inside of the car, "Dee? Dee, this ain't going to do no good."

Without breaking stride, Darlene leaped the rain-clogged ditch, landing on the slope of the other side, the wet grass giving way to the mud underneath. Darlene fell. She climbed out of the ditch and stumbled, dropping to her knees in the rain.

Cassie ran off the porch. "Darlene, what are you doing?"

"I'm dying." Darlene held her arms up to Cassie. "Your

brother's killed me."

Cassie pulled Darlene to her feet. "Ben? Dee, what are you saying?"

"Ben, oh, Ben." Darlene stumbled. "That bastard. Oh, Cassie, I loved him so. Ceilia's visiting. I got her to take me down to see him. He's a goddamn liar."

Cassie led Darlene toward the porch. "Dee, what in heaven's name are you talking about? Are you drunk?"

Darlene stood as if she hadn't noticed the rain soaking through hers and Cassie's clothes. "Your brother don't sing in his band no more. Hell, he ain't even got a band no more. Ceilia bought me some beer. I drank two cans."

"Come on," Cassie said. She pulled Darlene toward the back of the house. Her folk's bedroom was too close to the open front door. "We've got to get you out of this rain."

They stood underneath the small roof of the kitchen stoop. Even in the dark Cassie could see Darlene's mascara running in two wide lines down her face. Mud spotted Darlene's white blouse, now transparent and stuck to her, her ribs visible even in the darkness lit only by the distant barn light as Darlene gasped for breaths between sobs. "Cassie, Cassie, I love you so much. I loved your brother so much. There wasn't nothing I wouldn't do for him. But he's a liar. Purdy's already gone to college and Jimmy's going to be a sheriff. He's gone to some academy."

Cassie held tightly to Darlene's hand, afraid she'd run off. With her free hand she attempted to keep her soaked nightgown from clinging to her and revealing her nakedness underneath. "How can you know all this, Dee?"

"I knew all the time. Ben told me. We been seeing each other on the sly up to about three weeks ago. Then Ben quit coming around. He didn't call me, Cassie, and you even got a phone now."

Cassie stepped away from Darlene. "I don't understand. How could you and Ben have been seeing each other? I mean, why didn't one of you tell me? Don't you think I wanted you to fall in love?"

"Ben said your ma and pa wouldn't understand right away." Darlene attempted to hug Cassie.

Cassie stepped back another foot. "No, no you've got to be wrong. Ben couldn't of said that. He knows how we care about you."

Darlene attempted to stand erect, wobbling slightly. "You like me as a friend and your folks like me as your friend — but a future wife to their boy, that's something else. Nobody wants their son to marry below them. Ben was going to smooth it over with them. He and Guy's been playing with those hippie bands from that commune up in the woods. He told me. Guy left. He went to San Francisco."

"Guy left?" Lightning flashed and for a second the light pierced the wet clothing. Both girls seemed to stand naked before each other.

Water dripped from Darlene's chin. "Yeah, and your brother's a liar. Don't you know I loved him? Couldn't no one tell? Cassie, he done me real wrong." Darlene wiped her running nose with her wrist. She reached over and touched Cassie's face brushing her thumb gently across Cassie's cheek. "I love you," she said. "And I love Ben, but I can't ever see you again."

Cassie touched her hand. "No, Dee, we can work this out. Let's wait right here until Ben comes home."

Darlene pulled her hand away. "I saw him tonight. He was kissing up one of those hippie girls. She was sitting on his lap and I was stone sober at the time, which is more than I can say for him." Darlene stared into Cassie's eyes. "I can't see him ever again, so's that means I can't see you ever again."

"That doesn't make any sense, Dee," Cassie said. "I can still stop over. We can still go berry picking. When Jake and I are married you can visit all the time."

Darlene started crying again. She nodded her head. "Okay,

okay, but I got to go. Okay?" The storm had weakened, the rain falling lightly into the puddles, errant light from distant barn lamps dancing on the dark mirrors.

"Yeah, Dee, okay. Just go home and get yourself fixed up. I'll call you tomorrow. Come on." Cassie grabbed Darlene's hand. "I'll walk you to the car."

Ceilia opened the door. She was smoking. She held a can of beer with her left hand. She flicked the cigarette out through the open door toward Cassie, just missing her.

"Your brother's a bastard," Ceilia said. "My sister ain't never done nothing to deserve this. You people think you're so damn good. Well, let me tell you something Miss High-and-Mighty, Darlene's better than ten of you folks. I ought to have Art come down here and kick your brother's ass."

"No," Darlene screamed dropping into the front seat. "Don't you understand, Ceilia, you can't." Darlene laid her head against the dashboard. Her body shook in spasms. Water ran off her hair, down the dash dripping onto the floor or the car.

Her sister gently scratched her back. "I didn't really mean it, Dee. I was just trying to put the fear of God into them. You know I'd never have Art hurt..." Ceilia glanced from Darlene to Cassie. "Never have him hurt Ben."

Cassie glanced down at her nightgown. The rain had made the cloth as transparent as Darlene's blouse. Cassie pulled it away from her. "I'm so sorry," Cassie said to Ceilia. "He didn't really mean it."

"Oh, he did," she replied. "Dee thinks the world of you, so I'll give you a little advice. Kick them between the balls before they kick you. Get them down and keep them down. It's dog eat dog and don't be the bitch that gets taken. Now, shut the goddamn-door."

"Dee," Cassie said. "I'll straighten all this out, okay? I'll come over tomorrow." Cassie closed the door. Ceilia drove away. Cassie stood on the empty road in her bare feet, the rain soaking her, naked and wet. When the one working red taillight disappeared, Cassie went into the house. She dried herself off and changed her nightgown, then sat at the kitchen table in the dark waiting for Ben, listening to the storm ebb. Soon only the lonely sound of wayward drops falling from the trees and off the eaves, and the ticking of the kitchen clock could be heard. Cassie tried to figure out why Darlene and Ben had both hid their love. Why Ben, all this time? There were other things she needed to think about too, but she didn't want to, not in the quiet of the dark.

She still waited at two-thirty. The bars closed at one. The bars in Carter County closed at three-thirty. If Ben were a drinking man he might have gone over there. Was he? She didn't know. She'd never stayed up this late to see Ben when he came home. A year ago she would have said he wasn't, but now she wasn't sure what he was. Ben had become a liar, that was for sure, and worse, he'd lied to Darlene. Why didn't he say something? Why hadn't Darlene? The reason was obvious, but she didn't want to believe Ben was like that. One thing they'd always been, her, her parents, and Ben was honest—honest and poor. One made the other honorable, a covenant with God. It didn't matter how much money you had as long as you were decent folk. Ben wasn't honest. Neither was she, not now. What did that make them, make the last of the Wolphes?

At two-forty-five in the morning, in the distant rain-clear air, a car traveled slowly over wet pavement coming up the valley from the south. A car traveling this time of night up their road would most likely be Ben. She tiptoed the door and slipped out onto the stoop.

The air was washed clean and the grass sparkled with drops of rain. She'd always loved the clear smell of a rain-soaked summer night. Cassie stepped around the front of the car after Ben had parked in the driveway. Ben's head bobbed against the steering wheel. The door creaked open.

"Hey, Cassie girl, what brings you out this time of night?" His eyes widened. "You're not looking too good there. You sick?" Ben twisted quickly around to face the house.

Cassie stepped over the wet grass to stand between Ben and the door. "Just tell me one thing. You been going out with Darlene?"

"What?" He rocked forward and backwards trying to focus on her face. "Who told you that?"

"She did. She was here tonight and she don't lie. How could you? She seen you with another woman." Cassie slapped him across the face.

Ben closed his hand over his eyes pinching the bridge of his nose. "Okay, I deserved that."

Cassie wanted to slap him again—again and again until he got some brains back in his head. "Why, Ben? Why'd you lie to her, why to me?"

"I never lied to you."

"Yes, you did. You should of told me. That's as bad as a lie. You should of never lied to her and told her we wouldn't understand. Why, that's like calling her a whore."

Ben started to pull himself out of the car. "No, it ain't. Can I get out?"

"No!" she shouted, pushing him down onto the seat.

Ben held his finger to his lips.

"Why, Ben? Don't tell me it was just because you wanted— just don't tell me. You can't be that selfish."

His eyes glared back at her, his face flushed. He didn't have to say. She saw his shame for what he'd done and more importantly how he'd done it. But she felt his shame too, because he was kin and she'd been no better in the end.

Ben stared at the ground. "No, Cassie," he said quietly. "I was in love with her. I thought I loved her, I truly did."

The words shocked Cassie more than if he'd told her he'd never loved Darlene. "How could you? You up and left her." How was it possible for men to change their minds so easily?

"Things happen. I was just a kid. It was J.W.'s funeral and I was scared I'd be next. I felt all alone. Don't you see?"

"That was only seven months ago."

"It was a damn lifetime ago," he said loudly. He pulled himself from the car. "Cassie, you don't know. These times boys grow up real fast. Jake's changing, you know that."

Of course she knew. Her life was changed because she knew. Hadn't she done what Dee had done for love? "But you done her wrong." Cassie backed out of his way. Despite what Dee had done for her brother, he had left her.

Ben slipped around the door, closing it, pushing the door closed the last inch with his hip. "What'd she say?"

"Damn it, Ben, I don't need a picture drawn to figure out what you've been taking her to the barn for."

He gazed off toward the barn with its single light. "I didn't know you knew."

"Now you got some hippie girl sitting on your lap," Cassie said.

Ben leaned hard against the car, breathing through his mouth. "Her name's Penny, Penny Lane."

"Oh, my God," Cassie said. "What are you doing with people like that?" Soaked-up rain dragged the hem of her nightgown into the mud of the driveway. Cassie pinched the seams of her gown, pulling it up to mid-calf.

"I love her. So's she's a hippie. Why not? It's better than slaving all your life for some rich bastard, always smiling and saying yes'm and no'm. Do you know what it's like to be looking at forty-six years of hard labor? Do you know what kind of sentence that is?"

"That's what you're born to." The alcohol smell of his breath was stifling, almost turning her stomach. "You grow up. You do what's right."

"No, Cassie, there's got to be something better. Penny's got the right idea."

Cassie clutched her gown with her one hand and waved the other in front of her face. "Ben, I can't believe you. I bet you don't even know her real name."

Ben inhaled a prolonged breath and stared up at the dark night. "I don't need to. Look, I've been singing with some of the people from the colony. They're real good musicians. I got a chance with them."

"That's got nothing to do with Dee."

Her brother paced along side his car, more to sober up, she knew, than from guilt. "I just fell out of love with her a couple of weeks ago."

Cassie stood her ground. Someone had to. The mud of the driveway squished between her toes as she swung to face him as he walked. More importantly, she needed to know why a woman could give a man everything she had and it wasn't good enough. "A couple of weeks ago? Then why didn't you at least tell her? How many sins you going to cast on your soul?"

"Stop it. You sound like Teresa. God's dead, Cassie. When you going to see that?" Ben stepped toward her. "We're walking, talking proof. Where's the equity? Don't tell me in Heaven, okay? Don't tell me that shit. Religion's just the opiate of the people." He fell back against the car. "People like me and you are going to spend all our lives doing what people tell us is right and inside we're dying."

"What are you saying? I never heard you speak like this. You're like another man. Where's the Ben I use to know? That woman's changed you." Cassie turned away from her brother. There was nothing else to say or do. A woman could twist a man all up and there was nothing anyone could do about it until he came to his senses. She swung back to him and said, "You got to do right by Dee. At least go there, tell her you're sorry. Be a man and end it like a man's supposed to."

"Cassie, I'll do it for you and Darlene." Ben slipped back into the car. "Will you be happy then—will you forgive me?"

She nodded. "Yes, in a while." She couldn't make Ben love Darlene again, if he ever had, no matter what she said.

Ben drove off in the direction of Darlene's mother's house. She'd done the best she could for Darlene. After all, Ben hadn't been the only person who'd walked into the barn and Jake wasn't the only one in the bed today. A woman took what she got, right or wrong, good or bad. She only hoped with Jake the bad had been settled.

Cassie fell into a fitful sleep, waking before dawn to the sound of someone moving around in the house. She slipped out of bed. Ben stood in the dark holding three feed sacks full of clothes, his eyes wide with fear. He put his finger up to his lips then pointed toward the door. She followed him to his car.

The night still glistened with fallen rain. A girl with long red-orange hair slept in the front seat. Yellow tinted glasses perched on the top of her head. Her clothes looked several sizes too large.

"Ben, what are you doing?" Cassie asked. The girl in the front stirred.

"I'm leaving. I'm going to find Guy. I'm going out to San Francisco."

"You can't. You can't. Ben, don't go," Cassie said.

"Ben," the girl in the front seat said sarcastically, dragging the pronunciation of his name out. "Man, your name just doesn't make it, man. When we get to Frisco we'll get you another name, man."

Ben opened the back door and threw the feed sacks onto a pile of clothes and an old guitar. "If you love me at all, please don't do anything to stop me. Please, Cassie?"

"You can't go, Ben. We need you." The girl was the cause of all this.

Ben hugged Cassie tightly. "Cassie, Cassie, believe me, please, when I say I love you. I love Ma and Pa, but I can't do it."

Cassie held her arms around him as tightly as she could. "Ben, you're acting crazy."

"I won't do it, Cassie. They're not worth it." He kissed her on her ear. "Teresa, all the Wolphes, the people in church, all of them."

Cassie broke away from him. "What about me? What about Ma and Pa?"

"Why you want to do this to me? What have I got to look to, huh? Nothing—being poor and living poor and dying poor. I got to live before I die. Please just let me go."

Jake had said the same thing. Cassie tried to hug Ben again. "Please don't go, Ben."

He held her away. Ben reached for a folded piece of paper lying on the front seat. "Here's a note for Ma and Pa. All it says is that I'm okay and don't worry. If you don't hear that I'm dead, I ain't."

"Come on, Ben, man," the redheaded girl said. "Quit fucking around, man."

"Cassie," Ben said. "If I stay here, I'll die. If I leave, I got a chance to live. Let me live, Cassie, please?" He kissed her on her forehead. Ben pulled open the door and got in next to the girl. She leaned her head on his shoulder and glared at Cassie.

"What'll we do?" Cassie asked. The door had closed and her brother was leaving, but there was more than just a door between them. She'd taken a side for her mother and father and this life, and Ben for someone and something else. Maybe with the redheaded girl in the car she'd already lost. She couldn't pull her brother back. He had to come back because he wanted to come back.

Ben backed the car down the driveway, turning north. He put the car in drive and was gone.

Cassie began to cry, not just because her heart broke for him. Something else had gone. Something she couldn't put a name to had seemed to have ridden away with Ben.

Cassie sat at the table waiting for her parents to wake. She held the note in her hand. Fatigue jumbled her thoughts. She had made love to Jake to keep him and now her brother was gone. She had sinned, not the making love. The giving, that wasn't her sin, maybe. The taking pleasure in sex was her sin.

Her mother saw her first. "Cal," she called. "Cal, get up." Cassie's father hurried out to the kitchen. They stared at Cassie, her hair uncombed, her eyes red and puffy, the note in her hand.

"Ben's gone. He's gone and he ain't coming back."

The three of them watched the sun break the hold of the night. Another day had dawned.

Cassie's father said, "I best be getting to the chores. It don't look like we'll be making it to church."

Her mother said, "Cassie girl, we best be getting you to bed."

Chapter 8

Jake drove Cassie over to Darlene's mother's house to console Darlene and to apologize to her for Ben and for herself, but Darlene had left early in the morning, backed up and driven away by her big sister, gone to live with a great aunt in Cincinnati. Her mother refused to give Cassie Darlene's new address or telephone number. She refused to say why, but Ben had wronged her. Without Cassie pushing them toward each other, though, he might not have been able to, or even thought of it. So the fault could be laid on her.

At home, especially at dinner, loneliness hung heavy in the air, her father refusing to sit at the table, taking his meals in the living room while he watched TV. Cassie's mother soon joined him, and only Cassie alone, or with Jake, ate in the kitchen.

In one of the last warm days of the autumn of 1969, when the hills were just turning their colors and the nights were becoming colder, Cassie and Jake rode the motorcycle up to Flat River, searching for the commune. Jake thought Ben might have decided to stay there. Jake drove deep into the hills, along winding country roads, to a washboard gravel road, using the directions an attendant at a gas station had given him. Cassie sat upright behind Jake determined to find the commune, get Ben back, get her family back.

An old Volkswagen van painted in a multitude of colors in the shapes of flowers and peace signs was parked on the opposite shoulder in the tall grass. Several people sat cross-legged next to the van, one playing a guitar. Cassie had just leaned forward to tell Jake to stop to get directions when a man with very long hair stepped from the back and flagged them down. Cassie dismounted. The man held out his hand as he walked toward them appearing like a raggedy Christ. A woman stepped from the passenger-side of the van while the people sitting on the grass kept singing.

"Name's Bart," the raggedy Christ figure said. He pointed toward the woman. "This is my old lady, Moon."

"Moon?" Cassie said.

"Mother Moon," the woman replied. "I watched over Valentine Flats, the commune." She held out her hand to Cassie. Cassie stared at her. Moon shrugged, turned, and walked back to the van.

Bart pointed toward the rear of the van. "You know any about fixing cars?"

Jake shrugged moving along with Bart to the rear of the van.

"I'm looking for my brother Ben," Cassie said following Moon, searching the people singing even though Ben would have never ignored her if he saw her. She peered inside. No one was there. "He's a singer."

"Don't know anyone by that name," Moon said. Several of the people on the grass were just kids around her age, most in ill-fitting clothes, dirty and tattered. Some looked as if they could use a good scrubbing and a good meal.

"I need some tools," Jake said from the back of the van. Bart rushed into the van to reappear with a red-painted, rust-covered toolbox.

Moon leaned into the open back above the engine compartment examining the contents of several boxes. "Ha, here's some graham crackers." She dug down to the bottom of a moisture-swelling box. "We have a lot of musicians that come through here heading for San Francisco."

Cassie could almost taste the staleness of the crackers. "He was with a girl with long red hair and wore these little yellow sunglasses." How good could the crackers be sitting out in the open?

Moon bit down on one as if they were brand new, right from the store. As far away as Cassie stood, she could see they were stale.

"I remember her," Moon said.

Jake began rummaging through the rusted tools in Bart's toolbox, picking out a wrench wiping off the dirt, then placing it back to pick out something else.

Moon moved out of his way, picking a spot halfway up the van to lean against on the side away from the singers as if wanting to speak to Cassie alone.

"You do?" Cassie turned toward Jake's bike as if ready to find them. "Are they still there? Can you tell me where they went? Give me an address or something?"

"Honey, I wish I could, but she wasn't really one of us." Moon held the open end of the carton toward Cassie. Cassie shook her head. Moon sighed and looked down at herself. "None of them are like us anymore. People like you and I, Cassie, we believe there's more to life than money and material wealth. Most of them nowadays, like Penny, are just in it for the good times. Not that it's my business, but this whole thing with the drugs is going to be one bad trip."

Cassie reached for the open box. The crackers were moist, almost soggy. "Ben never took drugs. He drank some, but that was all."

Moon glanced at the sky as if worried about the weather or looking at something far off. "The commune's empty. We're heading for San Francisco. We've some friends there. If you and Jake want to follow me and my old man out, you're welcome. But honey, can I be honest? It's over. The movement's over. It was over before most people knew it existed. What your brother went out to, what you'd be going out to, isn't what you think."

Cassie took a step back from the tall woman. "What do you mean?" She could figure what Ben had gone out to, worse than what he had here.

Moon wiped crumbs of cracker from her shirt. "Look, honey, whatever it is at home that's got you troubled, it's got to be as good as what's happening out there. What you've got to do is find it and deal with it. You've got to face the bad times. Running away won't help. I'll tell you what. When I get out to the coast, I'll look your brother up and I'll tell him you love him and miss him and you want him back home."

"Will you do that? Oh, God, Moon. If you could just do that." Cassie grabbed her hand. "If you could just send him back where he belongs. There can't be anyone who could possibly love him more than us."

The woman squeezed Cassie's hand the way Cassie's mother used to do. "I can't promise you anything. He might not have even gone to San Francisco, but there's a grapevine, and if he's anywhere around, I'll try to get word to him. Now, if I promise I'll do this, will you go home?"

Bart rushed to the driver's side. Jake said, "Try it now." The van started, blowing gray-white smoke from the back, covering Jake in the cloud. He stumbled back waving it away. The kids sitting around singing filed back into the van.

Bart stepped out of the van and walked back to Jake, slapping him on his back. "When you get to San Francisco, look me up." Jake nodded.

Cassie turned to Moon and asked, "Why do you people have to do this? Why can't you just live like everyone else?"

Moon slowly scanned the late fall fields, dormant and waiting for winter. "Because," she said. She sighed as if running all the years and memories of a world Cassie had never known through her head. "Because, times, they are a changin'."

Cassie stared up at the taller woman wondering what kind of a world Moon had come from that she would be like this. Then she wondered if Moon was thinking the same thing about her. Cassie wanted to turn away to think about the fact that at some time she'd stopped thinking of herself as a girl, but as a woman who had inside her a world different than Moon's and maybe a world threatened by the changing times, by Moon's world. This was a standoff, a sizing up of foes. Not her and Moon, but everything that had made them and maybe, too, they were on the same side now.

Cassie finally gave up hope of finding Ben or Darlene. Jake struggled to comfort her, buying her presents, taking her to movies and even out to eat so she wouldn't have to sit alone. At night they sat on the porch and watched the leaves of the late fall burn from scarlet and gold, to brown and withered, scattering to the wind. When winter gave hints of its return, Jake said, "Cassie, we need to move on."

"How can I, Jake? How can you say that?"

"Cassie, I'm not being cruel, but think of it. Sooner or later you would have lost them." Jake brushed his fingers through her hair, holding her close to him. "Ben would have found a wife. Darlene would have found a husband. Who says they'd of stayed here?"

She turned her face to his chest. "But Ben had a job."

"Yeah, but who says he wouldn't have had better opportunities somewhere's else?" Jake pulled her to his chest. "Who says he's not better off in San Francisco? Who says that Darlene hasn't found the perfect man now? Think about it. Nobody knows her in Cincinnati. She's a smart, good-looking sort of girl. I bet there's good-looking guys falling all over her."

Cold wind finally drove them inside where Cassie's parents watched television, not speaking, not laughing or crying. Jake and Cassie sat in the kitchen not speaking. No music came from Ben's room. Cassie had no news from school to tell Jake. She sat alone on the bus, sat alone at lunch, glancing up quickly at the people who stared at her. Jake glanced at his new watch. He did that quite often. His world seemed to be divided into hours and minutes now, time and space, how long it took to do something, to drive some place.

"I've got to be getting home soon," he said. "I've got to get some sleep for work."

Cassie nodded. She carried their teacups to the sink.

Jake swung his coat off the chair onto his back, stuffing his arms through the sleeves. "Well, I'll see you."

"Yeah, tomorrow," Cassie said.

"Tomorrow," Jake said, walking out the door.

The deeper notes of the used car Jake had bought using his motorcycle as a down payment faded. Cassie jumped up and ran to the window. The raggedy Christ figure, Bart, had said to look him up. Jake still had thoughts of leaving and he hadn't kissed her. She hadn't asked. "God, it's all falling apart."

The Saturday after the Thursday-night missed kiss, her mother and father drove over to Teresa's. She said the invitation was to comfort them in the loss of their son. Cassie suspected it was an underhanded way for Teresa to get a chance to boast about Rancy and how he was making good money and had the respect of the whole county.

Cassie and Jake sat on the couch watching television, Jake's arm around her, her head on his shoulder. Jake absentmindedly stroked her hair. His fingers were warm where they rubbed against her face. He had not touched her in a long time. He was too decent to do that while she grieved. A cold wind blew outside, rattling the windows.

Cassie wanted his touch. "Jake, I love you. I really do." She reached across him, moving her body against him as she reached to shut off the light. He kissed her on her forehead. He kissed her lips, her eyes. Cassie kissed his neck and his chest below his open collar. She pulled her sweater over her head and took off her bra. A kiss, a touch, the pressure of her body against his, her hand placed on his inner thigh. Cassie knew what she was doing, and was ashamed of the thought, a little of the deed, but in a way proud of her ability.

"Cassie?" Jake whispered. "Do you want to?"

Cassie rested her fingers on his lips. Wearing only her good underwear, she led Jake into her bedroom. She didn't hold back, letting the feelings take her, swallow her until oceans of fire rushed over her in waves, ever-larger waves until the whole ocean crashed down on her. Gasping for air, she screamed wordlessly, clutching Jake, thrusting up against him, until he fell sweating, gasping onto her, his breath against her ear.

In stages they separated, always hugging and kissing, until he was dressed and she had on her nightgown. They kissed at the door before he left and she went to bed. That night she slept with the smell of Jake and sex around her. She slept the best she had in months.

Cassie was sure, as she lay in bed the next morning, she was pregnant; she almost hoped she was. There would be shame, and deservedly so, but they could be married right after her sixteenth birthday when she would be a little more than two months along.

Chapter 9

The summer sun pressed down hard on Cassie's back through her thin cotton blouse. The air smelled of heat and dried hay, of thirsty plants and parched barn wood and sun-dried cow manure. Cassie dug at the stubborn weeds between the rows of potato plants, her hoe sparking against the rocks, small clouds of dust exploding from the blade and floating away on the heavy lazy wind.

Three seasons had come and gone and she still missed Ben and Darlene, no longer with the heavy feeling of loss, but wondering if they were all right, what they were doing at the moment. She missed being Ben's little sister. Cassie had thought she and Darlene would grow into women together. There were few girls in school Cassie would have cared to be with, still less she would have wanted to call her friend. During those school years, when she had been singled out for the plain clothes she wore until they were threadbare, and the shoes whose heels were worn to the nails, Darlene had always stood by her, and when Darlene had been singled out for being a Tillman, Cassie had been there.

Her father had been sick quite a bit, and the phone had been shut off. He'd sold the cows and rented what little pasture and tillable land he had to the Cantrells. Cassie had finally found comfort in Jake and in the small bit of land her parents had left, but she couldn't help the wanting for it to end—for her to leave her mother's and father's life and find a new one with Jake.

Her mother carried a basket of laundry from the woodshed. "You about done?"

Cassie stretched her back. He thin cotton blouse stuck to her breasts. Her bras were all in the wash. It was cooler anyhow and she'd heard some women were burning theirs. A waste of good money and bras. She slowly twisted her upper body left then right to relieve cramped muscles from four hours of hoeing. "The weeding's almost done. There's still the watering yet. The garden's in desperate need of water."

"Do that after lunch." Her mother walked to the side yard and hung up the load of wash, coming back around the house and disappearing into the shed where the wringer washer chugged out a lazy rhythm.

Cassie wiped the sweat from her forehead and stared at cows that were not theirs, clustered under a single tree standing magnificently alone, a single oasis in a sea of heat. They calmly chewed on regurgitated grass. Their tails swished lazily, half-heartedly trying to keep the flies off their heavy bodies. The day would get hotter until the air buzzed like the flies, the only creatures that weren't affected by the heat, until the heat bent the light and objects began to shimmer and undulate. The whole world would lose focus before the sun dipped below the tips of the mountains, the shadows cooled the valleys, and the air condensed to heavy mists.

Her mother called to her. "Cassie, come help me with this washtub."

Cassie laid down her hoe, stepping over the rows of vegetables, her knees stiff from the effort of digging out the weeds. The two women hauled the large tub to the driveway and dumped it. The dirty, sudsy water flowed down to the ditch by the road. They walked the galvanized tub back to its sawhorses. "Ma, you need some help with getting more water?" Cassie asked.

Her mother yanked the side lever of the wringer down, banging the rollers into gear. "No, you got enough work to do."

The hoe struck again. Cassie and her mother ran the farm. Without his son, her father had quit caring, but Cassie had come to appreciate the steadiness of the work, how the plants grew day after day. The young bull her mother had bought for beef would be large enough by next spring to butcher. It stood by itself in its own small pasture and grew at an unvarying, unhurried pace watching the cows in the larger pasture as if waiting for his time, not knowing he'd been born to be butchered. The spring pigs Cassie slopped would be ready by first frost and soon there'd be tomatoes followed by beans and corn. It was harmony, like the song of birds that sang different melodies, but never out of tune with each other.

Her mother threw a tin bucket under the hand pump in the yard, easier than going into the kitchen. A few pumps and well water gushed from the spout.

Dust scraped against Cassie's skin as she wiped her face with her arm. "You want me to do that, Ma?"

"No, you just do your part and I'll do mine." She now struggled with one pail at a time.

Cassie remembered when she'd carried two. "Ma, you sure you don't need no help?"

Her mother set the bucket down on the lawn. "Who's to help us, Cassie?"

Cassie dug at a stubborn weed with the corner of the blade. Her mother was right. Her father did what he was able to do and Jake helped out some of the time, but he worked his father's farm and worked at the mill, working all the overtime he could get. Cassie didn't know anyone so worried about money. He had no faith. She wanted to soothe him, but she couldn't, not in the way he needed.

With the fourth pail, her mother stumbled, spilling the water over the grass. Cassie laid the hoe down. "Ma, take it easy."

Her mother held up her hand. "I'm all right." She picked up the pail and walked back to the pump.

The real problem was that Jake grew quieter every day. Would a family make him happy? And why hadn't she become pregnant? Could she? She had not tried to become pregnant. She just didn't care one way or another. After all, even with putting the wedding off until she graduated from high school, as Jake now insisted, in less than two years they should be married. It would serve Darlene and Ben right if they weren't there for the wedding or the birth of their first nephew or niece. After the night in her bedroom, Cassie had given herself to Jake twice more, but never again like that. She had vowed to never again let herself go like that. If she had not understood what was meant by sins of the flesh, she understood now. If she could, how many times? She'd like to make love several times a week, at least once a week. How many times would it take her to get pregnant? Sweat trickled into her eyes. Cassie wiped her face with the tail of her blouse. If she made love to him every night he might suspect she had those desires like, well, like men had. She smiled thinking about it. What would he think of her if she didn't lie there silently? What if they made love twice a night? Cassie shook her head not wanting to think of it anymore, to feel what she was starting to feel.

Her mother carried the last load of wash out to the line. Cassie grunted as she crashed the hoe into the hard dirt. The handle twisted in her hand. She clenched her jaw, stepped backwards and repeated the movement, flinging the blade down at the weeds. She had come to the end.

Rancy's county pickup truck wheeled into the driveway. Cassie stumbled backwards across a row of potato plants. After the lawn fete at the church and his new job, Rancy had pretty much disappeared. Teresa had told her father that Rancy had rented a house on one of the Cantrell's dairy farms. Rancy stepped from the truck wearing a green Fish and Game Department shirt and gray pants with a white stripe down the side. A gray, wide-brimmed hat shadowed his eyes. He walked to the back door ignoring Cassie standing alone and unprotected in her garden. He spoke into the dark interior of the shed. "Aunt Gert, how've you been?"

"Just fine." Her mother stepped into the light. Rancy bent down to let her kiss his cheek. "Come on in the house." She walked toward the kitchen door. "Let me fix you some lemonade."

Rancy motioned to Cassie. "Come on, girl. Let's get something to drink. You're looking mighty hot standing in that garden."

"No thank you," Cassie said. "I got more work to do." She picked up the pile of weeds from the row, gathering them together with the piles from the other rows, carrying them out to the pasture as two small dust devils danced across the field. Chaff, forgotten by the bailer, twisted up high into the vortexes. They spun close together, then quickly darted away, dancing unchoreographed, erratically, as if the steps were only vaguely known, bouncing across the field, always making their way towards the garden. They sucked up the dried earth, becoming gray-brown ghosts, then rushed through the corn and spun among the tomatoes, and turnips.

Cassie backed out of the garden. She'd seen dust devils before. In school she'd learned their science. There was nothing to do but get out of their way. They were a force of nature and one accepted one's powerlessness against these forces.

Her mother called her in for lunch. Rancy sat at the kitchen table, his hat hung on a chair, a large tumbler of lemonade sitting in front of him.

Cassie wiped the sweat from her eyes with the tail of her blouse. Cassie's mother handed her a tumbler of lemonade. She tilted the glass up, gulping the lemonade.

Rancy stared at her thin sweat-soaked blouse pressed against her chest.

Cassie's mother took her glass. "Tell her, Rancy."

Rancy cleared his throat. He turned the tumbler in his fingers. "Nothing really."

"Don't be shy," her mother said.

"I caught a couple of poachers this morning up on Snow Hill Run, back in the ravine," he said still looking into his glass. "They'd just got themselves a deer. Of course, it's out of season."

Rancy was leering again, but not at Cassie. "I get to keep all the game's been shot out of season. I been hunting these two guys down for months. I finally caught them. Had to do some reconnoitering." He leaned back against his chair. "Stuff I learned in Nam."

Cassie's mother handed her three plates, Cassie arranging them on the table, catching Rancy trying to look down her blouse. She scowled at him. *Who's the baby now?*

He pulled the plate to him. "Called the sheriffs, but first I made them dress and cut up the doe. Got it out in the truck. Thought you folks could use some meat."

Cassie's mother grabbed three knives and forks from a drawer. "Now ain't that nice of your cousin, Cassie?" her mother said.

"It's probably gone bad in this heat."

"What do you mean? I'd never give you bad meat. It ain't been sitting in the truck more than three-quarters of an hour."

Cassie's mother sat the pitcher of lemonade at the center of the table. "That's no way to talk to your cousin. Sorry, Rancy. I guess Cassie's a bit cranky from working out in the sun all day. Cassie, you go help Rancy pull it out of the truck and get it in the freezer. Your father can cut it up when he gets home."

"Aunt Gert, it'll keep until we eat. No sense ruining a good meal with the smell of deer on our hands."

Rancy kept up a running conversation with Cassie's mother, talking about family and job and how well he was doing. He sat opposite Cassie, speaking like he'd been coming over for years and hadn't tried to molest her most of her childhood. It didn't matter. No matter how much meat he gave her family, she'd never forgive him.

Rancy pushed his finished plate away and stood. "About time to get back to work, Cassie." He wrapped his arm around her shoulders. He half-walked, half-dragged her outside.

On the lawn Cassie spun from his grasp. "You just leave me

alone." She backed up, fists clenched. It was about time someone found out what he was really like and she'd be only too happy to show them.

Rancy stepped toward her. "I just come to give you meat." He walked off to the truck. "I got myself all the women I want."

He was lying. Nobody was going to put up with the likes of him, nobody.

A tarp lay in the bed of the truck. Hundreds of flies buzzed around it attracted by the acrid odor of dried blood. Rancy threw open the tarp. The skinned body of the deer lay in pieces stacked one on the other. The head, unskinned, was tossed in the corner, still looking innocent with its large brown eyes.

"Pretty, wasn't she?" Rancy picked up a front quarter. "It's all meat, one way or another. Here," he said. "It's yours."

Cassie grabbed the haunch of venison. "The family appreciates it," she said, hating saying it. The side of meat was almost too heavy to carry, soft in her hands. Blood oozed from it and ran between her fingers. Rancy picked up the two hindquarters and held them like turkey drumsticks walking behind Cassie to the shed as the blood made its way toward her elbows. Her mother stood in front of the open doors of the chest freezer. She'd already laid newspaper down inside.

Cassie dumped the leg onto the paper. Her hands were covered with blood. A small rivulet ran down her arm to the point of her elbow. She held her hands out to her side, not wanting any more blood to get on her. She thought she might be sick. "Oh, God."

Her mother handed her a wet rag. "Here, you're getting pretty uppity, young woman."

Cassie scoured at the blood on her arm. While Rancy threw the two hindquarters into the freezer.

He laughed when he saw Cassie frantically scrubbing the blood. "You sure the hell wouldn't make much of a soldier." He reached for the rag.

Cassie threw the rag at him.

Rancy said, "Fine, I'll get the rest."

"Then if you ain't going to do nothing else, Cassie," her mother said, "close everything up when Rancy gets it all in." Her mother walked out of the shed behind Rancy. Cassie scratched at the pinkish stain on her left arm.

Rancy came back with the ribs in one hand and a front leg in the other. Cassie backed away from him. He placed the meat on the paper, staring down at the carcass for a second. He turned and walked past her.

Cassie's mother stood in the sun outside and peered in at Cassie and Rancy. She held a bucket. "I'm going blackberry picking. Cassie you get supper ready."

"Thanks for the lunch," Rancy said. He picked up the rag and started to clean himself.

Her mother disappeared around the house heading up the road.

Cassie stepped up to the freezer, not taking her eyes off Rancy who was busy wiping the blood off his hands with the red-stained rag. She latched the freezer top, checking to see that the rubber gasket was sealed.

Rancy pinned her against the freezer, his hip against her pelvis, his hand under her chin forcing it back so far she couldn't scream. "Girl, I'm really getting tired of you treating me like I was dirt."

She pushed her hands against her chest.

Rancy chuckled. He slid his hand over her throat.

She forced the words out from between her teeth. "You got too much to lose to hurt me." She didn't know why she'd let him corner her. She'd been too over confident that he'd changed or she'd grown enough to handle him. "People'll find out." Cassie moved her legs; Rancy pushed harder into her. "And you know it," she said, with what little breath she had.

Rancy's hand loosened. "You'd be right about everyone else. I

---

drag them half-naked little girls out of the cars all the time on the back roads in the middle of the night." Rancy leaned harder, pushing Cassie further onto the chest freezer. "You want to know what I do?

Cassie shook her head.

"I like to make them get out of the car and stand there naked. A back hand usually straightens the boys right out." Rancy leaned over and whispered in her ear. "Some of them girls, they're real pretty. Some's so scared I'm going to arrest them, they even offer. You don't do that, do you, Cassie?"

Cassie shook her head again.

"You wouldn't be lying to me?" He pressed his face to her cheek.

She shook her head again.

Rancy moved slightly back. "They ain't worth losing my job over." With his free hand he grabbed her by her behind, forcing himself between her legs, hoisting her up, so that she straddle him.

"I think of you and what'd I do if I ever found you up in the hills naked," he said. While he spoke, he rhythmically moved his hips. "I wouldn't care about anything. I'd give it all up for you. I'd beat your boyfriend senseless and do things to you you'd never forget. You'll remember that, won't you, Cassie?"

Cassie nodded. Rancy was getting excited. She tried to slide further back on the freezer.

Rancy took his hand from her throat, pulling her tighter to him with the other. "If it weren't for my old man, you and me'd been kissing cousins for a long time and you wouldn't need to be fooling with them boys. What you got to learn is that you and I are just the same, like two sides of a mountain." He rubbed his hand against her cheek and whispered. "Hush." Rancy sat her on the freezer and walked out to his truck.

She hadn't escaped him. He'd let her go to show her how easy it would have been for him and how much he hated her, enough to lose his job, car, and maybe even his freedom.

After Rancy's truck had gone, Cassie walked into the house to start supper. She peeled three potatoes before her hands shook too much to peel more. She sat at the table and laid her head down. She tried to pray for forgiveness for whatever she'd done to be given the torment of Rancy, but she couldn't because she knew whatever she'd done must have been horrible and some day when God and Rancy felt it right, he'd savage her.

By the time her mother returned with two pints of raspberries, Cassie had recovered enough to finish the potatoes and open a jar of beans. She'd even gotten the water bucket and started to water the garden to keep from thinking about the afternoon and how she could still feel Rancy pressed against her. The chores took her mind off her cousin and gave her some sense of worth. If she didn't water the plants her time meant nothing. Jake understood his worth figured out in dollars and cents per hour. How much was she worth—a lifetime, a life? It seemed he'd forgotten about the good parts of life. She wished they'd married when she'd turned sixteen, but he'd insisted she get a high school diploma. How could it possibly help her raise kids or can vegetables? She could show him the good parts of life, but they weren't married, and she could only stand by and watch as he lost his beliefs and the farther Jake moved away, the closer Rancy and his world seemed to come.

Cassie wiped the table while her mother dried the last pan as Jake's car pulled into the driveway. His left forearm was wrapped in a band of gauze and tape. Cassie wiped her hands with the dishcloth, staring down at Jake's arm. "Jake, what happened?"

He glanced at the bandage as if he'd just noticed it. The skin around the bandage was stained yellow. "Caught a splinter today. It's nothing, just a scratch. There's guys who's missing fingers."

She reached for his arm. "Be careful, Jake, please? I'll change right now. It won't take but a minute," she said as she ran up the stairs.

Jake slid into a chair at the table. He put his head back against the wall and closed his eyes. "No, you don't have to," he said. "There's nothing planned."

Cassie dressed in the jeans and blouse Jake had bought her, then brushed out her hair, thinking. It been a long and hot day. Rancy had been Rancy, violent. Jake seemed the opposite. His enthusiasm for life was drained and not even an injury could move him. The poor deer had no choice. Did she?

Cassie ran back downstairs. "Okay, I'm ready."

Jake opened his eyes and started for the door. "Good." He walked out of the house

How many choices did she really have?

Chapter 10

The sun in Appalachia rises late in September and the mornings grow cold. The dew crystallizes on the grass, and the drying goldenrod shines like real gold. The night slowly turns into a day of weak blue sky and watery air.

A cup of tea sat next to a plate of buttered toast. The small radio on the counter played country-western music. Cassie pulled her hair behind her head and blew on her tea. Five nickels lay spread out in front of her. "Ma, what's this?"

Her mother slid the block of butter onto a shelf in the refrigerator. "It's your lunch money. We've got nothing around here 'til your father gets paid."

Cassie spread strawberry jam on her toast. The jam had been made from berries she'd picked last spring. "I thought he got paid last week?"

Cassie's mother sat down opposite her, a dishrag in one hand. "It took all the paycheck just to make up on the mortgage." She clutched the top of an old sky-blue housecoat. Cassie couldn't remember when her mother had had a new one.

"We're not still behind?" Cassie leaned in over the table to take a bite of toast, keeping it away from her clothes.

Cassie's mother scratched at a spot on the table with her short fingernails. "If your father can just keep working." Her voice trailed away. "But with cold weather coming on, I don't know."

Cassie sipped the tea. "We got any sugar? Ma, keep the money. Jake gave me some."

Her mother pushed the sugar bowl toward her. "Now, Cassie, you shouldn't be taking money from Jake."

"Ma, you should know Jake by now." Cassie carefully spooned out a half-teaspoon of sugar into her cup. She wanted more, but she could live with a half. Jake wanted to drive into the cities now, to movies and stores. He wanted to buy things they didn't need, as if the buying gave him pleasure. Jake had bought the skirt she wore, but hadn't liked the short length. Cassie, though, had seen how he stared at her bare legs, a look she saw seldom from him anymore.

Cassie's mother wiped the top of the sugar bowl with her dishrag, moving it in small circles. "I just don't understand the boys today. They go running away the moment things get tough, running away from their responsibilities."

"It ain't that," Cassie said. Jake got angry now and yelled—at anything, her, her parents, his family, but he never said anything bad about Ben. Jake talked about Ben after he finished blowing off steam, and Jake spoke of Ben quietly, wondering what Cassie's brother was doing and where he might be. She could only keep quiet, knowing why he thought that way.

"Then what is it? Please, I wish to God someone would tell me what it is?" her mother said, shaking her head, looking away toward the dim-lit window.

Cassie set her cup down. "The times, Ma. What can we do? How can we compete? There's a whole world out there different from anything we got. Just look at that place in New York, that Woodstock, where all those people got together. They just played music and danced."

Her mother walked over to the sink to stand on her toes. She pressed the palm of one hand against the counter. She blew on the window, almost kissing the frost clinging in leafy patterns to the glass, melting a small hole where they could watch for the school bus. "How can they not worry about anything—paying bills, where their next meal's coming from? They're fools. Maybe it's something else too." She leaned against the counter staring through the small hole at the frost-sprayed landscape. "All those things they see they'll never have—the stuff they show on TV. All those fancy cars and the clothes and those big houses. People get the idea everyone lives like that." Cassie's mother leaned against the sink. "Real people don't live like that. I mean it ain't all those things going to make you happy. You can be happy without them."

Cassie swallowed the last bit of toast. The school bus would be coming soon. She might not get to finish her tea. "Yeah, maybe, but maybe nobody knows that. Ma, maybe the whole world's like on TV, except in West Virginia."

Her mother said, "Could be Ben's out West making it big. He was a good carpenter." Her mother turned to the window. "Maybe he just don't want to be found?"

Cassie glanced at the clock. "Why?" She could figure what Jake had been thinking, and in bed alone she tried to figure out her options and it all came down to whether she'd do what Ben and Darlene had done or something that would convince Jake she could make life worth sacrificing worldly goods for.

"Men got their reasons. That's why I want to talk to you about Jake."

Cassie walked into the living room to get her books. "What do you want me to do?" She laid her books heavily on the table. They'd never spoken how Jake had changed, but how could her mother not see it? And she'd been expecting her mother to say something for a while. "I can't live without him."

Her mother turned to Cassie to stare at her bare legs, recognition showing in her eyes. "And what if you need to?" Her mother

Cassie felt herself blushing. She sat down and laid her chin on her books. "I should have gotten married the day I turned sixteen."

"Cassie, listen to me just for one minute. Okay? You're doing what you can do within what God deems fit for a good woman." Her mother seemed to think for a minute. "I just want to say that I'm here always, forever. Do you understand?" Her mother reached across the table and rubbed off some of the rouge Cassie wore.

Cassie pulled her cheek away. To say she understood was to

admit the possibility that things could get worse and that her mother did not suspect what she'd done. "Yes," she finally said. "Ma, the bus is going to be coming soon." If she had quit school, she'd be married now. Cassie disappeared upstairs looking for her purse. It hung on the footboard post. She flipped the strap over her head, pushing the trapped hair out from under it with the back of her hand, scurried back down to the kitchen hoping, by looking busy, her mother would leave her alone, but fearing her mother would ask and she'd be unable to lie well enough.

"I don't care if you miss the bus. Sit. In every woman's life there comes a time of decision. No, there are a lot of decisions, but there's always that big one, the one that changes your life forever." Cassie's mother reached across the table again. She pushed Cassie's bangs away from her eyes. "You've got to know what you want, what kind of life you want to live? Sometimes you've got to stand your ground and be willing to pay the consequences."

Cassie jumped up and walked over to the sink. "What are you saying, Ma?"

"You've got to decide what you want and if it ain't what Jake wants then he's got to make his choice, and you got to be strong enough to live with that choice."

Cassie leaned far over the sink and peered through shrinking hole in the frosted window. "The school bus is coming. I got to go."

"Cassie, do you understand? All you got is yourself."

"Yeah, I understand." Cassie ran from the house.

The bus bounced down country roads for a half-hour before it arrived at the central school. Cassie sat a while letting the younger kids scurry off before she slung her purse over her shoulder, clutched her books, flicked her hair back and walked off the bus.

Cassie attended school because Jake wanted her to attend. She did well in school because her teachers expected her to do well, and she always did what was expected of her and sometimes doing what was expected of her made her angry. She couldn't get the conversation with her mother out of her mind. Why had her mother brought it up? Because her mother knew what she'd been thinking, because she was desperate and might be willing to persuade Jake to stay for her own reasons. But what did her mother really understand about young love?

Every day several boys stood in the way of her locker, all gathered around Suzy Reese. Cassie didn't know every one of the five hundred plus students who attended kindergarten to twelfth grade, but she could place many of them by their resemblance to brothers, sisters, or cousins. She'd known the students in the single homeroom of her class most of her school life as acquaintances, not as friends. She'd had one friend and that had been Darlene.

Suzy was another country girl, a strange little girl less than five feet tall, similar to Cassie and Darlene, and most other country kids, in that their school day consisted of a forced routine: boarding the bus, attending classes, maintaining silence unless called upon, re-boarding the bus to be delivered back home and to their life.

Suzy smiled now, but only for boys who'd noticed her after she began to develop. For all her diminutive size, she exuded a strange, almost voluptuous, sexuality. Today Suzy exposed a good bit of her cleavage through the plunging neckline of a cable-knit pullover. Cassie saw nothing wrong with a plunging necklines but nothing so low. Short-shorts were one thing, but letting boys see your breasts was another. And Suzy had breasts, more than most girls in school despite her size, and a tiny waist and rounded hips with a full behind that swayed when she walked. It wasn't that she was sexy, just too blatantly sexual. And there were rumors about her step-father's barn and boys.

After history class, Cassie stopped at her locker to change books before lunch. Suzy rested against her locker while a town boy, Ricky Carbone, stood with her, his back turned toward Cassie's locker. Although Ricky was a senior, he stood only a couple inches taller than Cassie. His hair always looked like it'd just been cut. His clothes always looked new. Even his shoes were never scuffed, and he seemed to have more than several pairs. Ricky not only belonged to the town kids, but to the rich kids. His father, a lawyer, owned a real-estate business and sold car insurance. Cassie had never heard of anyone who'd used a lawyer. If you did something wrong you confessed and paid for it. No sense adding lawyer fees on top of a fine, or jail time, which most people who got arrested were forced to take.

Rickie turned to her when Cassie squeezed in behind him. "I'm sorry. I should have moved." He smiled a wide bright ortho-dontist-fixed smile, one of the few kids in school who had worn braces. Cassie turned to her locker, scowling, sure there'd be no way he'd be caught dead with Suzy outside of school, unless they were in her step-father's barn. Ricky said something to Suzy and walked away.

"Who the hell do you think you are?" Suzy said after Cassie shut the door to her locker frightening Cassie. Suzy leaned forward, staring up at Cassie. "You're walking around here like you're better than anybody else. You may be prettier than some, but you ain't that much." The part in Suzy's short hair showed a half-inch of dark roots. "You ain't no different than any one of us. You're country and you're poor, so's where's that get you? Just because you got yourself a steady boyfriend don't make you so high and mighty."

"I don't think like that." Cassie wanting to ask Suzy if she knew everyone could see she wasn't a real blonde.

"You're full of shit. You don't talk to no one now that Darlene McAlester's gone and she was nothing but a high-class whore." Suzy smelled heavily of perfume and hair spray, flowery and acrid at the same time.

Cassie's arms tightened around her books. "You got your

nerve, you little pint-sized slut. Everybody knows about the barn."

Suzy's eyes widened. She sat back on her heels, pressing a book over her exposed chest. "No, they don't. It ain't true. It's a lie. R.C. likes me. He don't know nothing about no barn."

"R.C.? You call him R.C. How quaint. Are there any more quaint little sayings you got? You're so cute being so—so petite."

Now Suzy's arms tightened around her books. "I thought you was nice, Cassie Wolphe, but you're nothing but a bitch."

Cassie wasn't really mad at Suzy anymore. She just wanted to be. "You don't know nothing about me or Darlene, but you go shooting your little mouth off."

Suzy stuttered something unintelligible, turned and walked away.

Cassie leaned against her locker. She had no reason to hurt Suzy out of spite, but Suzy had insulted Dee. She missed Dee so much, but the students that walked through the halls would all be gone someday. Soon some of the boys would be going off to college, some off to war. The girls would most likely be getting married, or getting jobs until they were married. She walked down the hall, down the stairs to the cafeteria. The school had become lonely without Dee and it was getting harder through the day now that Jake seemed to be slipping away. She'd hurt Suzy because of what was happening to Jake and her. It'd been Suzy's smile. She smiled because of new love, while Cassie struggled to hold on to old love.

When Jake and she were alone, in the car, sitting, or going someplace, or when they went to a movie, his quietness reminded her of a drying pool in high summer. Jake had headaches a lot now. Sometimes he leaned his head back with his eyes closed for hours. Sometimes he fell asleep. If they were married this storm could be weathered, some way—love, children, work. Hadn't she lived with her father's illness all her life? Ben had run from Darlene, and she held nothing to keep

Jake. Only Jake's love for her and sex. One she had no control over, the other—she wasn't foolish enough to believe a man didn't get his fill. If a Tillman couldn't hold on to a Wolphe, how could she expect to keep Jake?

Cassie ate alone at the end of a table by the far wall, away from anyone else, hers and Dee's spot. Suzy glanced over at Cassie. Cassie smiled hoping to make amends. Did Suzy really care about who laughed at all? Suzy ignored her at first, and then she waved, a little bend of her short fingers and palm.

At the end of the school day Cassie again stood at her locker muscling boys out of her way, and again, when she closed her locker door, Suzy was waiting, and again she frightened Cassie. "What?" Cassie said.

"Nothing," Suzy replied. She stared up at Cassie, her eyes big and round, her cheeks baby fat, still very much a little girl, looking oddly innocent. "I didn't mean nothing about Darlene McAlester." A town girl walked by wearing a new leather coat. The girl strolled down the middle of the hall. Neither Cassie nor Suzy could ever be so bold. "We got to stick together," Suzy said.

Cassie leaned against her locker. "Look, I didn't mean to say those things. I'm really not like that."

"That's what boys are for. When they look at you it makes you feel good about yourself. You know," Suzy said. "Tell you what. I'll keep the boys away from your locker if you want?"

"That'd be nice."

Cassie rode the bus silently back home. The early, autumn-harvested countryside slid by. Cassie crossed the road in front of the stopped bus. It wasn't much, nothing at all, their house, sitting squat on their piece of land. This was all her parents had to show for a lifetime of work. But there'd been her brother and her: Christmases, Easters, Thanksgivings and birthdays, cold winter nights, the house all closed up and cozy, days of sitting on the porch after a good dinner and a hard day's work of growing your own food and tilling your own land, and when you sat down to those meals, you sat down to an honest living. Simplicity was what she wanted, a house, children, and a good husband, not strange at all, but oh, she thought, those dreams now were so hard to come by.

Cassie sat on the porch in an old jacket watching the wind strip the early fall leaves from the trees, birds gathering in flocks, leaving, going to distant places. *Just one more winter, Jake. Just hold on for one more winter and a spring.*

Jake's old car rattled up the rutted grassy driveway. Cassie waited while he sat in the front seat, staring through the windshield. He shut the engine off and got out of the car. The engine sputtered and banged clumsily. The door squealed as he slammed it, the sun slowly dropping behind the hills, casting purple shadows over the slowly passing day. Jake stood at the front of his car glaring at her, the heat rising in waves off the hood behind him; the odor of cooked engine oil and fried rubber drifted slowly through the air.

Cassie held her arms out to him as he stepped on to the porch.

Jake stopped just out of reach. "How come you're wearing that dress? Where's the clothes I bought?"

"I was saving them for a more special time." She dropped her arms to her side glancing down at herself. The dress was old but not frayed or worn out. "I want to keep them nice and new." Dusk was setting in the valley. A cold night breeze ran past the two of them. The waning colors of the autumn hills were washing to gray as the light disappeared. They would argue.

He stepped onto the porch. "If you need some more clothes I'll get you some. I work hard, you know."

Cassie said, "This is good enough around the house. We need to save our money for more important things. Jake, no one's going to see me. Jake." Cassie kissed him and hugged his work-hardened body tightly not wanting to let him go, so much a man now, the boy, gone. "I've worn these clothes before and you never said anything about it. Jake, what's wrong? Someone give you a hard time today at work?" As soon as she said the words, Cassie wished she hadn't. The look on his face said it was true.

"Nobody gave me a hard time today." Jake stared out at the mountains again as if trying to see through them, sucking air in hard through his mouth, blowing it back out in long hard streams. "I think we need to talk. Let's go to the car." He marched back the way he'd come as if not worrying whether she followed, as if knowing she had no choice.

Jake's head lay back against the seat, his eyes closed. Cassie turned on the radio. Jake never listened to it anymore. "The Boxer" played. Cassie said, "Honey, what's wrong? If you don't want me to wear these old clothes I won't." A layer of dust lay on the sun-bleached dashboard. Small cracks ran through the vinyl.

Jake pinched the bridge of his nose with his finger and thumb, his eyes still closed. "It isn't that. It's just—what the hell are we doing?"

"When I get through with school, I thought we were fixing to get married." Cassie brushed her hair behind her ears. She wanted to take his hand and place it against her cheek, to remind him that she was the reward for all his labor.

He exhaled quickly through his nose. "With what, an old broken-down car and the clothes on our backs? I've got nothing except some stupid low-paying job that anyone can do and everybody knows it, and if I do one thing they don't like, or say something they don't like me saying, I'll be fired and there'll be six guys coming around the next day asking for my job."

Cassie rubbed Jake's shoulder. They were tight with the hardness of tired muscle after a long day's work. "It's not so bad. The car runs good enough for now. You can fix just about anything that goes wrong with it and Uncle Bill is giving us that hunting cabin. We got a jump on a lot of people."

Jake opened his eyes to glare at her. "That cabin only has a fireplace and no insulation, and besides, you just can't give someone a house. You've got to have a deed for it. That means you have to pay lawyers and surveyors." His head fell back against the seat. "We'd have to pay for it. Where're we going to get the kind of money it's going to take to fix up the place?"

The car's roof liner was faded. The inside of the car had once been a strange metallic green to match the outside, but the sun had marbled, and striped, and blotched the interior so it flowed from one shade to another.

Cassie brushed at the hair above his ears. He'd let it grow longer. She preferred it short. "Then I guess that's all the more reason we shouldn't be spending money on clothes I don't need." She took his hand, pressing it against her thigh. "Look, Jake, we got just a little over a year 'til I get out of school. We can save enough money if we don't spend it. I love you. You love me. That's all we need," she said reaching to fix his bangs, again needing to touch him, to know he was there.

Jake pushed her hand away. "No, it's not. There's a hell of a lot more we need."

In the distance cows walked slowly back into the field.

"Is there someone else?" Cassie's voice shook as the words tumbled out. "I mean, if you're having a fling with one of those girls, I'll understand. I mean, I know a guy's got to sow some wild oats when he's young, and I don't blame you, and I know I won't because, well, I'm trying to give you something, the only thing I can give you for a wedding gift." Cassie stared at the floor fearing she had given it all already and he wanted nothing more from her.

Jake's eyes widened. He opened his mouth as if to speak but not having the words as "Build Me up Buttercup" sang brightly from the speaker.

She whispered, "I know that sounds dumb because we already did it a couple of times, but I really do love you and, you know, sometimes I just couldn't help myself." Cassie hoped she'd see forgiveness in his eyes. "Jake, I'm sorry, but don't throw it all away for some fling." Nothing told her he still cared. "Please,

Jake, let's not wait any longer. I'll go with you right now. We can elope. I'll get birth control pills. I'll still go to school."

Jake's jaw clenched tightly. He trembled. "I don't have another woman," he said. "You really think I want some dumb stupid-ass job and some run-down shack in the woods with a bunch of snot -nosed brats running around and living from paycheck to paycheck? Is that what you really think? Do you really think I want to live like that?" Jake pointed to her house.

Cassie's gaze swung first to where he was pointing, then back to him. "I don't know what I think," she said. She turned away and covered her face with her hands. She began to cry. He had never said anything so cruel to her before. Even the boys in school who might have thought her below them, had never been so cruel. Minutes passed while she cried. "What do you want to do?" she finally asked.

Jake said, "I want to leave here."

Why had she cried? Not for the loss of Jake. He was still here. For his insults? No, there could be worse in the years yet to come. She cried because she had to make a decision. Yet, she had known for a while, maybe since the night Ben left she would have to make it. "Where do you want to go?"

"I don't know? I thought about Charleston or Charlotte."

"To a city?" Cassie sniffed back the drying tears, trying to understand why he wanted to leave. The ridges of the mountains etched a jagged line across the clear darkening sky. A hawk, black in the light of the setting sun, soared on the updrafts still lingering in the valley, soaring slowly across the hills. With a single flap of its wings it drove on.

Jake sat up, turning to her, his voice more powerful, his eyes wider. "There's money in a city, opportunity."

What did he see when he looked at the mountains? How could he leave it, just pick up and leave all of it? "Do you want me to go with you, now?"

"No, I thought I might send for you."

The hawk grew smaller disappearing into the coming night. He'd never send for her. He'd forget her eventually, forget it all. "I don't need no false hope, Jake. Don't tell me something you ain't going to do. There's one thing to go. There's another thing to run." They would live in an apartment in a building with a bunch of other people, people they didn't even know. They'd never see the sun. They'd never feel the breeze.

He stared at the hills. "I ain't running."

"Then take me with you," she demanded. "I'm old enough to get married."

Jake grabbed the steering wheel as if he were ready to drive both of them away from the mountains and the country. "Okay. In a couple of months we'll go."

"No, not in a couple of months." Cassie leaned her back against the door. The panel slid where the screw holes were worn. "You got money saved up. We can go now." She could say she'd wait and hope he'd change his mind and forget all about it, but if he didn't there'd be another reckoning, a good chance he'd bolt like Ben or find another woman, and better a reckoning now than to live in fear of it. That much she'd learned.

Jake took his hands off the wheel and rubbed them on his jeans. "Cassie, it'll be better in a couple of months. We can plan things."

Cassie forced herself to speak in an even manner, not slow, not hurried, keeping her voice calm and level. "Don't promise me nothing you're not going to deliver. Give me the keys. Give me your keys," she said. "Now, damn it. Jake, give me them."

He took the keys from the dash, holding the ring out to her.

Cassie clutched it. "Now, are we running or we sticking it out? Make up your mind." She lightly pounded the keys against her leg. "You got to make up your mind, stand or run." Cassie held up the ring. The keys jingled like miniscule wind chimes. "I give you these back, we go get married and we go to a city, or we get out of the car right now and go sit on the porch and I'll get you some cider and we'll work this thing out, whatever it is."

Jake sat quietly for several minutes. Her heart beat in her chest, counting the seconds of her life way.

"I can't stay here, Cassie. I got no life here." Jake stretched out his hand. "Give me the keys back. We'll go. We'll get married. I got enough in my pocket for a justice of the peace. Tomorrow I'll get the rest out of the bank."

Cassie closed her eyes. He had said what she had hoped he wouldn't say. He was running just like Ben. She wanted desperately to marry him, almost said she would. They could yell and scream and fight. He could become a philanderer or a drunk, lazy or hard working, but unless he had chosen to stay, to accept this life, the life she offered, they couldn't go on. As much as she wanted to be married, she couldn't accept life any other way but the way she and her kin had lived. It was what she wanted, had wanted from the beginning and Jake had been a part of it all, but he wasn't anymore. It'd been his decision.

The tall mountains were fading to gray as night set in. "I understand how you feel, but I got to be who I am and you got to be who you are." Her hands started to shake, the palsy moving quickly up her arms and down her body. "You can't stay here. I'll just hold you back, so I don't think you ought to come around here anymore. I love you, but that ain't enough anymore. I don't know what is." Cassie opened the door and got out, leaving the keys on the seat, walked back to the house, stepped onto the dilapidated porch, opened the rusted, cocked screen door, and walked into the cool darkness of the interior. Jake yelled her name. The screen door gave out a whining sound as it slammed shut, bounced then shut again. The sound echoed in the cold hollowness of her chest. He could follow her in and take her back. She desperately wanted him to, but she was afraid if he asked her again to go to the city, she wouldn't have the courage to refuse.

Cassie clutched the door jamb while the evening closed in around her. She waited to hear Jake's car door open, to hear it slam closed, and finally to hear his footsteps on the porch, to hear her life be put back in order. Instead, she heard the engine start and the sound of the car backing over the stones in the driveway. She heard it shift into drive and accelerate away as the darkness buzzed like flies hovering over a carcass.

Chapter 11

She should have been married now. They should have had their own home, their own life. Ben should have been home. He could have helped. Dee should have been her maid of honor. But now there was nothing, just the dimming light of the set sun and the shadows of the mountains reaching up the valley like long grasping fingers, nothing left, no strength, no anger, and no hope.

Cassie fell onto her bed shoving her face down into her pillow to cry long tearing wails that left nothing in her. The darkness was complete when her mother stepped quietly into her room and sat on the edge of the bed to gently rub Cassie's shoulder.

"It'll be all right." But her mother's eyes spoke the truth. Jake had been as much a part of their life, as Cassie's. "He'll be back," her mother said. She lied. He wouldn't. Jake wasn't like that. He made decisions, and this had been one.

Cassie cried through the night, whimpering, gasping little hiccupping sobs, falling to sleep before dawn. In the morning she listened to her father shuffle around the kitchen getting ready for work, the quiet click of dishes and the hurried closing of the door.

After the sun had risen, her mother brought Cassie in some tea and toast. "Eat," she said.

Cassie choked on the food. She could only swallow small bites, one or two at the most. In bed she burst into tears and cried for hours, but now she cried quietly, letting the tears fall down her cheeks. There had only been Jake. She could never be close to anyone else.

Sunday morning Cassie still lay in her bed wearing the same nightgown she had struggled to put on three days before. The day leaked between the curtains and the sill. Dust swam in the warmth of the light streaking across the wood floor. Cassie wished it was the shaft of light that lifted people up to heaven. She wanted to walk into it, to have it dissolve her into itself.

Her mother came in and sat on the edge of the bed. "Cassie," she said. "Now, we'll only be gone for a little while, okay? You just stay here and we'll be back." Her mother had put on her church perfume. "Look, honey, it's a real nice fall day out. Maybe one of the last of the year. I'll open the window and let some sun in." Her mother pulled the curtain back and slid the old window up. The brown shade flapped in the warm breeze. As she walked out of Cassie's bedroom she turned. "I'll pray you get better."

Downstairs her father asked her mother, "She coming?"

"No, she's still feeling bad," her mother replied.

"She's got to get over it. She can't be just lying around."

"You ought to talk."

Several minutes ticked by before her father said, "But she's strong. She just don't know it." The back door opened then closed. The car started, then drove away.

Cassie stared out through the window at the distant browning grass and the small dogwood tree stripped bare of its leaves. "It just keeps right on going, don't it?" she finally said. "I guess I ain't that important." She sucked in a breath and blew it out slowly, figuring she wasn't going to die from a broken heart even if she wanted to.

Her legs shook under her as she stood. Her nightgown stuck out stiffly and her hair fell in greasy strings, lying limply on her shoulders. Geese called to each other from somewhere over the house. Cassie walked outside to search the sky for the living vee flying south. Shots echoed off the hills. A faint hint of wood smoke was in the air. It'd be cold soon: Halloween in a month and apple cider, new-baked apple pies. Thanksgiving was coming. At least there'd be her, her mother, and father, alone but still a family of sorts.

A bushel of apples sat just inside the shed. She squeezed an apple testing its just-picked ripeness. Cassie polished the fruit on her flannel nightgown until it shined and reflected the autumn sun in a glass-clear sky. The apple snapped crisply as she bit into it. A little tart, but it'd make a good pie. She took a deep breath of air. It felt new. Cassie bit down on the apple holding it between her teeth. She made a pocket at the waist of her nightgown and filled it with the biggest apples she could find. One half-hour later two pies were in the oven.

Cassie bathed and washed her hair twice. Wrapping a towel around her she walked into her bedroom. A girl with stringy wet hair and dark crescent moons under her eyes stared back at her from her mirror. Cassie let the towel fall to the floor touching the hollow of her neck, running her hands across her shoulders, over her breasts, down across her thighs. Once her body had been Jake's, as a promise. Whose it was now?

Cassie set her milk on the empty table next to her lunch of sliced roast beef on homemade bread and a slice of her pie. She promised her parents she would to try to eat, but she had no appetite. She took small bites trying to chew them in a dry mouth, concentrating on swallowing.

Suzy slid into a chair next to Cassie pinching off a bit of the crust from the pie. She rubbed the flakes into crumbs that scattered across the table. "Who made the pie?"

"I did," Cassie said. She kept her head down unable to disguise the hurt she knew showed in her eyes.

"Looks pretty good. Better than mine. My specialty is biscuits. My daddy, well, he ain't really my daddy, says they's the best he's ever had and he's had a lot." Suzy motioned to her friends to come over. No one addressed Cassie, but they spoke in a way to include her, little jokes, snide little remarks about town kids, trying to get her to laugh. She smiled a bit only so they wouldn't feel their efforts were wasted.

Country poor, especially boys, were the most put upon and the most retaliatory. The boys in Suzy's entourage were poor— Gabe, Orlen, Davey, and their families. Judd Cantrell and Rancy had refused the hierarchy of city over country, rich over poor. They aligned themselves with no one, or maybe with anyone who had the courage, or was foolish enough to stick around.

"There's the shrimp and the big old dufus," Gabe said as R.C. and his companion Andy walked in to the cafeteria lining up in the queue for lunch.

"Don't ever call him a shrimp." Suzy's face colored in anger. "You're just jealous because they're on the football team."

Gabe leaned his chair back. "Shit, I got better things to do than playing football." He spoke loudly.

Orlen spoke with pie in his mouth having nodded toward the pie then Cassie as a way of asking. Cassie had nodded back. "Yeah, like getting beat by your old man for getting kicked out of school for fighting, which is going to happen any minute. Cassie, girl," Orlen said, pointing the plastic fork at Andy Furlong, "the big man on campus is eyeing you up."

Cassie turned to look behind her where Orlen's fork pointed. She caught Andy turning away, his face coloring. He was twice the size of Ricky Carbone. Andy glanced back for an instant and smiled. Cassie turned quickly away not wanting him to get the wrong idea about her. She wasn't available, never would be. She was Jake's whether he wanted her or not.

Suzy nudged her. "You could have one of the top guys in school calling on you."

Orlen cried, "What'd she want him to do that for?"

Davey had been staring down Ricky and Andy. "Jesus, Suzy, can't we even get a smell?"

"Damn it, Davey, I swear you got no couth," Suzy said. She hit him again.

Gabe laughed. "Couth, he's got. Manners he ain't." He slapped his hand down on the table. "Well, it's about time we get going. Same time, same place? Cassie?"

They'd made her laugh, but the boys were trouble, or little brothers of trouble. Then again, what'd she have to lose? She'd lost everything, Jake, Ben, and Dee. "Why not?"

Every day, at lunch, Cassie sat with her new friends, Suzy's old friends. They stood at their lockers and talked. Cassie cried less and less, but as the weather grew colder and as the stars grew brighter, she wondered where Jake was and if he were all right. By Halloween, Andy and Ricky were stopping at the girls' lockers. They were polite in a different way, not shy but confident and treated her as if she was somehow special, demanding a whole new set of rules, demanding of respect. Neither boy had asked either of them out yet. Cassie wasn't ready anyway. There was still the hurt, proving she still loved Jake and maybe he still loved her. Suzy acted too ready. Cassie wasn't sure if Suzy liked Ricky to the point of desperation, or desperately wanted him to like her.

On Halloween night a cold wet wind blew through the naked tree branches. The premonition of winter hung specter-like in the air. Cassie sat at the kitchen table finishing her Biology.

Cassie's mother walked into the kitchen gazing out through the kitchen window. "A car's slowing down. They're stopping. I ain't never seen the car before."

Cassie closed her book. "I'll get it, Ma." She carried the bowl of candy into the breezeway.

"Hi." Suzy spoke through the screen door. "Want to go for a ride?"

Cassie pushed open the door. "Come on in," she said, pulling Suzy into the kitchen. "Hey, Ma, this is Suzy." Cassie set the bowl back on the table next to her books.

Suzy peered questioningly at the open book, then at Cassie. "Hi, Mrs. Wolphe," Suzy said. "We're going to go to town and see all the kids trick-or-treating. We thought we'd ask Cassie if she wanted to come along. We might stop by my house for cider and doughnuts, Mrs. Wolphe. It might be late before Cassie gets home. Would that be all right?"

Cassie's mother said, "I think it'd be nice if you went for a ride into town. All those little children, they're so cute."

Cassie wedged her half-done homework into the book and

closed it. She guessed most kids didn't do their homework on Friday nights. She hadn't always, but with Jake gone there wasn't much else to do.

Gabe's car was even older than her father's. "Pinball Wizard" blasted from the speaker. Suzy slid in next to Gabe across the bench seat. Cassie sat next to the window.

"Nice car, Gabe. Big one," Cassie said. The automobile was long and round. The inside smelled of pine cleaner, polish, and cigarette smoke.

"Yeah, it's a fifty-three Buick Roadmaster. It's got a straight eight under the hood." Gabe backed the car down the driveway. He shifted into drive heading toward town. A fleece seat cover stretched across the front seat.

Suzy said, "We're going to find you brother right?"

Gabe reached for a pack of Marlboros sitting on the dash next to a greasy fingerprint-stained, hot-rod magazine and a couple of candy wrappers. "Yeah, don't worry." He shook a cigarette partway out of the pack, grabbing the filter with his lips. He passed the pack to Suzy.

"Want one?" she asked, offering the pack to Cassie. Cassie waved it off.

"Don't smoke?" The first guitar chords of "Along the Watchtower" boomed through the one speaker, vibrating the magazine. Cassie shook her head. "Too bad. It's cool," Suzy said. "God, I hate this song." Suzy stabbed the fourth button below the lighted dial. Another station came in, country-western. "What kind of shit your brother listen to?"

The cigarette hung from Gabe's lips as he spoke. "Hey, some of his girlfriends liked that shit. Hurry up. Light me up."

Suzy pushed in the car lighter. "God, I hate living out here."

"Why?" Cassie asked. "Mind if I open the window?"

The lighter popped out. Suzy stuck the end of Gabe's cigarette into the glowing recess of the lighter. He puffed on the cigarette three or four times. She repeated his motions with her own. They both dragged deeply, tilting their heads upwards, blowing long streams of smoke at the roof. "Can't breathe?"

"Not really," Cassie said.

The old car floated over the roads into town like a boat on a lake, each bump like a wave sending the car into a gentle rocking motion. They passed dark fields, fences, and lone farmhouses with their lonely pumpkins stupidly smiling at the night. Cassie wasn't sure if she trusted Gabe's driving. He acted too confident, as if he didn't know what he didn't know. She wished Jake would have still had some of his bravado and then she turned and gazed into the night.

The Buick bounced over the tracks at the edge of town. Gabe let the car coast down to the speed limit, passing children scurrying along the sidewalks up to houses carrying shopping bags, or paper bags, half-full of candy. Leaves, raked up to the curb to be picked up, rested in great red, yellow, and brown drifts. Only a year ago everyone burned their leaves in their backyards and the air was filled with the sweet pungent odor of fall. A new ordinance had been passed. No one could burn anything in town. Cassie raked all their leaves into the compost pile to be spread out over next year's garden.

Suzy pulled herself up to the dash. "Ain't that your brother's car there?"

"I see it," Gabe said.

"Gee, Gabe, don't you want to get some beer?" Suzy asked.

"Beer?" Cassie asked. Suzy had lied and implicated her in the lie.

Suzy smiled impishly. "Just a six pack or so. You don't drink either do you?"

"Well, a little bit. Not really." The truth was—she never drank, not even if she could have taken sips of her father's drinks.

Three men leaned against a large cream-colored convertible smoking cigarettes and staring at people passing by. Gabe pulled up to them.

Suzy said, "Cassie, roll down your window."

Gabe let out a breath like a balloon losing air.

"Don't worry," Suzy said. "I'll ask. Just watch."

A tall man wearing a short, brown, leather jacket walked into the street. Cassie figured him to be about twenty-two.

Suzy leaned over Cassie and smiled. "Hi, Raph."

Raph laid his arms against the door, resting his chin on them. "Gabe, little brother, nice ride." Gabe smiled but stared straight ahead. "Hi, Suzy. Who's this?" He nodded at Cassie.

Suzy answered. "This here's Cassie Wolphe."

"How do you do, Cassie?"

Cassie blushed. She didn't like Raph. He leered like Rancy. He walked and talked like him, too. One tooth was chipped, and a small scar on his left cheek showed pink through his two-day-old beard.

A man and woman walked out of the drugstore opposite them. The man glanced quickly over at the group standing and talking. He laid his hand against the small of the woman's back.

"Say, Raph, I was wondering, you know." Suzy's smile got even wider, "if you could buy us some beer?"

"Oh, that hurt," Raph said. "This ain't a social call? You mean you didn't come all the way into town just to introduce me to your new friend here?"

Cassie glanced sideways at him, blushing. She was in danger. She'd had enough experience with Rancy to know.

Raph seemed to be waiting for her to answer. He finally said, "Hang on a second." He slid back out into the street. "Open the back door." Raph slapped the fender.

Suzy stretched over the back of the seat and pulled the door lock up. "Anybody got some money?"

Cassie said, "No, not really." Another couple walked up the street to stop and talk with the people who'd just come out of the drugstore. The women were engrossed in their conversation, oblivious to what was happening across from them. The men, though, glanced over every dozen seconds or so at the people around Gabe's car.

"Got a couple of bucks, but I need it for gas." Children and teenagers, some in costumes, walked by on the sidewalk behind Raph's car. Some scurried along, speeding up as they approached. Others strolled by, casually watching the strange behavior of country folk.

A gauntly thin man around Raph's age opened the door and slid across the back seat. "Hey, Gabe," he said, cuffing him on the right ear.

Gabe winced. "Hey, Crank."

Raph jumped in next to Crank. A shorter man, with a pinkish face and white hair, climbed in and shut the door, all three men looking hard and edgy like some full-grown bulls and some mean dogs looked. People called it a short fuse.

"Shit," Suzy said, under her breath.

Gabe put the car in gear and drove toward the edge of town. Raph said, "This here's Whitey." He pointed to the pink-faced man on his right. "And this is Crank."

A mile out of town Gabe pulled onto the gravel lawn in front of a gray, unpainted house covered with paper signs announcing cheap beer for sale. Raph reached an open hand across the back of the seat. "Give me the money."

Suzy handed him a twenty-dollar bill. "Okay, but you better give me back the change. That's all I got."

"Where's a little thing like you get a twenty. You charging?" Whitey asked.

"You couldn't afford me," Suzy replied. "My old man. He gets real drunk. Leaves his pants all over the place. He don't even remember how much money he's got."

Suzy handed Raph the twenty. Whitey and Crank stood outside the car while Raph went in to the store.

"Here he comes," Whitey said. Raph slid into the car, carrying a brown paper bag. Whitey climbed in and shut the door.

"Change, please," Suzy said.

Raph passed her a handful of wadded bills and coins. "Here you go, honey pie."

She dropped the money into her lap to count it. "Hey, what kind of beer did you buy? You shorted me."

"Ain't nobody got to do that," Raph said.

Gabe backed out onto the road. Raph pulled a six-pack of cans out of the bag and handed it to Suzy. "Now, I just bought a little more than you expected. Got to pay the delivery man." He pulled another six-pack out and handed it to Crank

Suzy opened a beer for Gabe and another for Cassie. Cassie clutched at it wishing Gabe would take her home, but she didn't want any of the men in the back to know where she lived.

As Gabe drove back into town, Raph said, "Cassie, you got yourself a boyfriend?" Cassie shook her head. Raph belched. "Drink up, girl. It'll loosen you tongue, although we've got enough blabbering around here now from one female."

"You're an asshole, Raph," Suzy said without turning around.

Cassie tipped the can up. The beer tasted cold and bitter like a handful of cold, wet oats. She swallowed it. The aftertaste was even worse.

"Now that's better," Crank said.

Gabe had reached the village limits, slowing to thirty miles an hour. "Hey, you guys need off?"

"Naw, drive around," his brother said. "Well, Cassie, would you like one?" He spoke softly, smoothly, as though he were trying to speak romantically. It sounded more like a threat.

Suzy squeezed Cassie's hand. "Don't worry, Cassie, they're only picking on you."

Cassie squeezed back. Why her, why always her? Why did those kinds of men always find her? Just because she was poor? All she knew for certain was she was scared.

Crank said, matter-of-factly, "She don't need no boyfriend. What she needs is a man."

"I agree," Raph said.

"Shut up, you guys," Gabe said.

Raph cuffed Gabe's right ear. "Speak when you're spoken to." Raph motioned to Whitey to roll his window down. Whitey obliged, pushing himself back against the seat as Raph threw out his empty beer can. "Okay, boys, I guess we overstayed our welcome. Pull over at my car."

Whitey opened the door and stepped out. Raph slid over. Crank closed his door and walked around the back of the car. In the red glow of taillights he looked like the Devil himself. Cassie had prayed that they got out of this without getting hurt. She swore this would be the one and only time she'd ever go out with Suzy or Gabe.

Raph banged on Cassie's window. She rolled it down. He leaned in through the open window. "Gabe, someday you and I are going to have a little talk."

Gabe slowly turned to his brother. "It better be soon."

"Ha, you ain't never going to be big enough to take me. Here." Raph dropped the remaining three cans in Cassie's lap. "A gift for first timers." He smiled at Cassie, showing his chipped tooth. "You know, we ain't really bad. Gabe, he knows anybody fucks with him and they fuck with his big brother and friends. Anybody fucks with his friends, fucks with us too. Us poor country boys, it ain't that we don't have manners, it's just we like to tease the kid a bit."

As Gabe drove off, Cassie said, "Oh, God."

Suzy slumped in her seat clutching her beer. "Assholes."

Gabe stared straight ahead. "You're the one wanted to get them to buy the beer."

"How'd I know your brother was such an asshole?"

"I told you so." Gabe tilted his beer back and took three large gulps. "Drink up." He took four more gulps then threw the can into the street. It buried itself in a pile of leaves.

Cassie took two large swallows, gagging, almost spitting it up.

She'd started to feel a bit light-headed.

Suzy had finished hers. "It's like taking medicine. It makes you feel better."

They opened more beers and drove around on dark country roads until they finished them and Suzy nuzzled against Gabe's shoulder.

Cassie tried to pretend she didn't notice. The realization she wasn't with Jake hit her strangely. Maybe someone else was? She wasn't with anybody. Until that moment she'd still thought of him as her boyfriend. "Teach me how to smoke."

Gabe threw the pack into Cassie's lap.

Cassie struggled to get a cigarette out of the pack, Suzy taking it from her, holding the opening down, shaking once. The filter of a cigarette appeared as if by magic. Suzy tapped out another and put it between her lips. A third, she gave to Gabe. Cassie held the cigarette in her fingers. She hadn't realized they were so delicate. She could crush it if she squeezed just a little bit. Cassie stuck the cigarette between her lips as if kissing it.

Suzy lit the end. "Now suck in," she said.

Cassie inhaled. The smoke burned her mouth, her lungs, and her throat. Her stomach twisted. She laid her head between her knees, coughing and spitting. Gabe and Suzy laughed.

"Okay, silly, now that you've done that, here's how." Suzy slowly drew on the cigarette; the fire, smoldering at the tip, swelled to a brilliant red. She blew the smoke out slowly. "What you do is only take in a little bit. Hold it in your mouth, and then suck in air with it. Got it? Here." She handed Cassie back her cigarette.

Cassie hadn't remembered losing it. She tried it again. The second time didn't hurt so badly. Her eyes watered just a little.

"There you go," Suzy said. "Now we're all family."

Early on the first day of November, Gabe, Suzy, and Cassie drove through the cloud-covered darkness between the mountains. The radio played and the engine roared as the Buick floated down macadam country roads. Finally, when the beer started to wear off and was replaced by sleepiness, Gabe and Suzy delivered Cassie home.

Suzy asked, "You want to do this again sometime?"

Cassie thought about the offer. Her head no longer spun, but she could feel a headache coming on. "Yeah."

Suzy said, "Next week, maybe. If we don't have nothing better to do."

Cassie stepped out of the car. "Okay, seems like a pretty good idea. Beats the hell out of staying home." She shut the door.

Chapter 12

Suzy had refused a job babysitting the children of some of her relatives, dumping it off on Cassie who thought it a godsend to have the extra money, enough to put in her share for the beer and cigarettes, giving her mother the extra. Gabe found a place that didn't care that he wasn't eighteen, making getting beer a lot more pleasurable than having to ask Raph.

Six inches of new snow powdered the ground on the last day before Christmas vacation. Large clouds crowded the sky, turning the day a dark gray. Soon large soft flakes floated to the earth from the heavens, stippling the air. Ricky and Andy had invited Suzy and Cassie to a Christmas party. To Suzy, being invited meant they'd finally made it with the rich kids. "No telling what could happen once you hooked up with them," she'd said. Cassie promised Suzy she'd go even though she still thought Andy conceited. She did like how she could make him blush, or lose his train of thought right in the middle of a sentence with an exaggerated flick of her hair or batting her eyes and smiling.

Gabe drove the big Buick through town, its wipers clicking at the end of each stroke. He leaned forward over the steering wheel, not speaking. In front of the house where the party was taking place, cars lined both sides of the road for a hundred yards. Snow fell and the street was two sets of tracks between the cars

"Wow," Suzy said, staring at the cars. She blew smoke out in a long hard stream. An old Christmas carol played through the car's speaker reminding Cassie of the Christmases with Jake.

Cassie snuffed her cigarette out in the side ashtray. "Gabe, I wish you'd come." Suzy elbowed her.

He slowed down so they could get a good look. "Shit, I'd have to fight my way in and fight my way out. You know you don't have to go."

Suzy drew hard on her cigarette, trying to get as much smoke as possible before she had to put it out. "Yes, we do. Gabe, don't be like that." She touched his hand. "It's our chance to be somebody in this town."

Gabe stopped the car and rolled down his window. He flicked his cigarette against a snow-covered window of the car parked across the road. "Fuck, Suzy, it's bad enough people brand you like they do, but you don't have to go kissing their asses too."

"You're wrong," Suzy said. "You can be anything you want to be if you're smart."

"Go kiss their asses. It won't do you no good." Gabe stared out at the snow covering everything.

Suzy pushed against Cassie as if trying to shove her through the closed door. "I ain't doing that. R.C. likes me and you're just jealous, so you can go to hell. Let's get out, Cassie."

Cassie rested her hand on the door handle. "Maybe we should think about this?"

Suzy picked up her purse. "About what? I might of been born dirt, but I don't have to stay dirt." She turned to Gabe. "And you—you ever hear about fighting fire with fire? I can show them a thing or two." Suzy pushed against Cassie. "Come on, Cassie, get out."

Cassie stepped into the snow. The frozen air ran up her coat and under her skirt. The coat was too old to wear inside. She'd have to take it off on the porch before there was good light. She turned to thank Gabe, but Suzy slammed the door and Gabe drove off.

Cassie followed Suzy. A maple tree stood in the front lawn draped with strips of snow and colored lights. The snow chilled her bare ankles. "You think they could of at least shoveled the walk."

Several boys and girls stood drinking on the open porch illuminated by large yellow, green, red, blue, and orange teardrop lights gleaming through the fat lather of snow covering the large shrubs, running across the roof of the porch and down the pillars, across the rails and around the two front windows. Music blared from the open doorway and kids shouted above it as Suzy walked inside as if it were her own place, Cassie following, removing her coat before she passed through the door.

"Hey, Cassie," Andy shouted, pushing through the crowd. "Here," he said, handing her a drink.

Other boys smiled at her, a couple of them winked. She smiled back, dropping her coat on a chair, sniffing the clear liquid smelling of mint. "What's this?"

"It's schnapps. Try it."

She took a taste. "Oh, this is nasty stuff." Girls stared at her, their gazes running the length of her body. The way they glared at her assured Cassie she looked good. She'd already lost Suzy to R.C.

"You'll get used to it." Andy grabbed her hand pulling her into a dining room. "Drink up. Come on, you're already behind."

She took a large swallow. The liquor burned going down. "Who are all these people?"

"Everybody."

Cassie took another drink, thinking she should slow down, as a boy came by and held mistletoe above their heads. Andy's lips were thin and hard as if he didn't really care how a kiss felt, as if the kissing was more important than the kiss. She pulled away and smiled at him. The other boy walked away and said, "Remember, New Year's."

"What about New Year's?" Cassie asked.

"Nothing." Andy held up his glass and said, "To Christmas." He drank it all.

"To Christmas," Cassie repeated, drinking hers, swallowing hard, the fumes making her want to sneeze.

Andy took her glass. "I'll be right back. Don't go away." He walked into the crowd, leaving her alone.

Cassie searched the rooms for Suzy. Kids she only knew by sight, some she'd never seen before, out-of-towners, glanced at her as they flowed along the slow-moving stream of people as if she stood on the bank watching a river of people go by and not belonging there. Maybe Suzy felt as uncomfortable as she did? They could find Gabe, go up on a ridge and watch it snow.

Suzy held a drink in one hand. Her short chubby fingers of the other hand were entwined with R.C.'s. "Hi," Suzy said. "Can you believe this? This is wild. They got more booze here than I've ever seen. Where's Andy?"

Cassie wished she could feel half as happy as Suzy at being there. "I don't know," she shouted. "He took my glass and left. I thought maybe I ought to find you." She could see Suzy had no intention of leaving.

Andy came up behind Cassie, reaching his arm around her, his breath on her neck. "Here you are. I was afraid you'd left."

She took the glass and held it while Andy and R.C. talked about all the parties they'd gone to and how this one wasn't the best, but it was up there. Cassie listened and watched people watch her. Maybe Suzy had been right and she could be a part of this world. Her looks got her in. That's how girls did it. How foolish she'd been. How easy it was to move into a world filled with new shoes, nice clothes, food, movies, booze, and music. No wonder Ben left and Dee disappeared. Driving around the countryside with a six-pack of beer and a pack of cigarettes was one thing. It was completely another to stand hob-knobbing with the best kids in town, drinking someone else's expensive liquor.

Kids came by with more mistletoe and more drinks and in a while Suzy and R.C. found a wingback chair they could both snuggle into. Andy pulled Cassie back into the dining room. They kissed more.

The drinks had gone to her head, yet Andy seemed stone sober. Several times she moved his hands away from places they were getting too close to, even though she wouldn't have minded being touched in those places, just not now, and not by him. Making out was making out for Andy. A lot of kids were doing it. Although her kisses excited him, Cassie felt no love. She had loved Jake and that'd been part of the whole, of lovemaking.

She did miss sex, mostly the foreplay. There'd been mostly foreplay with Jake, almost never letting him go all the way. Cassie had let him think it was because she was a good girl. She'd been selfish, many nights going home satisfied, sending him home frustrated. She'd wondered if Jake took care of his own needs like he took care of hers. And then she felt guilty, but she couldn't do what Dee had said other girls did to keep their men happy. Now the tension was always there in her, and sometimes she was tempted to do things to herself, but that was definitely a sin.

R.C. pulled Suzy through the dining room toward the stairs. She smiled and waved as they disappeared upstairs. Cassie stared hard at the clock, finally deciphering that it was twelve-twenty-three, unable to figure out how it had gotten so late.

Andy took her hand, pulling her toward the stairs. Cassie pulled away. "No."

"Why don't we go upstairs where we can be alone." His right hand ran up her leg under her skirt.

"Stop it," she said. She didn't understand this. Weren't boys, especially town boys, supposed to be nice to good-looking girls? Cassie shoved him away, pushing herself back against the wall.

Andy leaned into her. "Why the hell did you come here for then?" Andy's forehead was almost touching hers. It didn't feel romantic, just threatening. "How come you're playing hard to get? You want me to dump Cindy? Sure, come on upstairs and I'll get rid of her."

"No, you've got it wrong." She closed her eyes trying to clear her head.

"No, you've got it wrong." Anger edged his voice. "You don't think I'm going to dump her without something from you. How stupid do you think I am? Everyone knows you and Suzy."

Rancy's and Raph's threats had been mostly implied, and compared to Andy's, almost compliments. "Wait a minute." Cassie stepped away from him. He tried to corner her, but Rancy had taught her too well. She slipped around him. "You had some kind of a bet, didn't you? I thought you liked me." She wanted to run away, but she had no way home. She'd been a fool. She needed to get out of there, go find Gabe.

"Cassie, you got it wrong," he said, moving close to her. He put his arms around her waist to swing her back against the wall. "I do like you, but you know." Andy slowly lifted her sweater and ran his thumb around the inside of her skirt waist.

She could let him do it. Just go upstairs and lie down and let him do what he wanted. She'd be popular, for a while. Cassie yanked his hand away. "Fuck you." She slapped him. Cassie staggered out of the room, grabbed at her coat, stumbling over the chair, some boy she didn't know keeping her from falling. She lurched through the crowd onto the porch.

Andy came up behind her and grabbed her left arm, spinning her around. "Who the fuck do you think you are?" The back of his right hand hit the side of Cassie's face.

She fell against the porch rail, pain burning in her cheek. "Oh, God," she said, clinging desperately to the post. Clarity came to her. This was the other side of the game Suzy played—she played. Maybe her looks made men love her. Maybe dressing up made them want her, but it also was so easy for it all to turn to hate. She slid down to the floor sitting on trampled snow as legs moved around her. There was no one here to save her from Andy, from all of them. This was the house of the real enemy. How much would the beating hurt before it was over, before he was through with her?

Someone tramped out of the house, the strides long and quick, tall thin legs in blue jeans, boot heels pounding the frozen planks of the porch through the snow. The man stood for a second, then said, "Aw fuck." There was a loud smack of a fist against a face, and a short cry, and a body landing beside her. Cassie opened her eyes to see a blurred vision of Andy sprawled next to her. Blood gushed from his nose running over his face onto the white snow. She stumbled down the stairs and onto the lawn and threw up while Andy screamed, "Oh my God, oh my God." A girl screamed and started crying hysterically. Cassie stood up, staggering over to the maple tree.

"You all right?" someone said. Cassie fell to her knees and threw up again. A pair of strong hands held her under her arms, lifting her. She looked up to see Judd Cantrell. Cassie leaned against the tree. He was smiling. She tried to focus. "What the hell you do?"

"I decked him." Judd brushed away the hair covering her face.

Cassie pushed his hand away. "Why? Who the hell told you to do that?"

Judd stepped back and glared at her. "Jesus, he hit you. The bastard hit you."

"You're all bastards," she shouted. "Every one of you, every single fucking man. I hate you all." Cassie leaned over and threw up again.

Judd laughed. "Yeah, maybe we are, but you're pretty fucked up yourself. Come on, I'll take you for some coffee." He reached for her. Cassie slapped his hand. He walked off to a car parked on the side of the road and opened the passenger door. "Okay, princess, your carriage awaits. All you got to do is make it to the door. Don't you worry none. I wouldn't think of sullying your perfect person with my crude hands. You got another way home?"

"Fine," Cassie said. She struggled to put on her coat as she staggered through the snow, getting one arm through a sleeve.

Judd held her coat for her when she reached the car. Someone on the porch yelled, "Fuck you, Cantrell."

"Fuck you too," he replied. "You're nothing but a bunch of mommy's boys. You want some of me? Come on down."

"Stop it," Cassie screamed, half-falling, half-crawling into the front seat. Judd slammed the door. Cassie leaned against it.

He drove her to an all-night diner where he fed her coffee, then eggs and bacon. She told him what an asshole he was, what an asshole Andy was, how all men were assholes except her father and brother. No, her brother was an asshole too.

Finally, when the room had stopped spinning, Judd drove her home and let her off in the driveway. "Merry Christmas, Cassie Wolphe," he said.

She pulled herself out of the car and trudged through the snow to her house, to try to sleep and forget.

After Christmas vacation Cassie expected things to have changed. The party would not be forgotten. What happened was irreversible. Suzy held Ricky's hand in front of her locker. A smile stretched across his face; a face almost blushed with love. Suzy had done her trick, fire with fire. Cassie opened her locker and shoved her books in. R.C. kissed Suzy good-bye and walked off.

Suzy peeked around the door. "I can't ever talk to you," she whispered. "Everybody in school hates you. Judd Cantrell? Why him?"

Cassie closed her locker, turned and faced Suzy. Suzy edged away uncomfortably, glancing quickly up and down the hall. "It ain't him, but he saved me," Cassie said. "I mean, he actually saved me. Andy, he was beating me up."

Suzy stared up at Cassie. There was a look of disbelief, but more so, a look of needing to not believe. "No, those boys don't do that. Country trash does that."

Cassie touched her cheek where Andy had hit her. "Damn it, Suzy, my face still hurts. Why do you think Judd decked him?"

"I heard you'd been secretly going out with Judd Cantrell and he showed up to see who was cutting his time." Suzy turned back to her locker.

"You know better than that."

Suzy leaned her head against the locker, playing with the dial. "I don't know nothing. It's just that you blew it. Cassie, you really fucked up. They got you down as country trash and there's no way you're going to change that now."

"You mean I should have let Andy screw me like R.C. did you?"

Suzy closed her eyes for a second. She sighed. "I had that coming. I guess we choose our own kind of prisons. It's just some are better than others." Suzy looked away for a minute, then back. "Would it have been so bad?" she asked. Suzy's eyes, though, seemed to be asking another question.

Neither question Cassie felt she could answer. "Don't worry, I won't try to be your friend. Lord knows I've screwed up my life enough."

"Thanks," Suzy said, seeming to finally realize she wouldn't get an answer. She leaned closer to Cassie. "Cassie, I just got to tell you that Cindy's after you and the jocks are after anybody who sits with you or goes out with you, you know."

At least nobody really thought Judd Cantrell was her boyfriend. If they had, there'd be no threats.

At lunch Suzy and Ricky sat at their own table. Davey, Orlen, and Gabe sat alone. Some people pretended not to stare, others stared blatantly. Cassie sat down at her table, spreading out her lunch, trying not to think of what each person was thinking. None of this would have happened if she still had Jake. School would have been just another chore to get through, like when they came to town to buy groceries. She wouldn't have turned into such a—she wasn't sure what she'd become. Some boys would have called her a tease. She couldn't be.

A shadow passed behind her. Andy's steady girl, Cindy, leaned her elbow on the table and stared into Cassie's face. Her arms were pudgy, almost fat. Cassie wondered why boys found her attractive. Did they only look at her breasts and not her stomach, her hips, the double chin threatening to develop a year or two out of high school?

Cindy pushed her cherub-like face close to Cassie's. "You must think you're pretty hot shit getting my boyfriend beat up?"

Cassie stared into light-blue eyes. She wanted to say that it had all been a horrible mistake, that she wasn't like Suzy at all, but maybe she was after all. She'd known Andy and Cindy were going together. Didn't she try to steal him away from her? Hadn't that been her and Suzy's plan, sort of? No, she'd just been stupid, not even thinking of the consequences.

"I ought to slap you right here, but I wouldn't dirty my hands on the likes of you. If you ever come near Andy again, well, I won't even think about it now." Cindy walked back to her table with her girlfriends. Her back was heavy and thick, her hips already squaring off.

There were cheers from the other girls. Andy sat opposite Cindy, both eyes blackened; a bandage across his nose. A year and a half left, Cassie thought. How could she survive being alone and half the school hating her?

The chair across from her chattered as Gabe pulled it out. Two more chattered in unison. The boys sat down. "Screw them all," Davey yelled. He laid his head on the table and looked up at Cassie. "Except Judd Cantrell."

"He's not my boyfriend."

Gabe said, "You could do worse."

Orlen said loudly, "Yeah, like that pimple-headed Andy Furlong."

Cassie smiled. "Okay, guys, no sense starting trouble."

Gabe picked up one half of Cassie's peanut butter and jelly sandwich. He bit off a large chunk. "You can make good bread. That's worth going to war for."

"Yeah," Orlen said. "Who's that broad all them Greeks was fighting for?"

Cassie said, "It was Helen of Troy, but it was her face that launched the ships, not her bread. It was all my fault. I should have known better. You know that, Gabe."

Davey grabbed her paper lunch bag. "You want this?" Cassie shook her head, no.

"Don't you ever think that," Gabe said. He tore off the piece of sandwich that had his bite mark in it and gave the rest back to Cassie. "You didn't know what they were planning. They were all using you, R.C., Andy." He glanced down the row of tables to where Ricky and Suzy sat. "Why should anyone of us know shit like that? We're good people, or we're bad people, but we're honest people. Suzy, she's a special case."

Davey blew into the sack. He slammed it against the table. The bag exploded. Girls screamed and boys jumped.

Cassie waited a week before she followed Cindy into the bathroom. She had thought about it a lot, about who she was and who were her friends. Cassie pushed in the stall door before Cindy had a chance to lock it. Fear sparked in Cindy's eyes. "Now," Cassie said, leaning hard against the door. "Let's you and I get something straight. I'm more of a virgin than you'll ever be again, from what I hear. Your boyfriend had a bet that he could sleep with me before New Year's. Where I come from that's pretty low." Cindy set her jaw as if to speak. "Don't, unless you're ready to back it up." Inside Cassie was scared, but she knew most of the threats she'd heard going around school depended on her and her friends being scared. She wasn't going to live like that, no matter what, not anymore. "Nothing's going to hurt my reputation at all in this school. So, if you ever embarrass me again, I'll hunt you down just like this and it won't be a tongue lashing I'll be giving you." Cassie shoved Cindy down onto the toilet seat. "And another thing, I don't want to hear about your boys hassling my boys. If they do, you'll never be safe in this town again. Got it?" Cindy only nodded.

Cassie walked out of the bathroom toward her bus. In a way

she'd been deflowered more cruelly than if she'd let Andy have her. The inner truth had come out. It had sought her and found her and now everyone knew what she had known in her heart, maybe since she'd been a little girl. She was that type of woman, the kind they thought Suzy and Dee were. Maybe Suzy knew how to use her sexuality? Maybe someday she'd know how to also, but it'd be on her own terms, her own time, and her own choosing, and neither God nor man would change that.

A month later in the cold deadness of winter, Cassie sat on the fender of Gabe's car, a wool cap pulled down tightly on her head, the heat of the engine warming her through her old jeans. She searched the stars in the winter sky.

Gabe sat next to her, staring out at the twinkling points of light. "Of all the planets in the universe, we're stuck on this god-forsaken one."

Cassie blew smoke out her nose. "Yeah, but of all the places where else is there?" The night laid out before them in the valley below where farmhouses sat, darkened square boxes in an icy landscape. Cassie opened her third beer. "Gabe, did you ever wonder what it'd be like to leave?"

"Nope," he said. He tilted his beer can up. "Well, yeah, but it'd be no better anywheres else. We are who we are, Cassie."

"Are we, or are we what they make us?" She sucked hard on her cigarette. "If we leave, go somewhere else, we could be someone else. It's just that it's like being torn apart. I mean, I bet there isn't a better place to live, you know. I mean, how could someone want to live in the city? Used to be so peaceful, too."

Gabe lit a cigarette, inhaling the smoke, holding it in his lungs for a half-minute and then slowly blowing it out. He peered off across to the gray hills streaked with bare trees. "They'd know me. Maybe you could get away. Go to college. Maybe you could still pretend you were someone else. I got no education. Got no prospects, but you could get something, then nobody would know."

Cassie tilted her head back to peer at the stars. There'd be all those strangers with different ideas, people living differently than she knew how. "There's probably a bunch of R.C.s, Andys, and Cindys at college too. That's where they go. You can't change your stripes."

"Some think they can." Gabe rubbed his hands together.

"You really love her, don't you? I really loved someone like that once," Cassie said. "He's gone and I got to learn to live without him. He wanted to leave and I said no. I'm afraid if I left I'd never come back."

"Yeah, but you don't have to see him every day. He don't call you to talk." Gabe stared at the can of beer clamped between his legs. "It ain't even sex. It's more. Hell, I ought to be getting you drunk like that other asshole and getting you in the back of the car."

"I ought to let you," Cassie said, staring back at Gabe through the dark. "Just to get back at all of them. No matter what I do, nobody's going to treat me worth a shit. I'm sick of all of it. But don't get your hopes up." Cassie blew out the last of the smoke. "I don't know what kind of girl I am. You know it wasn't all Andy's fault, or Suzy's either. It takes two to tango. There were other girls he could have gone after. I was just telling him, somehow, that I could be had."

"It doesn't mean anything. Men are men." Gabe kicked his heel against the front tire.

"And women are women." Cassie drank two gulps of beer, wondering why she drank cold beer on cold nights.

The shadow of the truck with its lights off drove up on them from out of the darkness. "Oh, shit," Cassie screamed. She flung her beer can into the snow and leaped from the fender. "Gabe, get out of here."

Gabe leaped off the fender and ran toward the driver's side. The truck slid past him as it skidded to a stop in front of the Buick. He jumped back out of the way. Cassie yanked open her door and jumped in, locking it. Gabe slid between both vehicles grabbing the door handle, but Rancy latched on to the collar of Gabe's jacket and flung him into the road. Gabe jumped up facing the large man. "You got no right."

"Sure I do." Rancy pulled a long flashlight from his back pocket. "Got to see if you and your girlie are jack-lighting deer or just poon-tanging." Rancy turned the beam of the flashlight on Gabe's face. "You're a Thompson boy, aren't you?" Gabe didn't answer him. "Fine," Rancy said. "You just get your ass over here next to the car." Rancy knocked on the window. He shined his light into the car at Cassie hiding her face. "Hey, you, get out here on the double."

Gabe said, "We ain't done nothing."

"Watch it, boy." Rancy stepped away from Gabe's car, giving Gabe and Cassie enough room to stand against it. "You're a bit stringy to be giving me lip."

Cassie walked around the car. She had yanked her cap down on her head and pulled more of her hair in front of her face. It made no difference.

As soon as she faced him, Rancy yanked her head back by her hair. He aimed the beam of light into her eyes and said, "Well, lookie here. If it ain't my dear sweet cousin. I'll be damned."

Cassie tried not to stare into the beam, but he held her tightly. Pain shot up her neck. "We're not doing nothing wrong. Least ways, we're not sneaking up on people."

Rancy banged her head back against the automobile. "Not yet, but if I leave you alone for an hour, you'll be screwing this skinny little bastard like there's no tomorrow."

Cassie's knees wobbled from the pain. She braced herself against the car. "You got no right saying that."

"Damn it," he said. "Ain't there no time you ain't going to give me lip?" Rancy leaned close to her. Cassie could smell the whiskey on his breath. "I got all the right in the world, you whoring around. I told you I ever found you like this what'd I do."

Rancy lifted Cassie by the seat of her pants, shoving himself against her, pinning her against the car. Gabe jammed his shoulder into Rancy's ribs knocking Rancy to the ground, Cassie sprawling between them. Gabe stepped out into the road, his fists raised. Cassie scrambled up and ran down the road, turning, waiting for Gabe to follow. Rancy slowly pick himself up and brushed the snow from his pants, as if he had all the time in the world. There wouldn't be much of a fight.

Gabe hit Rancy in the face with his right hand. Rancy backhanded him, knocking him to the ground. He picked Gabe up and threw him against the car, chuckling as he walked over and yanked Gabe up by his coat. Cassie ran back to the man and boy to grab Rancy's wrist before he could hit her friend.

"What the hell?" Rancy looked at her as if surprised to see her.

Rancy finally had her. She'd been stupid being out at night. Whatever happened would be her own damn fault, all of it had been her own fault. There was no sense in Gabe getting killed for her stupidity and he would have fought until there was no strength left in him. Rancy would have her anyway. Like everything else happening to her, it was predestined. "You stupid dumb mother-fucker," she said to Rancy.

Rancy dropped Gabe. He planted his foot on Gabe's leg. Gabe cried out in pain.

Cassie said. "You want me? You hurt him and you'll have to kill me to get it."

"Well, I'll be." Rancy chuckled motioning toward his vehicle.

Cassie backed away toward the truck. "Leave him alone and you got what you been trying to get all your life."

Rancy took his foot off Gabe, kicking him against the car.

Cassie held her hand down to Gabe. "Gabe, this is between me and my cousin, always been. No sense getting someone else hurt."

Gabe grabbed her hand pulling himself up to sitting. "Jesus, Cassie, no."

Rancy stepped toward Cassie. She turned and walked around his truck letting herself in the driver's side, sliding across the long seat to the middle as Rancy crawled into the cab. He looked at her and smiled. "Finally," he said, staring at her as if waiting for her to do something.

Cassie had been prepared to be raped the moment Rancy got in. She'd even left room so her head wouldn't hit the passenger's door when he threw her down. "Well, go to it," Cassie said. "Go to it. Get it over with," she screamed. Rancy gazed at her as if he'd never seen her before. "All your life you've been hounding me," Cassie said. "You got me now."

Rancy seemed to be waiting for her to fight or to cry. She'd already decided he wasn't going to get that from her, not that kind of satisfaction. No one would again. And why hadn't Gabe left? His silhouette sat unmoving in his car.

Cassie threw her cap onto the floor. She unbuttoned her coat, pulling it off and laying it on the cap. Rancy touched her cheek. Cassie pulled away. "Here, I'll get you started." She grabbed the front of her blouse and yanked it open. "I'm sorry I don't have a dress on to make it easier for you."

Rancy clutched her shoulder, feeling as if he might crush her bones, running his other hand over the skin of her chest, pressing gently against her breast. Cassie swallowed hard, knowing it was beginning and hoping the end would be soon. Rancy pushed her bra aside. Three large fingers cupped the bottom of her breast. Cassie closed her eyes. If she accepted it, tried not to fight, it wouldn't hurt as much when he crushed her beneath him.

"Get out," Rancy whispered. He pulled his hand away. "Get out, before I change my mind."

Cassie opened the passenger-side door, grabbed her coat and hat and ran to Gabe's car. Rancy started his truck, backed it onto the road and was gone.

Cassie stepped into Gabe's car. He still stared straight ahead. He clutched a lock-back hunting knife. His hand shook so much, Cassie had a hard time getting the knife away from him. She closed it, then lit two cigarettes, putting one into Gabe's mouth.

They each smoked two more cigarettes before he spoke. "What the hell was that?"

"Nothing, nothing," she said. "He just don't like me." Cassie stared into the dark where Rancy's pickup had gone. She wondered herself. Cassie pulled her coat tightly around her. She could still feel Rancy's large fingers holding her breast as tenderly as if it had been a baby chick.

Chapter 13

Cassie woke early to a warm spring Saturday. Her head throbbed as it did most Saturdays after being out drinking with Gabe, but last night would be the last night for a while. Gabe had informed her Suzy was back with a vengeance, Ricky deciding their love needed to cool down for a while. He'd invited another girl to the spring prom. Suzy wanted Gabe back without Cassie the leper, Gabe having protested, but Cassie wasn't stupid enough to get into that contest. What she needed was someone steady, a relationship sort of like Suzy and Gabe's, except a bit less weird.

An ache pulsed behind her eyes and her sinuses felt like they might explode at any minute. She wanted a drink of water and needed to brush her teeth, her mouth tasting of old smoke and stale beer. The stink of old beer ran up her throat and out her nose. She had no idea why she went out drinking. She liked to listen to the radio on the old back roads, but they could do that without cigarettes and beer. Then again life was all right when she'd had a couple. For a while Gabe drove all the way to Allegheny County to drink on the dirt roads, knowing it was out of Rancy's jurisdiction, never asking and Cassie never volunteering any more information about Rancy, but Cassie wanted to know why Rancy had let her go and why now people said Rancy no longer prowled the roads after dark. Some nights, when she was drunk, Cassie could almost feel him touching her.

Her mother and father were out in back spreading the compost pile over the unplowed garden. Cassie figured a farmer would be down to plow the winter-fallow garden under. She finished her breakfast and walked out into the spring sunshine. The day would be warm. She loved spring the most of all the seasons, but only one more spring and no more school. Her teachers and guidance counselor thought she should try for college. They'd said she could receive a scholarship and they'd help her find some money. She'd promised to think about it.

"Hey, Ma," Cassie shouted. Her mother attacked the large pile of rotting food stuff with an old garden rake while her father dragged shovels full of it across the soft ground, dumping it in clumps. "You guys want some help?"

Her mother stared at Cassie for a minute as if trying to decide what to say. She shook her head as if upset. "You could maybe gather up all the sticks and branches in the lawn and put them in the burning barrel."

Her father shouted from the southeast corner of the garden. "Have her get some gravel from the side of the road and fill in the holes in the driveway."

Cassie waved to him. She dug out a small shovel and the old wheelbarrow from behind the washing machine and then walked down the road toward Mrs. Fowley's, looking for spots where the plows' blades had torn up the shoulder to scoop the gravel into the wheelbarrow. Days like this, when the air was warm and moist and the ground still wet below anxious plants, were when she missed Jake the most.

Cassie shoveled the stones into the holes in the driveway, patting them down with the back of the shovel. On the wind she heard a distant rumble of an engine echoing through the mountains. Jake, she thought. He could have sold his car and bought another bike. Her heart beat faster. Should she wave if he rode by? Yes, definitely yes. This was no time to play coy. Maybe he finally got a good job, maybe in the mines, and he could afford both the car and the bike? Maybe he was coming back for her? Cassie listened carefully until she could make out the sound of a tractor.

Cassie stored the wheelbarrow next to the house. She'd use it later to carry the leaves into the garden. She passed slowly across the front and back yards several times to pick up broken twigs and small limbs. The tractor's sound grew louder as Cassie stacked the wood in the burning barrel and picked up a lawn rake.

A large tractor pulled up the driveway around their car. Judd Cantrell sat high in the seat, shifting the gears and working the throttle. He seemed to have mastery of it all. He throttled down and set the hand brake. The tractor idled like some giant reptile, a rhythmic croaking rumbling from its innards. He jumped down off the tractor. "How are you?"

Cassie took a step back still clutching the lawn rake. "I'm fine," she said.

Judd said, "You sure look better than the last time I saw you."

Cassie blushed. She stepped further away from him. "Last time you were pretty beastly."

Judd's hand reached for the metal hand loop to pull himself back up on the tractor. "Didn't know you were such a bitch when you're sober."

"At least I'm not some criminal, beating somebody up all the time. The garden's over there." Cassie nodded towards her parents.

"Thanks for nothing." Judd climbed back onto the tractor. The beast roared to attention and Judd drove off to her parents who had been watching and smiling.

A man walked up the road, a thin emaciated figure wearing filthy clothes. A knapsack balanced high on his back, his face hiding behind a bristly brown beard. Cassie began to rake the dead blades of grass and the winter-blown leaves, glancing up once in a while to judge the man's progress. To her surprise he walked over to her. "Can I help you?" she asked.

A rip ran along the lower left leg of his jeans. Grease and dirt were ground into his jacket. "Yeah, is this the Wolphe place?" He spoke with a strange city accent. He wore a half-dozen necklaces of cheap plastic beads around his neck. "I'm supposed to give you guys a message from Ben."

Cassie tucked the handle of the rake under her arm. She cupped her hands around her mouth. "Ma, Ma, come quick." Her mother hadn't heard her over the noise of Judd's diesel engine. Cassie waved her arms above her head.

"He told me if I stopped in you'd give me something to eat."

Cassie set her rake down. "Come on to the house." At the back door Cassie cried out again, "Ma, Ma, come on."

Her mother looked up from the compost pile. She dropped her rake and made her way toward the house.

Inside Cassie pointed to the kitchen table. "Sit down." Her mother scurried through the open door. "This guy knows Ben. He wants something to eat."

Her mother bumped Cassie aside as she opened the refrigerator bringing out the butter and a plate of cold chicken. "You know my Ben?"

"Yeah, we met at Woodstock. Great party, man." The hippie picked up a chicken breast and started tearing the meat off with his dirty hands, shoving long strips into his mouth.

"Woodstock?" Cassie asked. "He was in New York and didn't even take time to stop down here? You sure it was our Ben?"

The hippie stuffed another piece of chicken into his full mouth. "I found this place didn't I? Nobody around here likes flower children. I could have starved to death."

"You could of had worse," Cassie replied. "A lot of people around here don't like strangers." She thought of Rancy. Maybe he really didn't go out at night anymore.

Cassie's mother cut off a slice of bread from a loaf. "How's Ben? Is he okay?"

"Great, he was living it up."

Cassie said, "Ma, that was last summer. Why couldn't he of stopped in to let us know he was still alive? We don't know anything about what he's doing now." She turned back to the young man. "Does he have anybody? Was he with a girl with red hair?"

Pieces of chicken clung to the man's hands and beard. "Nope, he had a black woman with him."

"Good God." Cassie's mother sat down in the chair opposite their new guest.

Cassie rubbed her mother's shoulders. "Ben's having a good time, that's what, while we're here struggling to survive." Her mother took Cassie's hand. Cassie patted her shoulder. "What's important is that we know he's okay. Don't think of nothing more." She looked over at the young man devouring their chicken. "Do you know anything else, or is that all we get for what was going to be our supper?"

"Well, man, he hooked up with this commune." The young man spoke with a mouthful of chicken so that both Cassie and her mother looked away. "It's in New Mexico. He's working as a carpenter. Man, did they think that was one righteous profession. You know, Jesus and all."

Cassie knelt down by her mother. "See, Ma, Ben's all right. He's got a good job. I bet this man's told us all he knows. Why don't you just go out and make sure Judd's plowing the garden right. You know Pa will never tell him he's doing it wrong."

Her mother slowly stood and left without saying another word, glancing back at the hippie once as if she wanted to say something.

Cassie took her mother's place at the table. "Okay, what else do you know? What's he doing now? Was she pregnant? Were they married?" The hippie shrugged as if to say he didn't know anymore. "He should be here with us." As the hippie ate, she couldn't help but ask herself why. To suffer with them was her answer. Was that what she was doing?

The hippie stood, pushing the chair back with his legs. "Can I take some of this food?"

"Yeah, go right ahead." Cassie wanted to think about what he'd said, about what she'd been thinking, about Ben living in a commune.

The hippie stuffed the rest of the bread in his jacket and clutched the chicken in his hand. He left grease-loosened-dirt stains on the door jambs and knobs as he left. Cassie took her rake back up as the hippie walked on down the road, going to who-knew-where, but at least going. Judd seemed to have finished plowing. Why had she been so coarse? Andy deserved to have his nose broken after all, if for nothing else, then for his ignorance of life. Maybe Judd understood what life was really about, how tough it was to live?

Cassie went back into the house to bring out a pitcher of ice water and a glass. She stood near the driveway holding the pitcher up as the tractor came by. When Judd pulled up to her and shut off the engine, she said, "I thought you might want a drink."

"Sure." He reached down and took the glass and pitcher from her and set them on the hood. He held his hand down to Cassie. She took it and he lifted her lightly up.

"Welcome to my place," he said.

"Why thank you. It looks mighty fine." She laughed. "I just wanted to say I'm sorry for being so bitchy."

Judd poured the water into the glass. In one long drink he gulped it down.

"It's just, you know, the whole thing was so bad," she said.

He poured another half-glass. "You mean you getting drunk and all?"

Cassie leaned back against the fender. "Well, not so much that. It's what they thought. It's as if they don't even like us. They live in their little world and that's all that matters to them."

Judd's smile was strong; his face was strong. "You want to meet some real country people? I know it ain't a date or nothing like that, but if you've got nothing to do tonight, I got to play some pool over to Buddy's." He pointed in a south-east direction as if she could see the place through the mountains. "You could ride along. They got a band playing. It's just a little hole in the wall on Shimer road." He poured more water into the glass until it was about half full. He drank it in three gulps smacking his lips afterwards. He handed the glass and pitcher to Cassie.

He wasn't so bad. "Okay."

Her parents thought Cassie and Judd going out was a great idea. They were a little disappointed, though, when Judd only stopped in front of the house and honked his horn.

"It's not a date. We're just going out for a ride." She couldn't tell them she was going to a bar. They didn't think much of women who went to bars.

Cassie slid into the front seat of Judd's car. She wore cut-off shorts and a plaid short-sleeved blouse, nothing fancy, not even pretty, but Judd grinned when he saw her. "You're looking nice. I think you're looking a little too good for Buddy's." Judd put the car in gear and drove off. "Don't worry, you're safe with me. Just don't think I'm going to be busting someone's nose again tonight if you get yourself in hot water." The radio played "Let It Be" quietly in the background.

Cassie said, "I'm not going to make that mistake again. Now that you warned me, I ain't letting no man step within ten feet of me."

"Here." Judd threw a pack of Marlboros into her lap. "I know you smoke. I seen you once." An open pack of Winstons sat on the dash. "I think that's your brand?"

Cassie picked the pack up not sure she should accept them.

"Hey, they don't mean nothing. I invited you out." Judd grabbed his cigarettes off the dash. "I guess I got to share my butts with you. No sense you smoking a brand you don't like. It's only right."

Judd drove through town and out the other end. Lawns were raked and mowed. Some flowerbeds had been dug up. A few people still worked on their lawns in the early twilight.

Judd's car was old, not as old as Jake's, not even as old as her father's. It smelled of cigarette ashes. Cassie was pretty sure it wasn't the same car he'd driven her home in after the party. There'd been stories about Judd's driving. If worse came to worse, she'd drive home. She'd driven her father's tractor a couple of times.

"Do me a favor," Judd said. "Look under the seat and get the bottle that's there."

Cassie reached down between her legs. She pulled a square bottle out—whiskey, half gone.

"Give it here." Judd unscrewed the cap and took two long swallows. "Damn, that's nasty. You want some?"

"I don't know," Cassie said. "You always drink like this?"

"What's the matter?" he asked. "Don't worry, I'm not trying to pull none of that shit." Judd screwed the cap back on. "If a girl don't want to get in the sack with me when she's conscious, I sure the hell don't want her unconscious."

"No," Cassie said. "It's just that you've got a reputation of not being able to drive when you're drinking."

Judd laughed. "Hell, I drive real good when I'm drinking. It's when I'm passed out I can't drive worth a shit. I ain't going to take no chances of getting you hurt. This is just to take the edge off. Besides, I'm playing for money tonight. Can't be getting drunk if you're playing for money." He handed the bottle back to her. "If you want some, fine. They ain't going to serve you there, but if not, put it back under the seat."

Cassie swallowed two mouthfuls. The whiskey burned worse than the schnapps had. "God, this is awful." By the time they reached Buddy's, Cassie felt as happy as she had on Friday nights with Gabe.

Buddy's stretched out long and low, a one-story building with a low-pitched roof. An unlit wooden sign, white with purple script spelling out "Buddy's," was tacked to a telephone pole that stood in the dirt parking lot. Only the neon beer signs hanging in the four windows in the front, the one on the side, and a dozen vehicles pressing their noses up against the building made it distinct from any other house on the darkened road.

Judd stepped inside carrying a long, thin leather case he'd

taken from the back seat of his car. Several of the patrons grunted hello. Cassie peeked around him. Eyes glanced quickly her way out from under old baseball caps and cowboy hats.

Back lighting made the inside of the building soft and shadowy. Two pool tables, with long low lights, stretched across the room in front of a mahogany bar. A large mirror reflected the dozens of bottles stacked behind the counter. Though she'd never been inside a bar, this world and its people, existing on the edges of humanity, the Rancy's and the Raphs, the Cranks and the Whiteys seemed familiar to her.

At the bar a balding man with a stomach that protruded straight out from his body as if he carried a large unborn child, asked, "How's it going, Judd?"

"Great, Ray. Give me a shot and a beer."

"A soda for the little lady?" Ray said. He twisted a glass around and over his dishtowel. Ray's grin was large and toothy. "I'll be glad to serve you miss, if you got some proof."

Cassie flushed red. "No."

"Soda it is then." Ray put the glass he'd been drying in a row with other glasses. He pulled down a tall glass and filled it with ice and bar cola.

Judd drank his shot all at once. He turned and leaned against the bar. He spoke out to the room. "Who's up?"

A man in a plaid flannel shirt said, "I guess you are."

Judd pulled a quarter from his pocket and laid it in the slot. He pointed to a couple of tall stools in a corner near the door. "Let's go over there and sit down until it's my turn."

The men played pool intensely with a certain etiquette that Cassie had never realized that type of man could muster. They spoke almost politely to each other and were quiet when someone shot, apologized for being unskillful, removed themselves from the other's way, a dance of arcs and circles in and away from the pool table and around each other while their eyes flashed and jumped and watched.

The bang of a bass drum startled Cassie. She peered around Judd, trying to see what the band looked like, hoping it was someone she knew. All she could see was one-half of a large room lined with booths and tables.

The man in the flannel shirt said, "Judd, you playing?"

"Yeah," he said, "Be right there, Frank." There hadn't been a word said, not a "hurrah" or even an "oh shit," not a "you won," or an "I lost." One of the players tossed a couple of wrinkled bills on the green felt of the table then walked over to the bar and ordered a drink. Judd methodically unzipped the case, pulled out two halves of a pool stick and screwed it together. The real problem, Cassie found, was that Judd could play pool. He won three games in a row.

Sporadically, people walked into the tavern, most going straight to the bar then out to the other room. Three women slipped quietly through the open door as several men called out their names. Cassie figured the women to be in their mid-thirties, their faces sun-hardened. The stocky one, Alma, had long thick hair going in several directions at once even though there was no breeze tonight. The other two, Ruth and Irene, had reddish-blonde hair with almost an inch of dark roots showing. Irene's hair hung loose to her shoulders, Ruth's pulled to the back and held with barrettes. "Hey, boys," she said.

The women bought their drinks and sauntered into the other room, but not before they took good long hard looks at Cassie sitting by herself on her stool in the corner.

Judd finally lost a game. He went to the bar and bought a beer and a soda. He gave the soda to Cassie as the band started to play. The shooter stood up for a second as if thinking the music was going to stop. Sighing, he bent back over and lined up his next shot.

Irene walked out to the bar. Ray gave her change for a dollar. She smiled at Judd and Cassie. Cassie smiled back as Irene sauntered to the cigarette machine, put in her money and pulled the lever, fished the pack of cigarettes out of the tray, and walked straight over to Cassie and Judd.

"So, you're the one with the jail bait. No offense, honey," Irene said to Cassie. To Judd she said, "Figured it'd be you. Knowed nobody else in here could hook up with someone like her. No offense, honey, but I thought maybe one of these old fellas here might of brought his granddaughter down to watch him play." The other men laughed.

"Hey, Irene, that ain't very nice," Judd said. "This here's Cassie. Cassie, this here's Irene. She's one of the regulars, if you know what I mean."

"Watch it," Irene said. "Honey, he'll let you sit here all night just so's he can show you off. Most likely he brought you along to distract these old codgers."

"You know I don't need no help," Judd said.

"Uh-huh, sure. Well, I'm taking jail bait here in with us where we can keep an eye on her. You want her, you come in and ask politely." Irene held out her hand. "Come on, honey."

Cassie glanced at Judd. He shrugged. She slid off the stool, taking Irene's hand. At least she'd be able to watch the band.

People were filling the other room, most coming in through a side door. A tall, thin waitress with short brown hair hopped from table to table, collecting orders and money. Irene brought Cassie to a booth on the near wall. "Hey, girls, I got her. Can you believe it, she was Judd's?"

Cassie slid in next to Alma. Ruth sat next to Irene. They looked as if they could be sisters. "Cassie Wolphe."

Alma said, "Wolphe? There was a guy sang in a band named Wolphe."

"Yeah," Ruth said, "with Jimmy Marshal. You know he became a sheriff?" She drank from a longneck beer bottle, a clean glass sat beside it. "Don't know how because his brothers and old man's been in trouble for years. Think that'd disqualify him right off."

"Ben Wolphe," Cassie said. "Ben, he's my brother. I think he's in New Mexico. He went to San Francisco, but I guess he moved."

"Woman trouble, wasn't it?" Irene said. Ruth elbowed her. "No, that must've been some other guy. Hey, jail bait, you want a smoke?"

"I got my own." Cassie pulled out her pack and set them on the table.

In two quick motions of her thumb, Alma flicked open a Zippo and spun the wheel. "You drink, honey?" Cassie smiled. "Yeah, you drink." Alma fished around in a large black purse. She pulled out a flask of rum and poured some into Cassie's drink. "Ray sells soda for almost nothing. It's his rum that he screws you on. This is just in case I got to buy all my own drinks."

The four women drank, smoked cigarettes, and listened to the band. Cassie danced with the women and with a few men, but most were too old for her. She really didn't want them holding her, though she didn't mind dancing fast with them. Once in a while Judd came in to watch. He smiled at her when she danced with the girls, but stared at her when she danced with a man. He was jealous, she could tell. When Cassie sat by herself, or with Alma during the slow songs, Judd came in and sat and had a cigarette. Then he smiled broadly. She liked Judd. Yes, there was that madness in him like in Rancy and Raph, but not as bad. Like just a little bit of pepper. Too much of it ruined the food; just enough made it exciting. This is where she belonged. She knew these women like she'd known Dee and knew Suzy, but unlike Suzy, these three women where happy with their lot.

Late in the night Cassie slouched in the booth, a bit giddy from Alma's rum, dragging on her cigarette, rolling the taste of the smoke around in her mouth, satisfied with the low ache in her muscles, the itchiness of her eyes, trying to decide if she should dance again.

"Hello, girls." Judd stood at the end of the booth holding his leather carrying case.

Ruth looked at him, her head dancing slightly on her thin neck. "What do you care?"

"Sorry. You got no reason to be upset, Ruth. I just thought I ought to be getting Cassie home."

"Well, you done gone left her all alone," Irene said. Cassie had noticed that after Irene had a few, she spoke in county-western song verse. Cassie had known people who'd spoken mostly in Bible verse. She guessed you could speak country-western, too.

Cassie dropped her cigarettes into her purse. "No, it's all right. We're just friends. He brought me along so's I'd have something to do instead of sitting home."

Alma turned to Judd. "That's mighty nice of you, Judd, mighty Christian, seeing she's so damn ugly and all."

"Okay," Judd said. "I just thought I better get her home is all—before you three get her too drunk to walk."

Judd asked, as he drove away from Buddy's, "You have a good time?"

Cassie thought about it. "Yeah, I really did." She leaned her head against the cool window. "Did you?"

He smiled. "Yeah, but I always do when I shoot pool or play cards. I was just hoping you weren't all pissed because I shot pool all night long."

"Why should I be?" She sat up and looked out at the highway. The sugar maples were springing back to life, dropping little red and brown husks from their buds over the road. "I knew what you were going to do."

"Good, because most girls don't seem to understand that I got to do those things."

"What things?" she asked. Cassie reached into her purse. She clutched the half-pack of cigarettes.

"Men things."

"Oh, no problem. I don't care." She didn't, although she had the feeling of wasting time, spinning her wheels in deep mud and going nowhere. Cassie lit a cigarette. She had time for one last smoke before they reached home.

After Judd pulled up in front of her house he reached over and took her hand. "It was real nice you coming along and watching me. It made me feel real good."

Cassie squeezed his hand. "Thanks for asking me along."

Judd leaned over to kiss her. Cassie leaned over to accept it. She wanted to giggle. She was still a bit drunk. The kiss wasn't the best she'd ever had, but at least he only tried to touch her lips. He smiled sheepishly at her. Judd said, as Cassie stepped out of the car. "Hey, do you want to do something next weekend?"

She peered back into the car. The small dome light shadowed Judd's face, making him look tired, haggard, as though he were much older. "You mean watch you play pool?"

Judd sat behind the wheel staring out at her. "Those girls will be there, but maybe we could dance a couple of dances, you know, slow?"

He appeared more male than Cassie had first realized. His body was thin, not wiry, with a good square chest and well-developed arms. "Are you asking me for a date?"

"Not a date, exactly. A get-together where we hang around with each other. Maybe we can go for a ride Sunday?"

"Why don't we try for next Friday and see what happens?" Cassie closed the door. Judd drove off while Cassie jumped the ditch. She walked across the newly raked grass. She liked Alma, Ruth, and Irene. Judd was okay. At least she knew him, his kind. Judd was a good time and that's what she wanted now. She'd suffered enough, and to be truthful, he was pretty good-looking. Cassie walked to the door and let herself in. She hadn't even noticed the stars.

Chapter 14

When Judd first started calling on her, he'd stopped in to talk to her parents. After a few weeks he'd gone back to pulling along the shoulder of the road and honking his horn. By the time summer vacation came around they'd become girlfriend and boyfriend by default. They'd even gone out on some official dates, to several movies, once to dinner, but she hadn't been invited to his parents' home as of yet. He was free with his money and he liked a good time. He liked to drink. Cassie had learned to like to drink like he did, also. She became the center of the world instead of being small and insignificant.

They hadn't had sex yet, although she had let him grope a little more each week. Being drunk made her feel less guilty she didn't really love the man she let touch her and it just felt good, but Cassie figured the time was getting near where she'd have to let him or she'd lose him. She considered breaking it off, but Judd was her only link to the outside world. "Judd," she said, as he drove away from the house. "What do you want to do?"

Judd grabbed the bottle from beneath the seat. "Some of the guys are going to the Stone Road Bar to play pool. Maybe we ought to go there?"

Cassie took the bottle from him after he drank, wiping off the lip with the palm of her hand. She'd been to the bar several times before. It bored the hell out of her. Life was starting to bore the hell out of her. "Can't we do something else? All I get to do is sit there all night and watch you play pool." She tilted the bottle back against her upraised lips, bracing herself for the awful taste, holding her throat open to let the whiskey slide quickly down. She had learned, the larger the gulp, the quicker the buzz.

"Leave some for me."

"Don't worry, there's plenty." She wiped her mouth with the back of her hand. Cassie leaned her head out of the window. Her hair flew around her face while she searched for the sun. "Do we have to go?"

Judd drove quickly over the country roads, steering the car down the center when he could see a stretch of road clearly, only edging over to the side when approaching a hill or meeting another car. "Yeah, I promised the guys. You're my girl. You're supposed to sit there and watch me." The car roared and bounced down the highway, the right rear tire, an old snow recap, humming loudly.

Cassie turned up the volume on the radio. Judd didn't seem to even hear the music, never singing along or even tapping his fingers to the beat. Cassie fussed with the dial trying to find a clear station that wasn't country-western, although she didn't seem to mind her mother's stations all that much anymore. She stopped on a station playing "American Woman." "All I do is watch." She handed Judd the bottle then laid her head on his shoulder.

Judd took a long drink. "You want to go up to the old sugar shack, you know just to talk?" He didn't mean just talk.

"No, I thought maybe a movie or something." She really wanted to go up to the lake and watch the sunset, maybe listen to the band.

"Jake always took you to movies, didn't he? What a pussy."

"At least he took me out," she said. The sun would be setting in an hour. "Okay." Cassie moved away from Judd, sitting up and staring at the road going by. "Let's go to the shack. We're not getting nowhere riding around like this."

Judd turned the car around and headed back towards his father's farm. On a promontory behind the farm sat the remnants of a collapsed sugar shack. Once someone had boiled off maple sap in the late winter after the first thaw and made syrup or candy. The Cantrells weren't interested. Years of heavy snow had finally crushed the old building. Now the promontory stood as a junkyard, a memorial to Judd's inability to drive while drinking.

If one thing could be said about their relationship, he cared enough to never get that drunk while she was in the car.

Judd threaded his way along the tire tracks between the rusting, junked automobiles, trying not to splash mud onto his car. He steered past the rotting pile of lumber, the metal roof lying twisted, red and rusted above it all. Judd parked near the edge of the promontory.

The sun settled over the mountains, and long shadows streaked the valley below as Cassie stepped from the car and walked to a few feet from the edge. The Cantrell farm lay below, big and ugly. Old tractors sat rusting in the fields. Green and red farm equipment lay haphazardly around an unpainted barn. The paddock behind it wallowed thick with mud and manure; the whole place reeked of mud, manure, and weeds. Even the dairy cows making their way slowly down the lane to the night pasture were dirty. Cassie peered down at the tops of the trees. Some people ended it this way, she thought.

Cassie sat down to watch the day turn into night, Judd sitting next to her, putting his arm around her waist. He handed her the bottle. She took another long drink. The last of the sun reflected off the windows of the farm houses below as if all of them were on fire, as if all the people burned inside—a few tiny colored dots spread over a darkening green world, insignificant against all the immense beauty.

Judd's hand slid through the open neck of her blouse and into her bra. Cassie closed her eyes to shut out the world, wanting only to let the feelings come. She leaned her head against his chest while he unbuttoned her blouse. He kissed her and laid her down against the blanket. She let him undress her. The evening wind ran its hands over her and for once she felt free. Cassie lay on the blanket drowning in her nakedness letting Judd slide his hand between her legs. Judd pulled his pants down around his knees and rolled on top of her.

She pushed him off. "No," she said. Having sex with Judd

didn't seem right, not there, not out in the open. It wasn't modesty but something else, maybe just Judd. "Not here," she said without thinking. "Let's go to the car." Cassie picked up her clothes and walked naked back to the car for God and everyone to see.

Judd stripped off his shirt and pants throwing them on the front seat trying in one motion to gain entrance to the car and her. She guided him between her legs. "Wait a minute. Wait a minute until I get situated," she said. Cassie slid further down the seat and wrapped her legs around his back as he forced his way into her. It hurt a bit, but the whiskey dulled some of the pain. The way he was going, she feared he'd be too quick. Judd might have been right about Jake not being the man he was, but Jake had paid attention to her. He had been attentive to her feelings, and Judd had all the sensitivity of a young bull and about the same technique.

Cassie closed her eyes and felt him move inside her, rolling her hips to meet him as he pushed forward, shoving harder against him as the feeling grew, Judd's grunts getting louder and coming quicker. In desperation she grabbed him and pulled herself to him hard. She wanted the feeling to be so strong it would wipe out everything. His sweat dripped into her eyes. A small puddle formed in the hollow of her stomach. Judd strained to match her. Cassie's breaths came in shouts. Her head slammed against the armrest. In one great burst something exploded inside her. Cassie screamed out. Judd let out one last loud gasp and fell on her, Cassie's hips still moving in spasm, a whimpering sound escaping from deep inside her throat. Soon there was only the silence between their breaths.

Judd slid from the car, slid on his pants and walked off into the darkness.

Cassie stared at the ceiling, sweat covering her. *So he knows now. What do they want?*

Cassie found Judd sitting on the grass staring at the few lights in the valley. She reached for his cigarettes that lay beside him. "Mind if I have one?"

"Suit yourself." They sat in silence for a while, the tips of the cigarettes lighting up their flushed faces. "We ought to get going," he said. "We're almost out of whiskey." He held the bottle up without looking at her.

Cassie held the cigarette up to her mouth, the lighter poised. "Wouldn't you just like to sit here for a while and talk?"

"I got to meet the guys."

She'd lost in some way, but in a larger way she'd won, as if she had just taken revenge on something.

Cassie sat in a corner drinking her fourth cola. Judd had been playing pool for three hours, ignoring her. She could figure out the signs. He would most likely take her home later and never see her again. She kind of liked him, but it'd clear the way for other men. What was he to her anyhow? Cassie wanted to leave now, but it was just too far to walk and she couldn't call anybody to pick her up, wondering, as a way of passing the time, if he would try to have sex once more before he took her home? She wondered if she'd let him?

A large man blocked her view of the table. He said, "Hey, honey, you look bored." She glanced up to see Rancy wearing expensive-looking clothes. He'd let his hair grow out. His straight leering smile had been replaced with a large open one.

The old fear came back. Instinctively Cassie peeked around Rancy to the four men playing pool, including Judd. "Yeah, I'm bored. Why shouldn't I be? I can't play pool and I can't get served. What's there to do but smoke cigarettes, and they're almost gone?"

"Here, have one of mine." Rancy had never smoked. He gave her one and lit it, then walked off and left her alone. It was menthol.

Judd walked over to her and leaned on his pool cue. "What's he want?"

Cassie looked up at him making sure he could read the anger and boredom on her face. "Nothing. He just asked me what I was doing. I said I was just sitting here, that's all." She would have rather been home asleep. Judd went off to take a shot.

Rancy came back. "Here, sweetheart. I got you a drink." He set a tall glass of cola down next to her and slid into a chair. When he was dressed nicely, he was almost a handsome man. "Try it. I know you're going to like it."

Cassie took a sip. The double shot of rum bit at her tongue. "Thanks," she said. Rancy buying her drinks, now that was something.

He sat next to her smoking a cigarette, not talking. After ten minutes, he said, "Got myself a new car."

"I see you got new clothes too," Cassie said. She could be nice to him, maybe. If he bought her drinks.

"Yeah, been doing real good," he said. "They put me on permanent and gave me a raise because I done such a good job catching poachers and jack-lighters. Got the county damn near cleaned up."

Cassie sipped at her rum and cola. "I heard you got a reputation, you know—for being a little rough on violators."

"Yeah." Rancy finished his cigarette. He didn't inhale. He butted it out in a large glass ashtray half-full with the remnants of Cassie's efforts. "I ain't proud of it."

"What?" Cassie wanted to laugh, but she wasn't quite as drunk as she wanted to be. There was no sense screwing up the chance for free booze. "You spent your whole life working on it. You get religion?"

Rancy laughed. "You've changed yourself, Cassie Wolphe."

"I'm smartening up."

"I know what you mean." Rancy sipped his drink. "I'm trying something new. Hell, every time I turn around someone's giving me something or asking me for dinner."

Cassie's drink was getting low. She wondered if Rancy would

buy her another, or if she could talk him into it. "So what's wrong with that? You having trouble being a son-of-a-bitch with all those goody-two-shoes around?"

Rancy glanced at the pool players. When Rancy looked at other men they turned away. He held his glass in his hand watching the remnants of dark liquid lap at the sides. "You know how many good men died out there? Vietnam?"

"I thought you liked that sort of thing."

Rancy stood up and left the room. Cassie shrugged and turned her attention back to the players until Rancy returned with two more drinks. "Yeah, I do. There's just too many to kill anymore."

Cassie gulped the rest of her drink, setting the glass aside. She reached over and picked up the fresh one.

Rancy let his drink sit. "I didn't give a shit who died over there. Some's thought it was crazy. I thought it was the only place made sense. Some of them guys give their lives for their buddies."

"So what's your point?" Cassie asked. She wanted another cigarette. Maybe she'd take one of his.

"Point—is," Rancy almost shouted. For a second the old fear choked her again. Judd and several of the players glanced toward Cassie and Rancy. "Point is, I come back to this podunk county and I'm a hero for not dying. Other men's coming back getting spit on." Rancy laughed. He took a long swallow of his drink. "Seems you've gotten a bit cynical, don't you think? You're that way because you're still playing with boys."

Cassie shrugged. "Don't mean shit to me. Love 'em and leave 'em."

As the night moved on, he told her jokes and brought her more drinks. Cassie smoked three of her own cigarettes and had four drinks before she reached over and pulled a cigarette from Rancy's pack. She noticed he was looking down her blouse. The feeling of his fingers on her breast came back, such a light pressure for such large fingers.

Rancy pulled out his lighter; Cassie wrapped her small hands around his huge paw, pretending she was steadying herself, hoping Judd was looking. His hands felt like warm stone and were twice the size of hers. Cassie ran her fingers along fingers as thick as broom handles. They could grab a woman, crush her and yet they hadn't, not her, anyway. The word she'd been searching for all this time was, affectionately. "What kind of car you get?" she asked.

"A seventy Road Runner with a six pack. Right off of the showroom floor." He lit his own cigarette. "Boy, does she go." Rancy leaned back in his seat. "You want to go for a ride?"

"Sure, but I can't tonight." Buying a car like that took some hard money.

"Come on," Rancy said. He spoke loudly again. "It ain't like he's been paying much attention to you. I'm the one's been buying you drinks. I'm the one's been keeping you company. It'd do him some good if you went for a little ride. Might wake him up."

Rancy was right. "No funny stuff," Cassie said. "Rape's still a hanging offence." Although the thought came to her that in her state of drunkenness, they might not believe it'd been rape.

"Honest to God, I swear."

"Rancy?" Cassie said. "One thing you never did was lie to me."

"Still don't," he said. "That's for them little cowards."

One thing he'd never been was a coward. "Okay, let's go." Cassie got up to leave and found she had trouble standing. She was drunk again. She got drunk most weekends now.

Rancy grabbed her arm and walked her out the back door to a small porch lit by a bare bulb, and down a set of steps to the parking lot. Cassie leaned against his car.

Rancy had unlocked her door when Judd cried out from the porch, "Hey, where the hell you think you're going!"

"What's it to you?" Rancy yelled.

"I'm not talking to you." Judd's voice grew louder. "I'm talking to her." His boots crunched against the stones as he made his way toward Cassie and her cousin.

Cassie fell against the car as Rancy let go of her arm. She hung on to the mirror. "Damn."

"I'm taking her for a ride," Rancy said. "Go back inside with your little friends and play some pool." He flipped a quarter at Judd as he came walking up.

Judd slapped it out of the air. "Why don't you go home to that bitch that's keeping your house instead of trying to steal other men's women?"

"You little bastard," Rancy said. "I ought to kick your scrawny little ass." Rancy grabbed Cassie's arm. "Come on, girl, get in the car." He pulled Cassie away from the mirror.

Rancy had someone else? It made sense, the clothes, and the car. "No. You've got a woman," she yelled. "How could you do that?" Cassie tried to walk away but fell down. "I want to go home. Oh, God, Jake, please take me home. I think I'm going to be sick."

Rancy picked her up by her arm. "Come on, you little drunk. I best be taking you home."

"Leave me alone, you bastard." Cassie tried to steady herself, pulling her feet underneath her. "Go home to your woman. She loves you and you don't even give a damn." Cassie pulled her arm away. She stumbled, falling to her knees. Rancy picked her back up. She started to cry.

"Shit," he said. "Here, take her." He shoved her at Judd. Cassie sprawled across the gravel lot at his feet. Judd bent over to pick her up. Rancy hit him with a pawing left hand, knocking him to the ground. Judd jumped up. His nose was bloody and his lip split. He hit Rancy three times, knocking him back against his car.

"That's the best you can do," Rancy said, touching his jaw. "I almost feel sorry for you."

Another voice called out. "Leave him alone, Rancy. It ain't worth it." Judd's friends stood silhouetted on the porch. "You can't take on all of us."

Rancy stood over her with the old leering grin on his face. "It'd be a fair fight, but maybe some other time." He glared down at Cassie. "Girlie, they're right, you ain't worth it. Damn it all to hell, you really ain't worth it." He got into his car and left.

Cassie struggled to stand. "Jake, take me home, please."

Judd picked her up by the arm and dragged her to his car. He drove in silence for five miles in the opposite direction of Rancy's exit, turning up one road and down the next as if worried Rancy might double back. Judd pulled over to the side and lit a cigarette. "What the hell were you doing?" he said.

"I'm sorry, Judd. I didn't mean it." Her stomach was beginning to twist up, the muscles of her abdomen tightening.

Judd hit her hard with the back of his fist. Her head slammed against the seat. She screamed from the pain between her eyes, wailing loudly as the blood ran into her cupped hand.

"You're nothing but a little slut," he said. "You made me look like a fool."

The blood ran down her throat. Cassie opened the door and fell into the grass, rolled up on her knees and threw up.

Judd put a hanky under her nose and told her to hold it tight. After she quit throwing up, he helped her into the car. "I'm sorry," he said. "But you made me do it."

She leaned her head back against the seat, pinching her nose. For a long time no one said anything. She finally whispered, "You bastard."

Judd stared at the road. "You've got no right saying that."

"Yes I do. You're a bastard and I'm a little whore. None of us around here is any good."

"God damn it, Cassie, you were so different when we first started going out. I thought you were a good girl."

"I thought you were a decent man."

"Yeah, I'm a man. I ain't no pussy. I like to have a good time." Judd dragged hard on his cigarette, wincing from the pain of his split lip.

"So don't I." Would she have black eyes like Andy had when Judd had hit him. "You're just scared you can't keep up with me. You're scared I'm going to show you up, or worse, that I'll get bored with you and move on."

"That's not the kind of girl I'm looking for." He spoke slowly, as if admitting a shameful secret.

Cassie knew almost every road in the county, but she couldn't tell where they were. "You were looking pretty hard this afternoon. I'm not going to be one of those women who sit home doing their duty birthing kids while you men tramp around. And I ain't going to play the little wilting flower, not anymore." Cassie searched the stars, trying to figure their position. "I don't want no more lies or games. If I can't have it all, I don't want any of it. You understand?"

"Just tell me, where'd you ever learn how to fuck like that? I know that wimp-ass Jake McCullom wouldn't of been able to teach you that."

"Don't you say nothing about Jake. He doesn't even belong in this conversation." She closed her eyes, opening them again as the world started to spin. "I was inspired. Can't a person think for herself? You liked it, didn't you?" Cassie touched her nostrils to see if she still bled. She rubbed her fingers together feeling for wetness. "You liked it one hell of a lot." There was no blood. They were pointed roughly toward Orion, south, but how south depended on what time it was, and she was too drunk to tell. "Well, I want to like it too. So now you're going to run home and not call until you get good and horny. But you know something? I won't be there. I'll be out screwing some other guy. And I'll keep on fucking guys' brains out until I can find one who ain't afraid of me and won't leave me sitting all night."

He rubbed his fingers across his eyes. "You want me to hit you again, is that it?"

Cassie spoke slowly, making sure he heard every word. "Don't you even think of hitting me ever again." She shoved her fingers through her hair, combing her bangs back. "If you do, you better kill me because I swear I'll kill you."

A car drove up the road from behind them. The headlights reflected off the rearview mirror into Judd's face. Dried blood stained his nose. His lip was swollen. "What the hell do you want from me?"

Now they both had the same afflictions. "We deserve each other. Neither one of us gives a damn enough anymore to be decent. You want me to be your girl? You better make up your mind. The way you are, you ain't going to be able to keep nothing better."

Judd seemed to think about it for several minutes. "Yeah, you're right. I've never been able to keep nobody decent. I always fuck it up. But I got to see my friends once in a while."

Cassie dug an almost empty pack of cigarettes out of her purse. "Maybe they can screw you in the back of this car, because I sure won't be." Judd watched the car approach through the mirror. His neck muscles tightened waiting to see if it would pass or stop. He pulled himself up by the steering wheel.

She turned the pack upside down and smacked it against her index finger. "It's all or nothing." The car could be a county sheriff, or maybe Rancy looking for revenge on both of them.

The car moved over to the left to go around them. Judd sank back in his seat. "You think you're that good." Judd pushed the bulge of his lighter up to the opening of his jeans' pocket. He yanked it out. "You ain't that good."

"Light me." In the light his face looked drained, almost sickly. She blew smoke at Judd, leaning back against the door. "Well, I'll get better. Will you?"

"What's that supposed to mean?" He was looking away from

her again.

An old song, "Green River," played on the radio. It reminded her of Jake. Cassie reached over and turned it off. "What do you want? I want to live a little, and the hell with what other people think. I'm in all the way if you're in."

Judd started the car and put it in gear. "This is going to be one hell of a ride."

Chapter 15

Cassie and Judd sat across the road from her parents' house. "Come on," Judd said, yanking at her blouse attempting to pull it out of her pants.

"No." Cassie grabbed his wrists. "You just done it an hour ago."

"So, you never cared before?" Judd slurred the word through his crooked smile.

"I'm tired and drunk and it's after three in the morning and I ain't feeling that well."

Judd slid back over behind the wheel. "Damn it, Cass. I keep telling you to watch how you drink. You know you can't hold it worth a shit." Judd exhaled hard while reaching for the cigarettes on the dash. "You're going to be puking up in the toilet, pissing your mother off again." He lit his cigarette, blowing the smoke at the windshield.

Cassie tucked her shirttail back in her pants. The cigarette smoke nauseated her. "I'm sick of her shit anyhow. What she expect?"

Judd dragged slowly on his cigarette. "Maybe that you're still a little virgin."

"Fuck you. I'm out of here." Cassie shoved open the door with her shoulder. The door had a habit of sticking. Sometimes she wished he'd wreck the car and get one where her door worked. Cassie waved without looking back. A kind of sickness churned in the bottom of her gut different than when she drank too much. Maybe she was coming down with something?

Judd drove away as Cassie stumbled through the kitchen. The tiny shadow of her mother stood in the living room. For a moment they stared at each other. Cassie braced herself against the back of a chair.

"Cassie," her mother said.

"What choice did you give me?" Cassie struggled upstairs and into bed.

She woke to a cold and drizzly, fall Sunday morning. Her stomach churned. It'd been queasy for several days and her lower back ached. Lying still in bed, her breasts hurt as if they were trying to burst out of her skin. Her stomach worried her, and now she was a bit dizzy but not a drunken dizziness.

Cassie jumped out of bed, falling against her dresser. She reeled out through the closed curtain, banging against the door molding, stumbled into the bathroom, and threw up in the toilet. Cassie knelt in front of the toilet, her forehead against the seat as the swish of her mother's old slippers dragged across the hallway floor, the sound of the inevitable, of the truth coming to find her out. This day had been coming. She'd denied it even though it'd been almost two months since she'd had her period. She'd blamed it on too much drinking and too much rough sex, even as her body changed.

Cassie's mother took several minutes before speaking, her voice low, and her words spoken slowly. "Cassie, you best do what's right soon, or at least attempt to. You best stay home from church today. Lord knows you need to be going, but you best call him and get this thing settled."

Cassie nodded her head against the cold porcelain. She waited until the sound of her mother's slippers faded down the stairs before she struggled back to bed to stare at the ceiling as her parents got ready for church, listening intently to the movements of her father, waiting for his heavy footsteps to pound up the stairs and into her room to condemn her and throw her out. She didn't think of what she would say. There was nothing to say. Her head swirled—her life swirled. Who she had thought she was, she hadn't been for some time.

As the sound of her father's car faded, Cassie tucked her nightgown into a pair of old jeans, put on her shoes and coat, and walked up to Mrs. Fowley's house under a gray sky threatening rain again. The phone rang twenty-four times before Judd answered.

He growled into the phone, "What do you want?"

Cassie spoke quietly. "Judd, we got to talk." The house smelled of cat fur and kitty litter mixed with burnt butter from eggs and the heavy air of fat-back fried in its own thick grease, a smell she'd loved for its heralding of a new day, but now it made her nauseous. Cassie peeked around the corner of the kitchen to see Mrs. Fowley sitting on the edge of the couch, her small frame perched stiffly erect watching a Sunday morning gospel hour. "Now, but I can't tell you here. You got to come and get me before your parents or mine get back from church." A cat brushed up against Cassie's leg, arching its back, vibrating like an electric motor.

"Hell, Cass, do you know what time it is? I ain't even had six hours' sleep yet." He'd renamed her, saying Cassie sounded too sweet and innocent. People wanted to treat them like girlfriend and boyfriend. She once foolishly said they were. He'd replied that no, they were partners, remember? She'd agreed.

Cassie lifted her foot from underneath the cat's fat belly and tossed it a few feet. "Damn it, Judd," she whispered. "Get your ass over here now, in the next half-an-hour. We're in one hell of a lot of trouble. Understand?" Cassie hung up the phone. She smiled and said goodbye to Mrs. Fowley, then walked back to their home to bathe and change not believing how dense Judd could be not getting one hint.

Judd arrived fifteen minutes before her parents would be home if they hadn't gone to Teresa's. Cassie jumped into the car, pulled a cigarette out of her purse and lit it. Judd stared at her, his neck muscles tight. He didn't know. He was just too bull-headed to have tried to figure it out. "Drive. Get off of this road." She had the urge to throw up again. "Go up to the bluff."

"What the fuck's the matter with you all of a sudden?" He put the car in gear and stomped on the gas pedal, squealing the tires and throwing Cassie back in the seat. "You kill somebody or something?" Judd's hair stuck out away from his head in little tufts, like battered oats in a field after a disastrous hailstorm. He had on the same clothes he had on and off last night. He'd probably slept in them.

Cassie reached over and fixed his collar, folding it over with her fingers. "Okay, would you, just for little old me, take me up to the bluff so I can see it raining all over my whole goddamn life."

He shoved her hand away with his shoulder. "Fuck," he said. "What's gotten into you?"

They drove on in silence. Cassie smoked another cigarette before they got to the bluff. Judd drove slowly through the muddy path between the wrecked cars. They'd all been his, since sixteen. Maybe some were his sisters'? He had destroyed quite a few of them. The wrecked automobiles sat on both sides of the parallel ruts. Some had their wheels torn out from under them, some with front ends smashed to a vee, one with a spider-web crack in the windshield in a place where Judd's head would have contacted it. Cassie had noticed a scar high on his forehead while making love on a hot summer day with the sound of their sweat-covered bodies peeling away and re-sticking to each other. Some cars looked tortured as if in pain. A few cars sat serenely on flat tires, as pristine as old cars could be, quietly resting, as if for some reason Judd had just lost interest in them and cast them aside to end their days in quiet solitude.

She'd never been in a wreck with him, the loss of control, the screeching of tires, maybe flipping over several times, then a sudden stop, silence, just the creaking of metal and the seeping knowledge you were alive, maybe even okay. The time was past to think about things like that.

Judd parked the car. He rolled down his window. Cold air rushed in, wet and moist with the hint of newly decaying leaves. Cassie drank it like cold water. Judd took a long drag on the stub of his cigarette then tossed it out. "You going to tell me what this is about?"

"Look around," she said. "It started right here in this junkyard. Hell, we just made a wreck of our lives. The only thing I don't know is, are you going to tow me off to some field and abandon me?"

"What the hell, abandon you?" Recognition jumped into his eyes. "God, no. How?"

Cassie punched him in the shoulder as hard as she could. "What the hell you mean how? You know damn well how. What'd we expect? There wasn't a Friday or Saturday night you weren't on top of me, grunting away."

Judd slammed his fist against the steering wheel. "Hey, I wasn't always the one on top doing the grunting." He reached under the seat for the bottle. "I need a drink." Judd drank three large swallows. "You want some?" Judd stared out at the bluff, tears welling up in his eyes, his face turning a deeper shade of red. "My ma's going to kill me. Hell, a kid, a little bastard."

Cassie wanted a drink but she didn't think she could hold it down. "No, not now, not anymore. Judd, we got to decide what to do." Her voice quivered a bit more than she'd hoped. Now was way past the time for being scared. The car smelled of whiskey and smoke and something else, of old sex, of him and her, of love making, of the results of love making, and the anticipation. "It don't have to be a bastard," she said. She leaned closer to Judd hoping he'd put his arm around her, searching for a bit of tenderness in his face, but there was none. "Damn it, Judd. Do I have to hit you upside your head with a two by four? I've been waiting for you to say it, but I guess I got to be the one, don't I? You only got two choices. You make me an honest woman, or you have a bastard for a kid."

Judd laid his arms on the wheel and rested his head against them. He seemed to think for a moment. "You bitch," he whispered. "You mother-fucking bitch. You're like all the rest of them. You fucked me one way or the other, didn't you? I ought to strangle the life right out of you and the thing you got growing inside of you."

She hadn't expected him to panic. Cassie shoved open the door, running toward the bluff before realizing she could be running in the wrong direction. Judd could easily drag her to the edge and throw her over. Nobody would know she hadn't jumped. But for some reason being dead didn't seem like it would be the worst of all the arrangements. People would think it sad and feel sorry for her, forgive her in a way. If he wasn't angry enough to do it now, she could easily provoke him.

Judd stood beside the car. The wind blew the ends of his open jacket. It threw rain into their faces. He walked toward her in the drizzle, Cassie backing away trying to decide which way to run. This was her life, the one she'd been born for, the reality, not the dreams of a young girl, no college, no finishing high school, but of raising kids, doing the wash, fixing meals, and maybe struggling alone. Knowing the kind of husband Judd would be, she didn't give a damn if he married her or not. She didn't love him that much and now she had someone else to worry about beside herself.

Cassie laid her hand on her stomach. Maybe she was wrong. Her mother had known for a while, but for how long? Had she been watching, keeping track of her pads? Why hadn't she said something, stopped her?

"You know, this changes everything." Judd forced his voice through the sound of the wind.

Cassie turned toward him. "Don't worry." She wiped her nose on her sleeve. Droplets of water dripped from her matted bangs. "I got myself into this. I guess I can handle it." She didn't know if she could, but she'd have to try.

Judd pulled a pack of Marlboros from his jacket pocket, lit one and held it out to her.

Cassie took the cigarette from his hand, cupped it in hers, and put it between her lips.

"I ain't going to push you over," he said.

Cassie blew the blue-gray smoke into the wet air. "Wouldn't have to be much of a push. Maybe I just ought to jump. Save everyone a lot of trouble. They could write a song about it." The bluff was more dramatic, more redeeming, maybe in a way more honorable, but spring would be coming with newborn birds and new calves and maybe she could see the world through new eyes, her own eyes in a fresh new soul.

Judd lit a cigarette for himself. "Naw, don't do that. I'd have to jump so I wouldn't look like a coward that maybe I am. Besides, neither one of us deserves the easy way out. What the fuck we ever did, I don't know, but we pissed somebody off. I ain't got a ring and it's too wet to kneel, but I guess I'm asking you to marry me." He held out his hand, palm up.

"It ain't going to be that easy." Cassie wiped a wet strand of hair from his face. "It ain't going to be that easy to get out of it either, but you got to get a real job and we got to get a place."

Judd let the smoke tumble out of his mouth as he spoke. "Hell, that ain't no big deal. I'll just tell my old man we're moving into one of the old farm houses we got sitting not being used and he's got to raise my pay because I just got him another slave. Pays his hands better than me because they got responsibilities. Guess I got them now. The old lady, Ma, she's going to be one pissed-off bitch, being so religious and all." Judd quit smiling. "She don't deserve no better from me. If she thinks I'm going to be working for her the rest of my life, she's dead wrong." He pulled Cassie to him and held her against his chest. "It's still you and me, babe. You and me against the world."

Cassie should have felt warm and safe against his chest, but his hold was a little too tight, a little too strong.

"Sunday supper is around three," Judd said. "I'll take you home. You get all fixed up real nice and I'll pick you up at two."

Cassie pulled away from him. "At supper you're going to tell her we've been screwing?"

"Hell, no. I'm going to tell her I asked you to marry me. Fuck her. I ain't going to give her the pleasure of making a scene."

"She's going to figure it out sooner or later." The wind blew wet hair over her face and into her mouth. It tasted like the cigarette had tasted—dirty and gritty.

"Fuck her. We'll tell her when we're married." Judd kissed Cassie. "Let's go back to the car, you know." He slid his arms under her coat and around her waist.

"What, you want to do it at a time like this?"

"Yeah, why not? No sense getting all uptight just because we're in deep shit. We're in deep shit whether we do it or not, now."

Cassie thought about it. "What the hell, why not."

Cassie dried her hair as she listened to her father's car turn into the driveway. She tried to stay calm, but her heart raced. Why blame Judd? It'd been Jake that had taken her virginity. Cassie spoke to her reflection in the mirror. "It won't help any saying that."

The door opened. The door closed. No one called her name. Her father was angry. The quieter he got, the angrier he was. That's what he did and then he waited until the situation fixed itself or went away. That was probably why he never mentioned her carousing or the fights she'd had with her mother in the early mornings.

Cassie's father read the paper Carl always gave him, tucked in his chair in the corner of the living room. Carl had it delivered early. He said he'd read everything he'd wanted to read by church time. Her father's black suit coat lay thrown on the end of the couch next to her mother. His faded, red tie hung from the chair arm. His shoes were off and his toes twitched nervously in his good white socks.

Cassie's mother sat knitting, her faced drained, the hollows of her cheeks gray dishes under sharp bone. Once in a while her mother sniffed. Other than that, only the crinkling of the paper and the ping of the stove could be heard.

"Pa?" Cassie said. He didn't answer. She stood in front of him dressed up, hoping she looked like the lady grown from the little girl he'd loved so much. "Pa?" she repeated. "I'm sorry." Why had she done it, all of it? Why had she been so selfish not to see how she could hurt him so much? Ben's running away had been so hurtful. Had she done any better? Her father dropped the paper into his lap. He exhaled slowly through his mouth.

Cassie sat on the floor next to her father and laid her head on his leg. "Pa, don't be mad. I ain't bad, honestly. I'm just dumb. It ain't Judd's fault, it's mine."

He placed his hand on her head and stroked her hair. "It ain't nobody's fault. People are just people. God knows, I know that. It's just—why'd your mother have to tell me at Teresa's? That damn woman. See," he said to Cassie's mother. "They got me swearing on a Sunday. I thought Teresa's face was going to split right in half, her smile was so wide. Carl, that damn fool, all he could say was, little Cassie's going to have a baby, like he was going to be the granddaddy or something. Your ma could of told me some other place."

Her mother put down her knitting. "Where? If I'd told you in the car, you'd a run into a ditch for sure. I sure wasn't going to tell you in church. Teresa's was the only place."

Cassie reached over and held her mother's hand. That wasn't the reason her mother had spoken of it at Teresa's. Her mother had picked the perfect spot to deflect the anger onto herself and now Cassie's job was to pull them together again.

Judd honked the horn in front of Cassie's house at two. "Shouldn't he be coming in?" her father asked.

"Would you?" her mother said.

Judd wore a white shirt and black tie. "What's this?" she asked.

"We dress for Sunday supper." Judd pulled the car onto the

road. From the radio, Three Dog Night screamed in three-part harmony, "Mamma told me not to come." Judd had the car pointed toward his house before he said, "I don't eat with them most times."

"Oh, good Lord," Cassie said. Neither spoke as they drove to the farm, each smoking two cigarettes on the way.

Judd pulled the car into the muddy driveway. The Cantrells had never bothered to lay a decent load of gravel down. Cassie stepped from stone to rut, trying to keep the mud off her shoes. The door swung open to the big farmhouse. An old woman in a navy and white polka-dotted dress appeared on the porch studying them as they picked their way toward the house.

"Shit," Judd said under his breath. He grabbed Cassie's hand and walked up the broken flagstone walk straight toward the plump woman with the white hair. Cassie knew her as Mrs. Cantrell.

When their shoes echoed off the wooden steps, the woman's eyes moved down Cassie. "Well," she said. "When she due?"

Judd flushed crimson. "We come to dinner. Ain't that enough?" Cassie leaned against Judd afraid her knees might buckle.

Knotty-pine cupboards ringed the large farmhouse kitchen, the air heavy with vegetable-scented steam and the odor of drippings caramelizing against the inner rim of a roaster in a hot oven. Plants hung from hooks and a large oak table sat starkly in the center. The kitchen was newer and better than Teresa's, but for all its newness, it exuded a coldness, almost chilling, a kitchen beautiful and unloved. At least Teresa and Carl's kitchen lived.

Tawny gold wallpaper with a dark velveteen fleur-de-lis pattern covered the walls of the dining room. The thin chandelier hanging above a long cherry table did nothing to make the room feel homey. China, crystal, and heavy silverware that Cassie though to be real silver, sat on the table. Cassie had only seen tables like this set up in Sears. She never thought she'd know someone who owned one, let alone eat from it. A hutch and bureau stood back against the wall displaying the rest of the china and crystal.

Judd and Cassie hid in the sunroom, a glassed-in porch on the south side of the house facing a muddy pasture, the only place anyone was allowed to smoke in the house. The room smelled of the sun baking wet wood. Old tables and stands held potted plants. Ferns hung from hooks in the ceiling. The Cantrell farm seemed to grow mud. Judd and Cassie sat on an old couch still better than the one her parents had. Judd lit up a cigarette, held her hand, but didn't speak.

His two sisters arrived with short bitter greetings. An hour later Judd's father peeked his round face into the sunroom. "Time for dinner."

Judd butted his cigarette. "Let's get this over with."

A chubby boy sat at the kitchen table coloring from a box of crayons as big as a lunch box. A small girl with blonde curly hair and searching blue eyes, stood in the doorway, either unwilling to step into the dining room, or not allowed. She addressed her grandmother as Mother Cantrell. They all addressed her as Mother Cantrell. They were Maybelle's kids and they ate in the kitchen served by their mother and grandmother.

The dinner consisted of a large roast, a heaping bowl of potatoes, corn, squash, peas, and a basket of hot rolls. Judd pulled out a chair and sat. Cassie sat in one next to him unable to believe they ate this way every Sunday but more so why. Judd's parents sat at each end of the table in tall-backed chairs. The sisters sat opposite Cassie and Judd. She knew of them, enough to know Maybelle from Maddie. They were both blonde, not as much as they pretended, and both had a mop of hair as reluctant to mind as the two quiet children who squirmed alone at the kitchen table.

Maybelle stood tall and gawky thin. Her eyes bulged. The younger of the two, she appeared to be made of skin-wrapped bone. Maddie stood only slightly taller than her sister, but almost twice her size, big-boned, heavy around the middle with large forearms, resembling her father more than Judd did, with the same manly jaw and a heavy brow ridge.

Maybelle motioned toward Cassie. "Who's this?" Judd opened his mouth to say something when their mother walked into the room and sat down. No one attempted to start eating.

"Madeline, where's Howard?" Mother Cantrell said. "I don't expect to see your sister's no-account husband, but you'd think you'd of got this one to mind you a bit."

"Who you calling no-account?" Maybelle sat forward in her chair.

Maddie said, "He's home with Simon. He's got a cold. You don't like them to come when they got colds."

Cassie fingered a butter knife not wanting to act as though she was paying too much attention to the conversation. The knife felt unnecessarily heavy, the water glass, too daintily light. It'd break easily and need to be replaced constantly. Cassie had never touched real crystal before. It was beautiful but impractical.

After grace the plates were passed counter-clockwise starting with Judd's father, to Cassie, to Judd, to Mother Cantrell, who passed them on to Maddie, and then to Maybelle. Spoons clicked against plates, knives and forks slid together, the sound of six people eating earnestly breaking the heavy silence of the room.

"So," Maybelle said, leaning back in her chair after finishing her first helping. "Are you going to introduce us to your lady friend?"

Judd swallowed hard. "This here's Cass Wolphe."

Maddie smiled. "My, how you've grown. I hear your cousin Rancy up and re-enlisted. A lot of folks didn't like him, but I thought he wasn't all that bad." She gazed at the plates and bowls of food as if trying to decide what should be her next helping. "Used to see you all gussied up in church. I figured it was you the moment I seen you. About time we got some looks in this clan."

"My Crystal Jean is pretty," Maybelle said. Maddie wrinkled up her nose. "She sure the hell beats Sara Lynn in the looks department."

Maddie set her knife and fork down. "No, she don't. Who the hell are you to go talking about looks, you old horse?"

"Old horse? Ain't half the men in this county rode me like they rode you."

A fist hammered against the long cherry table. Plates and silverware jumped into the air. Cassie almost screamed.

Heads turned to face their father who sat reposed, his red face appearing relaxed, the pink skin of his scalp showing through his thin bristly hair. "From where I'm looking, it seems as though the seed of the Cantrells is cursed. Now I knowed the Wolphes since I was a boy. Never been no nicer man walked these hills than Cal. And as far as your mother, Miss Cassie, you may be the only girl been more prettier than her." Mr. Cantrell held his knife in one hand, his fork upside-down in the other, a man serious about eating. "Most of us tear our living from these hills with a vengeance. Cal and Gertie always were happy to take what the land give them. The way I see it, adding the Wolphes to the Cantrells, we get the better of the deal."

"What, they getting married?" Maddie asked.

Maybelle said, "Of course, you idiot. Why'd you think he brought her home for?"

Judd's mother pressed her hands against the table, standing slowly. "She'll marry him over my dead body."

Maybelle whispered down at her plate, "We can only hope."

Maddie laughed. "May, now you just take that back. That's so sinful saying that with how old our mother's getting."

"Madeline, shut up," her mother said. Maybelle laughed, covering her mouth. Judd's mother turned to Cassie, "Oh, no, missy, I got your number. You may have the rest of them fooled, but I know you. I can see you're pure evil with your makeup and your stockings and your short dress. You don't hide nothing and you ain't ashamed a bit. You bat your eyes at my only boy and you rub up against him 'til he can't even think straight."

Cassie had thought she looked pretty. The way Mother Cantrell described her she felt cheap.

Mr. Cantrell cut a piece of meat and dunked it into his potatoes. He sat back in his chair and chewed while watching his wife.

"He don't go to church no more," Mother Cantrell said. "Then you fornicate with him in the most vile ways." Both daughters snickered. "You mix his seed with yours and you think you can bring a devil into this house and call him a Cantrell." She turned to Judd, pointing at Cassie. "You marry this—this, and I swear you'll never step foot in my house again. And just forget about the good money we give you to laze around and call it work. You'll never see another red cent."

Cassie stared down at her plate. Her stomach wanting to reject what she'd eaten.

Judd stood and walked into the kitchen. Cassie started to stand to follow but Judd never looked back as he yanked open the kitchen door and slammed it shut after he passed through. A half-minute later a car started and backed out of the driveway. His mother sat back down. Judd's father closed his eyes and shook his head.

"Well," Maybelle said. "This is why I like to come to dinner. Just about the time I start wondering why I'm such a screw-up, I come here and know why."

"I think we've done enough arguing for one meal," Maddie said. "Someone best take the sacrificial lamb back home."

"No," Cassie said loudly. "I'll call somebody."

"Who?" Mrs. Cantrell said. "You don't even have a phone."

"Don't you worry about me. Some of us have friends." She could call Jake. And say what—that the grandmother of her unborn child wouldn't allow the father to marry her and he turned tail and ran? So Jake would pity her and why hadn't she called him the day after he'd left, a week a month? Suzy or Gabe would come, if they were home. "I'll call my Uncle Carl."

Mother Cantrell stiffened in her chair. Judd's father grunted. Cassie could see she had unwittingly taken sides in the battle of the left pews. Now the war would be between mother and grandmother to be played out over the years. Cassie bounced out of her chair. "Just point me to the phone and I'll be happy to call my Aunt Teresa and tell her to come and get me."

"There's no need for that," Judd's mother said. "One of us will take you home. It's the least we can do."

"The least," Maybelle said.

"I'll take her," Maddie replied, getting up, leaving her napkin folded on her chair.

Maybelle said, "Why you?"

Mother Cantrell leaned forward. "Let her. She knows better than you. You just might decide to take her out and get drunk or something."

Maybelle stood up, her eyes wide. "I will not. What the hell are you saying?"

Cassie smiled. This was the game the Cantrells played.

Mother Cantrell sat down. "Shut up, Maybelle, and stay here and take care of your brats, or maybe we'll just have to give them some old-fashioned discipline. Lord knows they need it."

Maybelle slid back down into her chair, her jaw clenched so tightly that her head shook and the veins in her neck bulged. Mr. Cantrell busily chewed, swallowed and went at his food again as if what was happening before him was nothing. He would be harder to figure out.

Cassie kicked her chair back violently as she threw her cloth napkin into the gravy on her plate. She retrieved her coat and purse. "Thank you for the supper," she said to Mother Cantrell. "It was so nice meeting you. I know we're going to be seeing a lot of each other." She slid her hand over her stomach, then turned and walked out onto the porch, hearing Maybelle laugh behind her.

Maddie's car still had its new-car odor. Jake had taken her to a car dealer just to look, he'd said.

Maddie backed slowly down the driveway. "Damn shit hole. Where the hell my mother gets off thinking she's so damn high and mighty living in a pig sty like this?"

"I thought you were on your mother's side," Cassie said. The big bench seat was still factory stiff, encased in a thick clear plastic cover protecting it from the backsides of the passengers. Cassie couldn't get comfortable on it.

Maddie grabbed at a pack of cigarettes from her purse. "You want one? Honey, just because I try to keep the family from killing each other don't mean I agree with what they do." A built-in eight-track player quietly played Credence Clearwater Revival.

Cassie shook her head. "I just quit. They taste like hell anyhow. How come nobody stands up to her?"

"Ha, I figured you'd a got it by now. None of us Cantrells got a piss ant's chance in hell of making anything of our lives. Pa's about the best farmer around. We got—they got four dairy farms and rent the land off of other farms. You know how much money they got socked away?" Maddie stopped at the end of the driveway peering up and down an empty road. "No, you don't, but I bet the old biddy thinks you do. If she's got a will, and I'm betting she does, ain't one of us going to piss her off enough to get written out of it." Maddie's thighs bulged against her slacks. Except for her small breasts jutting from her thick chest she looked like a man.

A pile of eight-track tapes lay scattered on the floor by Cassie's feet. "Not even Judd?"

"I'm kind of hoping he shoots her," Maddie said. "Then the old man would split everything evenly." Maddie knocked the ashes of her cigarette into a still shiny ashtray. She drove on in silence, chewing on her lower lip. As they turned on to Cassie's road, about three miles from her home, Maddie said, "Cassie, you know if I could get some money together, maybe me and you should take a trip. Solve all our problems."

Cassie read the titles on the tapes, Three Dog Night, Dawn, Simon and Garfunkel, "Bridge over Troubled Water." "Where?"

"Just listen to me, okay? Don't say nothing until I'm done." Maddie sat hunched over the wheel, un-relaxed, as if waiting for something to happen out on the road. "It's legal in New York now. We could drive up to Buffalo. It's only a day away. I'll get the money. We could go up and spend a couple of weeks." She tapped her cigarette against the edge of the ashtray again. "You ever stay at a real hotel? We could go up to Niagara Falls and get a hotel with room service and all that. It's just a quick little operation and you'd be in a hospital with doctors and nurses. You'd be fine."

"Oh, my God," Cassie said. "You want me to get an abortion?"

Maddie glanced at Cassie. "It'd be for the best. Don't you see, Judd isn't going to marry you. Farming's all he knows. He ain't going to take a chance of getting thrown out on his ass."

"You're wrong. Judd's already said he'll marry me."

Maddie sighed. "Judd says a lot of things. Hell, he wouldn't even have the guts to live with you if you were willing to shack up."

Cassie wanted out of Maddie's car. "I wouldn't do that." They were coming up on her house.

"Either way, you'll have that kid alone and you'll be alone the rest of your life. I'll guarantee it. This is your place, ain't it?" Maddie slowed down, her eyes riveted on Cassie's house.

"Yes," Cassie said. It wasn't even half the size of the Cantrell house, but it was a home and she'd hurt the people there, people who didn't deserve to be hurt.

After Maddie had stopped the car, she turned to Cassie. "Look, here's the deal. I get the old bat to stake the money for the operation and a small vacation for the both of us. We go first class. Maybe I can even get enough for you to have some left over. Then you can kick Judd's ass from here to kingdom come. You can be done with us once and for all. You don't know how lucky you'd be."

Cassie opened the door. "That's why she sent you, to talk me into getting rid of this baby." Cassie stepped out of the car. She peeked back in. "Get this straight so you don't misquote me. This ain't Judd's baby. Don't worry he's the father all right, but it ain't his or hers, it's mine. As long as we got each other, neither one of us is ever going to be alone." Cassie stepped off the road onto the wet grass. "You tell your mother she's going to be a grandmother again whether she likes it or not." The door gave out a solid new-car clunk as Cassie slammed it.

Maddie stared out at Cassie. She closed her eyes and shook her head, but she smiled as she drove off. The car had the nice purr of a well-tuned engine.

Cassie stood on the edge of the road before the ditch, peering at the old farmhouse with its sagging porch. The last night she'd seen Darlene, the girl had sounded desperate, alone, abandoned and now Cassie knew why.

"Well," Cassie said to her folks as she walked into the living room. "You won't have to pay for a wedding. That's the good news. The bad news is, you're going to have an unwed mother for a daughter."

Her father put down the paper. "I guess we'll fix up Ben's room for a nursery."

Cassie sat down on the couch next to her mother. She still knitted, but now she smiled that soft motherly smile she had. "Who knows, in a few years there could be a grandson running around and helping out with the chores. Get a couple of cows again."

Cassie's father replied, "Don't much matter what it is. I wouldn't mind having a little girl, either."

Cassie searched for the comics. "Could grow up to be a big disappointment."

Her father pulled the paper back up in front of him. "I don't see how that's possible. Ain't happened yet."

Cassie pulled the comics from the pile of disheveled papers, peeking over it at her parents. Did they know this child she was carrying wasn't their first grandchild?

Chapter 16

Judd never called, never came around. Cassie was pretty sure where she could find him, but a baby would be hard enough to rear without the troubles the Cantrells would bring. She had more pressing problems. Girls who became pregnant were asked to leave school when their womanliness became obvious. It didn't set a good example for the younger girls and somehow, a girl in her ripeness enticed the boys, supposedly, into thinking if one girl did it, they all did, but maybe the reason pregnant girls were asked to leave was something less obvious, something deeper and more earthly sensual.

On an early, November Friday night in late 1970, a car pulled into the driveway, a sixty-five Chevy. Cassie knew the year because it looked like one Teresa had owned, but this one shone mean black, moonlight reflecting off its glistening hide, around its curves and chrome, the grill a hideous leering smile, the lights, four eyes burning madness. A shiny silver sphere, like the moon itself, glowed intensely inside each huge black wheel. The car looked fast. With an automobile like that, Judd wouldn't have lasted a minute. She'd been sitting in the kitchen waiting for Suzy and Gabe, her hand on her stomach as if expecting it to rise like bread dough, for some outward change to show in her body reflecting the changes happening in her life.

Cassie and Suzy sat together at school, but school was not the place for this bit of news. Gabe had graduated last June, so had Davey and Orlen. They'd all found jobs. R.C. and Andy were off to college.

Suzy met Cassie in the yard. "Whose car's that?" Cassie asked.

Suzy laughed. "Gabe's. Ain't it neat? Goes like a bat out of hell. Come on. You got to get in the back because it's got buckets." She held the long single door for Cassie.

Cassie said, "You going to smoke?"

"Shit, yeah," Suzy said.

Cassie stepped away from the door. "Then I need the front window. I don't smoke anymore and it makes me sick a bit now."

"Wait a minute," Suzy said. "I always got the front."

Gabe leaned toward the open door to get a look at Cassie. "Aw, come on, Suzy, let her sit in front for once. Hi, Cassie. Long time no see."

"Hi, Gabe. Nice car." Gabe had grown taller and more muscular. In every respect the image of his older brother, except for the smile that still came easily. A thin beard hung off his cleft chin. A wispy mustache lay between his nose and lips that, if a little darker, might have been becoming. He'd grown his hair longer, swept back again like his brother's, but without the Butch Wax. Under his brown leather flight jacket, he wore a black t-shirt with the words "Blue Oyster Cult" printed on it. "You're looking pretty tonight."

The inside of the car glared bright red leather trimmed in black and chrome. Cassie slid into the front seat, wrapped between the leather of the door and the console separating her from Gabe dividing the car in half. "That's what they tell me." The interior of the car reminded her of a small room in Hell. If ever the Devil designed a car, this would be it.

As Gabe backed out of the driveway, Suzy, passed out the beer.

"None for me thanks," Cassie said. "I quit that, too. A little too late."

Sly and the Family Stone sang "Thank You" from speakers in the dash, the doors and even from the back. At first Cassie couldn't tell where the music came from, but she figured it originated from the strange little device in the dash below the radio, from a small slot hardly big enough for a decent size cracker. "What's this?" she asked, pointing to the slot.

Gabe pushed a button and a small, square, plastic tongue stuck out. "It's a cassette player." Gabe pointed at the glove compartment. "Open it."

Two-dozen, maybe three, of the small tapes sat neatly stacked in their clear boxes. Suzy said, "I told him to buy an eight track, but no, he buys these little things." She handed a can to Gabe. "Well, blurt it out. Might as well get it over with."

Cassie turned to look at Suzy, her small figure wedged into a corner of the seat. "You know?"

Suzy put down her beer. "I figured, the way you're acting."

Gabe tried to drive and look at their faces at the same time. "I don't have a clue."

Suzy replied, "Ain't none of you men got a clue."

Cassie pulled out a couple of cassettes, reading the names of the groups. Some she knew, some she didn't. "Well, Gabe," Cassie said. "It's like this—I'm pregnant and I ain't got a husband."

"Holy shit," he said slowly. "Ain't going to be no wedding?"

Suzy grabbed the backs of the seats sticking her head between them, straddling the console. "He ain't marrying you? You tell him?"

"Yeah, I told him. Hell, I think I even proposed to him, sort of." Cassie handed Gabe *The Best of the Bee Gees.* She'd noticed the song title "Massachusetts," the first song she and Jake had danced to on their first night. "We were going to, but his mother put the stops to that."

"Shit." Gabe said the word in one long breath. "He ran from his own mother." Gabe drove on through the dark, the three of them listening to the music and exhaust roar from underneath the car. The sound reminded Cassie of Jake's motorcycle, the way the pitch changed every time Gabe accelerated or slowed down. They were so far from each other now. If Cassie had ever thought Jake and she would get back together again, she knew now it'd never happen. She'd gone from being almost a child to a mother. Jake was still a young man, maybe. She was older than him now.

The three sat on a back road as the dark sky clouded up,

Cassie and Suzy on the hood of the car, Gabe standing beside them. Cassie drank a bottle of ginger ale Gabe had bought her to celebrate. "Here's to the baby," Gabe said. They held their drinks up to the moon.

Suzy peered up at Cassie and smiled. Very few times Cassie felt tall. Around Suzy, she always did. "You're going to have a baby."

The air smelled full of moisture and of the cold coming. "I'm quitting school," Cassie said.

"No," Suzy said. "Don't let them bastards scare you off."

"I can't make it anyhow." The moon was in its last crescent, lying on its fat belly. "The baby's due in the spring. I may be a little ashamed of how I got it, but I ain't ashamed of being a mother. I'm not going to be publicly humiliated; I won't give them the pleasure." A circle of ice crystals ringed the white Cheshire-cat smile of the moon. "Going to snow soon. Maybe next year baby and me will be making snow angels in the back yard. You know, I ain't had nothing all my life I could call my own."

"Don't cry. It'll be all right," Suzy said. She laid her head back on Cassie's shoulder.

Cassie put her arm around her. A strange comforting feeling came over her holding Suzy, as if she was already starting to become a mother. "I'm not going to cry. I'm done with that. The baby can cry for both of us."

Gabe tugged unconsciously at his wispy beard. "What you thinking of, Gabe?" Cassie asked.

He stared out at the moon. "Just how it's all changing. Don't know why. You being pregnant and your cousin—strange, him going back to Vietnam."

When she let herself think of Rancy, Cassie worried she'd had something to do with Rancy going away. "Not so strange," Cassie said. "Maybe we all do what we're supposed to do?"

They finished their drinks and Gabe drove Cassie home. She

hugged Suzy and Gabe goodbye on the lawn. They said they'd visit her. They wouldn't. Their lives were different now.

The next week Cassie quit school. A week later Davey came around and asked her to marry him. Cassie kissed him on the forehead and refused. He worked with Jake at the mill. Davey promised never to say anything to him. She didn't care if the world knew, but she didn't want Jake to know how far she had fallen. She wasn't sure if she was just ashamed or afraid he might show up. She'd heard he and his little brother were going down to Wytheville on the weekends and hanging out with city boys and dating city girls. She was happy for him. That was the kind of life he wanted.

During the holidays as Cassie felt the life grow inside her, news came of Rancy missing in action. Teresa rushed over to her brother's house sitting breathlessly at the kitchen table relating her woes while Cassie hid in her bedroom.

In late January the baby kicked for the first time. Cassie gasped in surprise. Her mother laughed placing her hand on Cassie's stomach waiting for the next sign of life. Cassie settled in to being a vessel of another's creation, a pea pod, growing larger every day. She worried that it wasn't all baby.

On a cold Sunday morning in late February, after her folks left for church, Cassie, in one of her brother's old flannel shirts she wore now for a dress, and an old sweater buttoned around her neck and wearing knitted woolen socks, sat down to watch a church service on TV. She feared that a godless mother might have a godless child. Within five minutes of her parents leaving, a car pulled into the driveway. The preacher's wife exited from the driver's side, Teresa from the other clutching a large square box. Teresa had started doing good deeds for the church and the parish. Cassie figured she was hoping to convince God to save her son. The loss of seemed to hang onto her, also, as if someone she'd loved had died.

"Oh, God," Cassie said. "Oh, God, not this." She put her

hands on her stomach as if to hide it. The door opened and Teresa walked in. "Just like her not to knock."

"Cassie," Teresa yelled. "Come on out so we can see you. No sense hiding."

Cassie walked into the kitchen. "I wasn't hiding, Aunt Teresa." Cassie had never felt so large until that moment, or so raggedy.

"Oh, my Lord," Teresa said. "You look a sight. If there ever was a child that looked like a street urchin, you do."

Cassie said, "Ma and Pa already left for church. If you come to get a look at me, well, you got it."

Teresa shoved the box at Cassie. "Here, now you go put these on. Don't you worry. Mrs. VanVleet picked them out herself."

Mrs. VanVleet gently nudged Teresa aside to take Cassie's hand and speaking quietly and slowly, her voice smooth and steady as if she had trained vocally for the moment, she said, "Cassie, it's time for you to come home. Yes, everyone knows." She spoke the words softly, as if the sin or the pregnancy had somehow addled Cassie's mind. "We know you've been abandoned."

Cassie forced herself not to cry. "Please don't. I can do this myself. I'm a lot stronger than I look."

Mrs. VanVleet sat down in a kitchen chair pulling Cassie into another one. "We know you are, but you don't have to do this alone. All of us want you to come back. Frank—the reverend, he's preaching a sermon especially for you today."

"God, no. I mean, I'm so sorry," Cassie said. "I can't. I can't sit there and watch her—watch people stare at me."

"Cassie," Teresa broke in. "You're sitting with Carl and me today. She'll stare at you and it'll shame her and maybe she'll do what's right. The Wolphes got nothing to be ashamed of, but the Cantrells, that's another story."

Cassie almost yanked her hand from Mrs. VanVleet's, the epiphany was so strong, almost like those people who suddenly found religion. All this fuss had nothing to do with God or faith, or her and her child, but the power structure of the left pews. The parish wanted her baby. They wanted to name it, to decide who it would be, what it would become just like they'd decided all those things about her. She could come back into the flock for her child. She would carry the shame anyhow. She could hide forever, but the baby couldn't. The decision had been made for her and the baby. All Cassie could do was change as quickly as possible.

The three women walked into church together as if nothing had ever happened and Cassie had no protruding abdomen underneath the gray double-breasted suit Teresa had bought her. Teresa had known Cassie's size, but Cassie wasn't so sure about panty hose instead of stockings.

Mother Cantrell sat catatonic in her anger, Cassie smiling as she walked to the pew where Uncle Carl sat. The pecking order of the left pews was being contested. All this, the suit, the panty hose, the shoes, a chess move. For years Rancy had been Teresa's weakness. She never out and out lied, but she had colored his actions, played them down as Mother Cantrell did with Judd. Now, no matter what Mother Cantrell said about her, Mother Cantrell's tow-headed boy was the one who'd refused to set things right. The suffering of childbirth, and Judd's refusal to own up to his sins, would emancipate her and her child. Why hadn't she seen it, all of it? How dumb she had been, no, not dumb, naive, innocent. She could play the game. She'd have to clean up her act, become the pious suffering mother, but the church would accept the role. She could live out her life with her parents and child, being the martyr, the fallen woman come back to God. "Now," she whispered to her unborn child. "Things will be all right."

Mrs. VanVleet, Bev, as Cassie began to know her from their Wednesday afternoon teas, not knowing how things were done in the hills, finally ran out of patience and contacted a lawyer over

Cassie's objections, insisting Cassie sign papers to take Judd, and thus his mother, to court to pay for the doctor bills and the birth of the child and to give Cassie some support. Two weeks later Cassie started receiving twenty dollars a week in the mail, a check signed by Mother Cantrell herself. She would get thirty dollars a week after the child was born.

The snow had melted and the wind had blown away the dead leaves. Uncle Carl had taught Cassie to drive. She was eighteen after all. Carl and Teresa were still doing good deeds even after Rancy had been found in some jungle village half-dead. Cassie guessed they'd just gotten into the habit.

Cassie sat on the porch and twined the shoots around the staves as she listened to a tractor make its way up the valley. Several minutes later it appeared down the road from her, monstrously clumsy, trying to masquerade as an automobile with a six-bottom plow jacked up behind like a bird's tail, zigzagging down the road, the driver barely in control. Not many farmers could afford a plow that size let alone a tractor that could pull it when it was sunk deeply into heavy wet dirt. The tractor had to be owned by the Cantrells.

Cassie lifted the basket off her stomach holding it in front of her, not so much to hide her stomach, but not to empathize it. The tractor throttled down, its brakes chattering as Judd worked the gearshift and throttle at the same time, his left arm stuck through the steering wheel, holding the tractor steady. The gears ground, the tractor jerked several times, losing speed. It pirouetted on its right rear wheel, swinging into the driveway. Judd accelerated across the lawn and onto the fallow garden to sink the plow deep into the earth, rev the tractor up, ripping the ground open. Diesel exhaust hung in the late-morning air. Cassie's mother wanted to go to Mrs. Fowley's house and call the sheriff. She thought Judd had gone crazy. Nobody had asked him to plow. Nobody would have asked him to plow.

Cassie walked out to the edge of the garden and stood with

her hands on her hips. Judd made two passes before he saw her. He idled down the tractor.

"What the hell are you doing?" she yelled. He said nothing but stepped down from the high seat. He stared intently at Cassie's stomach as he walked toward her, cigarettes rolled up in his sleeve. Cassie took several steps back. "I said, what the hell are you doing? Nobody asked you to come over here and plow. You got no right being on our land."

Judd reached for Cassie's stomach. Dirt streaked his face.

She grabbed his wrists. "You got no right."

"It's my child," he said.

Cassie backed farther away to make him look at her face. "It's my stomach. When the child's born you can come around and hold it. Until then, you just keep away from me."

The wind blew at his fine golden hair. "Marry me," he said.

"No, you had your chance." She pulled her father's shirt away from her abdomen, not wanting him to notice her pants couldn't be buttoned, but were fixed with a piece of elastic.

Wildness danced in his eyes. "Please, Cassie. I can't stand it. It ain't right, you and me not being married."

"Oh, my God." Cassie looked away at the tops of the mountains, not wanting to cry in her anger. "She sent your ass down here. See, see you've got me swearing again. I gave all that stuff up. I don't smoke or drink either, but I bet you'll get me doing those things before too long. Your mother's got you fit to be tied."

"I'm proposing to you. I'll get down on my knees if you want me to." Judd stepped up to her and took her hand. He dropped to one knee.

Cassie rolled her eyes. "Where's a camera when you need one? God, a hillbilly on his knees right off of his tractor proposing to his pregnant bride. All we need is my pa with a shotgun and it'd be perfect. You're just doing it because your mother made you."

Judd yanked her toward him. "I don't want my child to be a

bastard. Cassie, I want to make an honest woman out of you."

Cassie tugged her hand out of his. She stomped away a few yards and turned. "You bastard, I'm already an honest woman. If I'm anything, I'm an honest woman."

Judd followed her, his arms open. "You know what I mean. Please just don't say no. I'll finish plowing the garden and go home. You can call me, or in a couple of weeks when I disc, you can give me your answer." Judd turned back to his tractor.

"Shit." Cassie walked into the house.

Her mother sat at the table. She'd been watching through the window. Her whole life was spent watching through that window. "The child needs a name," her mother said.

Cassie slumped in a chair. The shiny skin of her stomach peeked out between the puckered openings of her shirt. She'd been set to live out her life in their small house, raising her child, maybe getting some sort of job to earn their keep, and then taking care of her parents in their old age. "The baby will have a name. It can still be a Cantrell, but right now I'd rather call it a Wolphe, especially if it's a girl. I don't attach too much pride to the name Cantrell."

Her mother walked over to the window. Judd had finished plowing, lifting the blades from the earth to drive out to the road, wiping his eyes with the back of his arm. "Cassie, the baby needs a father, and he's finally come around."

Cassie rubbed her temples trying to make the headache go away. "You mean that bitch did. I'm sorry, Ma, but I can't flatter myself thinking Judd did all of this on his own. At least with a lawyer I get it in writing how much I get out of them."

"Don't be so sure," her mother said. "He could just head for the hills and I don't mean the ones around here."

Cassie waited to talk to Bev. She laid out the complete story as politely as she could.

Bev sat her cup back on her saucer and sat up primly. "It's obvious why he's doing it and who put him up to it, but whether you think this is a good or bad idea, the Christian thing to do is give him a chance to make it right."

Mother Cantrell had lost the battle, not with Cassie, but with the parish. Cassie rubbed the life existing just under her skin. "Did Mother Cantrell speak to you?"

"She spoke to Frank. I don't know if she's lying or not. Frank thinks some of it is the truth, but Cassie, you have to turn the other cheek. You have to put your faith in God."

And there it was. She would be expected to do for Judd and his mother what the parish had done for her and maybe it had all been a set-up, Bev playing all of them as neatly as Mother Cantrell or Teresa could have ever hoped to do. When she married Judd everything in the parish would be fine. The church had won.

The garden would be disked the day before the wedding. Before anything was planted Cassie would have a new name and so would her baby. Judd might settle down, make a good husband, but a better chance he wouldn't. It was all she could expect. Maybe she'd been trapped since she'd been born?

Cassie woke well before sunrise on her wedding day, walking through the house touching chairs and counters, smelling the curtains. The old navy and gold Singer sat in its spot against the wall, idle. It had clothed her, given her warmth on cold nights. Her fingers had learned to touch it almost intimately. The new TV sat blind, its screen a blank brown-gray, the kitchen table, a bleak thing, down to two occupants. The house seemed to sigh around her. New life in it was over. It and its occupants could only go through the years.

Cassie drove her father's car to the gate of the logging road behind Mrs. Fowley's. Trees stood like shadows of the old dead, of all those women that had gone before her, standing and watching as she carefully threaded the car up the rutted logging road until she came to the opening onto the high meadow. She shut the engine off and stepped out of the car. She struggled up to the ridge where she and Dee had pick blueberries years ago. Day would soon be breaking. The birds had started singing. They were sure another day would dawn. A thin thread of light lay across the jagged eastern ridge beyond the valley. Above her it was still night, the Milky Way hanging in the sky.

She waited for the sun to rise, but it had risen someplace already, and other people lived and worked under it freely. The sky lightened above the smoke-black ragged silhouette of the distant range. Maybe Jake hadn't understood, but at least he'd had an inkling. A world waited out there where she could have been anyone she'd wanted. No, she was what she'd been born to, maybe not what she wanted, but then who was, especially women? The morning star stood gleaming in bright defiance of the coming sun. Cassie turned and walked back to the car to drive down and prepare for her wedding.

Two weeks after the wedding little Cody was born. As he lay against his mother, nursing, his father went out and got drunk to celebrate the birth of his boy, getting into a fight and ending in jail.

Chapter 17

Cassie woke to a cold house, the air frigid against her cheek. Why had she insisted on renting Uncle Carl's cottage even when he refused to give it to her, saying a Cantrell could afford to buy it? Today was her nineteenth birthday. She lay in bed listening to the wind howl up the dark valley and across the roof of the frozen little cottage; an asthmatic cry, weak and old, the leaf-frosted window refracted the pale luminescence of the pre-dawn sky. Judd hadn't come home again. She'd become used to it, no longer waking in the middle of the night worrying about whether he was hurt or not, about whether he was with some woman. She thought, like other times, he might be asleep on the couch, unable to stagger upstairs, or slept in his car and froze during the night. These things weren't unheard of, and she was pregnant again.

Cassie turned on the light. Prying enough money out of Mother Cantrell to buy the supplies, so her father and the utility company could wire the place had been a battle she'd won. The frigid floor stung her bare feet. Her boy, Cody, still slept. She held back the urge to cry for her little boy having to grow up like this. Maybe she and Judd didn't deserve anything better, but he did.

An empty couch greeted her downstairs. She stoked the embers in wood-burning insert Mr. Cantrell had put into the fireplace, Judd complaining it ruined the ambiance of the room, like he knew anything about ambiance. Cassie tore several pages from an old Sears catalogue, laying them on the smoldering embers, adding kindling, and a couple of split logs, blowing on the coals until the paper ignited. She twisted another page into a tight wand sticking it into the young flame, waiting for it to catch fire, walking the flame to the kitchen stove. At least they had wood for the winter. Judd's father had seen to that too. Cassie scraped the frost off the inside of a front window and peeked out. The snow had finally subsided. The sun still hid behind the eastern ridge, but enough light reflected off the pale sky and the dry clouds for her to see no car sat on the snow-drifted lawn.

She pulled on her boots and coat, grabbed a short-handled barn shovel and re-shoveled the path through the snowdrifts to the outhouse. The little money Judd chose to bring home after his binges was just enough to feed them, not nearly enough to get an indoor bathroom and she wasn't ready to take on Mother Cantrell again.

The wind scattered the smoke from the chimney smelling of burning paper and seasoned hardwood while small whirlwinds ground hard snow against Cassie's face. There'd be no real dawn, just the sky lightening to a watery gray.

She found the big milk bucket under a drift against the back wall, packed the snow down hard with her boot, added more snow until it became solid, carried it inside and set it on the stove to melt. They'd had to shut the water off before the pipes froze late November.

Cassie dumped more snow into the heating bucket, needing enough to wash herself and to bathe Cody. She'd make him oatmeal for breakfast. In another few days it would be gone and all they'd have left to eat would be a little corn meal, a bit of flour, and the canned vegetables she and her mother put up last fall. They had one gallon of milk left. She'd quit nursing Cody a month ago. When lunch came it was cornbread and applesauce again, and still no husband, only the hushed rattle of old windows and the soft clink of the stove.

After lunch, Cassie put Cody down for his nap. The wind had died down and the house became warm and intimate. The frost on the windows had melted. Outside, the trees stood gray and snow trimmed. A winter-white snowshoe rabbit bounced for several feet on its large hind legs making its way across the field in front of the cottage. It stopped and looked around, sniffing the air, sitting warm and fat and almost invisible in its winter coat.

The thought only half-formed in her mind as Cassie slipped

on her boots and hat, found her coat and dug through the closet for Judd's .22 rifle. A half box of cartridges lay on a joist. Her hands shaking, she dropped a half-dozen small brass slugs onto the floor while trying to watch the rabbit unhurriedly make its way toward the trees. She loaded eight bullets into the tube under the barrel, pushed the door open against a snowdrift, and stepped out onto the porch. The rabbit still sat in the yard.

Just line up the sights and slowly pull the trigger, the way she'd seen Judd shoot woodchucks. She pulled the bolt up and back, then forward and down, loading a bullet into the chamber. Cassie slid the barrel of the gun under one of the torn screens of the porch and sighted. The rifle smelled of gun oil and wood wax, of the faint acrid smell of spent bullets. She held her breath as she gently squeezed the trigger. Suddenly the rabbit hopped several feet further on toward the woods. Cassie breathed out slowly, re-sighted the gun and pulled back on the trigger. The shot rang out unexpectedly, the sound of it ricocheting off the hills.

At first Cassie couldn't find the rabbit, finally spotting a stain of red on the snow, then the rabbit flopping around crazily, trying to hop and falling on its side, jumping and twitching. It had almost dragged itself to the woods, trailing a streak of blood.

Cassie sprang off the porch, running through the deep snow to the dying animal, sliding the bolt back, discharging the small brass shell, kicking up another. Her hands shaking, she pushed the bolt forward. The snowshoe looked up at her, its breath coming in rapid pants as if it knew it would die. Sometimes, she thought, animals understand life and death better than humans do, but then a rabbit was low on the food chain and maybe it had always known its life would end this way. She held the end of the barrel to the animal's head, firing again.

Cassie stared down at her first kill as the wind flowed through the trees and the winter day, silent, the air stinging her face and biting at her lips. The animal lay dead in a dead world, half its head gone. It wasn't much. Hardly worth killing.

She picked up the bloody carcass and studied it. "There, damn it, Judd, we'll have some meat in spite of you. Got to get to be a better shot though, ruined half the meat and screwed up the pelt bad. Wonder how much rabbit pelt is going for these days?" If she had a phone or a car, she could get Ben's traps out of the barn, set up her own line. She'd ask her father how best to season the pelts and who'd buy them, but right now they needed food even if a few pelts were ruined.

Judd staggered home three days later, ramming the front end of his car into a snowdrift. He shoved the door open against the snow, cursing her for not having it shoveled. Judd staggered to the back of his car, cursing her again for the snow in his shoes.

A newer four-wheel-drive pickup pulled alongside his car. A tall gaunt man in a large army-green parka slid down from the cab. He walked with the help of a cane. The fur-trimmed hood of his coat was pulled tightly around his face, so only a heavy beard and two sunken eyes showed. Cassie went back to fixing her stew and sourdough biscuits.

"We're home," Judd called. "Why the fuck ain't the driveway shoveled?" He kicked his feet against the porch wall. "What's for supper?"

"Raccoon," Cassie said. She opened the oven door, wrapped a towel over the edge of the cookie sheet, pulling it out to poke one of the biscuits. Five more minutes. She lifted Cody into the highchair her father had repaired and let him gnaw on a leg bone.

"Bullshit," Judd said. He walked to the refrigerator and slid in two six-packs of beer, the only foodstuff he bothered to buy, studied them for a minute and then pulled out two bottles. "We're about out of food. When the hell you going to get some?" He handed a bottle to the man in the parka who'd pulled the hood down and unzipped the front.

Cassie wanted to say, when you start bringing home some money regularly, but they had company even if it was only another drinking buddy of Judd's.

The man pulled out a chair, threw his parka over the back and sat down. Stringy hair fell down past his shoulders. He took a long drink of beer and smiled at Cassie, two thin lips surrounded by a ball of hair.

Judd lifted the cover of the pot. "What's for dinner?"

"Raccoon," Cassie repeated.

"What's the fuck's wrong with you?" Judd said.

She was pushing him again. She could get away with it for a while, but if she went too far he'd remember when his buddy went home. "Judd, when's the last time you brought home a paycheck?"

Judd set the cover back on the pot. "I had to use it to live on. Ain't my fault we live in the boonies. I ain't eating no coon. Where'd you get it?"

"I shot it, myself," Cassie said. The stranger laughed.

"When'd you learn to shoot?" Judd asked.

Cassie stirred the stew. The potatoes seem about done. "When I started starving."

The stranger laughed again. "Raccoon stew sounds pretty good to me, but Cassie ain't said I could stay yet."

Cassie lifted the tray of biscuits from the oven, sitting them next to the pot. His voice was familiar in the way fear was familiar. "Sure, stay and eat. What the hell, I'm a pretty good shot."

"Well, girl, shouldn't be shooting nothing out of season," the man said. "Game Warden catch you and they'll be hell to pay."

"Fuck." Cassie backed away from the kitchen table. "Rancy, it's you." She stepped closer staring at the man's face, sliding into a chair next to him, trying to find a resemblance to the person who'd been the bane of her life.

Rancy said, "What's left of me."

"What happened?" Cassie spoke the words before she caught herself, thinking they weren't very polite, but then again, this was

Rancy.

Rancy tilted the bottle up and swallowed hard. He sat it on the table. "Got religion, sort of. Got blowed up. Almost died except for this old yellow woman who had no cause to keep me alive." He'd quit smiling. Rancy scraped at the label of his bottle with the long fingernail of his thumb. "Looked worse than I do now. All twisted up. Hell, they had to re-break some of my bones when they got me to Guam."

Judd said, "Get me over there and see what happens." He tilted his bottle up and drank. Rancy glared at him for a few seconds, then drank.

Cassie retrieved the pot from the stove, setting it in the middle of the table. She dished out a plate for her, Cody, and Judd. He only scowled at it.

Rancy dished out a large helping. "You know, I laid in the jungle only a few yards off a path for two days. People went by not even caring enough to check if we was dead. For a while I prayed I die. Then I prayed I'd live to see these mountains again. Now I'm just glad to have a beer and raccoon stew." They ate and talked a bit. When supper was over, Rancy and Judd took their beers and sat under the stag's head while Cassie picked up and put Cody to bed.

A week later, while both men sat and drank, Cassie took the paycheck, loaded up Cody, and went to get groceries. She stopped by a country store and bought another box of shells and raided her father's barn for the traps. She asked her father about the pelts, telling him Judd was doing the trapping.

Cassie found that pelts weren't paying that much, just enough to get seed by spring. Uncle Bill plowed a patch of ground across the side of the lawn where it seemed flattest, a large brown rectangle in a green lawn that would never be cut. A sewing machine, a car, and she could be done with Judd.

Her stomach was a small bulge below her light jacket as she and Cody began the planting, cutting the rows and dropping in the seeds by hand. Two weeks later they kneeled in the morning mist on the dew-wet earth and separated the young radish sprouts.

The sound of Rancy's truck echoed up the valley. He pulled up to the lawn and eased his gaunt body out of the truck. "Hey," he said. Judd never seemed to be happy anymore. Rancy never seemed to be sad or angry.

Cassie almost never saw Judd now that plowing and planting season had arrived. He worked from before sunrise to after dark, came home too tired to argue or to go out, ate and fell asleep on the couch watching TV. It was Sunday, the only day he didn't have to work and he slept in. If he was awake, she would know. He'd be at the front door demanding breakfast, if he was in the mood, or at least asking her why she couldn't find something like socks or shoes.

Cassie stood up, stretching her back. "The old man's not up yet."

Rancy leaned against the fender of his truck. "What a bum. It's time he got up."

"It's your funeral," she said.

He laughed and waved the comment off. "That'd be the day. Garden's looking good." Rancy limped into the house. A half-hour later both men walked out the back door heading for the woods. Judd had her rifle with him. It was his officially, but she cared for it, cleaned and oiled the barrel, polished the stock.

"Where're you going?" she asked.

Judd turned in her direction, raising the nose of the .22. "What's it to you?"

Cassie stood in front of Cody. "I don't really give a shit, but don't you go using up my bullets." She kept the boy as far away from the man as she could. He'd hit Cody several times already for nothing more than he'd been handy.

The barrel of the gun came up a little higher. "I'll use as many bullets as I want to."

Rancy put his hand on the barrel looking sideways at Judd. He pushed the barrel back toward the ground. Cassie thought she saw fear in Judd's eyes. Then she saw what Judd knew. Tucked into Rancy's pants was a small pistol with a walnut handle.

Judd said, "We're just going to do some scouting."

They followed the creek bed up between the trees and rocks, finally disappearing into the tunnel the creek made in the undergrowth. They'd follow the creek almost to its source, then cut through a mature stand of WPA pines, then back over the slope until they reached the top of the ridge and the old abandoned timber camp. She knew every bit of the woods now. It'd been part of her trap line. She'd shot a turkey there once. Judd cursed her for shooting it out of season.

She'd said, "So what, I ain't even got a hunting license, and I wouldn't be shooting nothing out of season if you'd bring home two paychecks in a row."

It'd been the second time he backhanded her that week. For a while Cassie had wanted to shoot him. She idly schemed, more daydreams than anything else, how she'd hike all day to the promontory waiting for him to come out of a barn, and then put a bullet between his eyes. Then she felt guilty for thinking those thoughts and changed to thoughts of running away, but it made no difference. He had her now and there was nothing she could do about it. She had no car, nor money, and she sure wasn't going to admit the beatings to anybody. So when he'd hit her again she took it and cried quietly so as not to wake Cody.

Judd reappeared at the opening of the woods besides the creek, walking over to the side of the house, picking up a long-handled spade and a garden rake where she'd stored them. As quickly as he'd come, he disappeared back into the forest.

The day neared supper as both men picked their way down through the moss-covered rocks, their clothes sweat stained, Rancy limping noticeably. They strolled in through the kitchen door. "Hey, Cass," Rancy said. "What's for supper?" Judd picked two beers out of the refrigerator and handed one to Rancy. Rancy pulled the small gun out of his pants and laid it on the table.

"We're having chicken, store-bought," Cassie said. "I made some potato salad. I figured you'd be hungry, so I made extra." She took out an extra plate from the cupboard.

"Damn, if I could find a wife like you, I'd think about getting married."

"No you wouldn't." Judd pointed his bottle at her. "Come home a little late once and see what happens."

Cassie spun around to face him. "I don't give a shit when you come home, but you buy beer for half the county out of the money we need around here."

Judd slammed his bottle down on the table and stood towering over her. "What the hell's wrong with you? It's my paycheck." Foam spilled onto the clean surface of the table. "Why don't you get off your lazy ass and go earn some money?"

She'd overstepped again. She'd pay for it later after Rancy left.

"Easy folks," Rancy said. "We're having a pretty good time here. No sense screwing it up." He handed Judd his beer still dripping foam. "Judd, let's you and me go out on the porch."

As they walked out of the kitchen, Cassie followed behind them carrying the guns. The pistol was light, almost dainty, blue-black and dark wood, made more for a woman than a man. She rested her thumb on the hammer, wanting pull it back, test its resistance, but beyond the end of the barrel was Judd's back and it'd be too easy to accidentally squeeze the trigger. She tucked both guns into the closet, hoping someday Rancy would let her shoot the pistol.

The two men came in for dinner when she called, and went out again while she cleaned up and put Cody to bed. When Cassie came back downstairs, a sweet smoky odor hung thickly in the air. She followed it out onto the darkening porch. Night had begun to roll over the eastern ridge, the blue sky fading to black, and Venus rising above the high horizon.

Both men were laughing. As she stepped from house to porch Rancy patted the empty side of the wicker couch. "Come on, Cassie, sit down here and let me turn you on." Judd looked on dumbfounded at what Rancy had said. "Let me turn you on to some dope. Maybe the only thing good come from Vietnam. It ain't going to hurt the bun in the oven. Better than booze or cigarettes," Rancy said.

Cassie said, "You don't know that. Besides, it's illegal."

Judd laughed. "Oh, yeah, you see any cops up here? I swear she's the dumbest woman alive."

Rancy said, "Hey, it takes the pain in my leg away. Better than that stuff the VA gave me. That stuff's got so many side effects, it really fucks you up."

Cassie lit an old half-burned candle, considering Rancy's suggestion and Judd's insult. Both men stared like children at the flame. She sat down next to Rancy as he rolled up some greenish shredded plant into a very poor rendition of a cigarette. Rancy showed her how to hold the joint, how to inhale and hold her breath. The smoke bit into her lungs like tiny bristles, piercing in a thousand places, not like cigarette smoke, not thick, heavy, drowning smoke.

Soon the night rolled in, a cool spring night just right for a light jacket or sweater. Starlight echoed the sound of the peepers calling for love. Neither men spoke much or she didn't bother to listen after a while. The muscles in her shoulders relaxed and the constant throbbing in her temples disappeared.

Rancy left just after midnight, saying something to Judd about him keeping the pistol close by, just in case.

A late moon rose huge over the mountain, Cassie dumbfounded its brilliance, and the night sounds that sang clearer than she'd ever heard them before. There were movements in their music working to a crescendo, soft movements, slow waltzing movements, loud strong movements.

She hadn't felt this close to the land in a long time. She loved the Earth, the trees, the birds singing out of newborn chicks, solitude, mountains, early morning. Her life could have been wonderful, might have been. The moon seemed to swallow her, to pull her out of her body and scatter her into air.

"Wow," Judd said.

Cassie laughed. Something seemed so funny to her. Everything seemed funny, that she was pregnant with a second child at nineteen, married to a man she didn't love, who she never had really loved, who didn't love her, probably never did and never could.

Judd started laughing. "It's funny, ain't it?"

The moon, silvering the long thin grass of the lawn, etching the edges of the trees, mesmerized Cassie, how the light had a sound surrounding her in an ocean of night, how it drenched her garden. "I was laughing at us, you and me."

"Yeah, that's really funny." Judd giggled like a little boy. "We're old people already. I've never been out of West Virginia. Never raced stock cars. Never did a lot of things. Going to live and die like my old man." He inhaled a long breath. "You got what you wanted."

"No, I didn't," she said.

"Really?" Judd said. "And what were you planning on doing—besides this I mean, having kids and shit?"

The moon outshone the stars. A breeze ran its cool tongue sensually over her skin—kissed her neck, whispered to Cassie to walk naked across the moonlit lawn into the dark silver-lit woods as the trees spoke a language she thought she could hear. "I don't know, go to college, travel. Go to Europe, maybe. Why not? None of us ever really gets what we want." This is what she wanted and had always wanted, for every night to be like this, except for Judd. But the nights couldn't be. She needed to deal in realities. The reality was she should have wanted more and for just a short while she had. "You could of just paid the money."

Judd's head lolled against the wall, his eyes closed. "You could of not asked for it."

There had been college, possibilities, independence, travel. "It wasn't for me. I didn't even want it. It was for your son."

An owl hooted somewhere deep in the woods. A small animal's life was slated to end. Judd kicked at a rotting two by four under a screen. "We were pretty good for a while."

Moonlight-drenched hills towered behind her husband. "We were hot shit," she said. "Except we were headed southbound on northbound tracks."

Judd lit up a cigarette. The moon washed him in tawny silver, aging him. "What do we do now?"

She asked, "You want to leave?"

Judd sat quietly smoking. He said, "What if I said I did? What if I said, yeah?"

"Just leave me the car." She was chains and shackles to him, but there were other chains that bound him here, family, community, a way of life as old as the hills and the hills, deep summer dawns, wooded creeks washing over ancient rocks, bursting from the folds of a hill like birth. There was the timeless call of the deep woods, and the smell of plowed earth and life planted by your own hands to watch grow, creation, and the birth. The most intoxicating drug of all, peace and a sense of knowing your place in the universe. The moonlight seemed to seep through Judd, and Cassie thought she finally saw the monster inside. He wasn't strong enough to break the bonds. Only dying could release him. But it wouldn't be enough for him to kill himself. He had to kill everything around him. "Hell, in a couple of weeks you'd have another car," Cassie said.

"That's true." Judd attempted to blow smoke rings. All he accomplished where little clouds. "You got any of that chicken left?"

"Not with that eating machine you got for a friend." A moth rushed at the flame of the candle, colliding with the repaired screens, grasping pathetically to the fine wire mesh.

Cassie brought out two plates of salad and two glasses of ice tea.

"You know," Judd said. "This stuff, the dope, it's sure different from booze. I think if a bear came up to me right now I'd hug it." Judd pinched the bridge of his nose. "You'd still want the money for the kid."

Cassie hadn't realized she'd been so hungry. She sat the plate on her stomach. Once she'd started eating she couldn't stop. "You wouldn't be willing to give money to your kid?"

"By fall we won't be worrying about money. Me and Rancy planted a ton of seeds. Rancy grows his own shit. He's been saving up the seeds just waiting to find someone like me. He figures if we let it grow until fall we'll clear ten grand apiece."

Cassie sat up. "Damn it, Judd, what if you get caught? We'll all go to jail."

Judd slid his empty plate onto the floor. He wiped his hands on his jeans. "We ain't going to get caught. This shit's the new white lightning. Rancy says he knows some boys growing it over by Wheeling that's clearing a hundred grand a year."

"That's why Rancy gave you the gun," she said. "If it's so safe, why do you need a gun?"

Judd yawned, tilting back his head, his mouth stretching open. "The gun ain't for the cops. I ain't stupid. It's in case someone tries to steal some, just to scare them."

Cassie set her plate on the floor. "But a hundred grand ain't enough to take the chance of losing Cody. God, Judd, they catch you and I'll go to jail too and then your mother gets Cody. You want that?"

"It ain't going to happen." He resituated his feet, banging the heels of his boots down on the porch rail. "I'll tell them you didn't know nothing about it, but I ain't going to get caught." He gestured with his right hand, saying, "See, what I did is, I planted them on the north side of the clearing like they were weeds. This way nobody's going to think they're being cultivated."

"I don't know." She needed to think about this. The money would be a godsend, if she got any of it. Maybe he'd run away? Maybe she'd run away?

"Just one year," Judd said. "Just one growing season. I swear I'll give you five grand and that old clunker out there. Five thousand dollars just to act stupid."

She could live a year on five thousand dollars cash, her and Cody and the baby. Get it, pack up the car and get away. Go someplace, find a job. Maybe go look for Ben, maybe Jake. Judd wouldn't follow if she went far enough. He was too lazy for that. He'd get caught someday and he wouldn't be man enough to sacrifice himself for her. "Sounds like a lot of marijuana. How are you going to get rid of it?"

Judd yawned again. "What do you think Rancy does? He don't work. The pension he gets ain't enough to live on, let alone get that nice truck he's got. He's got connections. It works just like the feed mill. We harvest and bale and sell it to them. They wholesale it."

He'd never leave the mountains, not in a million years. "One time, that's all, and I get five thousand dollars for keeping my mouth shut?"

Judd smiled widely. The moonlight reflected off his teeth. "Only one time." He was lying. That was clear enough. If there was a chance to make ten grand, Judd would sell his own mother, say nothing of a wife he hated and children he cared nothing about. He'd get away with it the first year if Rancy wasn't as stupid as Judd, but sooner or later they'd get caught.

"Fine," Cassie said. There was no longer a decision to make. Judd and Rancy had made it for her. As much as she loved the mountains, she'd have to leave. If she were smart, she could get all of it. What the hell, she knew better than to think Judd would hand over one red cent. She could play this game—who gets the money first. Ten grand would just about equal the child support she'd never get. Cassie gathered up the plates and went to bed thinking she really needed to speak to Rancy.

The spring grew into a bold summer. Cassie took care of her garden and Judd took care of his. In late summer the corn stood high, the ears almost ready to pick. She'd walked up on the hill several times and checked out Judd's plants. To her surprise, Judd was a fastidious gardener. The plants towered above her. The residue of insecticide spray and fertilizer lay on the leaves and the cultivated ground under the branches. Cassie figured Judd's garden to be about a half-acre. They could have gone into truck farming, or at least built a garden stand on the side of some main road where she could have sold the legitimate fruits of their labors. They could have done so much.

The sun floated in the western sky, but not yet behind the mountains. Judd ate while Cassie sweated over the dishes. By the way, he was going out and he'd stay out all night and come home late Sunday. She heard a vehicle making its way up the road. "Rancy's coming."

"I hear him." Judd hunched over his dinner plate like a dog over a bowl of scraps. "What the hell's he want today?" Cody was in the living room playing quietly, away from the large man who scared him so.

Cassie slid a plate into the strainer. Droplets of sweat stuck her bangs to her forehead and made her skin itch. "Probably checking up on his investment."

Judd stood up from his plate, staring down at his unfinished meal as if pondering which one should wait, the meal or Rancy. "I already told him how things are going. The bastard thinks I'm going to smoke it all up."

Cassie wiped her arm across her forehead. The cottage would be hot for the next two hours until the evening wind came up from the valley. If Rancy were smart, he'd worry.

Rancy called from the seat of his truck. "You want to go into town?"

Cassie wanted the car. She had enough money to get groceries. "Go ahead," she said.

Judd glanced back at her. He yelled out to Rancy. "I'm coming." He pulled on his boots and found a jacket then grabbed his half-eaten pork chop. Judd leaped off the porch and trotted down to the truck, ripping the meat off the bone with his teeth, throwing the bone into the yard.

In a few seconds the men were gone. No kiss, no goodbye. They only kissed for sex now and only once. One kiss, a polite introduction. Two would have meant they cared.

By the time she had finished her shopping, and they'd had their ice cream, night had fallen. Cody's head bobbed against her shoulder. Cassie laid him on the back seat and covered him with her coat. Having the car with no time to be home was a rare treat. She decided to drive to Buddy's just for old times and stop in to say hello.

Automobiles crowded the parking lot. The twanging sound of country-western music vibrated through the walls. A few people leaned against cars, speaking quickly, anticipation in their voices. When she walked in, those standing stepped back, those shooting stood up. They stared foolishly at her. No one laughed, smiled, or even said hello.

"Well, don't look so shocked. I'm just pregnant, not dead," she said.

Rancy walked out of the bathroom. "Oh, shit," he said when he saw Cassie.

In that instant she understood. If Rancy was here, then Judd was here also, and up to no good.

Cassie stepped into the other room. Alma and Irene were dancing. Ruth sat in the booth kissing a man, letting him run his hands all over her. Cassie recognized the man. "Damn you," she screamed. "You mother-fucking bastard!"

Judd quickly slid out of the booth. "What the hell you doing here?"

Cassie slapped him. "Don't you go asking me nothing, you son-of-a-bitch. I got your son out in the car and another one in my stomach and you got the nerve to ask me anything? And fuck you too, Ruth."

Ruth sat in the booth appearing stunned. "Cass, it ain't like that."

Judd clutched at Cassie's shirt. Cassie pivoted away. "When I get home I'm going to kill you for slapping me in front of everyone," he said.

People were staring. Cassie hit him as hard as she could because he'd made a fool of her and everyone here knew it and they'd made a fool of her, all of them.

She expected Judd to get her in the parking lot, but she reached the car safely. Maybe it wasn't even the sex she was angry at. It was the cheating, the unfairness of it all, treating her like she wasn't worth anything and all the time he was dirt, and her friends, her so-called friends, her so-called folk going along with it.

Cassie put Cody to bed and started unloading the groceries. She heard Rancy's truck coming up the valley. The significance of the sound didn't register until headlights came roaring up out of the darkness at her. Cassie dropped the bags and ran for the porch getting the screen door opened as the truck slammed into the steps, throwing her against the inside door.

She pulled herself up by the knob and opened the door. Before she could get into the house, Judd hit her in the back of her head. She fell against the outside wall, instinctively rolling over to see where the next blow would come from. He raised his foot to kick her in the stomach. She screamed and rolled again, catching his boot heel on her hip. Judd fell against the side of the porch. A loud crack rang out as his head hit the wall.

"Motherfucker," he screamed. "Goddamn you."

Cassie scrambled to her knees and then to her feet, leaned forward to run to the closet, reaching inside for the pistol. She cocked it as she swung around. "Stop," she shouted. "Stop or I swear to God I'll kill you."

Judd stood. Blood matted his hair behind his left ear. "Give me that gun. Give it to me, damn it."

"Or what, you mother-fucking son-of-a-bitch, you'll bleed all over the floor? I got all the right to kill you, Judd Cantrell, all the right in the world."

Cassie hadn't noticed the sheriff's car pull up. She hadn't heard it, or seen the lights. She thought they were alone.

Someone behind Judd calmly said, "Easy, Cassie, we don't have to do this." Judd attempted to step forward. A hand threw him to the floor. Jimmy Marshall stood above her husband in his uniform, tall and broad-shouldered, dressed in heavy gray and brass buttons, a wide-brimmed hat down over his eyes, his left arm held out, the palm up. His right hand was poised over his buckled holster.

Cassie re-aimed the pistol, pointing it squarely between Judd's eyes. "I got to do it, Jimmy. Don't you see? He's been beating me and he's tried to beat little Cody and he just tried to kill the baby. You see, this ain't never going to be over until one of us is dead. It can't be me because he won't take care of Cody or the baby."

"Arrest the bitch," Judd said looking defiantly and drunkenly at the barrel.

Cassie squeezed harder on the trigger. Her jaw tightened and she squinted her eyes in anticipation of the gun going off soon and of the pieces of her husband that would be flying around.

Jimmy yelled, "No, no don't." She wasn't sure who Jimmy spoke to, her or the other officer coming in behind him.

Judd's mouth flopped open and his eyes grew wide. She'd seen the look before on the faces of people who'd suddenly gotten religion. "Oh, God, she's going to do it," he cried. "Somebody shoot her."

"Shut up," Jimmy said. "Cassie, just take it easy. Don't get too hasty." He spoke calmly as if he was giving advice about fishing or directions, but neither officer moved his hand away from his holstered gun. "Just let me shoot him and then I'll give up. I won't harm no one else," she said.

"He ain't worth going to jail for or losing your kids, Cassie. Now, I'm just going to move around him real slow and come over to your side." Jimmy inched along the wall. The other officer took a position behind Judd. Jimmy reached over and put his hand around the gun, stuffing a large thumb between the hammer and the pin. He pulled the gun from her hand and slowly let the hammer down.

Cassie started to cry. She'd lost her chance. "It would of been self-defense, Jimmy. You know that. If you'd of come a minute later, it'd been all over."

Judd stood up. "I'm going to kick your ass." The other officer put his left hand on Judd's shoulder, enough to hold him.

Jimmy hefted the gun, studying the balance of the small piece, glancing from Cassie to her husband. Madness danced in Judd's eyes. Jimmy seemed to think for a moment. "Is this an unlicensed firearm?" He looked at Judd. Jimmy wrapped his large hand around the small butt of the pistol, feeling its weight. "This illegal?"

"It ain't mine," Judd said quickly.

Jimmy put his finger on the trigger, his thumb on the hammer. "You could kill somebody with this and nobody'd be able to trace it." He shoved the barrel against Judd's left temple and re-cocked the gun.

The other officer said, "Hell, Jimmy, what are you doing?"

Jimmy nodded toward the front door. "Go back out to the car, Henry. This ain't official business any more. This is family."

Henry looked at his partner and Cassie. He patted Judd on the shoulder as if to say goodbye, then turned around and walked off the porch, climbing back over the hood of Rancy's truck now sitting where the steps had been.

"The way I see it," Jimmy said. "There's a bullet in here that's got your name on it. It'd be doing the world a lot of good if it blew your brains out and it really don't matter who pulls the trigger, me, the wife you've been beating, or one of my brothers."

Judd stared at Cassie. She stared back half-hoping he'd do something stupid.

Jimmy said to Judd, "Now, I'm going to let you go, but I don't ever want to see you in this county again. The Cantrells may have some money, but the Marshall's got most of the mean. I'm giving this pistol to my kin and if you ever show your face in this county again, I'll make sure they kill you and bury you where no one will ever find your body. You understand you dumb hick bastard?"

Judd nodded.

"Then get."

Judd ran to Rancy's truck. He backed it around the patrol car, tearing away the rest of the steps.

Jimmy said, "It's going to be hard, girl, but at least you won't have him to worry about. Oh, and I ain't fooling about burying him. If he shows his face around here you just tell me and we'll take care of it. Okay?"

"Yeah," she said. "It's okay."

Chapter 18

The state police found Rancy's truck at the Virginia state line, Judd gone and those who searched the next day found a very pregnant girl picking and canning corn. Cassie had half the corn in before the labor pains came. She packed up Cody and delivered him to her mother, who was extremely troubled about the disappearance of her daughter's husband. Between pains Cassie said, "I figure he's got himself another woman by now and lit out. We're better off without him."

Her father drove her to the hospital and stayed during the birth of James. Cassie fell in love with little Jimmy from the first time he nursed, but with the love came the sudden realization that all three of them were in a deep mess.

Once home, Cassie settled in to a secluded peace as if her soul now rested to heal, adjusting to a life without the fear of violence. She canned the rest of the corn, waiting for the beans to ripen, digging up the potatoes and carrots when it became cold. She lived by the day. The years stringing out before her sat strange and gray in her mind and she refused, just for a little while, to peer into the mist to form the images of a future life.

Cody took his afternoon nap in the house. Jimmy lay asleep in a bushel basket stuffed with blankets on the side-yard next to Cassie while she hung wash on the line stretched from house to outhouse, humming an old ballad she'd heard somewhere when she'd been a child, one of those songs that had echoed around the mountains for a hundred years. Dull lifeless clouds rolled over the mountains. Rain would come before nightfall. A chill fall wind flapped the sheets like loose sails. They cracked and boomed. Cassie struggled against the life of them to hang the old cloth diapers, the wind whipping hair across her face and her dress against her legs.

A female voice shouted, "Hello." It came from the front of the house.

Cassie picked her sleeping baby up out of the basket. The cracking of the sheets and the wind had been too loud. Cassie hadn't been warned in time and she'd been caught in an insecure place, unable yet to meet people so soon after the birth of her child and the death of her marriage.

The heavyset woman, not fat but large, appeared at the corner of the house. She carried a green folder in her right hand. Her blue coat came to mid-calf.

Cassie edged toward the back door as the woman approached.

"My name's Dorothia Moressia," the woman shouted above the wind and the cracking of clothes. "Call me Dot." She stood for a moment below Cassie on the side-yard hill staring up at her as if taking stock of the young woman with her old dress and torn sweater, bare legs, and old shoes, clutching a baby, the wind blowing at her as if she were wildness itself. "I've come to see how you're doing. I'm from Social Services."

"I'd been expecting someone like you. You just tell Mother Cantrell to keep out of my and my boys' life. Her no-good son has abandoned us and that's fine by me."

Dot walked up the hill a few steps. "We can help you get support." The way the woman walked was familiar, all of her was, as if Cassie had seen her before.

Cassie backed away toward the kitchen door. "I don't want nothing from him. So you can just get back in your car and go back where you came from."

The woman still smiled and held up the green folder. "You've got children." She took another step closer. "I've got to see if they're all right. I'm not going to take them." Dot held her arms open as if to show she carried nothing dangerous. "Why don't we just sit and talk. I'm not going to report anything bad about you. It seems you're doing fine." Dot started walking up the hill.

Cassie stepped toward the back door trying to remember if

the front was still locked when the memory of the woman flashed in her mind. She pointed at the woman. "I know you. They used to call you Mother Moon, or something like that. I thought you were in San Francisco."

Dot stopped walking and laughed. "Well, I'll be. That's right. Did you stay at the commune?"

Cassie turned toward the wind to let it pull the hair from her face. "No, absolutely not. I went looking for my brother there."

Dot reached the top of the rise. "Did you ever find him?"

"No, but you got word to him and he got word back to us that he was all right." Cassie buttoned up her sweater to hide the old dress underneath. "Haven't heard from him since."

"Too bad," Dot said. She reached over and tugged Jimmy's cap down over his ear. "You wouldn't have a drink of water or something?"

Cassie smiled at her. "I could get you a drink of water without letting you into my house, but you'd stay 'til you found a way in. I got nothing to hide."

Dot followed Cassie into the cottage to stand on the threshold just inside the kitchen glancing around the room. "This is a nice place inside." She ran her finger along the kitchen counter. "Much nicer than the outside."

Cassie handed her baby to Dot and put a kettle on to boil. "The outside was a lot better before my husband ran a truck into it trying to kill me."

Dot sat at the table cooing at Jimmy. She pulled away the blankets. "You got a healthy boy here."

Cassie searched through her cups, sorting out the ones without chips. "Don't I know it. He never seems to stop eating. Nearly drains me dry."

"See, I think they're wrong about formula." Dot took the offered cup from Cassie. "I don't know why. It's just when I see you women nursing, I still see healthy babies."

The kettle whistled. Cassie dropped a tea bag in each cup then poured the water. "You women?" Cassie returned the kettle to the stove. "Poor women, or backwoods women?"

"I didn't mean anything by it," Dot said. "I'm sorry." She peered down into her cup as she dunked her tea bag.

"Nobody ever does mean it, but they say it anyhow," Cassie said. "I'm just a bit short of money right now. I'd wean Jimmy and get a job, but I can't afford store-bought formula. It's hard enough keeping enough milk in the house to feed Cody."

Dot pulled the tea bag from her cup, winding the string around her spoon, laying the paper tag over it all, and then squeezing.

"And in my spare time," Cassie said. "What little I have of it, I plan to make some baskets and maybe do some quilting and sell them around. Maybe sell enough to afford a babysitter. Then I'll get a real job."

Dot blew on her cup. "Have you considered welfare?"

Cassie slid into her chair. She pulled Jimmy from Dot's lap, laying him across her left shoulder. "You'll just go after Judd and I don't want him around." By now Judd had contacted his family and made up some lie. Jimmy began to cry. Cassie carried him into the living room to change him. Dot followed. Cassie laid her baby on the couch, unsnapped his pants, pausing after pulling them off. "So, why are you back?"

Dot sighed. "I don't know. I think the dream was too early, or maybe humans aren't God's creatures after all. The movement all fell apart. All that was left were the drugs."

Cassie wiped Jimmy's behind. "What happened to your husband, or boyfriend, or old man, or whatever you called him?"

Dot watched Cassie finish pinning up the clean diaper. "Bart? He left me for a sixteen-year-old runaway. Trying to recapture his youth, I guess, or maybe he was just a pedophile. I tried a couple of communes, all in the last throes of collapsing in on themselves."

Cassie raised Jimmy to her shoulder then walked back to the

kitchen.

"You keep a good clean house," Dot said. "I was talking to Bev—"

"No, I don't want to see her." Never again would she let them into her life. Then there was Mother Cantrell. Dot sat opposite Cassie now because the law gave Mother Cantrell the power to interfere with people's lives.

Dot sipped at her tea. She used no sugar, or thought Cassie wouldn't have any to spare. "You don't have to. They're leaving. They're going to Africa as missionaries."

Cassie sighed. "She'll hate it there more than here. She never said anything, but you could tell. I guess her husband was a little disappointed that we weren't more like wild natives or something—you know, going into deepest darkest Appalachia." Jimmy wiggled on Cassie's shoulder. "I think all she wanted was a nice stone church in the city where she could have tea every afternoon and the worst that happens is that someone gets divorced."

"She wasn't that bad," Dot said, but she laughed. She set her green folder in front of her. "Let's talk about getting you and your children some money."

"You'll go after Judd." Cassie undid her blouse and lifted her bra.

"We've got nothing to track him once he leaves the state. Can't touch his mother."

Cassie stroked the downy hair on Jimmy's head, combing it with her fingers. "When I get a job, I'll get off of it."

Dot opened her green folder. She laid out several papers, each thick with copies. "If you fill out these, you should be getting a check on the first of the month."

Cassie took her time reading them. Mother Cantrell had gotten Dot into her house not for Cassie or the children, but to have power over all of them when and if she needed it. "It'd help me more if you found me a babysitter when it was time for me to go to work." She signed on the bottom.

Dot slid the papers back in her folder. "I can do that. There are a lot of older girls in, well, in poor families that are in need of an extra dollar or two."

Dot stayed until Cody woke, and seeing he was in good health, left. The battle with Mother Cantrell was another draw. She'd kept her money, but lost her son. Now the next round was starting—whether Cassie could earn enough to keep her kids.

As Dot's car rolled away into the valley, Cassie said to her baby, "I'll give you another month, Jimmy, and then it's the bottle for you."

The welfare check arrived on schedule. After searching for several weeks, Cassie began to realize jobs were hard to come by. She couldn't type fast enough for secretarial work. For her size she was strong, but not strong enough to do a man's job, or so all the bosses figured. She'd even gone to the mill, hearing from Davey they were hiring and Jake had moved to Wytheville. She finally found a job tending bar and Dot found her a babysitter of sorts.

Amy was one of the few girls in the county who was willing to work for wages below the minimum scale, or not willing to put out the work bosses thought was needed to be paid minimum wage. She had her own car, which was the selling point to Cassie. This way her children could stay home and Amy looked as though she'd be around a while since she weighed over two hundred pounds and didn't seem to be in a hurry to do anything except get to dinner.

The bar lay in a narrow valley where two roads intersected, roads going to someplace, or from someplace, but nowhere right there. The small unpainted building stood by itself back from the road. Not even a gas station or general store kept it company. People just called it Darnel's, after the owner. Other than hunting season, the clientele consisted mostly of working men going home from the factories and mills. Around four they'd stop in;

the few tradesmen, carpenters, plumbers and electricians trickled in at six, and the miners from the second shift showed a little after twelve. Cassie worked day and night, sleeping only four hours on the days she tended bar, trying to clean and catch up on her sleep on the days she had off.

Men lingered to closing time buying Cassie shots, which at first she refused, but Darnel worked a deal with her. They kept a special bottle of Jack Daniel's, actually colored water. He split the price of the shots with her. The extra money came in handy, and knowing the money went to her children made this little sleight of hand, the short dresses and the tight blouses that got her the drinks, feel less perverse.

In late October the utility company sent her a third notice they'd be cutting off the electricity soon. The car needed snow tires. There were groceries to worry about, doctor bills, rent, and bullets. Without electricity the refrigerator wouldn't work and without snow tires, the car would never make it up and down the hills when the snow starting falling in earnest and to add to it Rancy walked in to the bar, standing the bar for two drinks and sitting for an hour before he got up the nerve to talk to her.

"Cassie," Rancy said. "You got a minute?"

She walked slowly over to him expecting an apology. She had a few things to say to him, too. She'd thought he'd become one of the family with all the meals she'd cooked and he'd eaten. She slapped a bar rag on the bar and started cleaning.

Rancy cupped his hand over his whiskey. "You know the deal I had with Judd?"

Rancy laid his hand on hers, stopping her cleaning. "It still goes—for me and you. I can't get up there on that mountain and lug all those plants down." He spoke down at his drink forcing Cassie to lean forward to hear. "There ain't another person I trust in the whole county except you and Judd."

Cassie neatly folded the bar rag in half, then in half again. The lost money had weighed heavy on her mind. Growing the dope had been wrong and illegal, but letting the plants rot was just a waste and things at home were in a desperate situation.

"I don't know what happened and I don't want to know, but he can't be found," Rancy said. "I figure he got what was coming to him."

"You were stupid to trust Judd. He would have double-crossed you." She walked away, squatting down to retrieve a beer for a customer.

"He fucked up my truck real good," Rancy said, when she walked back.

Cassie leaned over close to him. "If that fucker'd been a second sooner that'd been me you'd been picking out of the grill."

"I know he was bad. That's why I trusted him," he said. "He don't have the connections. Only I got the place to sell the stuff." Rancy swallowed the rest of his drink. "I was thinking, you already know about it, and you're a hell of a lot harder worker than Judd. How about it?" Rancy pushed the change she'd laid on the bar from the other drinks at her and nodded down at his empty glass. "You go up there and cut them and drag them down and pile them in the woods. I'll come up and we'll load them in the pickup."

With the money she could offer Uncle Bill five thousand dollars to buy the place, use a thousand for a better car, and whatever was left over from catching up on the bills, she could sock away for emergencies. "Then I get ten thousand dollars?" Cassie poured him another drink.

"No, I can't give you that." Rancy pressed the glass against his chin. "Where'd you hear that from?"

Cassie started wiping the bar again. "Judd. You'd never got him to do it for less. What happens if you get caught?"

Rancy sipped the new whiskey slowly. "Don't worry, I ain't going to."

Cassie pulled a dollar out of the pile in front of Rancy and rang up the drink. She leaned over the bar, putting her face close to his. "I'll tell you what happens. You send the cops to me figuring they'll go easy on you and me because I'm a single mother with two kids, except they'll grab those two kids lickety-split. Ten thousand or the plants rot."

Rancy pushed himself against the bar. "You don't understand," he said loudly. He settled back onto his stool and glanced around the bar. No one seemed to have taken notice. "The deal with Judd was he was going to cut it and bale it with one of his father's hay balers. You can't do that."

Cassie leaned back on her heels. She still wanted the money and she still wanted to make him sweat. "That's true, but that's hardly any work. The work's getting them down. I'll do it for five thousand."

Rancy counted his money on the bar, again. "You know, I can't sell it to the people I was going to, but I got somebody else who just might take it whole. I won't make almost nothing on it, but it's better than letting the stuff rot. I'll give you the money, but only after I get paid." Rancy picked up the bills, leaving a dollar and the change. "That was the arrangement I had with Judd."

Cassie walked away to draw a draft beer for a customer. She could have given Rancy the answer right then and there, but she wanted him to stew. She took her time getting back. "I'm not touching anything without something up front."

Rancy leaned over the bar, pulling his wallet from his back pocket. "I'll give you one hundred now. In fact I won't even deduct it from your share."

One hundred dollars out of five thousand wasn't much, but Rancy wasn't a man who could come up with a lot of cash on short notice. The one hundred would get her out of trouble for this month at least.

"One hundred now, one hundred before you get them on your truck."

Rancy pulled a wad of cash from his pocked, unfolded it and

peeled off five twenty-dollar bills. "Deal."

Cassie worked for a week during her children's naps, cutting and dragging the large plants off the hill. Rancy came over on Monday evening to load the plants. He got there before supper, bringing two six-packs of beer. He took care of Jimmy and played with Cody while she cooked. At dinner they talked about family, his parents, hers, how they were getting along in years, how people appreciated family once they got older and how he really didn't want the farm and just as soon give it to her or Ben if he could be found. He shared his beer with her. Speaking to someone close was nice. She'd been so lonely since she married Judd.

Rancy dried the dishes, leaning on his good leg, listing toward her. He smelled musky. He'd always smelled that way. The same way he'd smelled when she'd crawled into his bed and curled up next to him to sleep when she'd been innocent. She felt that close to him again. He helped put the boys to bed. Afterward, they loaded up the truck together, Cassie doing most of the work because Rancy had trouble balancing without his cane. They laughed and talked as they worked as if all those years between them had never happened.

"Well, it's all done," Rancy said. He leaned against the truck while tying down an end of the tarp Cassie had covered the plants with. "Let's go in and I'll pay you off."

Cassie held the screen door open for Rancy as he limped up the steps. "You want something to drink?" she asked.

"That's why I brought the beer," he said. Rancy tumbled into the glider. "This is about far enough for me." Sweat droplets had formed on his forehead. "Get yourself one."

Cassie brought out two bottles. The work had been hard, tearing at her muscles, fatiguing her, but it was work she liked and she liked sharing in it with someone. She sat down on the opposite side of the glider from him. How strange it was that, not only did she no longer fear the man who sat next to her, but she'd grown to welcome his visits—until she found out he'd been in cahoots with Judd and then she still had missed him. She hadn't missed Judd.

"Here's the other hundred." Rancy handed her five more bills. He stared out at the lawn and the autumn garden. "This is like old times."

Cassie folded the bills and put them in her pocket. She sat her beer on the floor. "What old times?"

Rancy sat quietly for a minute as if she'd said something to hurt him. "Remember, that one night?" He played with the bottle pretending to read the label in the dark. "You feel anything that night in the bar, or was it just a drunk to you?"

She'd forgotten about that night. The night in the truck was what she remembered when he'd asked, but the night in the bar had changed her, and maybe Rancy. "I'm not too proud of how I acted at the bar. I was pretty screwed up in my life by then. Usually, Rancy, I've never been too proud of this whole relationship."

Rancy scraped at the label on the bottle with his thumb. "No matter what I'd done you hated it and all I wanted was for you to like me."

The damp air chilled her now that the sun had set. She was a woman with two children to support by herself. Rancy was a man that had nothing left. Life had broken him. She almost said she was sorry. "Rancy?" Cassie asked. "That night in the truck, you had me."

Rancy glanced out at the lawn. He pulled his bum leg up on the glider, turning toward Cassie. "I seen men in Vietnam die for their buddies. Hell." He shook his head. "I didn't care about nothing else but the killing. When I came back, I was just the same."

Cassie stood pressing her hands against the rail of the porch trying to brace herself for Rancy's answer, turning to look into the garden. Only the pumpkins and gourds were left.

"But then you come to the truck to save that boy," he said. "And you shamed me."

"We'll always be family, Rancy," she said not looking back at him feeling his presence and the tension that'd always been between them. They'd closed the distance between them so much. If he reached out and pulled her back would she stop him? Was she that lonely? Maybe she had somehow redeemed herself. Her torment was over. She slid back into the recliner next to him. Did she care what people thought? But Rancy was going someplace she didn't want to go and maybe that was the only kind of men left for her. If so she needed to go it alone. "You're welcome to come over anytime, play with the kids, stay for supper."

"That'd be good," he said. "It'd be good to be family." Rancy reached for his cane. He patted her knee, and then stood. "I got to be getting along. Don't want to wear out my welcome." Two minutes later Rancy drove off with a truckload of dope.

A month later she asked Darnel, as she came in through the kitchen, "You see any sign of Rancy?"

"You know he lit out on you." Darnel flipped a patty of ground beef and pressed it into the griddle. "I don't want to know what he and your ex got you into, but it's best you're done with them both."

"Yeah, you're right." She could have used the money, any of it, especially after all the work she'd done. She'd been a fool again and her children suffered for it. She should have put a bullet in Judd's head or at least told Jimmy Marshall about the dope. She didn't know what made her angrier, them making her a fool or she being foolish enough to lose the money. People were getting while they could. She had to wise up and take care of herself.

Chapter 19

Cassie had hung up the season's icons, red, yellow, and orange leaves, and had cut out pumpkins. Soon she planned to make Pilgrims, Indians, and turkeys. Hunting season brought in quite a few new faces. She joked and chatted with the new patrons. Men bought her drinks and left. Other men came in and bought her more drinks. Three city men and two of the local girls, older women Cassie had seen before with other strangers, came in at around nine-thirty. They were the type who nursed their drinks until some of the hunters from the cities approached them. After eleven, the third man moved from the booth to the bar. His hat set back on his head. Gray hair lined his temples. He wore the uniform of the city hunters, a red plaid jacket, flannel shirt, and loose fitting jeans. His friends were getting drunkenly chummy with the girls.

"What'll you have?" Cassie asked.

"Give me a draft. What are you drinking?" he asked.

Cassie figured him for mid-forties. "J.D."

"Fine with me." Cassie poured herself a shot from her bottle. She let it sit off the bar for several minutes while she served other customers. She walked back and saluted the hunter with the shot glass, tilted her head back and drank it down. At eleven-fifteen he bought her another and one every fifteen minutes after that. At one, she told him she couldn't have any more. Taking a customer for a couple of drinks was one thing, another to make him pay for a whole bottle of colored water. At two-thirty in the morning only Cassie, the man, and two other people were left in the bar.

The man motioned to her to come over.

She said to him, "Sorry, but we've quit serving."

He pushed his hat further back on his head. Slightly slurring the words, he said, "Did you ever see one of these?" He slid a one hundred dollar bill at her.

"Of course." A lot of city hunters paid with large bills. The bills, though, reminded her of Rancy and the money he'd paid her now gone, not enough to catch her up.

He leaned over. The sickening stench of alcohol sweetened his breath. "It's yours if you come over to my motel with me."

Her first inclination was to slap him, but he was drunk and the amount made it less insulting. "What do you take me for?"

"Someone who'll let me buy her watered-down drinks all night. I know you need the money." The man sucked in a short breath through his mouth and then slowly exhaled. "I overheard you tell your friends about your kids and bills."

Cassie blushed. They weren't her friends, just regulars who'd understand her predicament. The one hundred dollars was a lot better than she got off of Rancy when she looked at it for time worked: a week chopping and stacking dope for only twice that. "Yeah, I could use the money," she said. "I'll just have to earn it some other way." She'd paid down the utility bill enough to keep the lights from being shut off, but there was next month's rent and snow tires and clothes, Christmas coming.

He pulled the bill back to his side of the bar. "How long will it take you to earn a hundred dollars, between what little you're paid and your tips, and let's not forget the little trick with the colored water?"

Cassie fell silent. The man made sense. "A week."

"You could earn that much for a few minutes work. Hell, you don't have to do nothing." The man folded the bill in half. "One hundred just to lie there. No funny stuff, nothing. I figure it's what my pals will spend on those floozies tonight and they aren't half as good-looking as you are."

Cassie started washing glasses, stacking them under the bar. "I'm sorry, I can't do that." But what other choices did she have? She couldn't borrow the money from anyone? No one had it and she'd never be able to pay it back. Worse, if Mother Cantrell got wind of her not being able to make ends meet, there'd be real trouble. Cassie glanced over to the man. God knows she'd done enough bad things. What was one more? She was between a rock and a hard place now because she'd let herself be cheated so much. It was her body, nobody trying to cheat her out of her labor. She'd get something out of it besides broken promises and an abusive husband. It wasn't like she'd ever do it again.

"Okay, but who's going to know?" he said. "A half-hour at the most. Cabin five at Sherman Hollow Inn." He put the bill into his shirt pocket and staggered to the door.

Cassie needed another half-hour to talk herself into going over to the motel. How many nights had she let Judd slobber all over her probably thinking of another woman? Yes, having sex for money was wrong, but not as wrong as what Andy had done, and Judd's beatings and Rancy cheating her out of money, no more wrong than growing and selling dope or chopping it down and loading it in a truck, not nearly as wrong as Bev, her mother, and the rest of them forcing her into an abusive marriage so they could think well of themselves.

"Fuck all those holier-than-thou bitches who have all the money in the world and really don't give a shit about anyone else including my boys." Cassie filled a shot glass with real whiskey. She poured it down her throat and then drove the five miles to the motel, almost turning around and going home twice.

The main building was a shabby little wooden structure in desperate need of paint. Ten small cottages circled it. Each had a window placed on each side of a dark door so the cabins looked like bawling children. The lights were out in number five and she half-hoped he'd be in a drunken stupor and wouldn't hear her knock, but the light went on. She almost turned and ran back to her car, but she'd come all that way and wasn't going to chicken out now. The man answered, his pants unbuckled and shirt unbuttoned.

"You got that hundred?" she asked. He reached into his pocket and pulled it out. Cassie snatched the bill as she walked in.

A bed and old dresser filled the little room. A TV sat on a high shelf. A bed stand and light made up the rest of the furniture. A gray carpet covered the floor, spattered and stained, worn to its threads by the door, the walls off-white, spattered yellow-brown. She sat on the bed. "Now what?"

"Undress," he said. "You can shut the light off if you want."

Cassie reached over and turned it off. She quickly undressed and sat on the bed, the bill still in her hand. She turned away as he undressed, laying down, closing her eyes and spreading her legs, folding the bill over and over as she prayed, just this once, not to get pregnant, and she promised to never do it again.

The man entered her immediately, hardly touching her with his hands. Cassie wadded the bill up in her hand as he moved above her, wishing she could see the one hundred printed on it. The metal bedsprings whined rhythmically sounding like old screen doors. She felt him moving inside her. His grunts grew stronger. She turned her face away from his breath. He'd been right; it was over quickly.

She dressed and left, stuffing the one hundred dollar bill into her wallet when she got back to the car. She drove home. Cool dry air kissed her face as she opened the door, but by the lack of smoke from the chimney she'd expected it, the fire all but embers. Amy slept on the couch, an empty cake dish on the floor next to her. Cassie woke Amy and sent her home, then stoked the fire, adding some paper and kindling and several chunks of maple. She kissed her boys and put their covers back in place where they'd kicked them off.

The first staying snow of the season fell three days after Cassie had her new snow tires, large languid flakes turning the sky gray and the earth white. Cassie watched it fall while waiting for Amy to once again lumber up her steps.

"I wish you'd move someplace flatter," Amy said between heavy breaths.

"Ain't a lot of that around here." Cassie picked Jimmy out of his playpen and hugged him. She chased down Cody, whose eyes were filled with tears. "No, baby, Mommy will be home soon. Tomorrow we'll play in the snow, okay?"

He nodded sadly. She kissed him, his eyes still shiny, Cassie's eyes clouding. She should be home like a good mother raising her children instead of working their childhood away. Why? she thought, as she walked to her car without looking back, not being able to watch Cody stand at the screen door. Why, did it have to be them? What had they done so wrong to have to live like this? Why punish children for the sins of their parents?

By the time she'd driven to work Cassie had worked up her courage again. "Hey, Darnel," she said, as she walked past him through the kitchen.

"Hey, Cass, what's new?"

Cassie grabbed a clean apron. "Snowing." She smelled the bar rag, wrinkled her nose and found a new one.

"Yep, good for the hunters. Brings them out like deer in the springtime."

The regulars filed in, stomping snow off their boots, shaking like old dogs and slapping their hats against their Carharts. They spoke louder than usual, smiled more. "Hey, Cass," they'd say. "Another round for my friends here." One by one they left to go to wife and child, home and hearth, to be replaced with another work-clothes-dressed man dusted with the early flakes of new snow. Cassie laughed and joked with them all. She let them buy her shots. She didn't mind their fawned proposals, mostly coming from married men, or even their off-color suggestions. They were all family to her now.

In the next week the snow started to fall more regularly in its early-winter, lazy descent, settling softly over the sleeping land. Cassie was glad to have new snow tires. Darnel had been right. The snow brought out hunters like spring rain brought out flowers. The men came from Charleston and Wheeling. Some were as close as Wytheville and some as far away as Charlotte and Pittsburgh. Many times she wanted to ask them if they knew Jake, but she'd learned the world was a big place and no one knew anyone, really. Cassie worked hard keeping up with them. She switched to blue jeans and tee shirts and low shoes. This way her feet didn't hurt as much when she got home at three in the morning and she didn't have to think about the proper way to bend down to get the beers out of the low coolers. Once in a while, though, they still whistled.

When she arrived on the Saturday before Thanksgiving, the bar was already full with tired hungry men. Darnel hustled from grill to deep fry, out to serve the customers and back. "Should of hired another waitress," he said to Cassie, as she took off her coat and boots.

Cassie tied an apron around her waist. "And split my tips? Don't worry, we'll get them all fed and settled in for the night." Cassie stepped out into the barroom. "Okay, who's waiting for food? Who wants to order, and who's here just to drink and don't want food getting in the way?"

The meal orders slowed down sometime after nine, but all the booths were full and the hunters lined two deep at the bar, sliding in between the men who'd staked out a bar stool. Cassie cleared away some dishes stacking up on the bar. She took them back to the sink and piled them on top of others. "You know," she said to Darnel. "I figured it'd be a little busy, but I didn't figure tonight was some national holiday."

"Oh, yeah," he said, pulling a rack out of the dishwasher. "This is the biggest week, and tonight's the biggest night. They all get out of work Friday and hightail it up here." He threw a rack of dishes over onto a stainless-steel work counter and slid another one into the dishwasher. "They hunted today. Can't hunt on Sunday, state law, so's might as well tie one on. They'll be home next Wednesday night so they can have turkey with the wife and kids."

Cassie turned to go back out front. "Yeah, national catting night." Cassie peeked out at the bar full of men. "The way I figure it, the only reason their wives let them go is because they're doing the same thing back home. Only these fools are too stupid to realize it."

Around eleven an older man slid off the end barstool and turned toward the door pulling his fleece-lined, orange hat down crookedly on his head. People called out goodbyes. A younger man took his place. He appeared to be late twenties, early thirties in age. He had stood behind the older man half the night. "Hi," he said to Cassie, "I'm Ron."

"Hi," she said back, "I'm Cass." His eyes were dark, lady's eyes, big ones with long lashes and thick dark eyebrows. He needed a shave. It accentuated the squareness of his jaw and his high cheekbones. The rest of him looked to be all man, from his hair, thick muscular neck, to his square shoulders. "What can I get you?"

"Give me a seven and seven." He pulled out a twenty. "Let me buy you a drink."

Cassie smiled. He smiled back. "Okay, but just one." She turned away from him to find the bottle of Seagrams. "Oh, God, he's gorgeous," she whispered to the bottle. She poured a shot from her bottle. "I don't need to get all silly when it's so busy."

She let Ron talk through the late night, walking away sometimes, but always being there before his drink was empty. He spaced them out. At one, Cassie announced last call. Ron ordered one more. The emptying bar allowed them to speak a bit more and quietly. Cassie leaned in closer to him, smiled more. He leaned closer to her, close enough for him to smell the perfume she'd put on in the kitchen. She drew little circles with her fingers in the waxy buildup of furniture oil on the bar while she spoke. She was sure he was interested in her, but how were they to get together? If he got up to leave she'd have to ask him to stay.

At one-thirty he still sat on his stool, a good sign as long as he didn't bolt. Three other men sat at the bar, down at the far end. Two others sat in a booth. At one-forty-five the bar echoed the quiet of the night outside. Cassie walked over to Ron, not being afraid to smile. He'd put in his time. She cleaned up, hoping at least to be walked to the car, to be kissed good night. Maybe she'd invite him over to Sunday dinner. She rehearsed the directions to her house in her mind, trying to remember the official names for the roads she'd known all her life. She set her elbows on the bar and her chin in one hand hoping he'd get the courage up to say what was on his mind.

He said to her, "Do you remember a guy named Bill Williams?"

Cassie laughed. "William Williams? Who'd name their kid that?"

"Was in here a couple of weeks ago." He searched for something in his breast pocket. "Maybe this will help." Ron slid a crisp new one-hundred-dollar bill toward Cassie, keeping it flat against the bar. "It's how much he paid you to turn a trick." Ron rested his chin on his hand. He smiled at her. "I want the same deal."

"Why do you want to do that?" Cassie said. "I mean, I thought we sort of hit it off?" In a couple of weeks he could have her and a whole lot more for nothing, just a little love, just some affection and it'd be returned tenfold?

Ron laid his left hand on the bar. He'd been drinking with his right all night. He slowly spun the gold band on his third finger.

"Why don't you go back to your wife?" Cassie said.

"I plan to next Wednesday, but now I'm with you. You know a hundred dollars is pretty steep. I know, I work vice in Pittsburgh."

"Then go to Pittsburgh." He hadn't cared at all, not at all, and she'd been strutting her stuff like a common whore. But it was a hundred dollars, and he was good-looking and she hadn't had sex that she'd enjoyed in a long time.

"Wednesday," Ron said. He kept his finger on the bill, but didn't pull it back.

"Fine," Cassie said sharply. She picked up the bill. "Where're you staying?" Cassie decided to forget about the one hundred dollars, pretend it didn't exist, make love to him for herself.

Cassie drove straight over to the motel this time, not wavering one bit, not even thinking about turning around. She was going to get laid and that was that.

Cassie lay on the bed afterwards, her chest heaving, thinking how good it was to have sex again and something else, to not have to worry about whether the man lying next to her would be a good husband or a bad one. She swung her legs off the bed.

"You leaving?" Ron asked.

"The deal's done." She wanted him to talk her back into bed.

He ran his finger along her bare shoulder. "You know, you're actually pretty good at this."

The finger across her shoulder could have gotten her back, until he'd spoken. She shrugged his hand away.

"I mean it." Ron rolled over on his back. "I know these things. You're good-looking. There'd be no competition."

She slid her underwear up her legs. "How many men did Williams tell?" How many more men would be expecting to get her in bed for a hundred?

Ron sat up pulling the blanket over him. "Not many. A few. Look, I see whores every day."

"I'm not a whore. If anybody's the whore it's you." Cassie pulled on her shirt. As far as she was concerned, Ron was the last. She'd been stupid taking chances like this.

"You're right, all men are whores," he said. "In Pittsburgh you'd really be something. You could go high class. If you know what I mean."

Cassie stuffed her bra into her purse. "I suppose you could fix me up?"

"I could. If you do decide to go pro. I'm at Pavlock's Cafe at least once a day. I could fix you up with someone who could make a lady out of you, if you know what I mean."

She slid into her jeans, her back to him. "You going to pimp me? Thanks, but no thanks. I got to go." Was this the best she could be? Maybe it was the best the world would let her have.

"I'll tell you this, you could be making a lot of money around here if you halved your price. For fifty bucks you'd have a lot more customers."

Cassie spoke unemotionally. "You going to spread the word?"

"I could do that, discreetly," he said.

Cassie nodded. She thought about it, what she had to offer. She could work at Darnel's for the rest of her life and never have two pennies to rub together. What else could she do that paid so well? She was going to have to work the rest of her life, leave her babies for someone else to raise. At least she could give them nice things. Without looking at Ron she buttoned her jeans, slid into her loafers, put her coat on and left.

Chapter 20

Cody stood beside his mother's bed, his big eyes dark brown wells of clear water, staring at her with rapt attention. How deeply innocent his soul was still, she thought. What little he understood of his poverty and his few choices. Did he know how close he had come to starving, malnutrition, to freezing? Had he been so deeply frightened he could not bring it out, could not say it, afraid if he voiced the thought it would make it happen? No, he didn't. He was safe for now. Love is knowing how far you'll sink for someone.

"Mommy, breakfast?" He was talking now.

"Sure, honey, and afterwards we'll go visit Aunt Dot." She pulled him into bed. He giggled and crawled under the covers. Just another hour's sleep and she would be fine, but she could hear Jimmy standing in his crib making his little bubbly noises like a baby tractor. In a few minutes he would start to shout, then speak to himself in his own language as if he were complaining nobody loved him.

Dot stacked some papers, banging the edges on her desk. "So, Cass, what brings you and your boys down here today?" Before Cassie answered, Dot said to Cody, "And how are you today, my big boy?" Cody hid his face in the crook of Cassie's arm. "Oh, now don't get shy with your Aunt Dottie."

Cassie pulled her son to her. "I got a small problem. I'll just tell you straight out. I think I found—well, I found a man I sort of like. Yeah, but you know, you know how it is now. I mean I'm no schoolgirl no more, that's for sure."

Dot raised her eyebrows and laughed a short muffled laugh through her nose.

"Yeah, maybe," Cassie said. "But I don't need no more little gifts." She gestured toward her boys.

"Gifts? Oh, gifts," Dot said. "No, no more gifts. So you need birth control?"

Cassie nervously brushed Cody's hair with her fingers. "Yeah, but I don't really know how to go about it. I can't go to my doctor. He'd never approve, me being without a husband and all. He'd just tell me to make him marry me first and I found out how that works. I'm thinking this might be a better way."

"Okay," Dot said. She put the phone up to her ear. "Go to mine. I'll call and get you in." Dot searched through a small leather notebook, and then dialed. "That's what I always liked about you, Cass. You take charge of your own life. Too many women around here think that God will provide, or that it's all a plan, or they just don't give two shits."

Cassie dropped her boys off at her parents' and drove the fifty miles to Dot's doctor, who explained to her how the pills worked and their side effects. Bigger breasts didn't seem like a bad side effect, but the others worried her. On the way home she calcu-lated—two years and she'd be done with it and men altogether, go to college maybe become a social worker like Dot, something, or a doctor, or a lawyer, maybe a botanist, or work for the State Agriculture Department.

Cassie arrived at her parents' home in time to have dinner. Her mother spoke less and less to her daughter, not being happy about Cassie having taken the job at the bar. Cassie got home in time to get her boys settled before witnessing the ritual of Amy ascending the repaired stairs, still thinking about what her mother expected of her—to go to church, find a God-fearing man, preferably poor and pious, marry again. There weren't any left. She grabbed her coat, barked instructions to Amy, who waved her acknowledgement, jogged down to her car, and headed down the valley toward Darnel's.

Men came in for Cassie through the seasons. Cassie could spot most of them before they sat down on the stool at the end of the bar. From a distance, they quietly searched her with their eyes. If someone sat on the stool, they sat somewhere within sight of it, and late at night they'd slide onto the stool, drink in one hand, their finger on a fifty or two twenties and a ten. Most never asked, only pushed the bills forward. Sometimes she'd pick them up and ask "Where?" Sometimes she'd leave the bills alone if she didn't like the looks of the man. Still, sometimes she had to slide the bills back at them.

By the time summer came and the business slowed, both Darnel's and hers, Cassie had caught up on her bills, had a good garden in, and a small electric water heater tucked in the front closet with an honest-to-god well. She'd stuffed more money into a mayonnaise jar, inside a coffee can she'd buried under the front porch. She even had a checking account where she kept a bit of money, hopefully not enough to make anyone suspicious. Uncle Bill was considering adding a room onto the back for a bathroom and a place for a washer and dryer, happy he was receiving full rent and on time, now hinting about working out a deal with her to take the place off his hands, but she had other plans. Still, she was thinking of building a shed off the back and putting in a chest freezer. Her father had agreed to help her build one, but there was only a fifty-fifty chance of him getting to it. She'd do it herself. There was enough deer in the woods to keep her and her boys in meat all next year without having to spend her savings on store bought. She'd bought a new rifle, a 30.06, big enough to bring down a deer.

In high summer Cassie preferred to be home with her children tending her garden, picking berries and canning, but she needed a newer car. She had enough extra money to float through the lean season before hunting began again. Still, Cassie was happy when the cold weather came and the canning was done. She'd gotten a better car, but not the shed, freezer, or bathroom. Jimmy was walking and Cody was talking a mile a minute. If business was as good as last year, they'd have a real Christmas, but more so, she'd be gone by next fall.

Small game season arrived in September and some hunters

were back limbering up their skills, getting cabins aired out and new truck campers broken in. Soon turkey was in season and the hunters were holding their own at the bar with the locals at Darnel's.

Heavy snow clouds had built and the setting sun tinted the air a strange pink the evening Gabe slid lithely into an empty booth, his body hardened by another year of manual labor and the loss of his youth. Cassie stood on her toes and waved excitedly. "Hi, Gabe. What do you want?" she asked, suddenly wondering why they hadn't gotten together in several years and then the memories of those years came flooding back and she remembered why.

"Just a beer," he said. His eyes were sunken deeper in his gaunt face. He'd shaved off the beard, but his mustache had grown thicker and his hair started down his back, tied off in a short ponytail.

Cassie drew the draft and walked it over. "Next time you're going to have to get it yourself, but seeing how this is your first time here, I'll do you a favor."

Gabe flashed a weak smile.

"You know I'm really sorry about not keeping in touch," she said. "It's been a little tough for the last year and a half. I've been pretty much a prisoner." If she had only known what she knew now, she'd have dragged Gabe to the altar, or at least taken up Davey's offer.

Jake had left the hills and state moving to Charlotte, married. His brother Chet stopped in during hunting season to track down the big-stakes card games the city men played. He'd grown tall and slender, but with a presence that exuded danger. She'd heard, through a few of her clients, that he fleeced the hunters pretty well and had, several times, been on the receiving end of their ire.

"So, where's Suzy?" she asked.

"In jail. The news ain't got here yet, I see." Gabe swept his hand over his hair checking his ponytail. "It's on the radio and everything. Not much, but they mention it, her name and everything. Most times those guys in the city wouldn't know if the earth opened up and swallowed us whole, but they got this one."

Cassie sat the beer on the table, forgetting about the napkin in her other hand. "Is it bad?" She shouted into the kitchen, "Darnel, I need my break. Come on out." She tossed the crumpled napkin on the bar.

Darnel shouted from the kitchen, "Damn it, Cass, now?" Darnel stepped out of the kitchen wiping his hands on his dirty apron.

Cassie sat down opposite Gabe. "Okay, what's going on?"

Gabe leaned back against the straight wooden booth. "She killed her old man. Stabbed him to death with a carving knife."

Cassie gasped. "Hell, God, Gabe, why?"

Gabe took a drink, wiping the foam off his mustache. "He'd been raping her off and on since she was twelve. That's what they told the judge, but I always sort of suspected it. It was always too easy for her to get his money. The pants were always at the end of the bed. That's why it got on the news. Good old hillbilly incest."

Cassie pushed her hair behind her ears. "Why now and not years ago?"

"They say she just went nuts. Didn't have any idea she'd done him in." Gabe glanced around the room at the men sitting hunched over their drinks at the bar, and those standing, elbows leaning and work boots up on the polished foot rail. "She's pregnant."

Cassie leaned over to him. "He got her pregnant? Oh God. Well, it ain't like he was her real father."

"It ain't his. He hadn't touched her in a while. Long enough for her to know. I think he went sort of crazy when she let it out she was pregnant. She's saying it's Ricky's." Gabe pulled a pack of cigarettes out of his pocket, stuck the filter end in his mouth and lit it with his Zippo. He threw the pack on the table. "He's going to Georgia now, first year of law school or something. I drove her down to see him once in a while."

Cassie picked up the pack and kicked one out. She wished she hadn't started smoking again. Smoking had just seemed the natural thing to do in her new line of work. "Does R.C. know?"

Gabe held his flame under her cigarette. The lighter clicked as Gabe closed it. "He knows it all. His father's defending her. He's come home to help get her out of jail. She's going to be living with them now, in their custody or something like that. Probably there as we speak."

Cassie sat back. She blew smoke above Gabe's head at a spot in the air, taking a minute to say it, wondering if she should, knowing that she had to. "Is it his?" Gabe turned away and looked out at the bar. Cassie leaned over to look at his face. "It isn't, is it?"

"Shit, Cass, that's what they call you now, I hear?"

She nodded her head.

"Her mother loved her, but that didn't stop her from letting her husband fuck her little girl for all those years. I mean, Suzy can't help it with all she's been through. She wanted out." Gabe slowly turned his glass around, watching the bottom rim lay a moisture circle on the table. "Cass, you ever hear of a cow bird?"

"Sure, I know what a cow bird is. It lays its eggs in another bird's nest."

"It does that because it knows the babies are better off with someone else." Gabe fingered his cigarette. The smoke lazily twist up through the heated winter air. "If I worked my ass off for the rest of my life I could never give Suzy or the kid what R.C. will be able to give them. Hell, even if she don't marry him, which it looks like she will, the child-support check the kid will get out of R.C., being a lawyer like his old man, will probably be more than I'll ever make." He stubbed his cigarette out in the ashtray. "Besides I just thought you'd want to know and that the

Cantrells keep pretty good track of you. I hear they know someone in Social Services. Watch your ass."

"Great, that's all I need." Cassie butted her cigarette. "Now they can know how poor I am. I should of never taken that check. It's hardly enough money anyhow, damn it."

Gabe slid out of the booth. He tossed a five-dollar bill on the table.

Cassie slid out behind him. "I'll get your change." He waved her off. Cassie hugged him. "Everything always works out for the better."

"Yeah, you're right—for some people. Others are pretty much fodder." Gabe stepped out into the snowy night.

Cassie packed up her sons early the next morning, making a surprise trip to her parents' house. "Ma," Cassie yelled, as she nudged Cody through the door. Cody ran to his grandma who picked him up and hugged him.

Her mother's jaw tightened when she saw Cassie. Her gaze ran the length of her daughter, scrutinizing her new clothes and makeup. "What brings you here?"

Cassie's father called from the living room, "Is my boy here?"

"Grandpa," Cody yelled. He ran into the living room still dressed for the outside.

"Ma," Cassie said, ignoring her mother's disapproving glance. "I got to go to town. Something terrible has happened to Suzy."

"We heard. Teresa stopped by." Cassie's mother turned away from her. "Cody," she called. "Come out here and get your coat off." Cody ran back to his grandmother. She said, "You got good kids here. You ought to be staying home with them and not associating with trash like that." Cassie's mother took off Cody's coat, mittens, hat, and boots. She patted him on his behind, sending him back to his grandfather. "It's bad enough you work in that place."

Cassie handed her mother Jimmy. "We went over this before. It's the best I can get."

Her mother held Jimmy who kicked and giggled while Cassie took off his coat, mittens, and hat. "You could get a decent man. You could make amends. Couldn't of been all Judd's fault."

"Ma." Cassie sighed. "Ma, I need to see Suzy. I got to know what happened. I got to let her know she's got someone. We don't abandon our friends just because they've become sinners. You know that. Bye, Pa," Cassie called.

He father called out from the living room, "Bye, Cassie."

Cassie drove into town to Ricky's parents' house. She parked her car behind a new station wagon on one of the few paved driveways in town. She rang the doorbell.

Suzy answered the door wearing a long shapeless brown dress and no makeup. "Cassie," she squealed. Suzy pulled Cassie hard to her. Suzy's hair had been re-dyed back to its original dark brown. "Oh," she said, looking back into the house. "Come on in."

"Who's that?" someone called from the back of the house.

"It's a high-school friend, mother." Suzy rolled her eyes. She brought Cassie through the house upstairs to a large bedroom at the end of the hall. They sat on a full-size bed with a football-printed spread neatly covering it. Cassie had never seen a room like it. The room had a padded leather chair, a desk, with a library lamp, two overstuffed chairs sat opposite a television and a stereo outfit as tall as Suzy. Bookshelves with model airplanes, cars, and sets of leather-bound books with gold lettering, ran down the inner wall. A thick brown carpet covered the floor, and posters of baseball players hung framed on the wall. And still, the room smelled flowery. The whole house smelled of flowers.

"It's R.C.'s. I mean R.C.'s and mine now. Ain't it great?" Suzy whispered. "It's bigger than half our old house. Look at this." She marched Cassie over to a door and swung it open. Beyond sat a full bathroom with a sink inside its own cabinet. Lights surrounded a long mirror. A modern tub sat opposite the sink and next to it was a walk-in shower large enough for two adults.

"Come here," Suzy said. They walked into another room half the size of Cassie's bedroom, a closet with rows of clothes. They were extra clothes Ricky hadn't bothered taking to college. Three suits were covered with heavy dry-cleaning bags. She'd only known her father to have three suits since she'd been born.

"Oh, my God. Real people don't live like this."

Suzy walked back into the bedroom and climbed onto the bed. "No, real people don't live like us."

Cassie sat on the bed next to her. "Hell, Suzy, what the hell happened?"

"What the hell happened?" Suzy said. "What the hell you do with your husband?"

"Me?" Cassie said. The bed was soft, but it seemed to resist her weight.

"Yeah, you. Either Judd Cantrell is dead and buried in the woods, or you put a scare into him that made him run like a rabbit, and I ain't never seen Judd run."

"I didn't kill him, that's for sure. Oh, God, Suzy," Cassie said. "I didn't mean that." Cassie hoped Suzy hadn't gotten the idea from the rumors about her.

"It's okay." Suzy folded her legs under her. "Truth is, I didn't know I'd done it. I still don't. I just come home from visiting R.C. I spent the weekend and Gabe picked me up."

Cassie whispered, "Is that before or after you knew you were carrying Gabe's baby?"

Suzy leaned against the myriad of pillows. Her eyes scanned the long rows of books. "So he told you. Is he going to screw this thing up? I'll swear I never slept with him, I will. Love ain't enough. I got to get out of it, out of this cycle that keeps putting everyone in poverty." Suzy lay flat on her back and stared up at the ceiling. "Someone's got to do it. My momma knew nothing but poverty, and her momma knew nothing but poverty. It's got to stop somewhere." Suzy turned to look at a draped window. "I remember arguing with R.C. about getting married. I remember arguing with Gabe about that, too. Only he wanted to and R.C. didn't. That's all. Next thing I woke up in the police car. Oh, God, I saw all this blood all over me and I thought I'd been shot or stabbed. I started screaming and everything. They had to stop the car. One of the sheriffs held me until I got to jail."

"Gabe won't say anything." Cassie propped herself up on her elbows. She could get used to a bed like this, a room like this. How wonderfully comfortable it all was. "Tell me one thing, Suzy. Who do you love? That's all I want to know. If you really love R.C. then marry him. If you love Gabe, marry him. It's that simple."

Suzy's face drained to blankness. "You know better than that. Nothing's that simple. I'm incapable of loving anyone ever since that bastard started screwing me." Suzy sat up. She pulled the skirt of her dress above her knees to free her legs. "You know what it's like to just be getting tits, not even knowing what they're for, let alone why you got what you got between your legs, and some dirty old drunken bastard crawls on top of you in the middle of the night and splits you in half? And your own momma in the next room crying, afraid if she stops him he'll leave her." Suzy wrapped her arms around her legs, pulling them close. "Why do you think I screwed half the boys in school? To get back at him. To make it mine again. I'll do damn well with it as I please. If that means whoring myself out, so what." Suzy laid her chin on her knees. "You think Mrs. Carbone didn't do the same thing? You think half the women who marry rich guys don't do it? She's good-looking. I bet she was a knockout in college. You ever see R.C.'s father? He's as small as R.C. What the hell would someone like her want with him?" Suzy shook her head. "It's money, security. It's all the same. Some women take it in cash, or booze and cigarettes. Some take it in houses and jewelry."

Suzy had a point. What was the difference between what she did and what Mrs. Carbone did? It was the same thing. Women sold their bodies for the security of their families and future families. It'd always been that way.

Suzy lay down next to Cassie, her body against hers, making Cassie feel uncomfortable, a woman touching her on a bed. "Will you sit with Gabe at the trial? No matter how this turns out, he's going to feel bad."

Cassie nodded.

They talked for another hour. Cassie drove back to her mother's home. She and her boys had supper there. Cassie's mother didn't ask about Suzy. Her father did.

After Cassie related all the facts, her mother said, "It's becoming a Godless world with Godless children."

"Well, if it is," Cassie said, "then it's God that let us down. I didn't ask for what I got and Suzy sure the hell didn't ask for what she got."

Cassie took her boys home, put Jimmy to bed and played with Cody in the snow. When Cody was tucked in and well asleep, Cassie walked out on the porch and stared up at the stars. It was January of 1974 and the dreams were gone. She was twenty-one and only stark reality was left, only survival. The only men who'd been honest with her at all had been the ones giving her money for sex.

Again hunting season had been good to Cassie. The word had spread slowly and discreetly. She turned down less than she accepted. Sometimes she accepted two or three a night if there were time, but she still turned some away, which she liked. She finally had control of her life and her body. Some men, she felt nothing. Some were decent sex.

A month before Christmas, on a Monday, her only day off, Cassie drove all the way to Charleston. Her mother watched Jimmy while she and Cody spent the day shopping. They strolled from store to store in the brisk air flowing along with the crowd of people, more than Cassie had ever seen in one place at one time. The main shopping street was decorated for the holidays,

Christmas lights strung in long looping upside-down arches over the streets. Drivers honked horns. Buses sent out blasts of air after letting off and taking on passengers. Everybody rushed. Everyone seemed to expend a lot of energy; they lived so critically, almost a madness. Men in long expensive coats, clutching attaché cases, turned their heads to watch her walk by.

The stores were huge and decorated finer than the streets. Everything was new and bright. Cody's gaze jumped from one shiny object to another, Cassie worrying that it might be a bad thing to have him see all this, or to have him see all this and then go back to their isolated cottage. One store, taking up five stories of a building, had big bright signs decorated for the seasons stating, "Moving to New Location in North Park Mall," whatever that meant. Male shoppers stood behind racks of clothes and watched her shop. Some men even spoke to her. She replied politely, but not shyly. She knew these men now, knew them better than they knew themselves. She wasn't fooled by their smiles, their polite talk. They wanted to own her. She would let them, but only for fifty dollars' worth of time. For lunch, Cassie and Cody ate at a real McDonald's.

She steered the old car toward home in light snow, the windshield wipers clicking out of time with the music on the radio. She listened absentmindedly until she heard Harry Chapin singing "Cat's in the Cradle." The song was beautiful, but she hated it for the pain she felt. Who had a choice? How many good people had no choice but to spend their life working as much as humanly possible?

Cody slept in the back seat curled up with a small teddy bear, a pre-Christmas present. The long drive gave Cassie time to think. She'd finally arrived at a place where she controlled her own life, where she wasn't dependent on one man to take care of her or her boys. Maybe Ben had seen it? Judd was clueless. Jake certainly had. What was it they said, he'd gone to school, owned a business?

"A year," Cassie said out loud, as she turned off the interstate. "That's what I need, just another year. I'll save up the money and go back to school. Maybe this spring I'll get my GED. I can work, save enough to take the kids and move, go to college. I'm out of it in a year."

The clouds hid the setting sun. Cassie drove on as it grew dark, only knowing that she was going home.

All through Christmas Day her mother sat sullen, hardly speaking, the house coat placed back in the box with the new slippers as if disapproving of the way she'd thought Cassie had earned the money. Cassie thought about telling her mother the secret truth, not to hurt her, but only to claim final independence.

The jury selection for Suzy's trial was held over until after the holidays. Suzy invited Cassie to a New Year's party. Cassie stopped in for a few minutes before going to work. She thought Suzy to be stunning in her blue and sequins gown with a very low neckline and a lower back, showing off the sculptured muscles of a young country girl. Maybe she could pull this off as well as Mrs. Carbone. Ricky was distinguished in his tux. They appeared to be a very normal well-to-do couple, as long as nobody stood next to them. Mrs. Carbone had taken Suzy to a beauty parlor to have her hair professionally cut and styled. There seemed to be no country left to her. Cassie turned down three men at Darnel's that night.

The county courthouse sat on manicured grounds with the county jail and the Department of Motor Vehicles. Inmates, wearing denim-blue shirts and pants with a yellow stripe running down each leg shoveled the sidewalks. The courtroom's vastness, with a tall sculptured ceiling, made it feel empty, though there were at least fifty people sitting in the rows of benches, like pews, facing a huge desk that reminded Cassie of an altar in some cathedral, dwarfing the white-haired, black-robed man who sat at its top and looked over his glasses at everybody and everything.

Suzy wore simple dresses and no makeup during the trial. As far as Cassie could tell, Mr. Carbone tried to establish Suzy's innocence as a simple backwoods girl whose mind had been twisted by a sadistically perverted man, a man who forced himself on a girl who didn't know any better. The jury, eight men and four women sat expressionless. The judge showed no emotion. Suzy showed no emotion. Cassie sat with Gabe; both had a habit of nervously bouncing their legs up and down every few minutes. Ricky was back at school.

The prosecutor was a balding young man, efficient and cruel in his work. He entered into the record an affidavit of men who would attest they had slept with Suzy. Suzy's future father-in-law did not question it. He cross-examined Suzy's mother, the only witness. She was warned many times by the judge that if she answered the question, she could get in trouble with the law. He said she could refuse to answer, so she refused many times.

The only other witnesses were the two county deputies that arrested Suzy. They told how they had found her standing perfectly still with a knife in her hand over the half-naked body, blood pooling at her feet. The two men figured she'd been that way for at least a half-hour. Catatonic, Mr. Carbone called it— proof of temporary insanity.

Cassie peered down at her new high heels. Did anybody in these parts believe in temporary insanity, or insanity at all— touched maybe, an addled mind, but still, did they feel that was justification for taking a man's life? She really didn't think so. Insanity was just too common in the area. Rancy, Judd, Raph, Whitey, Crank—maybe they were all insane, every single one of them who lived in the mountains. Wasn't believing in ghosts, spooks, angels, God, divine intervention, fate, faith, goodness of man, all a type of insanity?

Cassie dropped off Cody and Jimmy every day at her mother's, to her mother's increasing agitation at Cassie publicly supporting such an immoral person. Suzy had been a sinner all her life and justice should be swift, her mother said. Cassie couldn't help think her mother implied something more.

Cassie took Wednesday off, telling Amy not to come and not to think she was still going to get paid for it. Cassie felt too tired to work, but she couldn't sleep. Something about the trial made her feel she was witnessing the end of an age, a passing of something into history.

The trial lasted five days, Monday to Friday. The jury left at one o'clock. For two hours Cassie and Gabe stood outside the courtroom drinking weak, dirty coffee from Styrofoam cups, tasting of a poorly washed coffee urn. Suzy stood with Mr. Carbone, his arm around her shoulder.

Gabe pointed with his cup. "Suzy's happy now. Got a real father now, a real future for her and her kid."

The jury returned at three o'clock. With others, Cassie and Gabe moved back into the courtroom. "Is it a good sign?" Cassie shivered, her stomach in knots. Maybe she'd become a lawyer. She certainly had to quit being a hooker or someday she'd be caught and then this place would swallow her up whole. Gabe shrugged. Why or what she'd done with the money wouldn't matter. "I got to be more careful." When Gabe turned his head toward her she said, "I'm scared."

"Me too. I don't care how tough she is, Suzy's got to be shitting her pants."

The judge asked the foreman of the jury to state the verdict. "Guilty," he said, "of manslaughter in the second degree." Suzy dropped into her chair covering her head with her arms.

Cassie burst into tears. She didn't know why. She thought she had braced herself for this. Gabe squeezed her hand. The judge banged his gavel and announced that in thirty days there would be a sentencing. Suzy made no effort to move when two women grabbed her under her arms. They half-carried, half-walked her out of the courtroom.

The world cleared for Cassie as if a veil had been lifted. The world belonged to men, here at least, and Suzy had killed a man, a male, the king of the household. What men did to you made little difference. If she got caught, she could expect the same. Jimmy had done the right thing by her, putting the gun against Judd's head. If she'd killed him, she'd be going to jail just like Suzy. If she'd turned Judd in, he would have gotten thirty days in jail and she would have gotten a worse beating when he got out. Suzy's old man would have gotten nothing for raping her.

Cassie drove back to her father's farm. Her eyes burned from anger. She was scared of what they would do to her, but she was angrier at what they'd already done to her and Suzy and all those rich, holier-than-thou bastards would never own up to it. They'd justified Suzy's father's actions by their insistence that women cleave to their husbands or fathers, and when she'd fought back they put her away. "The bastards convicted her. Can you believe it?" she said to her mother.

Her mother brought out Cody's winter coat and Jimmy's snowsuit. "Cassie, they done what was right. She killed a man. It's against God's laws. It's the wages of sin. When will you change your ways?"

Cassie held Jimmy tightly to her. "My ways? What the hell are you talking about? You know, you've had a burr under you now for some time. Why don't you just come out and say what's got you so pissed off."

Her mother walked over to the window and peered out. She turned back toward Cassie. "You think I'm just an old woman that don't know nothing, but I can add things up pretty well. I know you don't get clothes like that and pay off your bills on bar wages and tips. I'm saying, the wages of sin, Cassie." Her mother pulled a wool hat over Cody's head and stuck his mittens on. "You got two good children that maybe you don't deserve. Lord knows they deserve better than what they'll be branded."

Cassie smiled down at Cody. She pushed him by his shoulder toward the door. "Go out and play for a minute, okay, honey?"

Cody grinned, nodded his head and walked out into the snow. Cassie turned to her mother. "Who are you to tell me what I deserve or not? These are my kids and I take care of them well by myself."

"And you shouldn't be. You got no business living by yourself up there in the hills. You got no business doing what you're doing." The light from the window backlit her mother's head. "Face it, Cassie, you're a floozy, nothing but a floozy and you ain't even ashamed of it. Look at you with all your makeup and tight skirts and blouses not even half buttoned, showing the world everything you got."

Cassie laughed at the words, but they stung like a hard slap. "Why don't you just spit it out, Ma."

"I can't say it. If I say it I'll believe it. Why don't you just take that makeup off and get some decent clothes. Come back to church and find a good man who'll take care of you before something bad happens." Her mother reached over to wipe Cassie's face with her thumb.

Cassie pulled away. "You want me to find a good man? Someone who'll drink up all his paycheck or spend it on some woman he's fucking every Saturday night, and then come home and beat the shit out of me because I couldn't make one paycheck last where four ought to?" Cassie tried to seem strong, but her voice rose tight and shrill. "Maybe I can find a man like Pa who'll only work two weeks out of a month, barely clothing or feeding his own children, letting the world look down on them like they were dirt."

"Don't you be saying nothing about your father," her mother said. She wiped the makeup from her thumb onto her dress, leaving a long beige streak. "He done right by you."

Cassie opened the breezeway door. Cold air rushed in through the outside door Cody had left cracked open. "No, Ma, it's all the men who made me like this. No, even worse, it's the place and all the people around here, all those church-going, God-fearing people, always telling me to submit and now you're calling me a whore. Say it, Ma. I'm a whore, a prostitute, a call girl. Then I've always been, one way or another, and you've always been one too because you put up with the shit people hand you. Suzy's the only woman who ain't a whore because she's finally refused to take this world's shit." Tears fell from her mother's eyes. Cassie hadn't wanted to cry, not here anyway, but her life in this house was over. "Don't you worry about me, Ma," she said, angrily wiping the tears away. "Not one bit. This whore won't be darkening your doorway again."

Cassie walked out to her car, calling out for Cody to follow. As she backed her car out of the driveway, she saw her mother staring at her from the kitchen window.

In the small visitors' room, Cassie sat in front of a yellow, oak desk with an ashtray bolted to it. The desk had been stained almost black in two large arcs opposite each other where, for years, elbows and forearms of prisoners and loved ones had reached.

A tall woman with orange hair brought Suzy into the room. Suzy's blue prison dress, with the name of the jail stenciled on the front and back, wide and collarless, threatened to slip off her shoulders. It hung to mid-calf. Her small arms stuck out of the oversized sleeves like thin twigs. She clutched a pack of cigarettes and matches. Her face had paled to a weak gray, her hair washed but not set, lying limply on her head. She wore no makeup or stockings, just low slip-on shoes.

Suzy smiled when she saw Cassie, no hint of collusion, no act, no hope. "Hi, Cass. Some mess I got myself into, huh?"

Cassie smiled back. "It'll be all right."

Suzy sat down in the other straight-backed wooden chair. "Sure, I could get life."

"Don't say that. Gabe said Mr. Carbone could get you an appeal."

"Why should he? He's got me right where he wants me." She

sighed. "I know when I've been had," Suzy finally said. "They'll keep me in here just long enough for Ricky to forget about what it's like to be in bed with me and find a good college girl, one long on bloodline, short on looks. They do a blood test, the kid's gone."

"They won't do that." Cassie didn't know what they'd do. But how could those people in their expensive homes and cars, with their big bank accounts, call either one of them a criminal? "It was all cut and dried to them wasn't it?"

Suzy exhaled at the ceiling. She blinked hard three times to clear her eyes. "I figure they all got together over lunch and figured this thing all out. The trial was just a play like we did in school, only the actors were a lot better. I should of got myself a real lawyer. What'd Carbone call it? Mitigating circumstances, temporary insanity? Shit, it's probably the only time I'd ever been sane. I don't know. I don't remember." Suzy sat back in her chair. "You know, I wish I was bull-shitting, but this is how life works. It's the first time I've been out of control since the first night he raped me. I got a real clear head the day after that. I knew who I was and what it was going to take to survive. You know, my mother didn't even have the courage to look at me the next day, let alone stop it. All she did was walk around the house balling to beat the band." Suzy reached out and grabbed Cassie's hand. "Cassie, they didn't convict me of killing the bastard. They convicted me of surviving. They could give a shit whether my old man lived or died. They just don't want trash moving up. Killing him was my mistake. Yeah," Suzy said, "I invited him in my bed a bunch of times. It saved on the beatings. He would of come anyhow and took it by force. But I always took it back a couple days later, in the hayloft or a car. Can you understand that?"

Cassie nodded. "Yes." That was how she felt now. Taking money from men and not being forced to sleep with them made her feel the same way. It was her body and if she sold it, so what? They didn't have to buy.

"They sent me to jail because I made a fool out of all of them. They won't even punish R.C. for slumming. Can't you see, they don't blame my old man or R.C. I'm trash."

The matron stared at the wall. Cassie said, "Don't say that. They can't be that cruel. How do they expect us to live?" Someday soon she'd have to quit, or she'd be on the other side of the desk and they'd be doing the same thing to her. There were locals now. The word was spreading slowly.

Suzy rubbed Cassie's arm nervously. "Oh, God, I don't think I can do it." The edges of her mouth twitched. "Twelve to twenty, that's what they're saying."

"You can," Cassie said. "You're damn near twenty-two now. That's twenty-two years you've served already. Twelve ain't nothing for you." Cassie ran her fingers up Suzy's inner arm feeling the soft sun-hidden skin.

Suzy's chin quivered. "Oh, God, Cass, it could be twenty-five years. I'll be forty-five when I get out."

Cassie laughed. "Don't say that. You can get time off for good behavior."

Suzy laughed, but tears were forming in her eyes. "Shit, I'll have to screw half the guards and the warden. Hope he's a man."

"Look," Cassie said, "play their game. Do your time, keep quiet, and get out. We've both done it before. Get your kid, and then get the hell out of here. Go as far away as you can, forever."

"Time," the matron called.

Suzy stood up walking to the side of the desk, clutching Cassie's hand, pulling Cassie to her. Suzy stared up into Cassie's eyes, running her right hand along Cassie's arm up behind her neck, pulling Cassie's head gently down and kissing her on the lips.

Cassie's first thought was to pull away, but she understood what the kiss really meant. There was a love between them, deeper than what any man had loved either one of them. Cassie kissed Suzy back. She wrapped her arms around Suzy's small body, bending over her. They held each other for a moment, and then Suzy walked toward the guard. She shrugged her bare right shoulder and waited for the matron to unlock the door. Suzy hand-waved good-bye. Cassie smiled and waved back as Suzy walked out of the room to wait for the sentencing. Cassie drove back home to continue her life.

On the day of the sentencing, Suzy traipsed into the courtroom, her hands cuffed in front of her. She strode between two tall women who had a time keeping up with her, her steps defiant, her hips swinging side to side, her head held high, her gaze meeting anyone's who had the will to stare, but in the end it made little difference to the men, Carbone, the prosecutor and the judge.

Carbone made an appeal for leniency. The prosecutor made a half-hearted attempt at painting Suzy as lascivious. Suzy was sentenced to twelve to twenty-five in the state correctional facility for women. When the final gavel fell, Cassie had the feeling that the sentence had been decided a long time ago.

Gabe sighed. "Well, at least I'll know where she's at now. I know that's rotten, but after she has the kid and the Carbones take it, who knows?"

The two of them walked toward the door, out of the courtroom to the rotunda. Cassie said, "They're going to take it?"

Gabe waited until Cassie walked through, and then followed. "Yeah, Suzy said it was all arranged. They walked under the marble rotunda, across the polished marble floor. "There's going to be a blood test. You can bet on that. Those things aren't foolproof. Raph's had a couple. Half the time they don't prove nothing. If they don't prove you ain't the daddy, then you are."

They stepped down the marble stairs. "What if it does prove R.C. ain't?" Cassie asked.

"I'll step forward. Tell them I always thought I was the daddy. Take it off their hands."

"What if it doesn't?" Cassie asked. "You going to wait twelve to twenty-five?"

Gabe held the door open to the outside. "No, she could be out in less than seven. Have a brother like mine and you know a lot about the law. I didn't tell anyone that. I suppose she'll learn it soon enough, but she's got to figure out Ricky ain't going to marry her. I ain't waiting seven. I figure prison ought to soften her up a little bit. I mean it's got to be better than what she had at home. It'd be okay with me if we had a prison wedding."

The two of them walked across the paved parking lot, walking several feet from each other. "You are a devious one there, Gabe."

Gabe smiled before unlocking his car door. "I learned from the best."

The massive building stood behind them. "Oh, God, Gabe, we're so alone."

"No, Cass, don't say that. It's when we give in to them and let them do what they want with us that it's over. Remember that, always."

Cassie nodded. Gabe got in his black car and drove away, squealing the tires out of the parking lot and down the street. Cassie glanced back at the tall building with the dome and the granite spike jutting straight into the sky as if trying to pierce the placid blue.

Chapter 21

A month after they took Suzy, springtime came—early spring between the melting snow and planting time, a wet cold time when the sun doesn't rise, but the night bleaches into a watery day. There were customers at the bar and customers after the bar closed. Cassie lost sleep, but there was the money, and as it came in and she stuffed it into the already stuffed jar under the porch, the flutter in her chest she'd had, maybe all her life but certainly since coming home with Jimmy, seemed to fade. She sat on the wet lawn and dug out the mayonnaise jar and counted the money, breathing in a slow clear breath and then deliberately breathing it out again.

And now trout season and spring turkey season were here. Darnel knew his business and unwittingly helped Cassie know her business, too. Things would slow down in the next month until the opening of bass season. More locals had picked up the thread, passed it to the outsiders who passed it back to the locals that the bartender at Darnel's could be had for, now, seventy-five dollars. She'd have been glad if her business would have been legitimate. Word of mouth was always the best advertising in the hills, but she needed to keep a lid on it for just another year. With the money she'd saved, a year would give her a grubstake to get out of the hills and start a new life.

On the mornings when Cody played quietly and Jimmy in his playpen, she sat on the porch as the day unfold in the mountains. Whose was it, really? The paradox bothered her so. Those who loved the life were crushed under the weight of it all. Those who cared nothing for the timelessness of a way of life, the rapture of living hand in hand with nature, ripped and tore a living from the land, giving nothing back and living well. But then it was their televisions, their fancy cars, their big houses, vacations, and clothes that made them happy. She'd get her GED between late

July and early September. Find a community college for two years and then a four-year college. She'd heard that's what Jake had done. She couldn't be a lawyer. She'd miss her boys growing up.

Men crowded the bar. Another long tiring night and Cassie was exhausted, the week long but profitable. She glanced over her right shoulder to see who'd walked in after hearing the familiar creak of the door opening, recognizing the first man as Chet McCullom. A tall well-groomed man followed him, someone she wouldn't think would be associated with Chet. The realization of the identity of the man caused Cassie to press herself against the back bar. She would have rushed into the kitchen, maybe to her car and home if she could have gotten her legs to move, but she needed to stand her ground, to earn money for her children and what would come would come.

He'd changed, but it was still Jake even through the expensive car coat hanging open showing a three-piece suit underneath. His hair was styled, but most of all he walked confidently through the bar as if all his shy country ways were gone, as if he feared no one or nothing.

A patron called three times before Cassie heard him. She poured the man's drink as Jake and his brother slid into a booth. Now was a time of reckoning and she'd been caught unprepared.

Chet strolled up to the bar and wedged himself between two men. "I'll have a draft," he said. "My brother will have a Dewars on the rocks."

Most locals didn't specify the brand, only whether it would be scotch or bar whiskey. Because city hunters liked the expensive stuff, Darnel kept a couple bottles, just in case.

Cassie tried to read Chet's face—did he know—had he told Jake? The room buzzed with sound and heat. She sucked in a hard breath at the thought Jake had come to buy her. Their first time was one of the few memories she still cherished. If he even tried, the memory would be gone.

Less than a minute after Cassie set the drinks on the bar a well-manicured hand with a wrist encircled with a gold watch and bracelet, held a twenty out to her.

She glanced quickly at Jake, smiling, her makeup and eyeliner feeling palpably heavy as if a mask. Cassie pulled the bill from his hand with her thumb and finger bringing back the change and counting it out as if he was just another customer. "There you go," she said. He dropped a five on the bar. She smiled at him but the tip stung even though it was expected.

Jake smiled back. He said, "How are you, Cassie?"

"Fine," she said. "And how are you, Jake?"

"Well," he said. Chet reached around his brother and grabbed his beer. He flicked a salute to both of them. Maybe a few seconds, maybe a whole minute passed between them before Jake laughed. "I'm usually not at a loss for words. I'm a broker. I've got my own investment business." Jake twisted the gold ring around on his left hand and looked away as if he hadn't planned to say what he'd said.

"Looks like you're doing all right for yourself." Cassie nodded at the watch, finding she disliked his wife, though she didn't know why. Maybe because Jake would never have spent money on such expensive things as fancy watches and bracelets or car coats. She had to be a city girl, someone from Charlotte or Charleston.

Jake tucked the watch under his coat sleeve and shrugged. His wife was spending his money, money Cassie felt she and Jake had suffered so much for. Cassie rinsed a couple of glasses and set them on a towel to dry. "Married, I see. Tried that one, didn't work out."

Jake took a slow deep swallow of his drink. She knew drinkers, those who practiced the craft, and the way he swallowed the liquor meant he'd been doing it for some time. Something else his wife had changed about him or maybe just city living had done all of it.

"Know what you mean," Jake said. "Sorry, I didn't mean anything by that." He reached inside his suit jacket and pulled out a large black wallet. He flipped out several photos, professional portraits of a wife and baby. "Only that every couple goes through rough times. My wife just gave birth to our first, Chloe."

Cassie picked up a photo of the baby and her mother. "She's beautiful—the baby. Well, the wife too." Cassie stared at the woman in the picture. The woman possessed beauty, but not the type she thought might attract Jake. She seemed too placid, not so much refined as lacking any definable character, as if the woman had worked very hard at being like everyone else who had a set of conventional options dictated by others. "I'm so happy for you, Jake," Cassie said, but now seeing him again, she wanted a crack in the porcelain of his life. Cassie held up her finger to say wait a minute; "I'll be right back." She walked down the bar checking drinks, trying to give herself time to figure out what she was really feeling. If given half a chance, she could steal him back or at least get him to cheat on his wife. She knew men, but she really knew Jake. It was wrong, but the world had taken him from her and she wanted revenge. As she walked back to him, she decided to let him have his perfect life. She took his empty glass and refilled it, waving off the payment. "So what brings you way out here?" When she looked at his face, his eyes still looking like a young boy's, she wasn't so sure she could let him go. She wanted some of her old life back, some of the innocence and belief. She wanted a good father for her boys.

He sipped the drink, and then smiled. "Visiting. Chet said he had a little surprise."

The air rushed from Cassie's lungs. Her throat refused to let more into her body. She was now sure Chet knew. It was a cruel joke. She was the cruel joke. "Jake." The business of the bar echoed around her, its clamor now taking on the weight of separation, her life from his as if he'd wandered into some awful space between heaven and hell.

"It's nice to see you again, Cassie. I didn't realize I'd missed you so much. How's the family?"

The question sounded absurd compared to what was going on around them, men drinking in earnest, lives balanced on a wire between survival and catastrophe. "Jake, sometimes things happen and we got to do what we got to do to survive."

His face paled. Jake stared at his drink. "I'm sorry," he said. "I know it was pretty lousy, leaving you like that. I should have come back." He brushed his hand through his hair. Some fell back over his forehead.

She wanted to reach over and brush it back for him, to touch him, to say she was sorry.

"I thought of coming back and asking you to forgive me a hundred times," he said. "I guess I knew you wouldn't have gone and I was just too weak to stay."

"No, that's not what I meant," Cassie said. Why hadn't she gone after him? Hell, she thought, she'd go with him now, wherever he wanted her to go.

"I know you won't believe this, but thinking of you got me through some hard times. Then I heard the news you'd gotten married and had a child."

"Well," Cassie said. She spit out a short laugh. "It was almost the other way around. God, did I screw that up. But I didn't mean that."

"No, let me finish," he said. "Maybe we both married the wrong people."

The words shocked her more than if he'd said he loved his wife with all his heart. "Don't say that, Jake. She's so beautiful."

Jake swallowed the rest of his drink. "Maybe you're right? I shouldn't have said that. I got what I deserved. She's selfish and self-centered. All she cares about is money and what it can buy." He stared at Cassie for a minute. "Seeing you seems so good. I never realized how much I missed you."

"Don't, Jake, I'm not worth it, really." She wanted to take his hand to comfort him. She knew how to comfort men now, but if she took it she'd never let go. Another part of her screamed to do whatever she had to in order to get him back. If that woman was foolish enough to give her an opening, she should make the most of it. Cassie reached to the back bar picking up the Dewars, refilling his drink. A man like Jake should watch how much he drank and she should tell him that, but if he were drunk stealing him would be easier.

Jake glanced down the bar at the other men who waited for drinks. He stood, clutching his glass staring into it for several seconds. "Nice seeing you again, Cassie."

He'd said it as if hoping this wouldn't be the last time they'd talk and she hoped the night wasn't over already, but if it were, she needed to leave him an opening. "Stop over to the house sometime. I live in the cottage behind my aunt and uncle."

"Really?" He smiled broadly.

Cassie returned his smile. They both remembered that time, their first time. "Tomorrow?"

"Tomorrow? I think I just might do that," he said.

"I'll fix dinner. We can sit on the porch and talk of old times."

"I'd like that. I miss the old time. Cassie, I miss you." Jake turned away a bit as if knowing he wasn't supposed to say that. "I'll be there." Jake stepped back over to the booth where his brother sat drinking his beer.

Cassie tried to busy herself, but her heart beat too quickly and she had the urge to laugh. Fine, it hadn't been perfect. They'd wandered a bit, but what they had could be resurrected. She'd happily pack up kit and kin and move to wherever he wanted. Once in a while she'd glance at Jake and Chet and prayed that her first fears had been wrong. *Chet,* she thought, *you don't screw this up for me and I'll be the best sister-in-law you'll ever have.*

But in less than ten minutes Jake yelled out, "Bullshit."

"Ask anybody," Chet yelled back.

"Fuck you," Jake said to his brother. Jake glared at Cassie as he walked out.

Chet slid from the booth. He laughed and walked down the bar toward the door, his arms held out. "Guy can't take a joke. Lucky we both drove." He leaned over the bar directly in front of Cassie. "Fucker deserves it. Not so all high and mighty now." He took three steps and stopped. "Guess I owe the barmaid a big tip." Chet searched his pockets. "Sorry, I'll have to catch you next time."

Cassie dropped the bar rag. She turned away from the men. Her reflection stared out at her from the mirror. Suddenly she didn't think she looked beautiful. She looked like what she was, a whore with a blouse a size too small, open halfway down her chest, the hem of her skirt higher than good taste called for and heavy makeup streaking across her eyelids. Rouge masked the natural color of her cheeks and her brows had been plucked to thin arcs above her eyes.

Cassie stumbled through the kitchen and out the back door. She braced her arm against the building, buried her head in the crook of her arm, and cried.

Darnel walked out behind her. "Are you okay?"

Cassie cried in loud rasping sobs. She shook her head. Darnel put his arm around her. "Go away," she gasped. "I'll be okay." She needed to get herself under control. Crying wasn't going to change a thing.

Darnel stood over her for a few minutes, not speaking, and then walked back into the kitchen of the bar. Cassie cried for a while; she didn't know how long it took until only whimpers were left, but redoing her makeup took another ten minutes. Staring into the small mirror in the women's restroom, she said, "You are what you are. There's no sense denying it." She needed three shots of real whiskey to continue her shift.

About eleven o'clock Ron slid onto the end barstool, a little early.

Cassie walked over to him. "What'll it be?"

"Hamburger and a cola."

Cassie took down a tall glass, bending over to scoop it half-full of ice, then filled it. "On the wagon?" She laid a small paper napkin down in front of Ron and sat the glass on it. He sipped the drink through his teeth, straining the soda from the cubes. Cassie peeked into the kitchen. "Darnel, burger, plain." She might refuse him, say she'd already been spoken for. He'd actually started it, gotten it going, maybe ruined her life, certainly destroyed her chances with Jake. Then again, Chet wouldn't have brought him across the county to embarrass him unless she'd done what she'd done. "So you're still married?"

"Yep. Let me buy you some of that colored water," he said.

She took an extra dollar. It'd still only be business—always business, but it was her business. "Let's just call it a tip. So what's up? Hunting or slumming?" The air still buzzed around her, her chest ached, and she wanted to cry, but she needed to go on.

"Party." He sipped his soda slowly. "So, you into group rates?" He said it easily. Most men were nervous asking the first time, even the second. Most times asking never got any easier for them and she didn't plan to make it any easier.

What Ron had said didn't insult her. How he said it had, as if she was selling nails or plumbing. It felt common. Maybe she was a whore, but not a common whore. "I'm not into that sort of thing."

"Too bad. A lot of horny old men. You could make a bundle," he said.

The whiskey and the fact that she was negotiating a deal made her feel a bit better. "I choose my men. They don't choose me." Cassie walked off to the other end of the bar. When Darnel called Ron's hamburger up, Cassie brought it over to him. "You know," she said, "you might be sitting in someone else's seat." She handed him the mustard and ketchup.

"You know," he said, "these aren't your normal dirty old men."

"I bet." Although she really didn't need another seventy-five tonight, Ron was taking up a space where another seventy-five could be possible. Then again, she was dog-tired, depressed and feeling pretty lousy about her occupation. "All dirty old men are pretty normal to me." Cassie turned to walk away. There were other men in the bar, drinking and talking, looking at her legs, peering down her blouse. She served them and spoke to them.

When she returned to his end of the bar, Ron said, "Just wait a minute. Just hear me out. I did you a favor so do me one. They're not really dirty old men."

"Just dirty middle-aged ones," Cassie said. "And don't ever think you did me a favor." The static of the jukebox getting ready to play a record buzzed in the speakers.

Ron finished his hamburger and played with the paper plate, tearing little slots along the edge, making petals, something a person would do for a child. "Okay, it wasn't much of a favor," he said when she was in earshot again. "But they've got this party going on and they're looking for female entertainment. What they found is pretty sorry. I sort of opened my mouth and told them I could get one a hell of a lot better. They're my bosses." He pouted.

"Brandy" played quietly out of the four speakers along the back of the bar and the small ones in the boxes at the booths. "You want me to do your boss?" Cassie said not understanding the guilt she was feeling. She poured herself another whiskey.

Ron smiled at the tone of her voice. "Him and a couple more."

"I told you I don't do that. One at a time, discreetly. I don't make them take me out or buy me dinner or nothing like that. I don't ask for anything else. It's strictly a one-at-a-time cash business." As the song played she decided some fool had probably thought the song was about whiskey. A car pulled into the lot, its lights strafing the bar through the high windows. Cassie stared at the door hoping it was Jake giving her a chance to explain, understanding what her situation had been and suddenly fearing he'd come back to buy her or to ask her to be his mistress or something crazy she didn't know. She didn't know anything anymore. An older man and his wife came in, two regulars.

Ron glanced at the flower-plate then dropped it on the bar. "Hell, by the time you get there a couple of them could be passed out, but don't worry, if worse comes to worse we can find someone. A thousand dollars."

Cassie leaned in toward Ron. "Why a thousand? What's so important?"

Ron smiled. "Influence, power, blackmail, whatever you want to call it."

Two local men came in and bellied up to the bar. Cassie served them both double shots of schnapps. She walked slowly back to Ron. "You taking pictures?"

"No." Ron laughed. "One grand for three guys, one at a time if they're still up."

The two men stood at the bar for a minute before they took their drinks to a booth. "I don't trust you. The money's too good," she said. But what really was the difference between one and three. It was what she did. Some men dug ditches. Some women cleaned toilets.

The door opened again. Cassie jumped. Three other men walked in, out-of-towners. What was she ashamed of? She fucked men for money and she was good at it. So what? Fuck Jake with his high-and-mighty morals. Rich people could afford them. Would she become his mistress if he asked? No, not his, not anyone's. "Where?"

"Peddlers Inn, room one." Another song started with the introduction static.

Cassie had the bar cleaned up by one-thirty. Two customers remained. She yelled into the kitchen, "I'm booking, Darnel." The effects of the whiskey she'd been drinking since Jake walked out had her a bit tipsy, but she poured herself a double and drank it.

The trip to the motel took twenty minutes. She had a bit of trouble parking her car, stumbling and almost falling in the gravel parking lot. Voices from a party spilled across the parking lot as she walked toward the door with the number one nailed to it. The door opened before she reached it, Ron silhouetted in the bright light of the room. Cassie walked into the room to shouts and whistles. She smiled despite herself.

On a large couch and several chairs, men sat in varying stages of drunkenness. Two sat on the floor with a couple of women, at least ten years her senior. Cassie knew them by reputation. Another girl, younger than the two, but heavier, sat on the counter of the little kitchenette stuck in an alcove in the rear of the unit. A man stood between her jean-covered legs, a glass in one hand, the other rubbing the inside of her right thigh. She giggled stupidly.

"Where are they?" Cassie asked.

Ron put his hand on her back and gently pushed her into the middle of the room. "Don't be in such a hurry. Have a drink." He handed her a drink and then ten one hundred dollar bills.

The drink was straight bourbon whiskey. It hit Cassie hard. She was too tired to be doing this, but for a grand, she better show at least a little patience. Ron guided her over to a red-faced, white-haired old gentleman who Cassie would have rejected if she hadn't already taken the money and been on her way to a drunk. She drank the rest of her drink and handed it to Ron. He brought her another, whispering, "It won't hurt so much."

She said, "You knew, didn't you?"

He laughed and walked away. It didn't matter to her. She had already decided to get drunker than she ever had.

Cassie woke to the smell of stale-beer breath and drunken snores. Someplace someone had thrown up. Her head spun and her body ached. She lay naked on a bed. She shivered. The sun shone through the crack between the blind and the window frame. Cassie turned on her back and rose up on her elbow. The room looked like a mass killing had taken place. Men lay everywhere in different states of unconscious drunkenness and nakedness. Two slept next to her, curled up in the covers like children.

The hotel alarm clock's red numbers said eleven-thirty. "Damn, oh, damn, what the hell happened?" How many drinks? How many men? "That son-of-a-bitch, I ought to kill him." Her skirt lay on the floor. Her shoes were under it, her blouse over a chair. Where her underwear was she had no idea. The girl from the kitchenette lay naked on the sofa with a man in his jockey shorts, her left breast hanging off the edge of the cushion. Three men lay around her. Cassie grimaced at the scene. She took her purse and coat off the pegs behind the front door. Hopefully no one had found the thousand dollars. She searched through her purse. It was still there, stuffed between the lining and the leather, through a small rip.

When Cassie arrived home, Amy's car was gone. Cassie ran up to the house and flung open the door. "Hello," she shouted. The house smelled steel-cold from the night. Amy had let the fire go out again. Cassie ran upstairs to check on the boys. Their beds were empty.

She ran back to her car and drove over to Amy's mother's house. Cassie banged on the door.

A woman from somewhere inside, yelled, "Come on in. The door ain't locked."

Open cans and bottles littered the table and counter tops of the kitchen. A rabbit scurried out of the room. Cassie picked her way around the slime-swollen cardboard boxes and paper bags to find a bulbous woman sitting on a broken couch watching an old black and white television. Her greasy hair lay matted on her head. She held a cracked bowl containing a brown paste that she spooned into her mouth while laughing at the screen. A small goat sat next to her.

"Where are my kids," Cassie said.

"They ain't here." The woman spoke to the television. "But I've been expecting you."

Cassie stood in the doorway to the room, reluctant to enter. "Where are they?"

Sunday-morning cartoons played across the screen. "We called the welfare woman when you didn't come home." She slid the spoon through rotting teeth.

"Dot? Does she have them?" Cassie asked.

"Yep, that's her name, but she ain't got them. I called up that old Cantrell woman. She was closer. She come and got them." Amy's mother smiled and bounced around on the old couch that whined as if it planned to fall apart any minute. "Me and her are good friends. Been that way since Amy started babysitting for you." The woman laughed, but Cassie wasn't so sure it was at the TV. "She's been giving me all sorts of stuff, like pots and pans and old curtains and dresses, can goods, you name it. Probably won't be doing much of that no more seeing she's got the kids now and you're in a heap of trouble. They was running over half the county looking for you."

Cassie drove to the Cantrell farm, pulling up behind Dot's car sitting parked in the mud that had swallowed up the even the flagstone walk. Mother Cantrell stood on the porch.

Cassie ran through the mud as Dot stepped out of the house. Cassie pushed by Mother Cantrell, but Dot grabbed Cassie's shoulders, pinning her against the building.

Cassie pushed against the large woman, but Dot pushed her further from the door.

"Let me through. I got to get my kids," Cassie said.

Dot spoke without emotion, as if she had done this before, maybe many times. "No, Cassie, you can't have them."

"You've got no right stealing my kids," Cassie cried.

"You got worse troubles than that, missy," Mother Cantrell said. "You've been fornicating with men for money." The old woman looked out at the road. "Here come the sheriffs now to take you away." She cackled a mad sort of giggle, her eyes dancing with the same mad fire Cassie had seen in Judd's.

The red and white car of the county sheriff pulled into the soup of a driveway. Cassie turned back to Dot. Dot's face was expressionless. Cassie said, "I don't know what you're talking about, but just let me have my kids and I'll get the hell out of here." Cassie pushed forward again, but Dot held her. "Don't do this, Dot, don't. You know the kids are better off with me. God, I'm their mother." The look in Dot's eyes said decisions had been made.

The barn door squealed and rumbled as rusted wheels slid over pitted rails. Mr. Cantrell stood at the edge of the dark barn interior, his coveralls manure spotted. Behind him stood the deep blackness of the interior of the barn, but still, across the dark empty space a crack of light stretched vertically showing a sliver of the world of the other side. He held his hands at his hips surveying the scene taking place in the spring mud of his driveway, then walked slowly toward the back of the house, his green, rubber barn boots splashing mud.

Other heavy footsteps sloshed through the mire. "Cassie," Jimmy Marshall called. He stood at the bottom of the steps in his gray uniform with his large brimmed hat, his spit-shined shoes covered with mud.

"Arrest her sheriff, arrest her. She's a whore," Mother Cantrell waved a lace hanky frantically as she spit out the words. "My poor boy's wife is a fornicator. It's no wonder he don't come home. Do your duty."

"Just be patient, Mrs. Cantrell," Jimmy said. He tipped his hat to say hello. "All in due time." He walked up onto the porch and took Cassie gently by the back of her upper arm. "Cass, let's walk down to the car."

There were too many of them to fight any longer. She had lost, absolutely and completely, and now she lay in the snow waiting for the bullet to her head. The mud splashed cold as needles against her ankles as she let herself be pushed away from the house and her children.

Jimmy stared down at his shoes. He shook his head. Cassie wasn't sure if the mess below their feet upset him or the mess she'd made of her life.

"You're in a lot of trouble, girl," he said. "Old lady Cantrell got a judge out of bed before dawn. Wanted a warrant issued for your arrest. She says she's got a dozen men who'll swear on a stack of Bibles you've been soliciting. What she's got is a rumor, but it's enough to rustle the bushes for real pigeons. I heard the call come in. I made sure I took it."

"You don't believe her, do you, Jimmy?" Cassie leaned against the car. Her voice was beginning to quiver. How had she been found out so quickly? Yes, she'd screwed up, but men kept their secrets, from women anyhow.

Jimmy stood between her and the porch, although he didn't seem worried about her running back. "I don't really give a shit, Cassie. People got to do what they got to do. But now the judge is got me picking you and Darnel up to take in for questioning." Jimmy nodded in the direction of the patrol car. "He's more pissed than anything else. All he wants is old lady Cantrell off his back. She's just a damn loudmouth troublemaker, always was. He'd just as soon not know anything about it."

Darnel sat slouched in the back of the patrol car, his hands cuffed together, his eyes peering out of the car, wild and scared. "Oh, God." The morning sky had washed out to a weak blue, the day into something surreal, the air too thick to breathe. Cassie was hardly able get it through her mouth while her lungs ached for a breath. The sun hung low in the sky a small orange ball, and the wind blew wet and cold, carrying the smell of the mud, decay, and death.

"Oh, God," Cassie cried. Only one woman knew — only one woman would have told Mother Cantrell her sins. "He didn't do nothing," she said. "Jimmy, Darnel didn't even know. He was in the kitchen. I was in the bar. He never knew."

"I got to take you in," he said. "I figure it'd be better me than someone else."

Cassie shivered even though she could no longer feel the temperature, not sure what was worse, being found out or that her mother had played Judas. She could almost see the sheriffs knocking on her mother's door. Her mother in her housecoat and slippers. Maybe Dot was there, maybe Mother Cantrell, all crowded in the small kitchen and her mother confessing her daughter's sins. "Are you going to let Darnel go? She don't want him."

Jimmy nodded to Henry who still sat in the car. He said something to Darnel who closed his eyes and hung his head. "Yeah, I figured as much. He keeps swearing you're innocent."

Cassie turned away, unable to look at Darnel. "But you can't arrest me. I can't go to jail. My kids'll be branded for the rest of their lives."

"Cassie, I can't do much else." He motioned back toward the porch. "She's got you pretty much hobbled."

Cassie reached into her purse and pulled out a pack of cigarettes and a lighter. Her hands shook so much she couldn't get the cigarette out of the pack. Jimmy picked one out by the filter. Her nose was running. She wiped it on her sleeve and took the cigarette from Jimmy, but her lips quivered so much she couldn't get the flame of her throwaway lighter to touch the tip. Jimmy pulled the cigarette gently from her lips, placed it in his and lit it, coughing when he tried to inhale. "Never could see what people saw in these." He placed it carefully between her lips.

Cassie took a long drag and blew it out harshly. "You'd know if you were in my place. God, Jimmy," she cried. "Don't I get a chance? Hell, you gave that bastard that caused all this a chance. Can't I get one too?"

"Run, get away? I can't do that. Shit, if it was me, I'd a left you alone. You weren't harming no one but yourself."

"I sure did that."

Jimmy nodded back over his shoulder toward the porch and the two women standing there. "It's her, Cass. She wants the kids."

"No, she doesn't. She wants blood. She just wants them out of spite."

Jimmy breathed hard through his nose. "Are you willing to give them up?"

Cassie bit down hard on her lip. Time, she needed a chance to get away. "No, but what choice do I have? I lose them either way. And people don't forget."

"Wait here." Jimmy walked back through the mud to the porch.

Mother Cantrell waved her hanky and stomped around on the porch as Jimmy spoke. Mr. Cantrell appeared from inside the house. There was an argument going on, sometimes two ways, sometimes four ways. Cassie smoked her cigarette and lit another, calmer now. Maybe her children wouldn't be branded the kids of a whore, but she'd pay one hell of a price, a price she'd pay for them.

The argument turned three against one. Mr. Cantrell walked three steps away from his wife. He turned, walked back, took her by her shoulders and sat her down in a rocker. The ease of his motions frightened Cassie. She had never seen anyone control Mother Cantrell that way.

Finally Jimmy and Dot walked off the porch to Cassie. Jimmy said, "She's agreed to forget about all of it as long as you're out of the county by sundown."

"Don't I get to see my boys first?" Cassie asked.

Dot said, "Cass, get going while the going's good. You try and see those kids and all deals are off."

"Yeah, I bet. You been trying to take them away from me since day one," Cassie said.

"I'm sorry, Cass. It was out of my hands." Dot glanced at Mother Cantrell who still sat in the rocker next to her husband.

Jimmy leaned in a bit as if about to tell her a secret. "Seven, Cass, seven years. That's how long you've got until she can't do nothing to you, but just a couple of years until this thing blows over and it's all a dirty lie she's trumped up. No one will believe it wasn't."

Dot nodded. "You leave now, Cass, and in a couple of years you find me and I'll say you gave them up voluntarily. Do what you've got to do, but stay clean. You can get them back easily. Mr. Cantrell promised he'd do what's best by them. You've got no choice."

Cassie threw her cigarette into the mud. "I never had a choice, never. I'm gone, but I'm coming back. You can tell her that." Jimmy nodded to the Cantrells with a little touch of a finger to the brim of his hat. Mr. Cantrell signaled back.

Cassie opened the door of her car and slid in. "Take Darnel home and tell him I'm truly sorry." She waited for the patrol car to back out of the driveway and head in the direction of Darnel's house. She put the car in gear and looked up at Dot. Dot kissed her fingers and pressed them against the car window.

Cassie drove home, packed her clothes, and then dug up the mayonnaise jar stuffing the money in her purse. She grasped the jar, weighed it. She could fill it with gasoline and burn the place to the ground. It'd never be hers. Cassie walked back into the house to take her rifles. She could get some food, go up to the bluff, no one would ever know. One good clean shot. That's all she'd need. She could come back in a week and do it. Nobody'd know. Probably half the county wanted to kill Mother Cantrell.

Her children were in Mother Cantrell's grasp. Mother Cantrell would turn them against her and it'd be a fight to get them back no matter what Dot said. How quickly could she fire from the bluff and get out of there? Mr. Cantrell would make a good grandfather. If she could avoid getting caught, get out of the county, she might just get away with it. If she got caught it might only be seven years. The same seven Jimmy talked about. She could do seven. Maybe she'd see Suzy. They'd do their time together, get out, get their kids and head to Pittsburgh or anywhere. Get Ron to hook her up with a madam or whomever he said he could hook her up with. Get them to be her alibi. Come back. She'd buy a scope. No, someone would remember her buying it, evidence. Besides, she needed to do it within a week or two at the most. Just enough time for her to be gone, not enough time for Mother Cantrell to get her claws into her kids. Cassie put the cartridges into her purse.

Cody had left his teddy bear. Cassie picked it up. She picked up the small monkey Jimmy slept with. She wanted to take them with her, but they'd need good things now, things to hold on to, things to hug. Cassie wanted to write a letter to her parents, to her children, tell them how much she loved them, tell her mother she forgave her. Cassie wanted to break down and cry, but she needed to survive. Mother Cantrell knew if she survived there'd be another day of reckoning. Everything would have to come later.

Cassie laid the rifles in to the trunk. She threw all her clothes and belongings in the back seat, not taking the time to pack. Mother Cantrell could still renege on her promise. Cassie drove down out of the mountains to the interstate, driving west toward the setting sun, a weak ball bleeding orange and yellow colors into the clouds. Spring was weeks away. She would see it for the first time alone. Cassie turned on the radio. It played, "The Night the Lights went out in Georgia." Gabe was wrong, cowbirds lay their eggs in other birds' nests because they have no choice.

The dim light of the morning sun replaced the buzzing light of the motel's neon sign somewhere in mid-Tennessee, close to Nashville. Cassie hadn't slept. She sat on the plastic chair looking out of the window toward the eastern sky. Maybe what she had done was wrong, maybe not. But she'd run—like Jake, Ben, Darlene, and even Rancy. No, not like them, she'd always been running, or hiding—from the changes that were taking place. Maybe she didn't understand it all, the riots, the war, the protesters, the hippies, the drugs, and people losing themselves in their possessions. Maybe no one understood it all, but that was no excuse. You deal with what God gives you. You don't give up or give in. She'd let herself become just another thing people bought and used. She needed to quit running and take a stand. It was the only way she was going to make it. Maybe that was it? Maybe there was no place for her in this new world, not for her kind, the person she'd been before she'd become a thing.

Cassie dressed in jeans and a shirt, tied up her old hunting boots, then dropped the keys off at the motel office. She started the car, and then shut it off. Cassie opened the trunk, yanked her rifles out, quickly loading eight bullets into the tube of the .22 and filled the clip of the 30.06. Her hands were rock-steady. She gazed up at the morning sun over West Virginia as she pulled back the bolt. A brass and copper cartridge popped up. She breathed hard through her nose, fatigued from lack of sleep. Her eyes burned, but her head was clear. For once in her life she knew for certain what to do. Cassie shoved the bolt forward, sliding the round into the chamber. She laid the rifles across the foot well of the back seat. Cassie drove toward the interstate, back east, back into West Virginia, toward the mountains.

The drive back on the interstate took six hours, much longer than it had seemed to take yesterday, but she'd been running away, afraid, letting Mother Cantrell and all the rest of them chase her out of the state and away from the only real thing she had left. And that was it, what Mother Cantrell wanted, the one thing she couldn't have, the children. It wasn't even for spite she'd taken them. It'd been greed.

When Cassie reached the county line she drove the back roads, avoiding the sheriffs and anyone she thought might know her car. The mist that splattered against her windshield had drenched the paved roads a slick gray, the dirt ones a soft brown. She'd ridden over all of them with Jake, knew them as well as he had, had been on them with Judd parked almost in a ditch humping like two mad dogs. She drove up to the bluff above the house, between all the wrecked cars that had been warning her all those years to get away before Judd and the rest of the Cantrells wrecked her and dragged her off to some back field.

She turned her car around in the mushy field full of the broken stalks of old grass, keeping the engine revved and the wheels spinning to keep up her momentum, circling back to the trail, facing out toward the road for a quick getaway. She pulled both rifles from under the seat. It'd stopped raining. The air was cold and wet, chilling her, but it'd be over quickly and running would keep her warm. It would end here, now.

Cassie walked down toward the edge, crawling on her hands and knees through the short wet grass the last fifty yards, trying to keep the rifles dry. She rested the 30.06 on a large rock near the precipice and then she sighted down to the kitchen door on the porch. She wished she'd bought a scope, but if she hit the old woman anywhere in the chest, it'd kill her, maybe not now but in a few hours or days. Cassie really didn't care.

Maddie's car sat in the mud-choked driveway next to Mr. Cantrell's truck. Mother Cantrell's car was gone. Fine, she'd have a better target when the old fat woman wallowed through the mud to the porch and she could die in the mud. It'd be fitting.

Cassie walked back up to the car listening for the approach of any automobile that might be Mother Cantrell coming home. She picked out an old coat to sit on and an old sweater to keep her warm. She'd waited twenty minutes when the door opened and Mr. Cantrell walked to the edge of the porch. He wasn't the person she wanted but she sighted down on him anyhow to check to see how hard it would be to hit a target that far away. She'd shot deer farther. He peered down at the mud then up at the bluff right at her and for a minute he seemed to be thinking about something. Then he waved as if he'd seen her.

They'd heard the car, hadn't seen it come to the corner and turn toward the house or away knowing it had to have stopped up on the bluff. She'd made too much noise turning her car around and they'd spotted her on the bluff waiting to kill Mother Cantrell. Maybe they'd known she'd be back and Mother Cantrell had taken her kids someplace, but she bet they hadn't figured she'd comeback to kill the old lady. It didn't matter now. They'd have surmised what she was up to and have called the sheriffs.

Cassie stood when Mr. Cantrell waved again. She glanced toward her car. She could still get away, maybe, but she doubted it. It'd only been the sheriffs yesterday. She'd only been a whore then. Now she was a killer or a potential killer. She couldn't even do that right. She could run and they would catch her and she'd never get her babies back.

A mist began to blow again wetting her face and hair. She sat down on her old coat dropping the .22 rifle on her lap but still cradling the deer rifle. Cassie lit a cigarette. They'd come and maybe in twenty years Cody would understand that his mother had made her stand here for him or maybe he'd just think she was some crazy-ass bitch. She didn't know, but this was as far as she'd go without them.

Mr. Cantrell walked back into the house. Cassie took a couple of hard drags on her cigarette then flicked it into the wet grass. He was calling them. They'd be coming soon. She'd be dead soon. She began to cry little tears, strange tears because she wasn't really sad, only disappointed. There was so much she'd wanted to do, to own a home with a garden, to teach Cody to read and Jimmy when he was ready, Sunday dinners inviting her mother and father, Teresa and Carl, all seven of them around the table and she still wanted to see the sun rise through the mountain fog, watch deer leap across an opening in a deep woods, listen to the creeks speak to each other, the limbs of tall trees rubbing together. She still wanted to experience lazy summer afternoons, to do all of it with her sons. There was so much she had wanted to do.

The door slamming echoed up to the bluff. Mr. Cantrell walked to the edge of the porch. He held Cody's hand. Cody was dressed to travel. Mr. Cantrell kneeled beside the boy and pointed up to the bluff. Cody smiled and waved. Cassie burst into tears. Mr. Cantrell waved at her to come down. She almost stood but it might just be a trick to get her where they could arrest her again. How could she kill someone in front of her baby? How could she let him see her die? Maddie came out on the porch struggling with two suitcases and Jimmy in her arms.

Cassie ran to her car and drove down to the Cantrell's farm. She ran through the mud to her sons. "Please," she shouted not having wanted to ask, wanting to grab them and take them, unable not to ask, meaning please let me have them and not force me to take them.

Mr. Cantrell pushed Cody toward her. "You got about four hours, before she gets home from her civic meeting, about a day before she starts to try to get the law to get you, but she let it all go and Dot dropped the paperwork so's you're really not stealing them yet."

Cassie grabbed her eldest son and ran to her car.

Maddie followed juggling the suitcases and Jimmy, splashing through the mud. Cassie opened the trunk throwing the rifles in the back.

Maddie handed her the suitcases. "I wanted to wait until you killed the old bitch, but Pa said it'd just complicate things too much."

Cassie cobbled together a nest for Jimmy on the back seat by wadding up her clothes. When Cassie turned to look at the older man standing on the porch, Maddie said, "He knew you'd be back. Wasn't sure you'd be on the ridge with a hunting rifle. He kind of liked you guts. But he got the old woman out of here and called me to get your boys ready. So get."

"Tell him I appreciate it," Cassie said stepping into her car. "Tell him I've learned a lot and plan to change my ways."

"I hope not too much. Ain't many of us willing to do what you were going to do for your kin, especially not a Cantrell. If we'd had any guts we'd of killed her long ago." Maddie slammed the door shut. "Just try to stay on this side of the law. I know my mother. There's going to be hell to pay for you beating her and she'll want revenge."

Cassie started the car putting it into gear. "What happens to you and your father after the old woman finds out?"

"I'm going to swear I was never here. He'll say he was in the barn and never even heard you come and steal them. He's going to say it's God's will. Good luck."

Cassie backed out of the driveway, the tires slipping a bit sideways in the mud. This time she headed straight for the interstate and south. Cody played for a while before falling asleep. Jimmy slept in the back. As she drove south the spring seemed to rush to meet them, the grass waking in its new-born light green, and soon the trees sprouted buds, and then greening too in that same new color.

As they crossed the Virginia state line Cassie said to herself, maybe to both her boys, now awake and playing, "Our family is back together. Ain't nothing going to get us separated from here on." She stopped for gas near the North Carolina border and to change Jimmy's diaper, getting her sons something to eat at the little diner in the station. As the people rushed in and out paying for gas or finding a table to rest and eat on their journey, they smiled at her and her children as if the three of them were a normal family, not fugitives on the run. Cassie didn't care, had no use for people anymore. She had plans, small plans, to live small, to stay away from the law, change her name, get an education, start over. She could do it. She had a lot of skills. She had her boys. It's when we give in to them and let them do what they want with us that it's over.

At Roundfire we publish great stories. We lean towards the spiritual and thought-provoking. But whether it's literary or popular, a gentle tale or a pulsating thriller, the connecting theme in all Roundfire fiction titles is that once you pick them up you won't want to put them down.